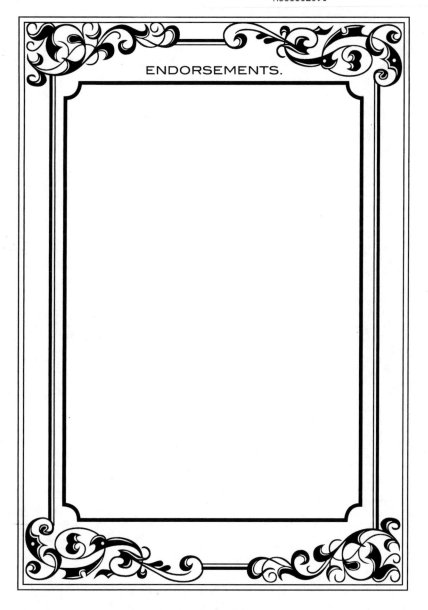

ENDORSEMENTS.

THRILLING TALES FROM LANDS OF YESTERYORE.
GUARANTEED TO PLEASE OR AT LEAST DISTRACT.

DISPATCHES
from
WONDERMARK
MANOR.

THE COMPLEAT TRILOGY.

BY

DAVID MALKI !

COVER ILLUSTRATION: WITHDRAWING THE FATEFUL HATCHET.

VENICE, CALIF.:
𝕭𝖊𝖆𝖗𝖘𝖙𝖆𝖈𝖍𝖊 𝕭𝖔𝖔𝖐𝖘.
2011.

ALSO BY DAVID MALKI !

The Annotated Wondermark
Wondermark: Beards of our Forefathers
Wondermark: Clever Tricks to Stave Off Death
Wondermark: Dapper Caps & Pedal-Copters
Hey World Here Are Some Suggestions (A Tweet Me Harder Collection)

A production of 𝔅earstache 𝔅ooks
2554 Lincoln Blvd #214 • Venice, CA 90291
BEARSTACHE.COM

The material in this book was originally published in three volumes.
THIS IS THE FIRST COLLECTED EDITION, printed *October, 2011.*

ISBN-13: 978-0-9821671-5-1

10 9 8 7 6 5 4 3 2 1

PRINTED IN THE UNITED STATES OF AMERICA

CONTENTS OF VOLUME I.
DISPATCHES FROM WONDERMARK MANOR

Prologue 7

Editors' Note 15

1. A Putrid Visitor 17

2. Gardening. 18

3. An Encounter With Neighbours 20

4. A Persistent Funk 24

5. Rabble. 27

6. The Key-Ring . . . . ; 30

7. A Delivery. 32

8. Bothersome Relations 37

9. The Great Purge. 40

10. Disturbance At Night-Time. 43

11. Saved By Instinct. 47

12. Remembrances. 50

13. Ill Portents 55

14. A New Acquaintance 59

15. In Dire Straits 64

16. A Ghostly Presence 68

17. The Arrivals 71

18. Violence. 75

19. Grave Injury. 77

20. A Shocking Revelation. 80

21. A Desperate Act 85

22. Unwelcome Visitors 89

23. Escape. 95

24. Into The Depths 99

25. A Shaft Of Light. 103

26. Return At Dawn. 108

27. Sifting Through The Ashes 112

28. To The Hospital 117

29. Confrontation. 122

30. A Desperate Plan. 125

31. Taking Flight 129

CONTENTS OF VOLUME II.
VOYAGE FROM WONDERMARK MANOR

32. Long At Sea 139
33. A Fateful Swell 145
34. Adrift 149
35. Uneasy Alliance 154
36. Grenadine At The Helm 160
37. On The Sand-Bar 166
38. Parting 169
39. Impact 172
40. An Unlikely Charade 176
41. Opportunism 180
42. The Surprising Saviour 184
43. Midnight Rendez-Vous 188
44. Face To Face 193
45. Peapoddy's Revelation 198
46. What Ails Him 203
47. The Cave In Question 208
48. A Mad Dash 213
49. The Old Man's Gift 217
50. Awakening 224
51. A Surfeit Of Thinks 230
52. Problems With Goats 235
53. The Pitiable Ascent 240
54. In The Razor-Chair 244
55. Commissioned 250
56. Stratagem 255
57. Meeting The Oaf 259
58. Dark Clouds Gather 265
59. Sky-Ward 270
60. Plunged To Earth 275
61. A Short Chapter 280
62. The Observatory 282
63. A Struggle 285
64. Bound For Else-Where 291

CONTENTS OF VOLUME III.
RETURN TO WONDERMARK MANOR

65. The Bon-Mot Gala 301
66. The Tangle Yet To Come 309
67. A Royal Commission 316
68. Ascent To Waverly 321
69. Ruins On The Old Hill. 325
70. An Awkward Tea 332
71. Dash Through Darkness 337
72. The Baron Of The Alley-Ways. 341
73. The Critical Prick 349
74. A Long Day As Beast-Cargo 354
75. Grim Voyage To Destiny 358
76. Step By Bloody Step. 364
77. Ashore On Prison-Isle 370
78. Master Tactician 376
79. A Blind Briefing. 382
80. The Scout, And What He Heralded 386
81. Air-Borne At Last 393
82. A Daring Rescue 398
83. Familiar Faces. 404
84. A Race Against Dawn 410
85. Fright At Pool-Party Plaza 414
86. Horrible Old Friends 420
87. Untold Power 425
88. A Ridiculous Plan 431
89. Aboard That Terrible Craft. 439
90. A Cunning Stratagem 444
91. Calm Before The Fight 451
92. Screaming To Earth 457
93. The Aftermath 463
94. A Reckoning Of Sorts 465
95. The Final Challenge 470
96. Looking Down On It All 481
Epilogue 485
Author's Note 490

Prologue.

A KNOCK UPON THE DOOR OF DESTINY.

I DISCOVERED QUITE EARLY IN MY TRAVELS that when faced with a talkative companion, it is often good practise to remain quiet, thus allowing the other party to volunteer all sorts of tidbits you never would have thought to ask after.

The couple seated across the carriage had asked me at the cab-stand if we could share a lift into town: penny-pinchers both, from the looks of them. The husband (I presume they were wed, if only because I doubted any besides each other would have them) was the fat, long-suffering type, constantly daubing his forehead with a sopping cloth and jetting me clandestine looks intended to confer that he, like I, was *above* the sort of idle prattle blasting incessantly from the cake-spout of the beast chained by ring-finger to his side forever-more. I didn't buy his camaraderie, and not just because I'd not a shilling in goods nor coin about me; no, he wanted it both ways, Ol' Roley-Pole did—the social benefit of marriage, ostensibly proving to strangers that he wasn't a weirdo, but retaining a cynical detachment characteristic of bachelor-hood as well. I might have sympathised with his aims, but I detested his two-facedness, if for no other reason than both of his faces had dripped sweat onto my battered valise as we'd clambered into the carriage.

The wife was an easy bird to peg; I'd had her number from the minute she fed me a fishhook-baited good-morning. It was a candy how-do-you-do, all sweetness with no substance, extended purely for the expectation of reprisal on my end. I knew that given such an opening, she'd launch in and fill the air for the duration of the whole ride into town. But I'd just debarked a steamer filled bilge-to-balls with peacocks, and was in no mood for further yowling.

Silence proved allergic for her, however, and she didn't take long to grow twitchy. Soon she was remarking on the trees passing by, or the foulness of the weather, or the fashions of the orphan-corpses that cluttered the roads. With no factory work to keep them busy since that great, flesh-grinding accident at the budget bottling-plant had poisoned thousands of thrifty beverage-patrons

THE CABBIE.

and resulted in great liability for manufacturers at large, the mischievous urchins had become a menace to urban travel, swarming intersections and snarling traffic for hours with ropes twisted 'twixt axles and beautiful mares trotted out to distract the carriage-horses.

Thanks to the endless spurt of noise spiralling out of Hades, up through the Earth's crust, and bursting volcanically from the throat seated three feet from me, I learned that a thriving trade of whelp-catchers had developed during my long absence from these environs, and that it was a "despicable practise" employing "far more knives" than, perhaps, were strictly necessary.

It was in response to this latter point that the beleaguered lard-mass poured into the corner finally gathered the gumption to interject. "Well, it's not *so* bad, really," he harrumphed, almost too softly to be heard, and I thought at first that the objection was purely a face-saving performance for my benefit, trying to look "cool" for the "cool guy." In any case, the nattering nag sped clean through his pipe-up with nary a pause for breath, though I had at this point resigned myself to the fact that the woman was inhuman and did not actually require respiration.

UNCLE.

"S-seriously," Role-Pole attempted again; "I think it's fine that they clean the streets of those disease-ridden brats. And to carry a cudgel in the service of one's employ—think of the lark *that* would be!"

It was clear that he was repressing violent tendencies. Surely he wanted to kill his wife; *I* wanted to kill her, and I'd only known her ten minutes. Even the horses pulling our carriage likely felt the same murderous impulse towards their passenger. But lacking the stones to carry out the act, R. P. was living vicariously through the scruffy whelp-catchers even now pulling small, limp bodies from the road-ruts, visible for fleeting moments through the thin windows of our conveyance. With one satisfying blow I could do the deed for the man, I briefly thought, but *why?* I stood nothing to gain; it's not like *his* companionship stood to be much more enjoyable. And it would serve my mission no good if I began offing citizens Willy H. Nilly on my first day back home.

True; once a resident of this city, I was now a stranger again—for the place had changed. The wharves where I had once hawked ropy strands of reconstituted cheese to tourists were crowded with smelly buskers and smellier seaman-tarts; the alley-ways were bustling with the sweating crush of an ever-growing population; and even the very roads were paved lumpily with child-flesh. It was not the Easthillshireborough-upon-Flats that I had cherished; but it was *an* Easthillshireborough-upon-Flats, and so long as *this* Easthillshireborough-upon-Flats featured as wealthy of an uncle as the Easthillshireborough-upon-Flats of my memory and imagination, then this Easthillshireborough-upon-Flats would do just fine for me.

"Ooh, there's where that nice old man lives," the chatter-box burbled perkily, pressing a smeary finger against the window. At first I thought she was indicating a post-box on the corner, and after that I followed the line of her gesture towards a bakery-oven. Par for the course for sense, I figured—but with a jolt I suddenly made out the silhouette of a tall château, barely visible through the late-morning fog, far off atop Waverly Hill. My destination.

Unfortunately, it seemed that the couple's stop was closer than the Hill; thus my plan to ditch them with the cab-fare unravelled quickly. In terms of spiteful comeuppance I settled for giving the woman a bit of a shove on her way out the door; she didn't fall and crack her brow on the cobblestones, though, so I did her cell-mate no favours there. His parting glance was wistful, so I tried my best to make mine mocking.

Once the door slammed shut I was alone in the carriage, and the quiet was like a density in the air, pressing against my ear-drums and massaging my contempt for humanity.

The cab-ride to the Manor itself was long, and would presumably be expensive, and each moment that seemed a capital chance to gather my thoughts I found my mind drifting towards a fear of the impending fare—I caught myself calculating wait times in dense areas, re-searching my valise for loose coins, and constantly arguing down my urge to simply off the driver and be done with it. But I had no use for a hansom-cab reeking with fatty-odour and scorn, and disposing of the body would take up valuable time, when I needed to see Uncle soon. My stomach churned—I'd been feeding it grog-slop and peacock-poop for weeks while at sea, and the promise of lucrative horizons ahead was making my gut-area antsy.

When the carriage rumbled to a stop, high atop Waverly with the whole of Easthillshireborough-upon-Flats spread before us, I waited for the driver to open the cabin door before budging a muscle, hoping that those few extra seconds might invent a solution to the problem of the fare. They didn't; nor did the ten extra seconds

I took ensuring that my valise was securely latched; nor did the solid eight minutes I spent searching the seat-cushion for an imaginary contact-lens. Finally, stumbling into the glare of midday, and clutching my valise tightly at the ready with my striking-

SOME KIND OF WIND-MILL.

hand, I offered a lame apology for the delay.

"Don't mind it m'self," the cabbie shrugged. "You're on the ol' man's coin, I reckon? No worries from me, then—he's good on account, an' I'll add it to his tab."

"Yes," I said. "Yes, that's fine. Add it to his tab."

After a moment in which nobody moved, the cabbie added "Be nice to pay down the tab a little today, though."

"Nice," I said. "But not compulsory?"

The cabbie spat and climbed back up to his seat. With the crack of a whip that I initially thought might have been meant for my back-side, the carriage clattered away, and I stood in front of the Manor.

The path-way to that wide front door was long and effortful, but the trek afforded a good examination of the grounds, which were well-groomed and verdant. It was a beautiful property, and I hoped that it was kept up largely by staff—as I had no plans, myself, to do a moment's labour ever again.

The thick brass knocker fell to the wood with a reverberant thump. Voices and shuffling sounds emanated from within. As the moment neared, my heart began to race. Mission time.

"Coming, coming," I heard Uncle say as he approached the door. I fumbled with the valise and wrapped hot fingers around the thick oak handle of my father's blunt-edged hatchet.

Today, the Manor would be mine. ✦

DISPATCHES *from*

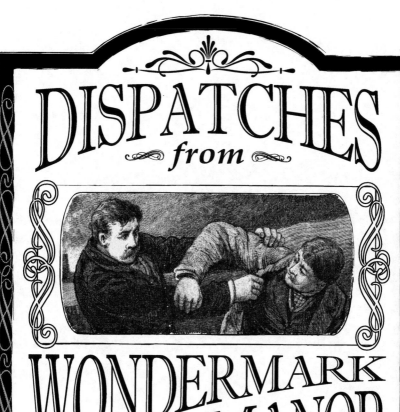

WONDERMARK MANOR

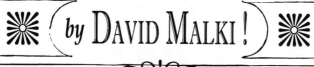

VOLUME I.

by DAVID MALKI !

a MAP of EASTHILLSHIREBOROUGH-upon-FLATS

➔ AND ENVIRONS ←

➤ *WHEREIN OUR TALE TAKES PLACE* ➤

Editors' Note.

IT HAS NOW BEEN SEVERAL YEARS since the day we arrived at the headquarters of our publishing concern and found, left for us on the stoop like an abandoned infant or a notice of foreclosure, a battered trunk containing ninety-seven white wax dictation-cylinders.

There was no note attached; the only markings the trunk bore were post-stamps indicating a trip through India, Russia and Europe. Also inside the trunk was a scrap of laundry-receipt in an Asian language, the only Roman characters decipherable being "M.X.Y.Z.D." Also enclosed were three weathered cards bearing images of a phonograph, a crowd, and the planet Earth.

The cylinders, set up for play-back, narrated a remarkable tale. We first published the account serially, via electric post, to the members of the Wondermark News-Letter and Humour-Strip Home Delivery (a free service of the Inter-Tube Site *wondermark.com*), and have now collected it here for the first time in a complete and unabridged edition. We believe the cylinders to have been recorded as a personal journal of sorts, and so far as we can determine, the events they describe are true.

Our belief is that the narrator has aimed to give expression to the truth that within every person, even if humble or debased, there may be some good worth lifting up and saving; that in each human being, though revered and seemingly immaculate, are some faults which deserve pointing out and correcting; and that all circumstances of life, however trivial they may appear, may possess those alternations of the comic and the pathetic, the good and the bad, the joyful and sorrowful, upon which walk the days and nights, the summers and winters, the lives and deaths, of this strange world. Or at least we suppose that was his aim, because otherwise we have no explanation.

—The Editors.

"I RAINED BLOWS UPON THE OLD MAN'S FACE, AND FOR SOME
REASON HIS COMPANIONS OBJECTED."—[SEE PAGE 516.]

1: A PUTRID VISITOR.

I ENTERTAINED A MAN-OF-TOWN AT THE mansion over the week-end. He was a rather shabby sort, a fellow one might see rooting about the waste-bins on Avenue T, that part of the wharf where the crab-smashers raise their mighty mallets and bring them down heavily on crustaceans with nary a care for who's walking besides or who might be gifted with the (rather prodigious) by-splatter of oils and shell-bits and general meaty leavings that cling to every nearby surface in a quite inextricable manner.

My guest, a certain Mr N____ , tried to keep his left side angled away from me throughout the evening, afraid, perhaps, that the tell-tale crabbings that stained his trousers would reveal him as a member of that loathsome cobblestone set, too proud to ask for proper crab-scraps from the smashers (a generally amenable class) yet too poor to buy even an eighth-ounce of rat-juice from the bellman's cart with the streamers, where the rats from the previous night's trappings are pressed and juiced with great fanfare at sunrise, the breeze plucking at the gay banners and lofting the bellman's ancient shanty from rooftop to rooftop in that great, old hallmark of morning.

I played Mr N____'s game against him, I must confess, by seating him close to the hearth, tacitly inviting the snapping flames to consume the greasy crab-oil from his dress like it was kerosene in winter—and when the blaze licked his tweed like an ostrich licks an orphan (that is, with vigour and no small measure of carnivorous desire), well, I knew that I'd had the last word in this measure of wits. For what is even the slightest of social intercourse, if not a test of cleverness?

"Fie," I shouted, leaping to my feat in as dramatic a fashion possible; "your becrabjuiced coat would have brought no shame to you, had you but held your head high and made no garrulous efforts to divert my attention—but instead your sly deceit has but piqued my zeal. Let this be a lesson," I intoned, and would have continued at great length and for the duration of several stanzas had I thought it necessary—instead, I saw that the fire was even now devouring Mr N_____'s earlobes and that the heat had caused his skin to liquefy; so it was with no small measure of irritability that I again took my seat, thinking, well, such is the fate of the working class.

Yet despite my unequivocal victory in that match of wits, the brandy in my snifter seemed sooted, of a sudden, with a certain dryness, and ash, and spite. My refined palate would not tolerate it.

And so, with a good and deliberate motion (yet briskly, so as not to be late for my afternoon squash), I poured the drink out for Mr N_____ —that desiccated, steaming husk who was nonetheless the closest I may ever come to having a homie.

2: GARDENING.

I HAVE, OF LATE, OBSERVED A SPATE OF shockingly shameful behaviour within the halls of this estate: it seems that my own servants, those wretched beasts whose very existence is owed to my volatile whim, have taken to delirious flights of intoxication—much to the detriment of their designated labours!

After a particularly vigourous bout of cannon-the-sheep one recent eve, I sought my usual refreshment in the dining wing—only to discover the entire kitchen-staff crouched and huddled like feral dogs about a half-empty dram of oven-cleaner (a turpentine of mine own formulation, made from ground russet turtle-shells and the sanded filings of king-cobra scales).

The whelps whipped about with surprise as I stormed into the room. I disrupted their chittering assembly with a brisk remonstration on the foreign concept of *minding one's travails,* emphasising

THE MANOR ON WAVERLY HILL.

key points with the cracking tip of my father's old horse-whip. My fondest childhood memories are of his imposing frame seated high upon our phaeton, speeding briskly down the meadow-lane, bound for the church or some municipal affair for which business prescribed his attendance; his arm moving gracefully and purposefully back and forth, cracking and snapping that long tail of hide-leather upon the heaving, sheening skin of the eighteen scrabbling orphan lads who drew our buggy across the cobbles.

To be sure that my firm-handed discipline would take root in the feeble soil of the kitchen-help's attention, I made a messy affair of troweling seedlings into their very flesh—uprooting some prized bulbs from the upper garden for just this purpose, and making sure the ingrates appreciated the damage it would do to my floral display come Spring. I found myself half-hoping that the sopping innards of these fools would prove somehow fertile for the bulbs, nascent blooms that I urged to sop whatever nutrients they could from the lazy sweet-meats they now found themselves rooted in. What the talk of the garden club I'd be then, I mused, and how the society folk of Waverly Hill would beg to hear the secrets of my cultivation! I quickly buried the servants to their crowns in soft soil, with just the delicate stems and petals protruding from the surface—I would let the blooms find their full majesty and then, come Spring, with a flourish I would pull their whole roots from the earth and reveal my genius method!

Alas, when I put my plan to action, the crane-and-lever system I'd devised failed spectacularly (cursed rotting timber!), and dark, sinewy skeletons that had spent the better part of the winter beneath the soil suddenly rained like clattering hail directly onto the society folk of Waverly Hill. It will take my whole cunning to manage an invitation to the Summer Garden Show now.

3: AN ENCOUNTER WITH NEIGHBOURS.

O NE NIGHT NOT LONG PAST, I WAS enjoying a rousing bout of brand-the-waif in the parlour when a frightful thumping-about sounded at the Manor's front door. As I'd already sent Armand the porch-boy to his quarters in shame (punishment for the withdrawal of his kin from the aforementioned romp), I reluctantly set down my blistering poker, gathered about myself my cloak and night-tweeds, and trudged that long, heavy distance to the door with nary a pony to bear my weight.

Wary of prowlers, salesmen, and religious types, who in past had weighed down this portico at hours later even than this (and several scalps of which now adorned my smoking-room shelf), I peered through the panes to find several members of the Committee for Genteel Relations among Neighbours, a local do-gooder group whose noses I'd long been espied along the narrow edges of. These brigands would fain demand tribute from each home on Waverly Hill, in exchange for invitations to their regular luncheons and teas, tedious affairs all that I imagined I would dispatch a flaming zeppelin into if it wouldn't adversely affect the neighbourhood's equity.

The doddering specimens persisted in pounding away until I flung the door wide and stood guard across the threshold: "What brings you here," I bellowed (the effect somewhat ruined by a last-second voice-crack, thanks to residual excitement from the

OUT-DOOR THEATRE IS FOR NINNIES—[SEE PAGE 570.]

afore-mentioned vigourous round of waif-branding, my heart still beating its staccato rhythm at the thought of tender flesh searing into the form of my sigil), "and why do you darken this already-black hour with your dour proclamations?"

In point of fact, they had made no proclamations of yet, but I thought it best to head this option off at the fore; this took them aback, as was my intent, and allowed me to follow my first pronouncement with another, this even *more* imposing: "Speak! Speak, thou wretched beings; for mine evening grows weary and my patience thin. Why are you here?"

The lead figure, a gaunt, drawn Mr S____ , who had a face like a sand-weasel and an intellect to match, was the first to volunteer an answer: "We've come," he babbled, "to ask your pardon to conduct a search on your grounds for a missing person, last seen in this vicinity."

"Missing person!" I shouted, blasting them back a step, causing them to clutch at their scarves and stumble. "Any missing

THE DR.

person trespassing in these environs would have already been destroyed by my ridiculous array of laser cannons, pneumatic wasps, and wolves with razor-blade teeth." This last was in accord with the posters I had erected about the boundaries of the property to discourage flea-merchants and smack-snorkelers from stashing their mothy bindles in crannies they'd carved in my enormous garden statue of Zeus straddling a pelican. Such offences were common in the summer, before the sandstone became too cold to dig at with leprous fingers half-split from exposure. In one key instance I had in fact become quite distraught, as I'd had the sculptor already flayed upon completion of the initial work, and was forced to hire second-rate gravellers to repair the damage. It was a thoroughly inferior arrangement all round, and I had docked their pay at each instance that they'd snickered at my insistence on precise anatomical detail.

"J-Just the same," Mr S＿＿ gulped at me, looking for all the world like a carp-trout high on speed-balls, as seemed to be the way of the excitable elderly of to-day—"could we take a brief look 'round? For they won't let us return without some perfunctory investigation."

Fearing that it was the only way to satisfy their gibbering curiosity, I at last relented, and accompanied the Committee on a perambulation about the grounds. They peered this way and that, shining their lanterns into the hollows of trees and towards oddly-shaped earth-mounds and of course sneaking long glances at Zeus's mighty extravagance, and just when I was quite ready to show them the gate and ram the point home with a rusty spade dipped in cholera that I kept for precisely such situations, I was aghast to discover *a small figure,* huddled in a makeshift trench and covered with mud and debris.

"Is this your person?" I called.

Mr S_____ and his loathsome entourage quickly hobbled over and confirmed that yes, this was the runaway; to their credit, they thanked me profusely as they wrestled the recalcitrant refugee to his feet and escorted him firmly past the bounds of my dominion. I watched them the whole lurching way, ensuring they didn't break ranks at the last instant and dart for the nook 'twixt the pelican's loins—but they continued steadily, more hastily with each step.

Just before I turned my body to the building and my thoughts once again to burning my emblem into quivering, living meat, the briefest flash of rippling colour caught my eye, and it took three long glances, two glimpses, and a full half-stare to confirm what I thought I saw. For this fellow—this *waif*—this sad being that had run from the Committee and sought refuge where he thought they could not follow—had a *brand,* a mark still red by moonlight that would cool to brown o'er the coming weeks. 'Twas a baroque ligature of *C-G-R-N:* Committee for Genteel Relations among Neighbours.

A moment later the troupe was swallowed by the night. I watched the non-descript patch of dust where they had last stood, feeling an involuntary smile stretch and creep and crawl hideously across my lips. It was nice to be reminded that we *all* had pokers in our hands, in one way or another—and perhaps that old Mr S_____ wasn't such a bad chap after all. ✦

"GIMME FIVE."—[SEE PAGE 548.]

4: A PERSISTENT FUNK.

PICADILLY DEFEATED PADDINGTON in junior-circuit boulder-cricket, and the unfortunate result as the universe grieved was a foul, pendulous fog and a miserable, sticky-wet dew that clung to every surface like a too-eager monkey or a thousand Royalist leeches. The sun, shamed at having given those Picadilly brats sufficient light to bat by, hid behind its gloomy cloak and did not reveal its searing nudity for a solid seven days.

Thus, no brilliant sunbeams pierced my boudoir to herald the coming of morning; thus, I stumbled from the chamber in a groggy state sometime late afternoon and let any in my path have the full brunt of my foul temper.

I set out at once in search of my alarm-boy, who should never have let me slumber beyond the stroke of eleven. Historically this precept has been reinforced with fierce lashings equal to the number of minutes I had been allowed to sleep beyond the allotted hour; on this day, however, I found myself quite too weak to draw the whip to its proper length. I was only able to summon a few score blows at best, and even these were of a middling intensity, drawing less blood than a lazy Sunday-afternoon bout of shank-scampering. As the weakness was clearly due to my over-rested state, and thus the lad's fault directly (not at all the result of the three gallons of cod-oil I'd imbibed in shame upon hearing the final match result from an altogether-too-snide score-pigeon), I bid him continue on his own behalf.

I slumped *ennui*-ly into a chaise as he finished the job, evidencing quite the propensity for't—capital form, excellent stamina, obviously simply aching for such an opportunity to prove his mettle at the lash. *I must remember this lad,* I thought to myself, *come recruiting time for the spring whip league.*

Stimulating as it may have been to watch a top athlete at the pinnacle of his game draw blood on himself for an hour (each strike landing on uncut skin, I noted with awe approaching lust, until his back looked like a pile of red toothpicks so thick that Rain-Man would simply shrug and soil himself), the cloud refused to lift from my spirit, and I began to worry. A tough jolt of Da's sledgehammer-to-the-toe technique sent a brief shock of adrenaline to the ol' ticker, but the vigour quickly subsided to a dull throb, and even then, the ambient Vicodin always present in my bloodstream since the "experiment" made short work of the sensation. Likewise, a belt of rye whiskey rustled from the servants' quarters did naught more than make me briefly resent my own caste and simultaneously hate and yearn for the amiable leisure of the bourgeoisie. Noting its effects, I confiscated the full supply of this tonic at once, and disposed of it in like fashion with shocking alacrity, lest the elixir continue to foster dark thoughts among the rabble.

At this point I am told I began to wail, rounding the parlour in ever-increasing gyrations and continuously making feverish demands for things unavailable—old friends long gone, perhaps, or particular items that I had no reason to expect would be on the premises (such as eighteen ounces of jellyfish-liquor; a child's boot, size 6, with the heel missing; and a copy of the American Articles of Confederation with all references to the monarchy replaced with crude but workably-accurate diagrams of my aunt's many tattoos). For reasons that escape me as fully now as they did then, I apparently dispatched search-parties after these items at massive expense, and when the first team sheepishly returned within minutes, clutching a child's boot with the heel hastily removed (for there is a cobbler's just down the lane, between the veterinary cooper and the goldfarmer's kiosk) I apparently struck them mightily with it and demanded they bring me something not so, you know, *easy.*

E'en now my malaise persists. This house is empty as a tomb, its denizens dispatched far and wide in search of whatever random crap I sputtered while deluded on jimmy-juice. No doubt even now they are scouring the wharf for the telltale blue cap of a jellyfisher, not realizing that this time of year only the poor and the lame and the politically obstinate have refrained from following the weather and the squishy-crop to the warm shores of South America. Also, I should probably give Aunt H_____ a ring, just to warn her—because it is very probable that my kitchen staff is even now attempting to penetrate the National Archives in Washington.

I suppose I should be grateful for their ceaseless dedication, but at the moment I just have to figure out how to heat up some soup or something.

5: RABBLE.

A FTER A LENGTHY ARGUMENT RESULTING in much vicious loss of life among the expendable class (who remain in my employ for just such a purpose, it should be noted), I was coerced into attending a lecture conducted by a visiting Dr P____ , some "learned" sort in the field of law and politick. The Dr (or, should I say, the *alleged* Dr, for I saw neither certificate nor stethoscope) rambled on at great length about the horrid state of affairs in Social Welfare, goading the audience all a-holler clamouring for "Change! Change," until they were all but scaling the church-spire and tolling the bell like a bunch of baboons left to mind a stack of brass hammers: there's not much they can do, but they'll cause an awful racket doing it.

I had been invited to the dreadful event because my boot-waxer's great-nephew was to bear the colours at the start of the affair, and my chap hadn't any transportation to see his lad's big day—it would be a stretch to say that I had *volunteered* my own carriage for the evening, but in point of fact after many hours of his wailing and bawling and threatening the patent-leather finish with a nasty cadre of awls and augers, I did relent and decide to accompany the man into town. Should the evening go well, I was promised, I would see my footwear again. As it turned out, the grand-nephew had been shanked by a thug en route to the Hall, and was in fact spending the lecture bleeding in a rotted alley-way, but as we didn't find this out till some days later we proceeded at once to the event via the normal route.

I hadn't been down Admiralty Way since I'd been a ropy young cheese-twirler, hawking steaming yellow ribbons of Gouda and sun-aged Jarlsberg and fresh-scraped Fromunda from an oaken smoke-trunk strapped to my then-significant torso. I'd trawl the haberdasheries and the society salons, hoping to find a parched young dairy fan or a corpulent lady who'd long ago given up the corset. It was a hard life, to be sure; the competition was stiff even among other cheese-men (each with his own gimmick—Johnny Fresca used to claim that his wares were "fresh from the feast," meaning he'd scavenged from scraps thrown into the alley behind the Baron's kitchen) to say nothing of the other hawkers and shills and street-wags that crowded you for space and shoved their rancid goop at every mark they figured might have a loose shilling in his vest-pocket. That was when I'd left this town for a spell in Peru—but the life of a cheeser in the guano-caves is tougher yet.

It was a life I'd not been reluctant to leave behind. When an opportunity arose for me to murder my uncle for his massive inheritance, I did it with a spring in my step and a hatchet in my hand, wearing the very leather boots that my impertinent wax-man now held hostage in his stinking hovel.

Perhaps it was because of my years spent elbowing my way through the same cutthroat (and cutpurse, and cutbuttock) street-level world that the besuited and bemonocled set claimed to be Expert in that I held no stock in, nor interest for, so-called "reformers" such as Dr P____. The Dr spoke at great length about the need for "bottom-up change," repairing the ills of society from what he perceived as their source—in essence, eradicating the "unseemly" classes whole-sale with extreme prejudice and battle-axes. While I was no stranger to the salving effect of indiscriminate murder, it dawned on me that the Dr perceived his proposed purge as a *social good*—and murder couched in *policy* has hardly the rewarding flavour of murder exercised simply as *pastime*.

And so the Dr blathered on, seeming to get off on the roaring support of the crowd. Once I realised that he had no interest in homicide's *æsthetic* dimension, I knew that it was time to disassemble his argument and de-podium his ego. For torment does not have to be fleshly to be gratifying.

"Tell me, sir," I bellowed, angling myself for maximal acoustic range (a trick I had developed with a cheese-pole in my sunburnt fist)—"Tell me, what is to stop the 'bottom,' as you so call it, from rising 'up' to seize control of these very institutions that threaten to help them?"

The room was silent in an instant. No one had yet dared call out Dr P____ on his poppycock platitudes and empty bargains. He adjusted his junk nervously, then addressed me directly.

"I'm not sure why you think they would react with such hostility to programmes and initiatives designed to benefit them," he said. In response I summoned up a laugh that would have rocked the bowels of Hades itself.

"Help them!" I roared. "We can help them by buying their cheese-wands, or scratching a hard-to-itch spot for them. Help them by putting their children to work earning a living in the factories, or giving them sixpence to run errands that require small bodies in tight spaces. But do not, sir"—and here I pointed a quivering finger, largely to watch the expressions on those seated nearby turn from bemusement to aghastment—"do not presume that they are lacking in the courage, the wherewithal, or the ingenious mercenary spite to graciously accept your hand up and then judo-flip you over their shoulder and into the path of a speeding autobus, or off a cliff, or maybe under a horse or something."

I left the lecture hall with vigour in my step and flourishing my awesome cape. (The discussion had continued for some time after my impromptu polemic, but I had stopped listening immediately after delivering my own opinion.) As I crossed the gaslit lane to mount my carriage, my gaze drifted into the shadowy alleys beyond the shallow pool of flickering light.

I had left that life behind for a reason. It was no way to live, always watching over one's shoulder expecting a shiv in the ribs for merely rubbing a man's toes in a friendly fashion, or for nicking his socks in a pinch. That life was one without servants, or port wine (besides what could be wrung from one's hair when one took a wild, naked run through the distillery in summer), or gigantic, ridiculous statuary of Zeus mounting a pelican, or brutality exercised as sport. It was a life not hardly worth living.

Unlike the Dr and his sheepish congregation, I *knew* what the wretches of Admiralty Way were capable of. I understood the cunning and hatred that the street honed in one's œsophagus. And now that I was no longer one of them, I knew that their eyes watched me the whole lonely way back to the mansion, my carriage rattling hastily through their darkened by-ways, my spirit afraid for the sharpest, brief instant before my front door clicked shut and locked against the darkness.

Beneath great grey mounds of night, I imagined, they were swivelling their yellow eyes and huddling beneath their thick, besmallpoxed blankets, coughing their deep phlegmy coughs and plotting their revenge.

6: THE KEY-RING.

ONCE EVERY GREAT WHILE, USUALLY after a particularly hearty swig of coot-barrel moonshine (brewed the old-fashioned way—by my servants in a marble bath-tub), I find myself digging through the old oaken bureau in my study and extracting my late uncle's great, thick key-ring from beneath mouldy mounds of old maps and tobacco-straws and spiked corsets. Without particularly intending to, I have on occasion let idle curiosity drift me slowly through the halls of the East Wing, where I may carefully try a key or three against the many rooms that have remained locked for the entirety of my residency.

Usually my patience disallows me more than a few rattling attempts at the knobs before I move to the next door in the hall; with near one hundred keys on the ring, I would be hard-pressed to suppose where all of their corresponding locks and latches might possibly lie. So many must be lost in the world, I reckoned, destined to forever yawn in wait for this rusted old ring of jangly metal.

But there were many locks in this hall-way as well, and there were many keys on the ring. Thus, on these odd week-end days when the whole of the staff was dutifully concerned with steam-cleaning my bedding and toilette, I often find myself leaning my weight on the creaking floor-boards of the East Wing, the heavy mass of keys in one hand and a doorknob in the other.

On each attempt, I would try three keys in each of three doors. I suppose I could have stood there shoving scores of keys into dozens of locks all the day long until one gave way, but such a cold method seemed wholly devoid of charm. I preferred to believe that my spare selection invited Fate to intervene, should she decide to do so. I would never make an empirical study of the many keys on the ring, full of check-lists and calipers and abacusi and no doubt one of Babbage's clanging pornography-engines rolled into my front garden; rather, I enjoyed prolonging the mystery for as long as Fate deemed appropriate, believing that which-ever door (if any) might open on this day, that it purposefully led to something she would have me find.

Not all of the keys on the ring were simple affairs of wrought metal. Some were highly stylised, having been picked up by my late Uncle M_____ on his merchant voyages to the Orient and New World. Uncle M_____ had made his early living trading furs, but when the coon-pelts of his native Brighamptonshire-upon-Grime began to decline in demand against exotic Russian sables and Chinese dragon-sloughs and Portuguese Incan-scalps, he raised a modest sum for an ambitious new expedition. He was next seen five years later, driven bat-scat mad by the sun and the sea, but helming an armada of merchant ships packed to the gill-staves with delightful foreign treasures—Formosan muskrat-snout for the ladies; West African juju dust, to cure gas (or, more precisely, to defer involuntary expulsions by a fixed 46 days, at which point one is revisited by the affliction—but still, a handy tincture in certain situations); a full, certified dram of snot from a Hindoo fakir with a moderate head cold; and a slim shard of bone that proved to be the left fore-knuckle of Simon of Cyrene, rescued during a minor crusade that (rumours indicate) led him down the Amazon, through Darkest Paraguay, and at one point, onto the very surface of the moon, which he insisted to the last that he conquered for Christendom—a claim none has been able to disprove.

With this newfound bounty Uncle M＿＿＿ was set for life. He established a curio shop where he hawked exotic merchandise and traded tales of the sea and far-off lands for piles and piles of raw seal blubber (with which he was secretly insulating the basement). At the end of each day he would pack the day's blubber into a waggon and begin the long trudge up Waverly Hill to the same estate that I now call my own home. His key-ring bore silent witness to those days of strange travel: here, a carved-ivory sawtooth; there, polished mahogany; and this—yes, this!—a fine bronze, the gentle green patina of which *just* matched the tarnished hue of the door-knob my fingers wrapped about now.

It turned easily. With a soft click the door swung open. Light entered the room for the first time in years. A musty smell greeted me. I held a handkerchief to my nose and pushed my lantern through a thick layer of cobwebs. What long-forgotten treasures would Fate's guided lamp-light finally from this dark alcove reveal?

I took three more steps and then stopped short. A dry mound in a chair. Dark, moth-eaten felt. Skin brittle as ashes. A gaze as blank as parchment. A neck split in twain by a single, ancient blow.

Right. I'd forgotten this was where I'd stashed his body.

7: A DELIVERY.

I SAW IT IN THEIR EYES—THEY WERE AFRAID to approach me, a well-learnt trait, but still they must have wondered: why does master pace so? What restless spirit inhabited his motions; why did he mark a steady, repetitive tread 'twixt the book-shelf and the mantel?

They attended to their various tasks dully, dusting the collection of Dostoyevsky erotica in the parlour or polishing the bronze buttocks of Heracles in the foyer with simple, disengaged motions, the corners of their eyes fixed on my nervous marathon. I would have admonished them, with the serving-spoon if necessary, but today my concentration lay elsewhere.

Scarcely had the parcel-boy rapped once but I had thrown the front door open wide. "Come in, come in," I indicated, clearing the way for him to trundle his hand-truck through the jamb, its vulgar wheels marring the glistening floor-boards with the squeak of un-varnished rubber. I cringed at the sound of the death of that perfect finish—but no matter. One of the leering ones would give it a buff as soon as I had retrieved my prize from within this looming crate.

The sweltering chap—an East Yorker, by his inflection—guided the crate into the foyer and set it near Heracles' divine toes. I scribbled on his claim-slip and snapped for a crow-bar! A hammer! Any implement would do!

My sudden bark startled the bronze-waxer out of her reverie—she scampered back to whatever wretched corner she loitered in whenever she wasn't busy waxing the bulbous loins of the cel-ebrated demi-god, returning quickly with a ball-peen hammer.

I stared at her for a long moment. This hammer had no claw; it had a ball on one face, a peen on the other. Neither could open a crate. "Do you expect me to smash it to splinters?" I growled.

Before she could reply I had buried the peen deep into her fore-head. "Bring me a claw hammer!" I bellowed. Sometimes you just have to spell it out.

As the call reverberated through the North Atrium, I heard the frantic shuffling of a dozen pairs of feet rushing to search a dozen tool-boxes, utility-bins, and hammer-foundries (the one in the Lower Annex had only recently been de-commissioned, once my enthusiasm for the hobby had dimmed with its difficulty. Freaking *hard*). Within moments I had thrust at me a goodly number of claw hammers; I took a delicate pause and chose a robust model, glimmering with chrome and with just the right hint of scuff that implied hardy labour. With vigour befitting a man of my hands-on quality, I applied the claw to the crate's lid and leaned my weight upon the handle.

At first I feared it was my spine making that horrible creaking. But no—it was the nails, slowly awakening from their woody slumber and drawing themselves reluctantly from the planks within which they had been interred.

Inside the crate was darkness. "Fetch me a lantern!" I cried. I was making stuff *happen*.

Flame in hand, I accosted the shadow, calling its mother various insulting names, but (like a true gentleman) restricting myself to those epithets I knew personally to be true. Within, I could barely discern the outline of a large device, packed tightly against damage with layers of saw-dust.

Saw-dust! The flakes swirled aloft, stirred by my exploration. I waved them away with my lantern. Then I thought about that for exactly one-half second before the dried shavings erupted suddenly into a blaze.

TURTLE-TURNING.

A roiling gout of flame consumed the saw-dust instantly, blasting me backwards with the heat, propelling me powerfully against Heracles' outstretched middle finger. The lantern slipped from my hands and crashed to the mahogany floor. The oil spread over the slick surface like dock-waifs over a fish-spill. The fire licked the walls; it licked the drapes. It licked Heracles, inappropriately.

I fumbled backwards, shrieking for water. My dutiful hydration-boy stepped forward from his alcove with a chilled bottle of Perrier and a swishing-glass; I had trained him well. But this was no time for sparkling pretentiousness. I heaved the lad full-force into the conflagration, hoping to staunch the blaze's ravenous appetite for misery. The heat-monster hissed, then spat; the lad went down without a cry, and I wondered for the briefest of seconds: if I hadn't cut his tongue out for telling idle mule-tales about his hee-haw days and high-burro time at the peasant-infested fairgrounds—would he have screamed?

But now was not the time for idle speculation! The blaze had reached the powder-kegs. I cringed as the tongues of flame enveloped the barrel-staves and dissolved the joint-pitch that held them tightly sealed.

The staves fell free. The powder billowed forth in great, cloudy bursts, settling heavily over the room.

With a sputter, and a hiss, and a final, angry crackle, the fire went out.

I peeked through my fingers. The room was empty; the staff had fled for their miserable lives. The charred skeleton with the ball-peen hammer lodged firmly in its skull tangled around my ankles as I approached the blackened kegs, as if pulling me back. I pulverised the thing against Heracles and approached the barrels. What luck! Fire-retardant powder in the North Atrium! How lucky that I hadn't disturbed these drums since my brief dally with open-air torch-juggling, those many months hence! Such was the foresight that kept the servants in constant awe of my worldly prowess. I ticked off "fire" on the list of disasters averted—we'll not have *that*

A CORPSE.

problem in here again, I wagered, now that we'd had it once and kicked it off yelping.

I ran the powder between my fingers, its fine white silt stinging my skin with chemical. I dropped the dust and ground a last glimmering ember into the charcoal floor. The shortsighted staff would have long days ahead of them refinishing these planks to my satisfaction.

My attention turned to the splintered crate. The saw-dust that had caused this whole mess was now a fine ash, painting everything grey. Heracles resembled a marble ghost. The Perrier bottle was a white funerary urn, flecked with airborne charcoal. The hydration-boy looked like a terribly-burnt corpse—the resemblance was simply uncanny.

With no concern for the black mess that crumbled in my fingers, I pushed the husk of the crate's remains away to reveal the device that sat still un-singed in the centre of the havoc; my shining new appliance, its steel surface marred with dust that brushed away with ease. I saw my face in that brilliant shine; it looked eager.

I raised the lid. Twisted the knob. Clicked the igniter. This would be some barbecue.

8: BOTHERSOME RELATIONS.

I CERTAINLY COULDN'T FAULT THE LAD for enthusiasm. He gibbered wildly, practically slobbering with delight as he led me from hall-way to hall-way, room to stifling room; the entire place was filled floor-to-ceiling with mounds of horrid clutter passing for his particular brand of whimsy, and I was fast growing sick of it all.

This was Josiah, the bothersome son of an insufferable half-sister—a near-stranger who'd dispatched the whelp to my door with the fool idea that I, as a well-known patron of the finer arts, would indulge the brat's ridiculous notions. For Josiah fancied himself an artist—and a "contemporary" artist at that, interested mainly in silly experiments with foodstuffs smeared on paper and the creation of endless wax-cylinders filled with dissonant recordings of lead plumbing being played with a horse-hair bow. These cylinders I inspected with feigned interest before casually placing them near the window, hoping they would melt down into sad yellow candles of wasted youth.

He'd brought me to his squalid hovel to expound at excruciating length about his newest project, some flotsam notion that had caught upon the craggy reefs of his barren brain, washed up on the shore of an absinthe-fuelled stupour, no doubt. With each dreadful step he drew me ever-deeper into this cavernous maze of misery, his mouth never ceasing all the while:

"I see this being the beginning of a new age of connectivity," he gushed, "where you and me and whoever else *gets it* can just take interpersonal relationships to a whole new level. See, what are we *missing* as a people? We already have verbal communication. We already have body language. We already have written communication. And *still* there are misunderstandings, problems when people just don't *get* each other."

I shook my head with dismay and rubbed my brow distressedly. My scalp was beginning to chill from the sheer idiocy of his breath. Josiah had taken my hat from me when we'd crossed the threshold, ages ago and much nearer the surface, and I was beginning to wonder if I would ever feel that fine felt nap again.

"My new method is about direct *idea-to-idea* communication," he went on, his back to me as we rounded yet another mildewed corner in yet another dark corridor. I found myself wondering how the penniless lout could afford a property as expansive as this, but figured he probably made up the balance lad-whoring to Germanics in the eve—no shame in't when the purse is tight; we've all been there.

Finally he trimmed his lantern and hung it from a sconce. We entered a large room filled with mouldy tarpaulins, and being allergic to tarpaulins, I promptly sneezed.

Josiah didn't even bother to extend me the basic courtesy of a "God bless you, kind sire, and may the Devil keep and protect you." I wiped my whiskers with my handkerchief and narrowed my gaze on the inconsiderate sot, too busy pulling the heavy brown rags from several standing easels.

"Each core idea is represented by a symbol, with varying grades of secondary and tertiary ideas," Josiah said, whipping the cloth from the easels with a quite-unnecessary flourish that raised a deadly swirl of dust and micro-tarpaulin-particles. I flapped my hands before my nose but could not help but unleash another mighty explosion.

When I looked up, I saw half-a-dozen easels in the dank space; each canvas decorated with a series of colourful picto-grammes. Vulgar simulacra of true talent all; I turned my nose at the lot. I was trying to find the door in the flickering glow of the lantern-light when Josiah came darting at me, reaching to offer me a series of stiff cards. Dabbing my running nose with one hand, I took the cards with the other, anything to hasten our egress from this damnable pit.

The cards were stamped with the same disgustingly-bright emblems as the canvases: in my hands, the three cards showed a heart (what treacle), a stack of money (of course!) and a palette with paintbrush (how original). Josiah's eyes practically begged me to understand with their fool-hardy earnestness.

"Don't you see," he said, "it's a whole new way of communicating. Words may be too surgical to express the full breadth of my meaning, but simple gestures or other visual cues may lack specificity. With the ideo-gramme cards, you are exposed to many facets of what I'm sharing simultaneously—all free for you to interpret."

I stared at his chittering face, then at the cards again. His concept was asinine. I could scarcely grasp the meaning behind the trio of cards he'd shoved at me. Was he asking for money? Claiming some relationship between art and commerce? Dis-avowing the same relationship? I raised my hand to dash the cards to the floor, preparing to immediately thereafter rain blows upon the lad until he led me back up to sunlight, back to my hat and my carriage and my home full of sanity. But he stopped my arm; caught my elbow halfway up. "Whatever you want to tell me, tell it with these," he said, pushing a tall stack of cards into my hand.

I tell you, I stared at the boy as if he'd grown goose-feathers. But it was clear there was no budging him from this wretched spot until I played along with his game, at least for a little while. Very well—I'd been in His Majesty's Dramatis Corps; I could certainly put on a game face.

I shuffled quickly through the cards, taking in their discrete images, looking for any appropriate to my situation. I chose a vicious-looking sword, a house on fire, and a skeleton doing a jig. Added to my hand were two horses engaged in coitus, a cactus with a skin disorder, and a witch drowning in æther. Then I found a leper-dog, and had a tough time choosing between it and the rotting corpse of Charlemagne. Finally I settled the issue by trumping them both with the Golden Scroll of the Lord's Judgment, rendered

in striking relief complete with tortured sinners and a writhing
Judas caught between the Saviour's toes, and handed the fanned
stack back to Josiah without ceremony.

His eyes went saucer-shaped at once. He looked up at me slowly,
and his heart seemed to shatter even as I watched. His spirit left
his face and took up residence in his bowel, settling firmly and
uncomfortably, and affecting his posture noticeably. "I'm sorry
you feel that way," he all but whispered, "but frankly, I've found
that largely, Mother's been right—*nobody's* ready for my unique
genius."

Meanwhile I'd found a large jug of umber house-paint and began
to unceremoniously dump it out over his precious canvases. It was
already tea-time, and at this rate I would never get my hat back.

9: THE GREAT PURGE.

T HIS TIME OF YEAR, THE NIGHTS BRING
with them a quite unseasonable chill as the heavy wetness of
Spring-time lay a stifling blanket of fog o'er the low country. This
night in particular, the windows of the mansion were steamed
white from the inside, glazing the night beyond with a fine silk of
wetness and warmth.

For in the Great Hall we endeavoured to make double-duty of
the evening; we could both clean out some musty store-rooms and
stave off the chill by stoking the central furnace with smelly stacks
of leather-bound tomes from my late uncle's library. I'd never given
much thought to that high-ceilinged room off the East Wing, its
windows angled towards the winter sunrise; tall shelves crammed
with dusty volumes never held much interest for me. Their spines
cracked and faded from use, the gilt text long-since cannibalised for
showy dental applications—why, who *knew* what was in all those
books, and whoever could be bothered to find out?

THE LIBRARY.

Certainly not me; I had the heftiest plucked first, loaded into wheel-barrows for the bumpy ride down the spiral steps to the Great Hall and its waiting, snapping stove. The thickest volumes burnt slowly, the flame almost dawdling as an orange line gradually ate away at the dense leaves, stacked a thousand deep like the world's least-fulfilling tea sandwich. The paper curled like a spider in the heat; it was great sport to see how gentle a touch could still send the fragile skeleton exploding into ash.

In this manner we burnt Uncle's entire vast library. Not a single book was left un-consumed. In fact, once we'd gotten into the swing of the thing, we scoured every nook of the estate to make it a clean sweep. We purged the pantry of cook-books, the better to make each meal the adventure it had once been in the early days of Man. A stack of ledgers from Uncle's old roll-top desk, appearing to contain a hand-written account of his many travels into Darkest Africa during the Zulu conflict—gone, blazed to a cinder. The shoe-shine boy's tearful illustrated diaries—giggled at, then reduced to ashes. "Val-Pak" coupon books too numerous to count—thrust into the flame with something approaching glee.

The whole of the staff got in on the action, volunteering whatever printed matter they could find, fighting each other for the privilege of adding to the smouldering pile. Phone books joined bank statements joined Sudoku collections joined a piñata, for some reason. (While not technically 'printed matter,' the piñata was in fact made of brilliantly-burning paper and besides, I didn't want to hurt the feelings of the poor lad who'd brought it down slowly from his sleeping-corner in the attic. I'd been meaning to have the beastly thing destroyed anyhow, so in a sense, this was win-win. A pity about the candy, though.)

After three days of marathon biblio-graphic bon-fire, we stopped to catch our breath, our collective chests heaving with the effort, our lungs choked with thick smoke and our fingernails dark with soot, a strange unity binding us once and forever with the indelible tattoo of shared destructive experience. We'd done it. We'd torched every piece of paper in the place. Towards the end of our frenzied crusade, wall-paper was being torn down in great sheets from the walls. Toilet-paper rolls were blazing up like giant marshmallows. An entire collection of drawings I'd made in the second grade was destroyed in an instant. (Rather rubbish anyhow—no sense of composition, shoddy control of the pen, and in retrospect, bloody derivative of the Ninja-Turtles.) We were exhilarated. We laughed. We grasped each other with charcoal-black hands and smeared the remains of *The Remains of the Day* on each others' glisten-ing, sweat-slicked torsos. We danced about the flame through the night and into the next day, and when the sun dawned in the East the following morning, penetrating the fog for the first time all week, it gazed into a starkly bare room in which every molecule of paper had been fed to the flame. The shelves stood skeletal in the sky-lit brightness.

The next night we got cold again, so we took to igniting the kitchen-help.

10: DISTURBANCE
AT NIGHT-TIME.

NOT YET A FORTNIGHT AGO, I WAS peaceably slumbering beneath my lady-hair comforter when a frightful crash startled me awake. Snatching a lantern from my doe-eyed lamp-man, who'd barely stirred at the racket (someday when I take a holiday I must allow the chap some sleep), I rushed to the veranda and gazed out over the North Atrium, where clouds of dust still settled from some mysterious impact.

At first glance, nothing seemed amiss, save for a few trinkets shaken to the tile and a few cripples thrown from their feet. (Which should teach *them* to loiter in the North Atrium.) Upon closer examination, however, I detected something most peculiar—a slowly spinning *wheel,* jutting distinctly through the Atrium's ceiling, having smashed its way clear through the roof-tiles.

I leaned over the railing to inspect the ground far below—sure enough, there was the debris, wood and stone and terra-cotta forming an impromptu burial-mound for one of those many doddering hobblers that infested this room every year, quivering, bebunnyslippered feet the only visible remnant of the ancient trespasser.

Just then the roof creaked with a sudden massive shifting of weight. I spied a graceful, shadowy form silhouetted against the night-misted sky-lights, moving gingerly from toe-tip to toe-tip, testing each inch of roof-tile before pressing his (her? its?) weight against it. A gentle *tap-tap-tap,* outlined in stark relief against the bright, moonlit night; I could make out a jaunty traveller's-scarf, dancing in a mid-night breeze, and even thought I espied the delicate seams and precise workmanship of fine kid-leather whelping-gloves. I shook my head to dislodge that last image, sending it crashing to the far-off cripple-floor. For surely my eyes had not *that* acuity, at this far distance. I would fain not let wistful wishfulness over-ride factual observation.

Tap-tap-tap—the cripples craned their waddle-necks heaven-wards in rapturous confusion, turkey-like, their watery, becataracked globes straining to track a vague form at the very limits of their perception. Yet who could blame them for pushing their senses to bursting? Their lives had suddenly grown interesting. As for me: I was none too thrilled about the sudden and indecorous rousing, nor the jagged gap that now yawned o'er my head, yet I had the most wretched trouble bringing my anger to bear against this most delicate of night-færies, this dark vision of grace from realms I knew not whereof.

Suddenly the silhouette slipped, and I felt a dreadful rumble in the rafters: with a terrible shriek of twisting hardwood and rending fabric, I spied for one terrible split second the angular shape of some man-made construct outlined sharply in the sky-lights—then the whole contraption came shattering through the lead-glass, sending rippling shards cascading onto the very veranda where I stood gaping. (Not to mention, because I care not to, the dangerous exposure faced by the league of cripples far below.) And then a mangled behemoth of wire-braces and triangular struts and flapping canvas came hurtling through the ceiling all at once, threatening quite imperiously to dash the brains from every last cripple indeed—but suddenly, quite haltingly, it *stopped* with a great heaving smash, its murderous fall arrested by the twin railings of my own veranda and a second, vacant balcony mirrored across the Atrium.

I am ashamed to admit that I shielded my head from the raining debris, like a scurrilous coward or a common marble-thief, or possibly a sooty chimney-tramp caught with arms full of mouldy beet-bread and cheeks stuffed with root-sprung potatoes. Indignant at my instincts, I raised my skull henceforth back into the dangerous open, the better to espy this uninvited interloper, the figure whose form had so intrigued me on the roof-top.

A-ha! Movement! "Come out, scoundrel or sylph, færie or fiend, whichever ye be," I blustered, putting on my best Authority tenor (though this particular voice had scarcely found exercise at this hour of night since my last dalliance with the Duchess in her gazebo on old Privy Lane)—

The figure stirred, deep within the wobbling innards of the smashed conveyance that even now swayed uneasily over the cripple-pit.

My first impression was of a tanned-leather riding-cap; this revealed a shock of white hair, snowy and mane-ish. Then a slim hand, steadied on the lip of the man-seat embedded in the contraption's centre. Finally, the figure turned to face me for the first time.

A slim form indeed! For there was hardly flesh at all on these bones; what meat there was seemed sunken to the skull like a vacuum-hose applied to a jellyfish. Eyes peered out at me from deep well-holes; teeth guarded a grave-yard of sorrows with their crooked tomb-stones of misery. The nose was hairy and gross. And the voice! Oh, the voice!

"With greatest apologies, kind Sir," it hoarsely began, struggling to wrench the very air from the room; "my navigat-ometer seems to have led me astray. See, I had attempted the first circumlocution of the—"

Not another word did I abide from that wrinkled jaw-trap. A fierce kick from my slipper and the whole wreck shifted quickly— until all that resounded from that rusty voice-box was one long, protracted syllable as the entire mess found its swift, destructive, and terribly loud path to the hard, cold Atrium floor.

Thus disgusted with the turn of the evening's events, I resolved to retire at once, to perhaps rescue some portion of my aborted respite—but curiosity got the better of me, as it has a favour to do in times such as these, and I afforded myself one last o'er-look over the veranda to peruse the tangled wreckage of my diversionment. The rattling old sop was *moving,* I noted with amazement—not running, not leaping nor skipping nor reciting the times tables in Pig-Esperanto, but certainly there was ghost yet left in that old meat-shape. Before mine eyes he seemed to find his feet—albeit

MR BERTRAND—[SEE PAGE 48.]

with a dodder that the surrounding pack of cripples
recognised as perhaps too
uncomfortably similar to
their own.

So they were on him,
rending his limbs and
sinking weak, waggling
teeth into rubbery skin
and tearing the intruder
apart; deftly, with precision
borne of a life-time of bitter
competition, feeling for the
knobby soft points that
rheumatism had scooped
from each round knuckle. They popped the pensioner's finger-joints
like pop-corn and spat the nails to the tile with disdain.

Within minutes, they had totally devoured the foreigner. This
was *their* turf, after all.

And then they sat, as if nothing had happened, as if the
destroyed wreck of a flying-machine had been their constant companion these many freezing months, as if it was in fact their own
splintered city-scape, as if the whole grisly affair were no more
remarkable than a slight drizzle during afternoon tea.

There they have sat these ten and more days, quietly inhabiting
the wreck, making it slowly and terribly their own.

Perhaps if I tossed down some wood-clamps and glue they
would fix the blasted thing and find some way out of here.

11: SAVED BY INSTINCT.

WHEN THE LION'S-HEAD DOOR-knocker roared its deep, fateful pounding, I somehow knew that the day was about to become bothersome. Each step down the velvety stair-case felt like submerging myself deeper and deeper into a clammy well of foreboding. When I passed the rising bucket at the halfway point I briefly debated sending a note up back to the world explaining my plight—but I sucked in my breath, kept on slithering into the dank, fearful depths, and when I eventually touched the doorknob it was like a stab of ice run through my palm into my very heart.

At that instant the dreadful pounding sounded again—*BOOM, BOOM, BOOM,* sharp and piercing, the knob trembling in my grasp. This morning's gentle sun-beams and cool spring breezes enjoyed from the high mount of my piggyback-oaf's knobby hunch seemed a thousand years ago. Swallowing the last of my late-morning Percoset, I seized the knob with purpose and flung the devilish slab wide.

The sunlight—blinding! I clawed at my eyes, letting something not unlike a shriek escape my throat. The snooty gentleman at the portico startled. His hand had been raised to resume that massive thumping, and at my sudden appearance he fiddled his snooty white-gloved fingers in alarm before regaining his snooty compo-sure and folding them, snootily, at his waist-coat.

The man inquired as to whether he had the correct name and address, and I resignedly informed him that yes, I was indeed the one he had come to see. As he took in this information I detected a subtle but definite resignation enter his stance. His shoulders slumped a half-inch, before freezing in the interests of propriety; I have no doubt that should he have been given information of like import in private, or rather in the company of any other but the very object, he would have fallen to the ground at once, a broken man.

As it was, however, he simply choked back down whatever bile had risen in his aristocratic gullet and extended a stiff, cotton hand. "I am Mr Bertrand," he said snootily, "from the assessor's."

From the assessor's! Those shiftless penny-mongers had been a thorn in my side since I'd inherited this property. Apparently my late uncle had accrued some outstanding debts in his time (no surprise there, the cootish lolly-wag) and his creditors have been quite keen to seize the estate as recompense. The value locked in these walls is the only thing keeping them from coming after my person for the sum, their purses flapping their tiny little pincer-jaws, straining at the leashes, waiting for the barest chance to lunge for my anatomy and rend it asunder until my veins spewed coins, or something.

And this man was here to report back to those nickel-hounds just how much value still remained as equity within these iron gates. To shut him out would risk his report indicating that the preferred target for their foul attentions was indeed my own person.

At this ugly conundrum I bared my teeth in what may only have been called a smile because the situation expected one. In truth, it was more of an expression one might make when the dentist prepares to examine one's teeth. *Look, see my incisors, my canines. I am an animal,* I indicated to this man on my stoop. Yet I heard myself say "Won't you come in."

After a moment I realised that I should, in fact, step aside to allow him to do what my voice had invited him to do. This took some doing, but was accomplished. Bertrand crossed the threshold, and I could tell the instant that his eyes adjusted to the dimness inside—for once he could see, he shuddered.

Dutifully he produced a loose-leaf pad and began paging through a series of documents. I craned my neck for any clue as to what he was expecting to see. Had Uncle claimed some overly-fantastic value to the place that Bertrand intended to verify?

I tried to make out the writing, but it had been set down in some bizarre system that was foreign to me. Each word was comprised entirely of individual glyphs and shapes, and to make it worse, the glyphs were repeated throughout the page in different arrangements and varying order—the whole affair was impossible for a layman to decipher.

But clearly the brainy Bertrand had no such trouble, for he lay right in with a to-see list that sent my stomach leaping to my throat. The North Atrium (with its aero-carriage damage to the roof still yawning sunlight and rain onto the bowed forms of the cripples)? The Great Hall (with its still-smouldering pile of ash and book-remnants)? Worst of all, the statue of Heracles just behind me in the foyer yet reeked of ash and lighter-fluid and the late-night oil-fighting that always seemed to follow, seamlessly, after a robust cook-out. There would be no hiding *this* indiscretion.

Bertrand's eyes took in the sooted figure even as I debated what to do—while my mind raced, he made arcane marks on his pad with some sort of sharpened wooden stick that left dark squiggles on the paper. What he was writing, I could scarcely imagine.

And then I lit upon a plan: I would gamely offer the staid inspector an utterly comprehensive tour of the entire garden, which would certainly occupy the better part of the afternoon. In that time the staff could easily clean the statue, sweep out the ashes from the Great Hall, repair the roof in the North Atrium, re-upholster the furniture in the sitting den, shovel out the dogs from the basement, find a home for the Gipsy band in the bottom orchard, add a water-closet to the servants' quarters in the attic as the housing code required, and then deport all of themselves before Bertrand could ring his pin-headed friends at the Naturalisation Service. Yes, this would take a fair amount of doing, but it could certainly work— after all, elaborate, perfectly-crafted plans such as these were what my considerable reputation was known for. To action!

I turned to Bertrand, eager to set my plan to the tracks, and was shocked to realise that in my reverie I had killed the man. My fists were drenched in dripping crimson, knuckles torn from where his teeth had (apparently) offered some resistance. The chap was a mangled mess atop the tile, battered almost beyond recognition. I stepped quickly aside to avoid staining my house-slippers in the growing pool of blood and fluids.

It has been said that often-times the body's instincts know what to do even when the mind is still reeling from the problem. In this case, my clever fists proved the axiom correct. I heaved a sigh of relief, and smiled for the first time in what felt like an age. Thank heavens I wasn't going to have to put in that bathroom. That would have been a bitch.

12: REMEMBRANCES.

IT HAPPENS TO THE BEST OF US: one gets too wrapped-up in a rousing game of swat-the-orphan-in-the-garden and one loses track of the hour. I should have noted the sun sweeping dangerously close to the far-off horizon, but alas, I was too enrapt in the frivolity at hand—such is the danger of beginning the game after luncheon; it often lasts late into the night, as the squat little devils simply do not tire.

It was the church-bells that reminded me of the time; they toll furiously throughout the day to keep the bat-creatures at bay. The Archbishop had issued the mandate after learning through bitter experience that only the resonant assault of those massive brass clangers could create the necessary disturbance in the sonic land-scape that would disorient (and, it should be said, nauseate) the vile, winged beasts' airborne equilibrium.

The cathedral down in Stamps-upon-Staves had been under relentless assault from the vicious pests for months, losing uncounted bushels of communion wafers in each blighted onslaught, with no defence proving the least bit effective. The bat-things simply soared above pitch-forks, and proved not at all receptive to entreaties read from the collected works of St. Augustine. The order discovered the bell stratagem quite by accident when, in an unrelated incident, a certain love-struck hunch-back hung himself from the pull-rope at the exact moment the flying beasts were darting through the nave. The invaders were routed within seconds, their keen sense of predatory cunning rendered utterly useless by the concussive pealing, and (so the report goes) they banged and flapped about inside the sanctuary, weaving and spewing putrid bile from churning innards, for as long as it took the abbot to cut the hunch-back from the rope and for the peals to echo away.

Then they left, it's told, amid much praise from the hapless, goop-drenched folk of the cathedral. Notwithstanding his smelly attire, the abbot had offered a prayer and a sacrifice in gratitude, then tracked down the lass who'd driven the hunch-back o'er the edge and made her a full citizen of Stamps-upon-Staves, her outstanding warrants for solicitation repealed and her name entered into the town register in majestic gilt ink (an honour redeemable for free cutlets at the cutleter's during cutlet season). The day was won, despite the fact that the cathedral of Stamps-upon-Staves smells of bat-bile still, and likely will for generations to come. But from that victorious day till this, the bells all 'cross the shire now ring out at random intervals to ward off future attacks.

Today, hearing the bells reminded me not of any particular hour, but rather of dead hunch-backs—which reminded me that it was time to feed my own, kept captive in the basement. I tossed a hock of indiscriminate meat his way and rushed to dress for my appointment in town—an important meeting with the municipal solicitor regarding my own unmistakable awesome-ness, among other topics as were sure to arise.

Within ten minutes the carriage was harnessed and ready; a mere four hours after that, I emerged at the door, irate at having only time for the hastiest of vinegar-soaks. Before visiting the town on any business, I'd taken up the habit of soaking in vinegar for a solid day, so as to pre-empt whatever odours might await me once I crossed the bounds of my estate. Largely this was to fend off the unpleasantness of that fecund set who made those urban alleys

CATHEDRAL AT
STAMPS-UPON-STAVES.

their miserable abode, and who thought nothing of saving their waste for later use as cooking-fuel or art-supply; but I must admit that part of the rationale for the admittedly absurd practise was to keep the tantalizing scent of twirled wharf-cheese from reaching my nostrils—for I feared losing control of all inhibition should a certain incident repeat itself, even in any minor capacity.

One week ago, I had no such compunctions about visiting the town un-self-odoured; in fact, should you be of a mind to suggest to me that I ought to soak in vinegar for eighteen hours before visiting the wharf, I would rightly have thought you mad, or a pervert, or else a mad pervert, or possibly a Minister of Parliament. *(Zing!)*

Yet six days ago, I had been strolling idly on the wharf-front, minding my business as wharf-strollers often do, taunting the crab-smashers with new-model mallets I'd procured for the express purpose of tossing in the water to watch their sad expressions. I gave no thought to the rabblish cheese-twirlers (younger every year!) harassing all, nor to my bygone days spent fighting for scraps in that sad, ignoble profession...when a peculiar aroma tickled my hind-brain, that primal centre of lizard-reflexes and subconscious associations more powerful, more dictatorial of the flesh than any realm of conscious thought could hope to aspire to. The scent was a rare blend of cheese-spice and meat-funk, in a proportion I'd only encountered once before, in the Indies, during my great pilgrimage to the holy shrine of cheese-twirlers, that fabled city atop the Himalayan peak of Tall-Mount. (So named for its *ta*lcum, *lla*mas, *mo*rdancy, and *unt*s.)

At Tall-Mount I was but one of many hundreds of eager supplicants come to wait outside the doors of the monastery of Abu Fromage, that ethnically-diverse grand-master of the sacred art of C. T., hoping but for a glimpse of that revered figure. For six weeks I waited, as acolytes came and went, gave up hope and renewed it; I subsisted only on the cheese that I had brought, carefully rationed, and the flesh of the men I could kill while in the frenzied rage that the cheese began to induce after about Week Three.

And then—unbelievably—as I was about to resign myself to a painful and horrifying Week Seven, in which I was totally willing to begin eating my own foot—the door opened.

I saw naught but a silhouette. No face, no features. Two hands, bronzed with fondue-splatter, holding a simple bucket. Waste-water from some arcane interiour ritual splashed on the doorstep and on my person. And a simple, pungent waft of the most divine cheese-mix I had ever sensed with my senses.

The door was open but for one second, and the odour lingered for barely three more before it dissipated, commingled with the historical funk of countless acolytes and the waste-smell from the skunk-farm across the street. Yet I knew my journey would never reap more treasure than this. I picked myself up and began the long trudge back down the slopes of Tall-mount, slurping the soaked-in waste-water from my tunic and breeches as I went.

From then till now I had never so much as turned my head at a cheese-smell, having once known the graceful perfection that had been Abu Fromage's wafty wisp.

And yet. And yet, here on the wharf, six days ago, there it was. I pegged the location behind me instantly—this old C. T. still has a nose for the business—and whirled, but found nothing.

For a moment, I had entertained the thought that Abu Fromage himself had crossed the Continent and was now ten yards from me, but then I dashed the prospect from my mind. Then I mused that he may have taken a successor, someone younger who would be more prone to travel—this, too, was discarded as ridiculous, for *I* hadn't gotten any letter, and who else could he have chosen? No, the explanation was simple: there was a new grand-master in town, and he would have to answer to—*There it was again!* And *closer!*

Six days ago, I found the heart of the aroma.

Six days ago, I met an old leper, dying in a vat of discarded cinnamon from a cinnamonery, waste-cheese poured atop him by some ignorant child, his leprous juices mixing with the enzymes and the what-not and somehow, by some wretched alchemy too awful to even contemplate, his rotting nastiness produced a scent indiscernible from the most heavenly Abu Fromage delicacy.

Too grossed out to conceive of any other option, I had resolved to block my nose from ever smelling anything at all in the town ever again. Hence the vinegar-soak.

But now, this instant, after only the most perfunctory of soaks, I was still late for my meeting. I simply would not have it.

I disembarked the carriage, dispatched a messenger to reschedule the meeting with the solicitor, citing unregulated levels of awesome that had overloaded a system still frail from orphan-slapping. And then I went back inside to cry for a bit.

Far-off, the bells of the church tolled, and then were still. Before I shut the door, I thought I heard a faint *screee!* of frustrated indignation coming from the direction of the hill-caves. *I know the feeling,* I thought. You think you leave a life behind but it comes back for you regardless, and the most elaborate vinegar-soaking (with crystals, even) can't wash away the longing.

Against the moon I thought I saw the fluttering silhouette of a leathery wing. Some had claimed they could smell the bat-creatures from miles below, as they passed abhorrently overhead. I don't know if that's true, but I suppose the vinegar came in handy tonight after all. Proof that all things work in concert for a purpose: tonight, whatever happens—at least I can't smell anything.

13: ILL PORTENTS.

I FOUND THE FLYER TACKILY TACKED to the front door: a gaudy waste of paper, splashed with vulgar-coloured inks and bedecked with the most garish of symbology. Pulling on the tacks hurt my powdered fingertips (I had spent the morning in the flour vat searching for meal-worms, as it was Thursday), so I summoned Armand, the porch-boy.

Ever eager to be of assistance, Armand clambered from his perch 'neath the front-yard gallows and plucked the circular from the door. The sun reflected irritatingly from its surface, so I shaded my eyes demurely. "What does it say, Armand," I sighed.

Clearing his massive throat, Armand read a long and rambling missive claiming that I was in violation of various housing codes and zoning ordinances and that I should appear at once before the magistrate down in town. Well, that was certainly not going to happen, not without a vinegar-bath; that had become my special rule, after all, and what good are rules if not to be followed to the letter at absolutely all times regardless of circumstance? (Otherwise, they might as well just be *laws,* which were clearly more akin to nanny-ish suggestions.) I plucked the paper from Armand's crooked fingers, rolled it into a ball, then unfolded it and deftly constructed an obscene origami—then dispatched Armand to deliver the paper-figure to the magistrate, no message necessary.

As his pumping flexors descended the drive, I turned my attention to the damage that the tacks had done to my front door. Whatever heartless fool had thrust his bedeviled points into my property had shown absolutely no respect for the structural integrity of the wood—two deep clefts split the grain in unattractive places. I stepped back to take a further look at the damage—

And then stopped short, my hand darting to my mouth. It couldn't be. It was impossible. It was just too inconceivable. But there it was.

A pattern.

It will be necessary to explain that my door had suffered a great number of bladed indignities o'er the years. The monks who'd once burrowed beneath my greenhouse had, at one point, nailed up a series of theses; these had left a dark gash in the oak that persisted long after their personages were dispatched to the hereafter by a series of crossbow bolts to the face. Another time, I had defended myself from rampaging loons hopped up on fizzy-brine and come to murder me in broad daylight (over some pitiable mis-understanding regarding who was betrothed to whom, as I recall, and who exactly could or couldn't claim the right of *prima nocte,* I claiming "me" and they claiming "not me"). That tussle of foils had left some shallow but looping furrows in the surface. And, of course, there was mine own first introduction to the manse, in which I had traipsed up the wide steps with hatchet in hand to demand audience with Uncle—I could still make out the faceted imprint that the jewelled hilt had smashed into the planed wood that long-ago winter's eve. Uncle's traitorous monkey-butler had opened the door then; but if he had not? I would have smashed it to smithereens with my ridiculous power. Such was my wroth! Such was my taste for traitorous monkey-flesh!

And yet! And yet if I had indeed smithereened the thing—this door would not be standing today. This pattern of grain and gash, of nail-hole and knot-hole, of tack-wound and imprint, would not present itself before me like a constellation across the wide heavens of my portico.

ARMAND THE PORCH-BOY.

I traced the fine lines with a finger-tip, leaving a faint trail of flour, feeling the texture of the grain beneath my skin. This discovery was more fascinating than any mealworm-hunt. To think that such patterns were anywhere we looked, just waiting for us to catch them in the right light and awaken to their latent majesty! I spun around, eager to take in my surroundings, to find whatever messages may be hidden in the design of everything around me.

Horse-falls reached my ears—a carriage approaching the gate. The gate-man turned the visitor away, as was his explicit charge; but for some reason, after some distant argument, the black iron creaked open. What treachery was this? What did I pay that dude for if not to keep out *freaking everybody?*

Even before the carriage's thin wheels had come to rest on the cobbles, the door was open and who should emerge but the magistrate himself, a certain Right Hon. Lord D_____, come straight from his bath, no doubt; his robe looked hastily donned, and his face bore the ruddiness of steam-soaking—that, or he was drunk this early in the day. He came to the ground heavily, without grace, and I saw the sheepish face of Armand within the carriage, refusing to meet my glance. How much time had passed? How deep had my pattern-reverie *been?*

As I saw the flash of colour in the magistrate's hand, I instantly knew why he had come. The Right Hon. drew himself up to his full, imposing height and thrust the origami in my face, its rude contours waggling in the sunlight—"What," he boomed, "is the meaning of *this?*"

But now, having anticipated this line of inquiry, I had an answer. "Cryptic, yes," I ventured, plucking the paper from his gnarled claw; "do not fault me for that. It was my way of bringing you here," I gushed, my mind racing.

"Bringing me here?" Lord D_____ shook his head. "I came here to serve you with this summons in person, since you so callously—"

He stopped. For he saw what I saw. I had traced the constellation with my flour-tipped fingers, and drawn its outline for him to see. "Is...is that...?"

"It is," I breathed, and smiled. Armand gaped from the carriage. The driver, seated high and still clutching the reins, stifled a giggle. For upon the door was the perfect outline of a phallus.

"Dude, that's hilarious," Lord D_____ boomed, and we high-fived in a dignified manner. Then he leaned close, in a whisper that could be heard from across the garden: "I hate to bring bad news to a fellow phallus-sketch enthusiast, but there's been a bit of a shake-up at the Town Council. The Solicitor-General's made designs after you."

"That rangy sot," I snorted. "He's pawed this gate before, but he knows where my predlictions lie. For the *ladies.*"

An uncomfortable pause. Then, Lord D_____ adjusted his robe and clambered his bulk back up the ladder to his carriage. "Well, then," he said. "I suppose I shall just *keep* your messenger-boy for the time being."

I sighed as I watched them rumble back down the path. Then I turned back to the house: "Draw the vinegar," I told anyone within ear-shot. "I'll be making the trip to town to-morrow."

14: A NEW ACQUAINTANCE.

THE SOLICITOR-GENERAL'S PASTY-FACED file-boy lasted about six minutes before beginning to gag at the vinegary aroma that filled the antechamber. I watched his expression turn sour in increments from my perch across the room, on a hard wooden bench; I twirled my walking-stick idly while shooting side-long glances at the wispy lad.

My mind twirled in time with the staff, as I considered witty remarks to call across the room. For example, to be spoken in a hushed, conspiratorial tone: *I'm sorry to ask, but do you smell something? Is it, er...the Solicitor-General?* was high on the list when the door to the far office burst open and the thin, reedy frame of His Honour himself came wafting into the room. With a curt gesture he bade me follow, and I departed, leaving my witticism un-vocalised but mentally filing it away for later.

We clambered down the front steps to the street, His Honour holding two twiggy fingers to his nostrils. "I really don't know what that awful stench is in my office," he said. Once outside, he drew in a deep draught of the exteriour air—and promptly coughed. "Out here, too, blast it! Has someone upset a vinegar-cart? Doused vinegar about willy-nilly? I should levy charges, conduct a fair trial by jury of peers, convict, and toss the rascal in the lock-up!"

I dared not inform His Honour that the scent of the vine was, in fact, emanating from my person; instead I simply lingered in my own aromatic island, olfactorily oblivious to the heaps of refuse (living and otherwise) that littered the eye-scape in every direction. To stave off further (potentially embarrassing) inquiries regarding the odour, I diverted His Honour's attention back to the purpose for which he had summoned me from the Manor down into the municipality, requiring me to immerse myself in manually de-virginised

ENTERING THE POLICE BUREAU.

vinegar for the better part of yester-eve and this morning. "Pray
tell," I entreated, "what manner of business is at hand, that concerns us both?"

"Ah, yes," he sniffed, stepping nimbly up to the kerb and making
for a low, stone building. A squat constable looked up from knitting
a vou-dou doll in the shape of Napoleon III long enough to pull the
iron door open for us. We ducked into the low hall-way and were
making our way down a brick-lined corridor before His Honour
continued: "I wanted to introduce you to our new Head Inspector."

Head Inspector? I felt my blood turn to ice and my spleen turn
to close the window against the chill. It took every ounce of resolve
to refrain from faltering in my step, or worse yet, knocking His
Honour in the skull with my walking-stick and making a run for
it—but that was exactly the sort of behaviour that put me in fear
of the law in the first place. No; I would restrain myself, and see
how this played out. "I look forward to making his acquaintance,"
I said.

His Honour turned to me with a knowing grin on his long, craggy face. "We are a bit more progressive in this township, I'll have you know," he said mysteriously.

As I tried to make sense of his comment, he pushed through another metal door, and suddenly we were in a well-appointed office—the dingy grey and red of the corridor's block walls giving way to rich mahogany panelling and softly-crackling lanterns set into silver sconces in the forms of fantastical creatures: unicorns, centaurs, Scotsmen. I blinked in the warm light, and scarcely made out a figure sitting at the long desk, face buried behind a leather-bound tome. This person looked up as we entered, and then rose: it was a woman.

"Welcome, Your Honour," she said to the Solicitor-General. With a fine voice like the tinkling of garden-chimes disturbed by a nun's gas (smelling like roses and good for the environment), she welcomed me as well, and bade us sit. His Honour took to a leather arm-chair like it was his bath-tub, sinking deeply into its plush contours; I had somewhat more difficulty with my own seat, afraid of losing my balance and appearing the fool. (If only I hadn't dropped out of jester-college, I might have been able to make awkward motions appear graceful; but those guys had been wankers all and deserved the punishment I had meted out.) His Honour, all elbows and knees, apparently had no such anxiety.

Once I was settled, however, I turned my attention to the fine figure now standing before me—first, I well noted the high cheekbones, as was proper for a lady of class; also, her hair was pinned up in a sensible fashion. So far, she matched my Ideal Mate check-list, tick for tick.

Additionally, she wore the uniform of the Head Inspector, which I thought was mighty forward of her; when the Head Inspector himself appeared (as I expected he would shortly) he would doubtless be upset to find her wearing his clothing, as it was a symbol of rank and authority, and as such would have to be *earned* by the wearer and not simply donned as if it were Darling Daddy's Career Day o'er at the nunnery.

"Good afternoon, Head Inspector," the Solicitor-General said, and I turned, expecting to find that man having entered the room— but to my amazement, it was to this woman that he had spoken. "You know my companion, of Wondermark Manor on Waverly Hill." At *companion,* I bristled.

"Only by reputation," the woman said, formally extending a hand to me. "Head Inspector Lara Q____, at your service."

Numbly, I took the hand. The touch of her skin was like an electric shock sent straight to my spinal cord. It took all of my motor-control not to collapse into a dribbling mess atop the bear-skin rug. "Charmed," I believe I squeaked. ("Not a pouf," I think I may have added, just for safety's sake.)

"Now then, Sir," she said, taking a serious tone, and I felt my heart leap into my throat. This delicate flower would be the death of me, in multiple ways at once. I could see it all un-spooling in my mind like a ball of twine bouncing down a hill towards a forest fire set by pillaging Vikings in historically-accurate non-horned hats: all the zoning violations, the liens against the property, the neighbours' complaints, the many, many murders that had taken place on the grounds since I had begun my tenancy. It was bad, all bad—and the worst of it all was that as she was prosecuting me for my many heinous crimes, she would likely never spare even a moment to lean over and kiss me. Our love was doomed before it had begun.

"Now then, Sir, I wish to make as my first order of business in this district a thorough accounting of the many outstanding reports we've filed regarding incidents at your property," she was saying. I could scarcely make out the words above the blood pounding in my ear-drums.

She consulted a thick ledger, stuffed to the bindings with yellowed papers of every shape, and began to talk from it: "Starting with this year alone: January the first, report of missing children in your area. January the third, six horses found mutilated on the grounds. January the fourth, burglary at neighbouring estate leads a trail back to your property. January the seventh, strange plume of smoke rises from your house, persists for the better part of a fort-night, neighbours complain of the stench of burning snake-skin. January eleventh, a bear is loosed and hunted for sport in the street. It goes on and on like this." She snapped the folder shut, startling me from the pleasant trip down memory-lane. January had been tame compared to, say, March, but there had certainly been some classics. I found my gaze drifting to the bear-skin rug at my feet and mentally comparing it to the one, twice as large with a musket-ball hole punched through the eye-socket, that sat in my front sitting-room.

THE CHIEF MAGISTRATE.

"I wonder if you've considered any possible explanation for this remarkable string of aberrant behaviour centred at your estate," she said, taking pains (I noticed) to keep her voice flat and even, the better to judge my reaction.

I played her game right back at her, with equal control: "I have my theories," I said, "but what evidence have you gathered?"

She flipped open the folder and began to page through the reports again. I felt my face flush. The vinegar aroma seemed to have become particularly pungent in this enclosed space, but she hadn't so much as wrinkled her nose. "I think you can help us put an end to all of this, with your coöperation," she said.

This was it. This was the end. She would throw me behind bars and the whole mansion would go to rot, or worse. All those carefully-planned homicides (to say nothing of the rash, impetuous ones) would come back to haunt me in court. This angelic creature would damn me to the foulest pits of Hades. I waited for the gates to come crashing down on my freedom.

"Tell me," she said, leaning closer—"have you ever given any thought to the idea that your estate may be haunted by a mischievous ghost?"

What.

I opened my eyes. "A g-g-g-ghost?"

"It fits the pattern," she said, looking back at her files. I looked incredulously at the Solicitor-General, who nodded his assent.

Head Inspector Lara began to spread tissue-thin pages delicately on her desk. "It's the only explanation that makes any sense. I would like to visit the estate with you—with your permission and coöperation, of course—and perhaps together we can crack this mystery and send any wayward spirits happily on their path towards the Great Beyond."

I grinned. "At my Lady's convenience," I said, and gave my walking-stick a twirl.

15: IN DIRE STRAITS.

I RUSHED HOME FROM THE HEAD INSPECTOR'S office with purpose. That lovely creature had inadvertently granted me a temporary reprieve from the charges of homicide that I richly deserved to face—but I now had two things to accomplish that would make that reprieve permanent: first, rid the estate of all outstanding evidence of said murders; second, create some sort of rigging, or lever-system, or perhaps hired saw-benders secreted away within the wall-boards creating spooky sound-effects—anything that would convince her that the crimes that took place on these grounds were, indeed, the work of a g-g-g-ghost.

The first order of business would be to sweep up the various corpses that littered the grounds. Impertinent servants, wayward

insurance salesmen, pros-
elytising door-knockers that
had gotten a bit too familiar—all of these would have
to be somehow disposed of.
I made to summon my body-
disposal team, but when they
did not respond to my snapping, nor to their dedicated
bell, I realised that I was in
fact staring at their remains,
stuffed unceremoniously into
the mouth of an ornate concrete bull-frog.

The frog had been a gift
from the Garden Society, on
the occasion of my inaugural

THE SOLICITOR-GENERAL.

hosting of the Autumn Gala Luncheon and Harvest Jamboree, an
event that had certainly *not* turned murderous. (I had been far too
tossed on Lady W____'s bitter brown dandelion-tonic.) The curious
demise of the body-disposal team, however, was somewhat more of
a mystery.

From the residue that caked their masses I was able to confirm
that alcohol had played a part (notably as flame accelerant); from
the varying integrity of the remains I pegged the event as having
occurred within the last two months. Blimey, it could have been
anything in that time; a body can't be expected to remember every
single murderous incident that happens in a week, much less six—
er, ten—er, *however*-many times that amount.

No matter; body-disposal engineers were tuppence-a-dozen in
this modern economy. In fact, quite a crowd of them had taken to
loitering about just outside the gates, watching my carriage traverse
the drive and making themselves available for day-labour. Should
my horses or orphans take the turn too slowly whilst merging with
the thorough-fare, they would saunter casually up to the hansom,

holding up fingers to signify their wage; I once made the mistake of not glancing out the window while flicking a boogie and ended up (quite accidentally) hiring three of them through lunchtime. I didn't have much work to assign them, but they gave the kitchen-staff the opportunity to use the guest china. (The guest china *himself* was not amused—I gathered from the way that his conical hat kept falling off during.)

That particular day, my temper had turned foul (a rare occurrence, I should say) and I'd had to venture to the gates and hire three more body-disposers to rid me of the first three. What they do with the bodies, I have no idea; although I would admit to curiosity, my new stay-out-of-irons policy holds me strictly to plausible deniability. I nursed my fourth vodka-and-beetle-juice of the hour, already well on my way to demolishing every last vestige of bothersome knowledge that cluttered my cranium.

But choking the life from my synapses did not accomplish the task at hand: preparing the estate for the forthcoming visit by the Head Inspector and her poltergeist squad. Once I'd (eagerly, natch) invited her to visit the Manor, she'd mentioned off-handedly that she would be bringing along her specially-trained ghost-detecting goons, a prospect at which I had audibly groaned—the guest china was exhausted enough as it was, the poor fellow. Also, it would mean that my faux-fantômes would have to be that much more convincing.

"If only I knew some real ghosts that could give me some tips on what exactly I should do," I mused aloud, staring at nothing in particular.

Nothing in particular moved a good three feet with a sliding crunch, and my vodka-and-beetle-juice slipped from my fingers to shatter on the floor.

"*You're in luck,*" came a deep, echoing voice, and I wet myself. ✦

THE TAKING TREE.

16: A GHOSTLY PRESENCE.

ORRORS! THE GHOSTLY VOICE HAD caused a *bona fide* trouser-accident. I patted at my pantaloons—sure enough, my fingers came away damp. I took the steps two at a ginger time back to my bed-chamber, holding fiercely in my gut to whatever power of autonomy I still retained. Once safely to the water-closet, I took a breath and let Nature's call continue in force, while thinking back on the last thirty seconds.

The incorporeal speech had seemed to come from everywhere at once, filling the room and reverberating from every fixture. What could it mean? And why had this mystery been fousted upon me at this very minute, with the Head Inspector mere moments from my doorstep?

As I attempted to thread my feet through the sopping trouser-legs, I reflected that it had been a solid year since the last time Nature, that haggard witch, had poked me in the bladder with her knobby cane and dashed my pride to pieces—on that day, like today, I had been anxiously awaiting the arrival of a fetching young lass. I had been in the antechamber, pacing a bit and rehearsing my smooth lines for the evening, when a sharp rap had sounded at the door—it was the Lady P_____'s footman, come to herald her arrival. At that moment, as I stepped forward to welcome the Lady to the estate, *at that very moment* Nature had leapt up and struck me full in the kidneys with her cruel, unheeding mockery, and I still hated her for it.

As I recall, I'd gurgled something more than a squawk but less than a word, yet still tried to play it off, hoping the Lady wouldn't notice. After all, I told myself, what well-bred Lady would even recognise the tell-tale spreading stain of self-soilage; if she knew what she was seeing, the thinking went, she was hardly a Lady proper enough for me.

Needless to say, within minutes the Lady P_____ had left me with my own P, and I sat alone in the North Atrium cursing Nature, cursing her vile, cackling pettiness and her immature sense of humour. The servants had found me there, squatting in my trousers, my sobs mingling sadly with the intermittent *drip-drip-drip* onto the cold marble floor. Anyway, this recollection was getting really gross, so I changed into clean pants and headed back for the stair-case.

My reverie of drippy moments past and present had all but distracted me from the ghostly voice I'd heard just prior to the, ah, *moisture incident,* but that was remedied the instant I set foot onto the first step—like a church-bell, the sound rang from the stone walls. *"Here I am,"* it boomed, and I stumbled and clutched the railing and felt my heart leap to my throat and beat thrummingly within my larynx.

"Who's there," I cried, whirling around; but the voice cut me off, seeming to descend from the rafters above my head one instant, then rise from the floor-boards far below.

"The better question," it said, wrapping its presence around me like a cloud of hot breath, *"is who are you, and what are you doing in my house?"*

I tightened my abdomen, determined to keep these pants as dry as a teetotaler's tankard in Tipperary on Tuesday. Totally. "Show yourself," I said, feeling the booming laughter of the spectre's response even in the quaking railing beneath my slick palm.

The laughter stopped abruptly, bringing silence once more. I caught my breath, startled by the sudden void. I turned, slowly, in every direction; nothing. The sounds of the room gradually became audible again: foremost, the wind, whistling through the still-gaping hole in the sky-light, that un-scabbed wound from the old man and his bizarre flying-craft. The hole had been hastily patched with some carpet-tacks and an old coat, as we'd had neither the time, nor the opportunity, nor the manpower, nor the inclination, nor the means, nor the know-how to repair it properly. (In fact, should the evening turn chilly I would probably rescue the coat from that duty and don it myself.)

And then: the far-off sound of creaking metal. The front gates! The Head Inspector, in her carriage, with her ghost-hunting goons. And here I had been so busy soiling my trousers and conversing with spectres that I had set up no levers or pulleys or saw-blades or crying statues or catsup-stigmata or comical slimy side-kicks or bad CGI effects to convince her that a murderous ghoul in fact inhabited the premises. With no ghost to blame my homicides on, I would be found out and my deeds discovered. I was ruined; I might as well start converting my cash into pesos now, for the long flight ahead.

Unless...

"Are you there?" I shouted into the emptiness.

Only echoes in reply. By the sound, the horses outside had cleared the cobblestones and were moving onto gravel. They would be at the door in moments.

"What do you want?" I called. "There must be *something* you need."

A low sigh, from everywhere—or just a breeze?

No. The lamps in their sconces had not so much as flickered. It was the g-g-g-ghost.

"Let us become partners, for this afternoon at least," I cried, seeing the shadows move through the drawn curtains of the front windows. "Please. You first spoke to me for a reason. You had some intent—let us execute it."

And then I had the most peculiar sensation—though I saw nothing, though my eyes lit upon only the empty air, somehow I knew that the voice was smiling.

"*She's here,*" it breathed, and downstairs, at that exact second, came the knocking.

17: THE ARRIVALS.

THAT DREADFUL POUNDING! WAS IT my heart within my ribs, or the visitors at the door? I could scarcely distinguish one from another. My hand fluttered to my breast—nerves making my limbs and innards into rubber and butterflies. The rubber sank to the floor and rebounded softly, having smeared my courage across the surface at my feet; with each weakening bounce it deposited more of my resolve at ground level. All this as the flighty creatures of my attention darted to and fro, nervously sucking nectar from every possible distraction in the foyer—the wall-sconces (their patina! How in need of polish); the brass doorknob (was that a scratch in its lustre?); the gaping statue of Heracles that yawned above me with arrogant disdain, his powdery skin still be-sooted from the bizarre conflagration not one month ago. As hummingbirds flitted about like fire ants and rubber un-spooled about the floor like molasses, I pushed myself through the deafening rumble of metaphors and focused instead on the steady knocking, growing more insistent by the second.

By now my servants had begun to appear, poking their heads from their quarters or crannies or with eyes pressed to cracks in the floor-boards, remembering my past fury when knocking doors had historically been left un-addressed. I could sense them thinking through the process in their simple minds: should we venture forth, and take this responsibility upon ourselves? Or stay put, and leave the master to his own devices? Each option was equally likely to incur wrath, and in fact it was this perpetual imperilment that had, indirectly, led the Head Inspector here today. My temper, in past, had been easily kindled and rarely sated, and such situations had often gleefully led to blood-shed.

Today, however, I would have to be on my best behaviour. With a glare they knew well, I sent the servants scurrying back to their respective nooks, before dispatching one last glance about the room in whole and tugging on my fancy-gloves, all the better to be proper.

"Are we in accord?" I asked the air, not knowing if the mysterious voice could hear me. In response, my collar stiffened with a not-entirely-tangible breeze.

"*Leave this to me,*" the whisper came; and I reached for the doorknob. In the moment of bright sunlight that followed I had the startling thought that I must have been imagining that terrible voice; but it was too late now: the door swung wide.

Two beefy types handling a log-shaped object were conferring with the Head Inspector near her carriage. These would be the ghost-hunters. I smoothed my hair with a glove and attempted a smile as all turned to regard me.

"Oh! We feared you weren't in," Lara purred, gliding across the gravel with a grace I would have thought impossible for anyone with joints. To the pair of brutes she directed: "We shan't need the battering-ram after all."

With some obvious reluctance they shrugged; I fingered my already-abused door with alarm. "You would have availed yourself of your inspection without me?"

"Now, now," she said, delicately lifting her hem and stepping across the threshold; "we are here on official police business." She softened this last statement with a beaming expression; I felt my innards melt and begin to leak from my belly-button in the most romantic way possible, but could scarcely take my eyes from her feet—for I had glimpsed a flash of pink skin. An ankle! I sucked in my breath.

"My eyes are up here," she added softly, and I jerked my chin away, tripping over a stray apology someone had left in the entryway. I looked back to the two gorillas, now encumbered with an armful each of technical-looking equipment: polished wood and brass adorned with all manners of gauges and widgets and peep-valves all capped by a large copper stop-cock.

AN ABSINTHE PARTY BEFORE IT GETS FREAKY.

The Head Inspector followed my gaze. "Our equipment, on loan from the Institute for the day," she said, as if I would know what she was talking about (of course, I feigned that I did). I hadn't the faintest idea what Institute she might be referring to. The Naval Institute? That didn't make any sense, as the devices were far too large to fit in anyone's navel; and the only other Institute I knew of was the Institute for the Cultivation of the Blind as Weavers, and *that* was an organization I had founded myself, as part of an elaborate prank that had my poor blind cousin Maynard enduring an hilarious battery of absurd applications and, later, the most brutal hazing that a ribald Ceylon steamer-crew could devise. Ah, the memories! I could still feel the slap of his sightless gaze on the back of my head on summer evenings, when I caught a whiff of curry on the breeze.

My fond recollections twisted in my gut, however, as I noticed the Head Inspector tracing a line of soot down the marble thigh of Heracles, blacking one perfect fingertip. This place was practically oozing with incriminating evidence, were one disposed to look for it; no doubt the basement would make for particularly awkward conversation. Of late I'd had to simply shove things down the steps—

old food, bodies, servants half-awake, orphans with limbs already harvested for other purposes—and I wasn't sure just *what* exactly still remained down there. I hadn't so much as taken one step actually into the wretched place in months; I'd simply been pulling open the door, heaving (or kicking) as necessary, and letting the heavy trap slam shut before I heard anything hit the ground. For all I knew, there was a whole rebellious colony of zombie freedom fighters down there, scheming and making tea from ham-leavings and rain-drops; though there couldn't be *that* many of them, as I'd had the place fumigated last Christmas.

But even here, many yards away from that dreadful basement door, here, not five feet from the welcome mat with the embroidered puppy-dog, here, thirty seconds into her inspection, Lara had already found cause for pause. I found it suddenly hard to swallow.

"What sort of fire was this, lit in the foyer?" she said. Her eyes were the most piercing blue of Law. When I opened my mouth to lie my tongue was dry as a medicine ball in my mouth.

I gagged for a few moments, fumbling for an explanation. In truth, all the fires of late had run together in my memory. Was this the book-burning? No, the barbecue? Or was it the signal-fire I had set for the zeppelin races? Possibly our latest religious immolation?

"Ah, that was, er..." I whirled, hoping to find something to jog my memory, something to inspire a particularly believable tale, something to make those gauges jump in the goons' hands—

And then they did. The needles jumped on the meters. The walls shook with an unearthly wind. Four sets of eyes widened at once—and every lamp snuffed out in that instant. The room plunged into darkness.

In the blackness, I grinned. My g-g-g-ghost had delivered.

18: VIOLENCE.

VOICES RANG OUT IN THE SUDDEN DARK—
"Lanterns!" and, imaginatively, "What foul devilry is this?"
from the two hulks of the spook-squad, insisting (in their irritating,
imperious way) on explanations for every erratic detail of existence.
I felt confident presuming that even in the safety of their respective
homes (not daring to imagine that they might share an abode; no,
that would be too deliciously scandalous a proposition to entertain
at a time of such stressful agitation—better to retain that thought
for a more savoury moment alone) they dashed their minds against
the sundry and storied mysteries of telegraphs, or pressed profes-
sors for digestible descriptions of the behaviour of radio-waves, or
provoked longhand equations to explain how the Internet might
still exist even in those dark hours at mid-night when its coal-
turbines fall silent. Yes, these boys wanted *answers,* and secretly,
I delighted in their momentary ignorance.

Head Inspector Lara had no doubt retained their service in
the interest of adding an empirical component to her own, perhaps
more *intuitive* investigative style...thus, plainly, the task before me
was to appeal to her predilection for the fantastic, for the sensual. It
was a mission I took upon myself gladly. As the buffoons continued
to call out for lights, bumping into each other and crashing about
the room, I gently tapped through the air in front of me, hoping to
encounter a soft dash of silk that would indicate close contact with
the Head Inspector.

And then—the noise! A terrible shuddering drowned out all
other sound. The walls creaked and the roof threatened to thunder
down onto our heads. I ducked to one knee, covering my head
against the inevitable collapse—and found the Head Inspector,
already on the floor, struggling to regain her footing. I opened my

mouth to speak, but the banging and clattering around us drowned all attempts at communication and shrieking both.

Suddenly, with a fearsome flash of light and a searing crackle that anyone could recognise as charring human flesh, every lamp in the room sprang to brilliant life. A terrible voice seemed to pour from the lips of the flame itself: *"Who dares enter my cavern of souls?"*

The sound echoed and rang from every surface. We cringed at

THE LIGHT-HOUSE OF DESPAIR—[SEE PAGE 326.]

the light; we shielded our ears against the assault. I wondered—far too late!—if cahooting with this ghoul (or whatever it truly was) was really as sensible a prospect as it had seemed ten minutes ago, when we had made our pact to deceive the Head Inspector.

I thought back to minor incidents that had, over time, not particularly stuck in my memory—various doors found open or closed; jam-jars, un-lidded, left in corridors; horses somehow introduced into the privy; a link of sausages somehow wended about the crystal chandelier at heights unreachable by any ladder on the premises. I had always attributed these bizarre (if rather benign) occurrences to sleepy servants, or unsociable house-guests, or burglars with a poorly-developed sense of prankery. There had always been enough bodies in the building to ascribe an inexplicable act to someone with more idle time than social grace.

But now...if indeed the sonorous spectre had been a long-time occupant of these halls...

Was *I*, in fact, trespassing on *his* domain?

The thought gave me a chill. I realised that nobody had responded to his booming inquiry—perhaps the task fell to me. In the waxing lamp-light I watched the oaf-twins gape at the flickering meters and tingling antennae of their detecto-matron, or whatever it was. Clearly, even according to their spook-ometer, the presence was real—and clearly, I would have to deal with it. The Head Inspector's eyes, wide in the night, took in my every move. I made sure of it.

"Treacherous fiend!" I cried. The entity was either playing along with my ruse to frighten and intimidate the Head Inspector (as it had earlier indicated it would), or it was diabolical in nature; either way I would play it as my adversary, at least for the moment. "Begone from these premises—your foul presence is not welcome here!"

I thought it quite a rousing call to action, myself. However, if in fact the fiend was play-acting against me, he seemed to be taking it a stroke too far—for in the next instant the giant statue of Heracles came to life, and dashed the Head Inspector against the wall.

19: GRAVE INJURY.

THE NORTH ATRIUM REVERBERATED WITH the terrific crash. Stone-dust and wood-splinters filled the air—as I ducked and protected my precious face I caught a flashing glimpse of the Head Inspector's badge, loosed from its clasp, spinning in a wild arc through the murk.

The blazing fire-light of now-toppled lanterns flickered and spat across the statue's gleaming marble skin, outlining fierce muscles that twisted and bulged in the smooth whiteness like armadillos wrestling in a pillow-case. Until ten seconds ago, this figure of

SMASHING SKULLS INTO DUST—[SEE PAGE 594.]

Heracles had been but a massive carving; now, it was destroying my home. What had I *done,* thought I, by agreeing in desperation to the vague terms the spectral voice had proposed?

"Stop this madness!" I cried. "Stop it! The deal is off! It's over!"

But no response came—my voice was swallowed by the crashing and collapsing of the entire sitting-room hearth. Soot-blacked stone crumbled like sand-châteaux before the massive creature; he clutched the Head Inspector in one sharp white hand like a blackjack or bobby-buster. She was limp; I knew not whether she still drew breath.

I suddenly began to feel flushed and tingly—what *was* this uncomfortable sensation? With a shock I came to realise that I was, against all odds, experiencing genuine concern for another human life. And this time, there was no time to drink the sentiment away.

The Head Inspector's two companions, the hulking brutes with the ghoul-ometers and spook-amatrons calibrated to register and amplify even the faintest æthereal stirrings, now stared dumbly at gauges pegged to their stops and popped free from their housings by the over-blast of signal; their fancy needles and brass valves had sprung and split from the pressure of straight-up g-g-g-ghost action. They scrabbled to keep their feet as a rushing wind blew from above—I looked up to see gaping hole in the sky-light, where a single carpet-tack still held fast the overcoat now fluttering and snapping like a pennant in a typhoon. With my eyes I traced the stair-case winding to near that gale-force flag; it was also very near the head of Heracles, who even now pounded his fists against the creaking railings.

A moment later I found myself flying up those steps, taking them three at a bound with a haste not usually in evidence when simply retiring to the boudoir. With a tremendous leap I planted one foot on the swaying bannister and reached for the coat with out-stretched fingers. For a single, awful second I felt the ground drop entirely away, as I floated between the blasting wind of heaven and the wretched Earth below, suspended by the dueling forces of gravity and jumping-ness.

And then I felt fabric 'twixt my fingers—I had the coat. I jerked it against the power of the carpet-tack, pulling the whole mess down to cover the head of the statue. I didn't really think that covering Heracles' stone eyes would prevent the monster from seeing—but then I hadn't really though it would've come to life, either.

It worked. The statue stopped, dropped Lara, and bellowed in rage. I tumbled heavily to the stair-case and scrambled to descend those swaying steps before the creature destroyed the structure. I met the brutes at the crumpled form of the Head Inspector.

She lay in a mangled heap; breathing or no, I could nary tell. Even in terrible injury she was beautiful; her head lolled back and forth on a limp, lovely neck. I took her by the shoulders and shook her viciously, trying to wake her; but the brutes took her hands and feet and yanked her from my grasp.

The two rushed her out the door to the carriage and made to set off at once. The cobblestone path no doubt assuaged her spinal injuries with its bouncy massage.

The front door slammed. And so the commotion stopped, as if a match had been snuffed. The lamps burnt merrily. A gentle breeze tousled the destroyed remnants of my stair-case and sitting-room. The walls sagged with bashed and shattered wounds. A tattered, fluttering scarf and a distinct Lara-shaped imprint in the sitting-room wall—accurate in shocking detail down to wide-eyed alarm— were the only evidence she'd been here at all.

"I have ridded you of those meddlers, as promised," Heracles boomed good-naturedly as if nothing at all untoward had occurred, his voice the strange grating sound of mill-stones rubbed against cliff-sides. My heart boiled with anger—but what could I say against a beast that could crush me as soon as blink a stony eye!

The statue settled with a heavy shuffle into a cross-legged position, wiping out a hearth as he did so. Those milky eyes fixed on me, somehow impossibly seeing, their veined blankness sending a chill to my very core—a chill that would only crystallise as the statue moved its very lips and said, quite calmly:

"Now, you are in my debt."

20: A SHOCKING REVELATION.

THE SOUND OF FAR-OFF CHURCH-BELLS drifted into the ruined foyer. The front door creaked on its hinges with each faint breath of wind, letting in the evening air. The ground at my feet was covered with rubble—splinters of wood; marble dust; chunks of brick. Lanterns jutted crookedly from sconces like the haggard teeth of a whale-man, burning dimly like the haggard teeth of a whale-man, smelling on the whole somewhat better than a whale-man, but then no burning substance in Christendom wouldn't. The servants were gone, or at least nowhere to be heard; probably they were taking advantage of the distraction to vulgarly thrash about in their quarters, the better to replenish their ilk.

As for me, I sat alone, next to the giant statue of Heracles, surveying the destruction of my home.

"She'll be back," I said, of the Head Inspector. "She'll bring the
whole Bureau with her. They'll call in Ghosty McGhosterton from
the Municipal Ghostery in Ghostershire-upon-Spook, and you don't
want *that* guy on your case; it's ghost-puns all day long with that
crowd. You have made this worse than it ever would have been.
I didn't want any of this. I didn't ask you to hurt her."

"I was not the one who cried to the æther for salvation," came a
soft, clear voice.

I looked up. This was not the granite rumbling of the statue's
stone throat, nor the booming thunder of the g-g-g-ghost that
had visited me on the stair-case, back when the stair-case still
stood. This was the voice of a man, approaching from the wreck
of a doorway, wearing a rakish cap and the most awful breeches.
He had the snooty air of a man out of time; like a spirit that had
decided to take the form of a man, but having as its only reference
lurid descriptions from second-rate dandy-rags.

He glowed, subtly, like a foppish algae. He did not look real.

Sensing my un-asked question, he looked down at himself.
"I have taken this form to make things easier on you," he said.
"When I was alive, I remember how horrendously ignorant I was of
the æthereal realm, how frightened I was at the simplest noise or
startle-bug or incubus encounter. Humans have such capacity for
stupidity." He took a moment to tug delicately on the fingers of a
white glove that seemed to shimmer in the lamp-light. "Man can be
such a dumb animal, jumping at shadows and believing the most
preposterous lies, anything that will make their narrow little world-
view make sense. Why, I remember when I thought that fire was
hot!" At this he passed a finger through the flame of a lamp, with
nary a change of expression, looking over at me as if he expected me
to leap to my feet in astonishment. "Eh? Eh? Really, you primitive
mortal folk are so bothersomely dense. Why, I remember the time
when I believed that the only way to digest food was to—"

"Enough," I said, forcing my aching body to its feet. "So you are elevated beyond the pale frailty of Man. What message have you brought from the hereafter?"

"Message?" At this he laughed, an annoying trill, the breath of which extinguished the lamp and plunged his face into shadow. "My dear boy, if I am here for any concrete reason at all—and I'm certainly not saying that I am—it's not to bring a *message*. How preposterous! How absurd! How absolutely like a man, to force some meaning onto every whim of chaos."

"Then why are you *here*," I grumbled, feeling rather the worse for the conversation. I was beginning to prefer the booming wind of mystery to this dandy's twinkling lilt.

He turned to face me, his eyes alight with purpose. Each word brought him another suddenly-terrifying step closer. "You have a book that belongs to me," he said. "I have searched through every unlocked room in this manor, and I have not found it."

"I don't think there are any books left here, and good riddance," I rejoindered. The still-smouldering soot-pile in the Great Hall's stove was testament to that. Oh, what warmth those innumerable volumes had provided! What a noble sacrifice they had made! I had been dreadfully close to actually shivering that night.

"I left it with your uncle, many, many years ago," he continued, as if he hadn't heard me, which was impossible, because I am loud. "It was a tall volume of necro-mancy that holds many secrets. He was the one living man I could trust." A far-off look drifted across his shimmering eyes. "I met him just the once, in Dublin—he'd had a bit too much to drink and made a pass at me. We'd spent some time in the darkness until he fell asleep at my ankles. You look like him, you know."

I thought of the cottony corpse upstairs in the East Wing, locked behind a coppery doorknob in a room that had been stripped of its many artifacts and treasures during the three-day paper-purge in the Great Hall. I pictured that stiff, dried hatchet-wound, and then I thought of this fop's ankles, and then I tried to make up gibberish-words to clear my mind of the image. Apparently I said them aloud, because I heard them echo, and it earned me a strange look from the dandy.

"There are no books remaining in this estate, none what-so-ever," I finally said. "It's a point of moral principle. I won't have them beneath my roof."

The man looked upwards, at the gaping hole in the sky-light through which the dusk was turning to night. "Right here would do fine, then," he said simply.

"We burnt them," I said. "We burnt them all. We burnt them gladly—the books, then the wall-paper, then the kitchen-help. I'm not sorry. I'm not sorry about them at all. We all do what we do in this life for reasons that we think are best, at the time."

His eyes narrowed. "That short-sighted philosophy is what dug you the hole you're in now," he said. "Are you *proud* of your pathological behaviour? When you pass to my plane you will have much to look back at with sorrow. Go on, brag—your debauchery does not impress me."

"Would that your lifeless husk was locked upstairs with the old man," I shot back. "And a pox on your detachment. I brand my servants because it's *fun*. I give free reign to my murderous impulses because it *makes me feel alive*. I swim naked in a vat of whale-blubber because *I heard it was good for my skin*. What was *in* your precious book? Words, like all the rest? If we'd known it was yours, we'd have burnt it first of all."

The man shook his head. "If you cannot give me the book, I will take my debt from you in other ways," he said. I felt a brief flash of panic, but he reassured me: "I have passed beyond the realm of carnal desires. My sole concern now is honour."

"Honour?" I spat the words. "You promised to help me! I wanted to *deceive* the Head Inspector, not *mangle* her! I wanted to *woo* her, not slam her against a wall and destroy my house—"

"Your *uncle's* house," he interrupted.

I kicked a chunk of marble and hit him in the thigh. "Ow," he added.

I stopped short.

"I thought you were a g-g-g-ghost," I said.

He looked at me, then looked down at his thigh, at the dusty smudge.

Then he looked slowly over at the front door, where stood the hulking figure of one of the Head Inspector's goons. From his expression, he'd clearly been listening for some time.

"Came back for her scarf," the man said slowly, pointing to the tattered silk that lay near my feet.

I stared at the man, and at the imposing figure of the Solicitor-General behind him, and at what appeared to be several thick-and-ready constables behind him.

Suddenly the giant statue of Heracles shifted behind me. I whirled—and for the first time saw the elaborate ropes-and-pulleys apparatus that controlled its movements.

It had been a set-up.

I turned to the dandy. Before I could say a word, he'd reached into the statue's throat and reset what sounded like a phonograph needle. *"I have ridded you of those meddlers, as promised,"* came the statue's 'voice,' suddenly less frightening than it had been an hour ago.

He moved the needle again. I heard a scratching sound as the needle jumped about—then the brassy tones of Herb Alpert ("blanks are expensive," the fop said apologetically), and finally, my *own* voice, waxy and thick but unmistakable: "I give free reign to my murderous impulses because it *makes me feel alive.*"

The 'ghost' extended a hand. "Special Investigator Peapoddy, at your service."

I stared at his hand, as real and solid as my own. Its faint phosphorescent glow, I now detected, was a powdering of Aboriginal algae-dust. The stuff was a penny-a-pinch down at the crab-shacks. Hardly supernatural in the least!

"Charmed," I managed, feeling my bladder give way to Nature once again.

21: A DESPERATE ACT.

THERE WASN'T MUCH TO EXPEL, THIS TIME; my bladder was still empty from the episode earlier. But it *tried,* that valiant organ, gifting its meagre contents to the wide world outside, for what good it would do. The net result: mildly damp trousers.

A mildly uncomfortable sensation by itself, without mentioning the stony silence from the cadre of law-enforcement assembled at my doorstep: Special Investigator Peapoddy, a dandy freak; one of the hulking ghost-hunters from the Head Inspector's newly-formed Ectology Division (as I later learnt it was called); a handful of tallow-liver'd constables; and the angular frame of the Solicitor-General himself, wearing a most sour expression.

"It was all a ridiculous farce," Peapoddy declared smugly. "And with your confession inscribed on the wax phonograph installed in Heracles, here"—with this he patted the statue, which was looking more like plaster and less like marble with each passing second— "your reign of violence over Easthillshireborough-upon-Flats has ended. The Head Inspector—"

"The Head Inspector!" I cried. "You've dashed her through my sitting-room wall! She's dead, by now, isn't she, you maniac!" I turned to the Ectologist. "You there—you chaps spirited her away after this madman as much as crushed her with his hands. How does she fare? Does she still breathe?"

Peapoddy spoke up before the brute could reply. "Any violence she has experienced; any excruciating pain she has felt, or is now feeling, is a direct result of your complicity," he said. I lunged at the man, but the constables rushed forward to restrain me—I managed no more than twenty or thirty hard blows about his head and neck before they pulled me away. How I yearned to sink a croquet-mallet into his spine! Should the Head Inspector ultimately perish

PEAPODDY.

from his assault—I pledged I would find *some* way to mallet the man, and *drat* the consequences.

He cowered in the corner, hands up to protect his precious face or whatever. I roughly shrugged the constables' hands from my person, and turned my attention to the statue of Heracles, looking closely for the first time at the dark pulleys and ropes that had given the statue its ambulatory character. Upon inspection it was clear that this jerking puppet was but a crude imitation of my glorious original. Instead of being carved from a single block of marble, this version had been assembled from a kit (the hastily duct-taped joins were painfully obvious even in the dimness); instead of heroic features withstanding all adversity, this one appeared to be wilting beneath a disagreeably humid afternoon. Most crucially, instead of depicting the demigod in the heroic act of slaying his music tutor with a lyre, this knock-off seemed to be in the midst of ordering replacement eyeglasses.

"Really, you must have been so shocked to see your statue come alive!" Peapoddy cackled. "Our plan was amazingly ingenious in every fashion. To think, you didn't even *notice* that we had spirited an alternate statue into your foyer, just *waiting* for the chance to lurch forth at any moment! And your servants have been *most* helpful in every facet of this investigation."

I jerked my gaze up to the fop. "Never," I breathed. "My servants remain loyal to me till death! They've even been branded with hot iron to seal the deal, my laughter drowning out their incessant squeals of pain. How could they feel anything *but* loyalty?"

"They positively *wel-comed* us in," Peapoddy grinned, seizing this opportunity to broaden the betrayal already clefting me in twain. The twain-conductor continued: "Armand the porch-boy gladly provided the magistrate with his front door-key, and I hear they are to be married soon, *mazel-tov.* Leonid the alarm-boy ensured that you'd sleep through the entire operation—"

"Leonid?" I scowled. "Was *that* that whelp's name? That's sort of a stupid name."

AN ECTOLOGIST.

"They have all turned against you," Peapoddy said, sharpening each word into a roof-tack and driving it deeply into the shingles of my soul with the hammer of his whiny tone.

"I thought they loved me," I rejoindered, lamely. "I had always worked under that assumption."

"Oh, woe is you! Two trousers soiled in as many hours. Taking up residence in your walls and speaking to you through an elaborate series of echoic tubes was really the most fun I've had on a Special Investigation since impersonating a mermaid to bust old Cap'n Narwhal for bilge-smuggling." Peapoddy leaned close, sensing my impotence, and also my inability to do anything. "Did you really think you could just *kill* the assessor? Pay off the magistrate with naughty origami and Armand? *Seduce* the *Head Inspector?*"

"My love for her remains pure," I huffed. Granted, such love was based strictly on the limited professional interactions we had so far enjoyed—but those had been pretty good, for the most part, except for the one thing. "Did *you* really think you could harm her so, and face no consequences? I will see to it that your gizzard-eggs are—"

Peapoddy waved my words away from his face. "Poppycock," he burbled. "Once you provide me with the Tome of the Cowering Sigil, the spells and directions within will instantly restore her to top form, all the better to prosecute you. Now"—he leaned close, and I felt his decidedly un-ghostly onion-breath batter my pores—*"where is that book."*

I held my tongue, but it started to get dry so I let go. I *knew* the book to be burnt; we hadn't left a scrap of paper un-lit during our Great Hall purge. But clearly *he* hadn't bought that explanation; he believed me to have secreted the volume away somewhere. Was this a chip I could use to bargain with? To buy time, if not necessarily freedom, and biscuits, if not necessarily time?

I realised that Peapoddy, for all his lacy cuffs and bravado, and despite apparently having lived cramped within my walls for some time, fundamentally misunderstood my character. He believed me possessed of at least *some* cunning, a sensible sort who wouldn't *dare* burn an obviously old and treasured book. In this he appeared to be ascribing to me some whit of reason.

In this, of course, he was totally mistaken.

This, added to the new information that the spells in the book would evidently bring the Head Inspector back to full health, gave me my plan.

I took a deep breath, before Peapoddy, the constables, the Ectologist, and the Solicitor-General. All men that would gleefully lock me away forever, given the slightest provocation.

Before this whole crowd, I told a blatant lie. "Fine," I said. "I'll take you to the book."

22: UNWELCOME VISITORS.

I THREADED THROUGH THE RUBBLE-STREWN
North Atrium, leading the caravan of constables towards the
East Wing. We stopped for some crisps in the kitchen; then I led
them 'round the chocolate-fountain, up a set of narrow stairs, and
towards that far point where my late uncle's library capped the
architecture like a jaunty wig. The troupe following me didn't know
that the shelves in said library were, in fact, bare as last Arbour
Day's chicken-bones.

The silence was what struck me most: the servants were gone.
No incessant chatter murmured behind locked doors; no ridiculous
hopscotch-playing or vou-dou chanting or pleas-for-mercy reached
my ears. I had long and ineffectually admonished the staff to
maintain a respectful noise-lessness, but now that I was granted
my wish, I longed for the barest peep from around a corner—just so
I could launch into a fury. Anything to sip from that gilded chalice
of power! My sense of authority within these walls was at a low ebb,
and it made me *sad*.

Special Inspector Peapoddy came up beside me, his flouncy
trousers incongruous in this hall-way of dark woods, sober colours,
and "no flouncing" signs. I made myself throttle my hatred for the
man, play it cool, not let my roiling abhorrence for him spill over
into violence. Self-restraint was a new discipline for me—this whole
experience, if nothing else, had been an education.

"There are many books in Uncle's library," I lied. Had I spoken
in the past tense, the statement would have been true. "Pray tell,
what distinguishes *this* book from any other? How am I to tell it
apart?"

"You said you would take us to it," Peapoddy hissed, "but you
don't know how to find it?"

Urp. "It is certainly with the other books of Uncle's," I added hastily. This was technically true—*all* the books were ash in the Great Hall's stove. "But he brought many volumes back from his travels. What characteristic will allow me to pluck the Tome of the Cowering Sigil immediately from the stacks?"

"I'll know it when I see it," Peapoddy said, and that seemed the end of it. But a few steps later, he seemed to relent: "The Tome is one of only two books written by Plaxus the Unwise, that great and learned scholar of antiquity. You've heard of him, certainly?"

Never in my life, but I nodded sagely. Peapoddy continued: "Plaxus lived at the time of Rubidarch the Orange and Mouseke- teer the Loud, the famed alchemists and water-heater repair-men. He worked closely with them as they progressively unlocked the æthereal mysteries of the human body. It was quite genius, really—through a systematic series of vivisections, Rubidarch and Mouseketeer examined and measured and recorded every system and process of human life, assigning a set of numerical values to each quality. Then medicine became a simple process of mathemat- ics—measuring the characteristics of, say, a diseased organ, and then working the abacus, seeing what must be done to make the equations balance again. It was remarkable research."

Vivisections, eh? "I've embarked on similar experiments myself, but not of that scale," I mused.

Peapoddy shot me a dark look. "Rubidarch and Mouseketeer were roundly condemned as heretics by the emergent Church, natu- rally."

"Naturally."

"They were burnt at the same stake that they had everything at, along with their research notes and figures, their knowledge largely lost to the ages. Imagine how we could build on their work today, with our current understanding of anærobic geometry, of the once-thought-magickal properties of calculus lard, of multi-variable long-division and other, even *more* ridiculous higher mathematics!" Peapoddy seemed to be angry at the air in front of him, barking at it as if it would choke him. "Plaxus the Unwise managed to escape

EATING HATS FOR PLEASURE—[SEE PAGE 537.]

the Church's death-otters and spent the rest of his life planning to transcribe what he remembered of Rubidarch and Mouseketeer's findings. But he waited until he was old, and once he finally started he only got through two books before he died. Ironically, scholars believe that he died of the very ailment he was describing as his pen faltered and fell from the page."

"What was that?" I asked. I wasn't sure how much ignorance of the subject I should admit—but Peapoddy seemed happy to blather on.

But he shrugged. "I don't know—that's in the Tome of the Precious Lore, the second of the two, and the one I haven't read. While the two are largely similar, they do differ in certain respects. Notoriously, the Precious Lore has a particularly hilarious cover-illustration. If only the Church would have allowed any copy to be made without sending the full force of the Vatican's Holy Avengers to destroy it immediately! So instead, we must put our full trust in anecdotes."

"Sounds like a solid plan."

A CHAIR.

"I was close on the tail of the Precious Lore in Dublin. I had the Cowering Sigil in my possession, and for safe keeping I entrusted it to your Uncle. He'd seemed like a nice guy. I'd thought he would at least stick around till morning." His expression soured. "The trail went cold, that steamy night. It has been a long, hard road working to find this estate. And once I detected your feelings for the Head Inspector, I knew I had to hurt her—you would never turn over the book otherwise."

What! I turned to see if the Solicitor-General was hearing this confession. This book-mad fiend had subverted the aims of Justice to further his own biblio-obsession. But if the Solicitor-General was firmly in the pocket of Peapoddy (or, it should be considered, whoever was backing his operation)—Justice here was a sham.

I wondered, not entirely idly, if the entire murder investigation had been but a front for Peapoddy to gain legitimate access to the Manor. Had the Head Inspector been in on the game? Or had she been Peapoddy's unwilling pawn this whole time?

"You should have come by a month ago, and asked nicely," I scowled. "I probably would have handed you the book at the front door. Things might have been different. I might not have figured this all out."

"Figured what out?" Peapoddy glared.

"The old Head Inspector wouldn't go along with your plan, now, would he?" I retorted. "He and I always had an understanding—he left me alone, and I didn't send people to poke him annoyingly while he slept. But he wasn't willing to play games with you, was he?

Of course not—look at you, you foppish foreigner. So you had him removed, and found a new Head Inspector. A beautiful one, to lower my defences. This has been your plan all along!" By the end I was shrieking—the constables rushed forward and seized my arms as the Solicitor-General strode over.

"Now see here, that's enough out of you," he growled. "These matters go far above *all* our heads. No matter how much it may seem like it—not everything revolves around you."

"Doesn't it?" I sneered in return. "Then why are you all in *my* house?"

We reached the end of the hall-way, and the door to the library stood solidly before us. "I can't reach the keys," I told the constables with a haughty smirk. They let me go, but not before glancing at the Solicitor-General for his reluctant assent.

I fished for Uncle's huge key-ring, trying to remember which of the many jangling shards fit this door. For Peapoddy's sake I had to look like I knew what I was doing. After a few fumbles I turned the lock and slowly swung the door open.

As it was by now quite dark outside, the sky-lights provided no illumination. The hulking shapes of towering book-shelves sat silhouetted against the night. It was impossible to see—yet—that they were empty.

"I'll just go and turn up some lamps," I offered, moving into the room—but the brutish form of the Ectologist stopped me. "You'll stay out here," he rumbled.

Peapoddy nodded to the constables. "Find the lamps," he told them. They and the Ectologist spread out into the room, and I knew it would be only a matter of seconds before the light would put an end to my charade. In a split-second, my master-tactician brain conceived of and discarded a dozen plans of action, from *start pretending not to understand English* to *go back to the kitchen for more crisps.*

Finally, I alighted on *claim that there's a secret compartment in the room,* as presumably there *would* be one of some sort, some-where in the room. Uncle loved him some secret compartments.

The lamps flared up. Peapoddy's eyes widened. But I spoke up quickly: "The room will look empty at first. There is a hidden passage."

Peapoddy inched into the room, his book-sense tingling, feeling the air for any evidence. The musty smell of aging paper, which I hadn't been able to totally eradicate with kerosene, reassured him, and his step quickened. The Solicitor-General followed, slowly.

And then, a terrific crash sounded from the direction of the North Atrium! The walls shook as a terrible screeching filled every inch of space. Could my luck be so fine? *Bat-creatures.* In the Manor.

Peapoddy and the others reeled. I felt the weight of the key-ring in my hand—and before I realised what I was about to do, I had already slammed the library door and bent the key in the lock. That terrible, shocking sound still reverberated in my skull—but the door was locked, and I was free. When Fortune hands you bat-creatures, by heaven, you *take* them.

I ran, my damp trousers chafing, the hall-way moving by in a blur. As I rounded the narrow stair-well, I heard the smashing sound of the roof collapsing in the North Atrium. The stairs bucked beneath me with the impact; I was thrown to the ground and tumbled several steps down the passage. The sounds before me were horrific—cries and screeches and the furious, leathery flapping of a hundred evil wings tore at the bounds of my sanity.

But there was no other way out, as I had long since barricaded all other doors in a particularly mischevious flaunting of the Fire Code.

I caught my breath, readied my spirit, and made for the heart of the terror.

23: ESCAPE.

MY EYES REELED AT THE SIGHT THAT greeted me: bat-creatures, over a dozen, each taller than a man and wider than a woman, more ugly than the lepers down on Leper Blvd., and more deadly than the Shiv-Packing Shiv-Master of Shiv-Master Lane.

I stumbled down the last few steps into what used to be the North Atrium—now simply rubble, the roof collapsed by the beasts' smashing entrance, and walls and columns brought down with it. The opposite stair-case was utterly destroyed, my bed-chamber unreachable; I was stuck with the (slightly sotted) trousers I currently wore. No matter, as groinal moisture was the second-to-least of my current problems. (The least being, where to change the Canadian nickel I had just found in my vest-coat pocket.)

The bat-creatures heard me immediately, of course; they had ears the size and shape of conch-shells, ugly, misshapen conch-shells the shape of bat-ears, and each beat of my fluttering heart was no doubt a thunderous bongo war-drum of terror to their delicate senses. They wheeled to face me, their eyes glowing a fierce red that reminded me of very angry blue-jays, if they were red and glowed. I was trapped like a lemur.

I considered everything I knew or had heard about the creatures. Their only known weakness was the sonic assault of a church-bell or gong, as the cathedral in Stamps-upon-Staves illustrated multiple times each day, but I had no such clanging-devices here—save for the old coal-fired Casio key-board that took up the large part of an upstairs bedroom. I'd acquired the piece from an Okinawan with a hare-lip in exchange for letting him borrow my moustache for a job interview, and had thought briefly that I could make a few coins busking some dope rhythms—but the device weighed three tonnes and required a team of oxen to transport and a full crew of shovelers to keep lit, and I was also really bad at playing, so business had been slim down at the board-walk. In any case, it was inaccessible now.

These creatures had probably been driven mad by church-bells o'er in Stamps and were seeking any form of refuge, and had been attracted to the faux-Heracles in the North Atrium foyer—that plaster-and-rope replica constructed by the slimy Peapoddy in order to tease me into confessing murder. I'd heard that the joint-wax much prized by oversized-marionette manufacturers was actually an extract of bat pheromone, harvested with great difficulty during summer middays while the bats slept in their freakish inverted fashion. Highly-trained wax-men using long, pointy hooks trod as silently as possible so as not to wake the slumbering creatures,   · sometimes moving as slowly as six inches per hour. (It was a guild one had to be born into—I'd looked into it, as they had excellent dental, and at the time I'd been eating a lot of glass for some reason.)

In any case, that dreadful combination of destroyed manor roof (thanks to the trespassing aero-carriage, an incident from which I was still waiting on the insurance payment) and joint-wax aroma wafting heavenward through the jagged opening seems to have brought a whole coven of them slavering hungrily into my house. I watched them smear that paraffin on themselves with a giddy sort of glee. It was a strangely stimulating display, and inspired in me an idea for a potentially-lucrative stage show that I might have pursued were the situation otherwise not so dire.

I shifted a bit and glimpsed the crushed fingers of Heracles protruding from the rubble of the stair-case, the automaton having been utterly destroyed by the manic fiends in search of that lumpy yellow aromatic. My heart soared—for the dictation-cylinder containing my murderous confession had been hidden within that lurching statue, and now, pray hope, it was flattened.

The present situation, however, left no time for even the most fleeting form of self-congratulation (and my bed-chamber was inac-cessible, anyhow). My motion had attracted attention. All frantic wax-love ceased as the bat-fiends reared to full height, extending their massive wings as far as the confines of the walls would allow and then further, brushing and knocking against each other and crashing everything within reach to the floor. I spied the front door, a far run across dangerous territory, and judged my chances of making a run for the open portico.

A horrific screech filled the room! The beasts were calling to me, rather than attacking outright; this was a good sign, so long as my ears didn't burst from the assault. Despite the horrible-ness of the sound, each second they screamed was one less that they were ripping the flesh from my meat-cloaked bones. No sense postponing the effort; I made for the door at once.

A great flurry blasted me from behind as massive wings rushed and twisted after me. The indoors blocked their manoeuvre-ability somewhat; I turned to shield my eyes from dust and swirling shards of debris. They headed me off, blocking the door, and I soon found myself swiftly surrounded by reeking fur and flashing talons.

And then, a flash of movement—a small figure scurried beneath them, hunched over and winding like a rugby-brat between the heavy hunks of marble and wood that littered the North Atrium. It was my basement hunch-back, running full-speed towards me, with something in his arms—"Follow me!" his gnarled throat croaked, and I complied without delay.

"Hunchy!" I cried, gasping for air as I pumped the ground at a sprint. "Where are your bells? You can rid us of this menace in an instant by tolling your graceful song!"

"I can't, Master!"

"Oh, I'm sure you're very good at it!" I said. "This no time to be ashamed. I'm sorry that I've never asked to hear you play before—"

"No, I can't because I haven't any bells," he hissed. "It's just a stereotype." He spun the object in his hands: a coil of rope with a weight at one end. "I haven't any bells, because *you* haven't any bells—it's *your* basement, Master, and I merely tend it." A great surge of pride quickened my step. I knew at once that this wretched, deformed creature was my man through and through.

A creature near us whirled, its red eyes flashing in the night, and the hunch-back let fly with the rope—it sailed through the dusty air, and with a sudden *clang* two gas-lamps were free from their sconces and airborne! Kerosene spattered through the dusty chamber, followed by white, hot light. Within moments the entire place was ablaze, the previous chaos of the evening having done nothing if not stock the room with ample kindling.

The bats screeched and fluttered towards the roof, smashing against one another, striking at anything that moved. Hunchy leapt over a flying claw, dodging what would have been a killing blow, and tucked-and-rolled impressively through a narrow opening in the wall. I realised that the opening used to be a hall-way, now mostly blocked by collapsed columns and sagging wall-boards.

Through the opening I saw him lever a panel up from the floor—"Quickly, into the basement, and away," he croaked.

There was no way—the opening was far too narrow for my robust, unhunchbacked frame. But in the other direction bright talons stretched for my person, so I ran and leapt, feeling the barest whisper of razor across my back—then, somehow, I was through, my coat falling into ribbons as I tumbled and rolled and, finally, stood.

The opening to the basement was dark, and it stank of all the horrible, fœtid things I'd dumped down there over the years. That place had seriously been my nasty-trash go-away hole.

But behind me the manor was ablaze, the bats still wheeling in burning agony, and before me the hunch-back was already three steps deep into that inky blackness where odours seemed to take on physical form.

I sucked in and coughed on a last, big breath of above-air, then pulled the floor-panel closed behind me and I descended.

24: INTO THE DEPTHS.

WITH EACH GROANING STEP I FELT HOT, oppressive fear settle with ever-greater weight into my bowel. The slick stone of the basement stair-way felt alien beneath my feet; it was covered in goop of some kind—whether alien or animal or simply rancid human, I cared not to discover.

Ahead of me, the curled-over form of the hunch-back led the way by the flickering light of a dented lantern clutched in one gnarled claw. "This way, Master," he spat, as he led me far beneath the surface.

Suddenly, I knew the goop: I was seeing, feeling, smelling, and tasting the remnants of my late uncle's grand seal-fat insulation scheme! This pursuit had overtaken the latter decades of his life, so assured was he that an estate of the Manor's prodigious size could only be protected from costly heat-loss by extensive subterranean blubbering. As the cellar-fatting was but one of the many eccentric projects of his that I had abandoned completely upon assuming residency (along with watering the garden where he'd planted a few shillings decades ago, hoping to grow a money tree; and, ironically, reinforcing the ceiling against sudden, severe bat-creature attacks), the oily mess was slowly seeping into the earth below through the joists and seams in the basement walls and floors, and soon it wouldn't be anyone's problem, ever again.

"This is catastrophic," the hunch-back suddenly said, gesturing to a large crack in the stonework, shining his lantern to spill a shaky pool of light on the surface. I nearly bowled the freakish little creep over, but managed to catch myself (but not without slicking my palms with seal-goo).

"The seals are leaking," he continued, regarding the shimmering, quivering wetness on the wall, then swiping a finger and taking a taste. He gargled for a moment, then nodded with confir-

"THE MUSKET-BALL CAUGHT HIM IN THE CROTCH."—[SEE PAGE 651.]

mation. "With the thinning of the seal, the integrity of the support beams has been severely compromised." He touched a wooden pole, black and rotting with blubber-stains. It creaked ominously, and he jerked back.

Then he pointed a gnarled finger in my general direction. I had no doubt he would have gestured at me more precisely, were his spine not massively deformed. "This is your doing, Master," he sputtered. "*Old* Master understood the level of care that these old structures require. He spent every day lovingly and conscientiously procuring and installing the necessary insulation. But what have you done for us? Nothing—left an entire eco-system to rot!" Spittle made an arc from his buck-tooth in the lamp-light.

"What would you have me do?" I retorted. "Spend every day negotiating and haggling for seal-blubber in the marketplace? There are no seals around here! Its trade is carefully regulated! My foolish uncle gave up untold treasures haggling with smelly merchants to pack this place with seal-fat. And you would have me do what, exactly?"

"He loved this house," Hunchy said softly. "You have brought shame to his legacy." He looked up, above our heads, towards where the North Atrium was surely burning to a cinder. As for Peapoddy and the others, trapped in the library as the flames grew ever closer—I shook my head to drive the thought from my mind. Dwelling on such things would only make me hungry.

"I fed you hunks of meat every day that I walked these halls," I told the creature. "You owe me that much."

"Aye, that you did," he nodded, a crude and savage approximation of reasonable human expression. "And that has purchased you your life today. Now, you must come with me, to the Council—and we will explain what you must do to save our civilisation."

"I have plenty of problems of my own!" I shot back. "And you want me to drop everything for—for *what*, exactly? Your crumbling empire? Some sprawling underground society, teeming with life and culture, existing for decades unseen beneath the feet of regular people?"

"Regular!" He snorted. "The 'people' you call 'regular' are not 'fit' to 'lick' the 'boots' of the heroes down here."

"Watch it," I breathed. "I own you."

"You don't even know my name."

I stopped short, my next witty riposte dying on my tongue and reincarnating as befuddlement. This beast had a *name?* Like *sentient* things might?

"Of course I do!" I said quickly. "It's...Kiefer."

"It's Sandy!"

Wait, now I was confused. Sandy? Was the thing a dude or a chick?

Suddenly the ground shook with a fearsome thunder that reverberated through the darkness. I stared vainly at the tunnel ceiling above me, but only a fine strand of dust, drifting through the lamplight, betrayed any commotion at all.

And then the ground heaved and shifted. I lost my footing on a heap of seal-fat. The hunch's lantern was lost to the darkness; the sound of the glass shattering against squishy seal-goop was the last thing I heard.

As I floundered for balance, reaching blindly in the darkness for any purchase, on any surface, the walls collapsed around me. My ears popped. Silence descended.

I stretched my jaw, trying to work it in a sort of chewing motion, and in the tumbling blackness I was rewarded with a mouthful of seal-fat, rock-slime, and something wet that I would later learn was dog-carcass. Remind me to share the recipe; it's surprisingly good over Melba toast, with a stiff chaser of turpentine to kill the regret.

Face stuffed with this delicacy, I struck the ground hard, my wrists twisting on unseen rocks, my ankles kicked out by falling timbers and slippery surfaces, all of it a bizarre, sightless, sound-less, purely tactile experience. My eyes ached for shapes in the nothingness; but this far underground, with the lamp gone, there was not even the barest hint of light.

As for my ears—well, who knew what *their* problem was. Between the fumes, and the pressure-gradient of the cave-in, and the many blows over time, and the bat-creatures' horrible sounds, and that brief burst of Herb Alpert a few hours ago, and all the years of ear-hole abuse with cotton-swabs *even though it says not to right on the package,* it frankly could have been anything. But the result was the same.

I was trapped underground in the darkness. I yelled and screamed my head off, beckoning for—what was his/her name? *Sandy*—or anyone at all to come save me, buried in the chaos of my own making.

But I couldn't tell if they heard me. *I* couldn't hear me. For I had been stricken deaf.

25: A SHAFT OF LIGHT.

I AWOKE TO ROCKING. I HAD HEARD nothing, of course, beyond a faint buzzing deep inside my ear-canal, as if a hornet had taken up residence and was now gently snoring its way through an afternoon knocked out on malt liquor and found pills. Bobbing yellow light bounced all around me; there were folk with lanterns here, and torches, and a single bio-luminescent swamp-frog, its glow the wan green of captivity and forced labour. The sad amphibian peered out from between lashed cell-bars of a makeshift wicker cage held at the end of a staff; its skin shone through the branches, casting cross-hatched shadows onto dark cavern walls. *Freedom,* it seemed to plead of me with its sad, black eyes, only one of which I could see at a time.

I was being carried by several small figures whose form I could not discern. It seemed to require about a dozen of them to bear my weight. From this I deduced that they were likely mythical gnomes, or else perhaps the mining-dwarves of lore, or else hopelessly stunted and disfigured human-like creatures worthy of nothing but my utter disgust. As we entered a large, lighted chamber I realised that my lattermost notion had been the correct one.

As my mind reeled with a sudden blast to my remaining senses, I became painfully aware of my deafness. I felt the ground shake, even through the many-fingered grasp of the sickly whelps who bore me at the end of their grabby-limbs. I saw a large audience of grotesqueries, stamping their probably-webbed feet, as I was borne into a sort of coliseum. It was a wide-open space, about the size of the Great Hall in the Manor, surrounded on every side by chipped stone blocks arranged into a makeshift amphitheatre.

On every level of the arena I espied the most vile and misshapen beings ever to huddle in cowering conspiracy beneath the varied by-ways of Civilisation. Why, this was a veritable colony of zombie

TOBOGGAN
SQUAD.

freedom fighters, as I'd once feared might reside in the dank depths of the Manor's lower realms—my nightmares had, here, once again, with great fervour, come to pass.

Everywhere I looked, new horrors greeted my eyes. These beasts schemed; they made tea from ham-leavings and raindrops; they cultivated a fearsome immunity to fumigation. Though I could not hear them, I could tell from their uniform gasping expressions that they were shouting at me. Some of them hurled dog-parts; others made rude motions with digits so twisted that every gesture inadvertently resembled an elaborate gang-sign. Others may have composed extemporaneous poetry decrying every facet of my character, for all I knew—I couldn't hear a thing.

But gradually it dawned on me this was a sham court-room. They were judging me, here in the Earth's rectum. I stood in the centre of their gathering, still weak on my feet from being crushed by rocks and buried alive. How much time had passed between that moment and this, I had no way of knowing; my trousers, formerly sopping with bladder-water, were at present caked with seven layers of nast but largely dry. That, plus a rapidly-growing hunger, were my only clues to the passage of time.

One figure stepped forward: it was my hunch-back. I'd already forgotten his (her?) name. I had a vague recollection that this gnarled beast may be a woman, for some reason; the notion seemed odd, however, as it would certainly make for an ugly example of the fairer sex. In my mind I had long labelled the creature Hunchy, because I'd once had a "hunch" that that was his (her?) name. Hunchy spoke to me quickly, in what were probably low tones. I responded with, "I'm quite sorry, but I'm utterly deaf."

Hunchy cocked his (her?) head at me quizzically, like I'd seen many a dog do in my time; I could tell that he (she? this confusion was becoming tiresome) was debating whether my handicap was sincere, or whether I was enacting some sort of ruse.

The twisted creature began to pace around me in a circle— I had the good sense not to follow it, as my dervish licence had been suspended ever since the ball-bearing incident, and the last thing I needed was an inquest by the Whirly-Dirvs on top of everything else.

Hunchy begain clapping its dusty claws at random, behind me, to gauge my reaction. I steeled myself to make no response, and in truth I felt my vigour begin to return as a thick well-spring of anger began to burble deep in my intestine.

Apparently satisfied, Hunchy addressed the audience. Whatever was said only riled them to greater heights of fury; and I could tell from their savage expressions what it was they longed for. It was a collective expression I'd grown plenty familar with over the years: they meant to hold me responsible for some long-standing ill.

I watched them ready themselves for imminent en-mobbing. This would end poorly for me, and Hunchy was having no luck pacifying them. In the dense dimness I could not make out more than their slavering thirst for blood.

Two of my senses sprang into full alertness:

A shaft of light suddenly penetrated the cavern from a fissure high above—a thin white beam cutting briskly through the dust-filled air.

And through the layered odours of seal-fat, dog-remnants, and misshapen civilisation, the far-off scent of wharf-cheese tickled my nostrils.

We were not far underground. The sun had risen. The cheese-twirlers would be winding their morning curds for the fishermen's brunch-hour. It was a time of day I knew well.

I was drawn toward the scent, finding myself scrabbling over rocks and boulders, wending my way towards a narrow passage that seemed to lead Above. The light continued to fill the arena.

I got my first good, illuminated look at the underground creatures when my way was blocked by their hulking champion—a menacing fellow of sour expression who stood about to my collar, and who must have weighed as much as my wet bathing-trousers. Deprivation of proper nutrition, revelry &c. had made these folks not just angry, but pitifully weak.

All at once they descended upon me, their many vicious blows like so many pummellings with marshmallows. I waded through them stiffly but steadily, dashing them against one another like swinging a cow's-leg through a wading-pool of eggshells, feeling their brittle, un-fortified skeletons shatter under my grip like so many glass swizzle-sticks.

From every passage-way I passed they piled onto me, attempting to choke me with their numbers, drawing their women and children and larvae and blobuous, mutated cripples from every cranny and cave, meaning to drown me with their slavering bulk. And they might have succeeded, too, as body after body added to the assault, holding my limbs, making my movements slow and un-deadly, the hornet's soft, snoring buzz echoing all the while. The sun's light faded as their continued battering forced me ever-deeper into the caverns, and with it, my strength; darkness returned until the only light was the sad green glow of the swamp-frog in his wicker cage, bobbing in the hands of the mob.

I stumbled sideways into a wide-open passage and saw Heracles. The *real* Heracles, the marble statue from the North Atrium that had been secreted out by Peapoddy and his minions and replaced with the soulless automaton that had, in turn, attracted the bat-creatures—*these* vile voles, these subterranean monsters had actually *performed* the exchange that had, indirectly, led to every problem I'd experienced to-day. *These* creatures were in league with *them.* The statue that had so bravely guarded the stairway to my bedchamber with its toned, alabaster physique was *down here,* lying in a pool of seal-fat, propped against what appeared to be a toilet-pit, no doubt cursing its own downfall and the conspirators that had forced it from its grand position.

I assumed that shame of Heracles and amplified it, grabbing the glowing frog from a gibbering creature and ripping the amphibian from its wicker prison, liberating it, watching it glow bright white with the pungent air of liberty, letting its light power me back out in the direction I hoped freedom lay, detecting and following the barest hints of that old familiar cheese-scent—feeling nothing in my veins but a blinding, fortifying rage, sensing it work its way from my thumping heart into my pounding fists, forcing my way forward through throngs of battered bodies inch by heavy inch, tossing those masses of twisted flesh aside one after the other after the other, wondering how many more of these things would have to die before—

I broke through. A sewage-grate. Cobblestones. The wharf-front. A sharp, tingly cheese-breese to wit.

I gave a snarling creature one last, desperate kick to the face, tossed the frog onto the street before me, and heaved myself out into the sunlight. ✤

26: RETURN AT DAWN.

THE SUN HAD JUST CRESTED THE SEA, and bands of golden light filtered through the fluttering pennants and sails being drunkenly raised for the day's mercantilism. I drank in the sight with a great, heaving breath of fresh morning air. I thought I detected a hint of smoke, but the sky farther inland hung dense with cloud; there was no way to tell if ash stained the atmosphere. The fate of the Manor was still a mystery, for the moment at least.

I thanked the frog and left it to its own devices; it hopped away and was promptly run over by a runaway kelp-waggon. As for me, I was still deaf as a post; the snoring-hornet buzz in my ear canal had settled to a dull thrum. No matter; I'd miss the wharf-rat cries for squid-for-a-quid, cheese-on-a-spun-rod, peanut-butter-and-jellyfish-on-multigrain, and whale-egg-on-a-platter-made-of-old-wood-crusted-with-what-are-probably-barnacles. I'd also miss the rat-juicers' shanty, but that was no great loss since as a child I'd heard it a million times on long buggy-rides (my parents had had it on tape).

It was the smells that swept over me like a wave: the terrible odour of the masses, all the spices of human exertion baked into churning vile sweat-cakes. After hours stewing in the stench of underground monsters drenched in seal-fat (a bitter flavour, but with a nutty after-taste) and bat-creatures (largely a sickly-sweet old-fruit tang with a dash of cardamon), the more familiar reek of Man-kind in General was a swift, sensory homecoming.

Still, there was a reason I'd instituted a strict vinegar-soaking policy before venturing to this part of town, and it was only secondarily because of the overwhelming unwashed-ness of People. For *there* it was: the distinctive, slightly porky odour of old Abu Fromage's secret cheese formula. Still here, on the waterfront, mingling

with the gull-poop and bilge-poop and clam-poop. Still wafting on
the sea-breeze like an ill wind of Fate.

But such a thing simply could not be! The last time I'd smelled
that sacred scent on this side of the world, I'd traced its source to a
leprous old pier-brawler mixing his inside-water with waste runoff
from a third-rate, un-pedigreed cheesery. And yet *here it was,* a
pungent boldness that cut through the sea-air like a steam-fired
torpedo. I would know what powered this aroma.

I cocked my nostrils and made my way for the source, honing in
with a power and a potency only enhanced by my lack of hearing.
Undistracted by jealous glares from longshoremen, unwiled by seamen's she-men plying their trade on the board-walk, undeterred by
urchins that I trampled to a pulp without pausing, I crossed wharf
and market, street and cobble-way, bridge and dale—until I found
myself unexpectedly fitting in with the environs, my filthy, bladder-
water-stain'd apparel positively *de rigueur* for the neighbourhood.
I had crossed Admiralty Way. I was in Kipper-town.

I was quickly surrounded by dirty thugs, bouncing black-
jacks in their hand and cudgels on their clavicles. The Kippers
were a band of street-toughs, bound by an iron code of honour
that included many ridiculous elements, such as requiring group
pooping—if one member was absent, they all had to wait. Due
largely to procedural rules such as this, they were a rather minor
player as far as the City on the whole went, but I happened to have a
connexion to this particular faction: I'd pledged as a Kipper during
the year of University I'd spent begging for old buttons, perfecting
the cheese-trade, and busking terribly using a wooden spoon and
my own skull. My Brotherhood in the Fellowship of Kippers may
have been long ago, but it was time to see if I still remembered the
secret gestures that would identify me as a friend.

I clapped twice, then spun around and imitated the swimming
pattern of the noble pickled herring. I struggled to remember the
mnemonic for how many flails to make with my flippers—the wrong
number and they would descend on me instantly, as a (presumably
hostile) infiltrator who'd gotten the pass-dance incorrect was many

THE WHARF-FRONT.

orders of magnitude more dangerous than a simple bystander who'd wandered down the wrong alley searching for pudding or sex.

It seemed to work; their gestures softened, and they turned on the fellow who'd first noticed me and pulled out his switch-blade. They killed him with several quick blows about the face, then strung his ceremonial shawl about my own neck, clapping several times in unison to welcome me. *One in, one out* was another of the ways of the Fellowship, and a hard man it made you.

I made use of my newfound authority at once. "Where is the cheese-smell coming from?" I asked. "And I'm deaf, so you'll have to gesture."

Suddenly, a familiar face rushed from the crowd, its lower half flapping. The lad was quite excited, tears streaming down his coal-stained face, revealing in stripes what had once been fair bourgeois skin, now soiled by a brutal life of labour under the sun. With a start I realised this was my stupid nephew Josiah.

He of the "contemporary" art; the tap-dancing rat-brigade, the deep-throated pipe-bowing, the fæcal paintings. I had lost a good hat when last I ventured into his deep hall-ways of idiotic exhibits, and here he was now, evidently ruined by his own preposterous attempts at novelty and bound up with the Kippers. He probably owed them all money, and was working off the debt on a peg. "Good to see you too," I said, possibly too loudly, as he leapt up and down and launched an awkward embrace. To stave off further conversation I promptly said, "I'm deaf, so you can shut your fool mouth."

The lad's eyes went positively saucer-shaped. He immediately produced a sketch-pad, where he began to write with a fury that amazed the gathered Kippers; they sucked in their jaws with positive bewilderment. I couldn't make heads nor tails of the scrawled characters, as I've not yet heard a decent argument for literacy; I could only tell him thus, to the effect of "I think reading and writing is for flopsies and Irishmen, and have had no part of it my many days."

This brutal fact of life was a bit harder for Josiah to swallow, but it was intriguing to watch the rusty old creative-gears work behind the boy's eyes. Then he seemed to have a notion, and departed my presence with haste. Finally, an outcome I could get behind! The boy thus banished from my mind, I turned to the nearest Kipper and tried to practise the old hand-shake, but fouled up the turn-around-reach-behind-stones-jostle.

Josiah soon returned, to my chagrin, holding a small wooden box in his white-flushed fingers, It was his set of picto-gramme cards, each emblazoned with a badly-rendered picture. He worked them deftly, I should admit, like a thirteen-card-monte player upon a cardboard stand with every audience member an accomplice.

And then a strange thing began to happen.

I understood his meaning.

Perhaps it was the otherwise total deprivation of communication I'd been subject to, but I actually fully grasped an understanding from his shuffling, displaying, and combining of picto-grammes. Fire + House + Moon = *The Manor burnt all night.* Sadness + Fire + Distance = *We were worried, but unsure.* Gold + Barrel + Man picking nose = *Treasure is hidden in my sinus cavity.* I took the hint and rubbed self-consciously at my face. The other guys thought I was scratching; I totally played it cool.

"In the Manor, when I left," I told the lad softly, unable to accurately gauge the volume of my speech but doing my best to approximate low tones, "were several constables, a certain Special Investigator Peapoddy, and the Solicitor-General. I fear they may not have escaped the conflagration."

At this every head turned towards us. Apparently I had not been as quiet as I'd intended. The Kippers had no great love for the constabulary, but neither did they ken to un-sanctioned violence that might throw off the delicate balance of power on the streets. I thought back to the many lonely nights I'd felt the heady menace of the Kippers and their many rival groups through the elevated windows of my rich-man's carriage. *Society is coming down, big man,* was what their gaze shouted; they were keenly attuned to any shifting zephyr in the howling gusts of City authority. I suddenly realised that this whole affair may yet have repercussions far from the grounds of the Manor.

Josiah worked the cards quickly and surely: Army + Boots + House.

We were going to the Manor. All of us, apparently.

27: SIFTING THROUGH THE ASHES.

A S WE MARCHED CLOSER TO THE ESTATE, the air steadily darkened with ash; the white mist of morning hung brown and acrid with soot o'er Waverly Hill. I was rather enjoying the freedom that deafness brought; it meant that I could be as talkative as I liked, and not have to trade blathering-duties with a conversation-partner. Normally I tired quickly of silently ticking the seconds like a metronome while some tiresome bore went on and on about this or that Matter of Great Import, waiting

NEIGHBOURS FLEE THE BLAZE.

for the chance to return the subject of the conversation to myself; in fact, in many such cases I'd simply said my piece and then murdered the other rather than suffer his constant chatter.

However, with my ears still groggily buzzing like a wasp's nest on Ambien, there was no risk of being forced to listen to any tedious yapping—so on I went, describing to my stupid nephew Josiah the many fierce adventures I'd suffered in the last day, from Peapoddy and the Tome to Hunchy, through to my daring, frog-assisted escape. I may have embellished the account here and there, as the finest bards are wont to do, maximising my prodigious feats of strength and quite frankly minimising the role of the freaky hunchback in the whole affair.

Suddenly I realised that, caught in a wild frenzy of orgiastic oration, I'd abandoned the audience some distance behind; they'd stopped, their attention diverted towards the smouldering embers visible even through the wrought-iron fence. We'd arrived at the Manor.

Not much was left—though it was hard to tell, really, because we were far from the only spectators gaping at the rails. I noted the wizened Mr S____ of the Committee for Genteel Relations among Neighbours, poking his weaselly nose between the bars and making a general nuisance of himself. He was probably an all-right sort, being a fellow man-brander, but probably oddly uncomfortable discussing the pastime in public, as was usually the case for devotées of the age-old sport.

Peering 'twixt hats, we caught sad sight of the once-formidable (and Garden-Society prize-winning) manse reduced to so much charcoal and bat-creature-leavings. I imagined the far-off bells of Stamps-upon-Staves poetically tolling their vigil; if only we'd had such a bell, to keep the fearsome winged beasts away, none of this might have happened.

Surveying the rubble, it seems that we *did* have a big bronze bell, and a bell-tower, even. In the South Courtyard. I thought back—I didn't recall *ever* being in the South Courtyard, or at least not since that visiting carnival had upended its trolley-cart of pin-heads in the square and we hadn't been able to flush them from the gum-trees—it had been far easier simply to lock the door and forget about them. As I surveyed the heap of charred, avocado-shaped skeletons in the vicinity of the South Courtyard, I realised that the creatures must have been multiplying the whole time—the remains were piled four deep in places. That might have become a problem later, save for the blaze. One crisis averted by another, it seemed— more proof that the Universe had a Plan.

Truthfully, it was hard to gauge a precise sense of the damage from this distance. The fire brigade had blockaded the gate, presumably to head off egress for escapees from the conflagration; their simple-minded ruthlessness impressed me, as I'd had the whole red-capped lot pegged for poufters and fops, always posing for calendars and such. The crowd blocked any closer view, but that's why I had Kippers; quickly, I bade them hoist me atop their bodies, and if they complained, I heard none of it. Three or four of the strapping chaps hefted me above head-level, and I surveyed the scene.

The structure was blackened nearly entirely, with many timbers half-burnt or eaten away totally, though the mighty statue of Zeus mounting a pelican seemed to be largely intact. The property was crawling with constables, most grunting heavily with spades, dumping bones by the score into thick yellow wheel-barrows. They were utterly destroying my garden, turning over fine, brown soil along with the blackened bones of last year's kitchen-help, each stroke of the spade further ruining any chances for champion bulbs this year.

And in the midst of it all—the Right Hon. Mr D____ , Chief Magistrate, sifted about the ruins of the East Wing, poking right about where I had ushered those five into the Library and locked the door. Peapoddy, the Solicitor-General, even the brutish Ectologist—had *they* survived the blaze?

A shadow fell over Mr D____'s wide brow and he looked up to see a bizarre flying-contraption, apparently manned by aged cripples, having emerged from the smoke and now looping in slow circles about the wreckage. So *they'd* made it out all right, at least.

One of the knobby fellows aloft spotted me in the crowd. I couldn't explain it; I'd have thought his eye-sight about as acute as a cinder-block. But the coot pointed a gnarled, accusatory finger directly at me from that creaking aero-carriage—which wouldn't have mattered, if the magistrate hadn't followed the gesture with his eyes.

D____ looked straight at me. Even a hundred yards away, dirtied in full Kipper-grime, I froze in fear. I dropped from my perch, nearly braining a Kipper in my haste. *(One out, one in*—we would've had to make a speedy recruit from the gathered crowd, and I don't know if old Mr S____ of the C.G.R.N. was limber enough to execute the secret handshake.) Peeking through the

"WE HUNKERED DOWN IN A GENTLY-SWAYING
HAY-WAGGON."—[SEE NEXT PAGE.]

shoulders of the gathered crowd, I saw the magistrate gesture to his constables—they were coming, they were in pursuit, and no naughty cartoon scrawled on the front door would stop the man now. I turned to Josiah and the Kippers, opening my mouth to bellow—

With a dreadful, crinkling, crunching *pop,* my hearing returned. A wave of fluid seemed to slosh along the under-side of my face. I stumbled, clutching at Mr S____, working my jaw, speaking too loudly—"Pardon, pardon," I told the old man, removing my hands before he got any ideas I simply didn't have time for.

The first thing I heard was the magistrate's voice from fifty yards away: "Ring the Head Inspector! Ring her warden at the hospital! I want an arrest warrant issued—"

I didn't hear the rest. Not due to deafness, but rather rapture:

Lara was alive.

28: TO THE HOSPITAL.

"I T WAS THAT MAD PEAPODDY WHO
nearly dashed her brains out," I explained to Josiah and the rest, as we hunkered down in a gently swaying hay-waggon. The most brazen of our troupe would occasionally peek betwixt the slats, peering thus and about for the navy-tinged brass of the constabulary on our tail, but so far we'd gotten away clean. A quick duck-and-run and we'd managed to clamber aboard this waggon headed for the Hospital, stocked high with enema-hay, premium-grade from Sweden if my nose was any indication. After such stressful minutes at the gates of the Manor, it was nice to lay back a bit and watch the sun burn the fog to ribbons.

The Kippers looked up to me, I could tell; one of their own made good in high society, so flush with wealth that I'd rather waste a new ham on meat-rugby than hand it to a drunkard; so above the cares of these grime-caked cobblestone cads that I'd fain spend eighteen hours soaking my body in vinegar before even considering coming 'round those rough alleys where they'd shank a man for the glimmer of a hope of a promise of a prospect of an empty can they could turn in for recycling. I was a hero to them, a prince made pauper but for the moment.

I wondered what they would expect of me once the present ugliness was resolved and I was back atop Waverly Hill wearing laundered trousers and bandying servants about with a riding-crop. I didn't dwell much on the prospect, for as it was said, reciprocity in this town could sting like a bull-dog if one wasn't careful to watch one's mill-wheels. (Or something like that.)

The Kippers didn't know exactly *why* we were headed for the Hospital, or that every agonizingly slow creak of the waggon's wheels was like a rusty nail being driven ever-deeper into my hollow gizzard. I wanted to spring from this butt-hay and bound down the road like a prancing gazelle in dirty trousers, wasting not a single moment before laying eyes on my dearest love, the fetching and wounded Lara. I yearned to take her gingerly in my muddy arms and cradle her to my filthy waist-coat. I wanted to rock her gently until her blood knit every last wound she had sustained from that fiendish Peapoddy with his overly artful hair-style.

I wanted to make her my own. And if she woke up it would be a nice bonus too.

I knew the Kippers were not posing as my personal mercenary beggar-army simply to further the aims of my romance; rather, they were forming shrewd alliances for the day soon to come when legions of leprous rag-swaddlers would rise from the streets and begin to throw metaphorical stones of revolution at the bourgeoisie. Already some had begun throwing literal stones, and with the Solicitor-General currently missing (perhaps burnt to a cinder in the Manor) and the Head Inspector ill abed, the Chief Magistrate certainly had his fat hands full with law-enforcement. I resolved to lay as low as necessary to avoid his ire—and if it meant stuffing my face deep into butt-hay for an hour and a half, well, that was just how things had to go. I wondered if Josiah had picto-gramme cards for "straw + stench + laxative".

Turns out, he did, and was oh-so-happy to discuss the matter— but thankfully, we arrived at the Hospital just before his lecture digressed into foot-notes. We burrowed deep into the hay as the waggon-driver (who must have been six hundred years of age, though he moved like a spry four-fifty) eased his cart up to the Hospital's back-door loading-dock—then we scurried from the waggon into the dark halls before he could reach the bales with his pitch-fork.

Once inside the Hospital, we remained suavely inconspicuous as we searched for Lara's room, or at least as inconspicuous as a dozen dirty men wearing questionable moustaches could remain in a hospital. There were so many rooms she could be in! Was she in the trepanation complex? Or perhaps having her humours bled in the leechery? We passed theatre after theatre as doctors practised the ground-breaking surgical techniques of the modern era—in one, the clinical application of jelly-fish as a treatment for acne; in another, bare-chested M.D.s ground away at a gangrenous torso with a lumberjack-saw while interns took careful notes between the regular goop-splurts endemic to the process. The net result was my queasy realization that I had no stomach for Science.

Josiah spotted a sign that he claimed read "Morgue/Chronic Coma Unit," and wanted to head that direction, but a horsey nurse in matronly garb stopped us in our tracks. "Hold it right there," she said, in a tone bespeaking a sense of impotent authority. "Where does yehs think *you're* all gettin' te?"

I flapped my tongue. I tried to work the ol' smooth-logic on her. It was actually going pretty well, until the terrifying image of spurting torso-goop returned unbidden to my mind's eye. I gagged on something chunky from my throat, then accidentally breathed it. I gaped at Josiah, wide-eyed—I needed a card with a picture of choking.

Right as the horse-nurse moved to call for us to be taken to the trespasser-incinerator, a raspy voice

"THE MONKEY SEEMED TO SENSE MY INTENTIONS."—[SEE PAGE 511.]

sounded to my right. "We're with them," one of the Kippers said, stepping forward and raising a knobby digit. The meagre chap indicated a raggy team of sailors across the lobby—tattooed and burly sorts, wharf-men through and through, poop-deckers to the grave sporting un-ironic beards. But they were dirty, like us, and to the female eye we must have all appeared a matched set.

With a huff the nurse let us be, though she kept eyes on us till we hesitantly shuffled over to the oar-dogs and pretended like we knew them. "Act like I'm saying something interesting," I told the first of them, adding a wide grin and a hearty handshake hello.

"Oi? Wot's that?" They had about three good eyes between six men, they smelled oppressively of tuna, and apparently they preferred brawling to hand-shaking. They burst into rum-soaked action, swinging wildly about with their hooks and peg-legs and cutlasses, at one point neatly cleaving an orderly in two. Instantly it was a ruckus, violence breaking out in every hall. Sailors lunged for Kippers; physicians were set upon by geriatric patients bearing grudges; a monkey-hater seized the chance to bum-rush a nearby organ-grinder. I was having a merry time smashing a wheel-chair about in a wide, crashing arc when suddenly I glimpsed a familiar face across the fray. A large, brutish, meaty face, clear on the other side of the hall.

It was the Ectologist. The second of the Head Inspector's twin ghost-detecting goons, the first of which I'd locked in the Library with the other crispy cops. This fellow seemed a bit lost without his spring-loaded doodads; he glanced quickly about at the developing mayhem, then ducked back into the doorway from which he'd emerged.

I looked back at Josiah and the Kippers, already girded for a fight to the salty finish. "I think she's over there," I called over the boisterous volume of the fray.

The ancient Kipper who'd spoken to the nurse nodded—crisply, serenely. Looking him full in the face, I couldn't shake the feeling that I knew him from somewhere, but in no way that I could place at the moment. "We'll handle affairs out here," was all he had to say.

THE BILGE-SMUGGLERS.

Keeping my head down, I barrelled full-steam across the melée, crashing through a few barnacled bodies on the way. I leapt off the back of a crouching cancer patient, gave the shrieking monkey a bit of a spank as I whipped by, then burst into a curtained-off resting room—finding myself abruptly face-to-face with the Ectologist.

And there was Lara, lying softly in a white-sheeted bed not three feet away. Her hair, un-bunned, striped her pillow with amber silk. Her skin was pale; her frame thin; her eyes closed. Her trunk rose and fell with the breath of a sparrow. She was alive. But just barely.

A shadow fell over her face. Frozen by the shock of seeing her, I hadn't noticed that the room was actually quite crowded.

Then came a voice that would echo in my nightmares if I ever slept again.

I didn't recognise the face—it was twisted and melted beyond the appearance of humanity. I didn't recognise the timbre of the words; fire had blackened that gruesome throat. But I recognised the foppy clothes.

Special Investigator Peapoddy stood at the window, the midday sun blasting him into silhouette.

"Well, hello again," he said. ✦

29: CONFRONTATION.

S O YOU MADE IT OUT ALIVE," PEAPODDY wheezed through a twisted mask of burnt flesh. His crisp white waist-coat and breeches stood in stark contrast to my grime-encrusted attire. "If just barely, it seems."

"The fire was unexpected," I replied in as even a tone as I could manage. With the lovely Lara in the room (despite her apparent unconsciousness) I would take no chances with rudeness, as simple civility was basically free points in the calculus of love. "The hunch-back was driving off the bat-creatures. He lit the drapes; it was out of my hands from the first. Also, I didn't lock you in the Library—it was a gust of wind that slammed the door, and drat that rusty lock! I was trying to open it when the floor collapsed." Maybe he was buying it. "Also, I am innocent of anything that you think I may have done, ever."

"Fantastic tales of hunch-backs and bat-things notwith-stand-ing," he said with what may have been a snarl, "that fire cost me too much to *ever* forgive."

At this, meaty fingers seized my delicate, bony wrists and wrenched me off-balance. I swung my neck around, but heavy hands clamped my shoulders to hold me still. I felt hot breath on my neck. This wasn't quite how I'd hoped my reunion with Lara would go, although I must admit there were a few key similarities.

Peapoddy traced one thin finger along Lara's silent face, the bridge of her nose luminous in the morning sunlight, her cheeks rosy with the flush of ailment. Her eyes did not stir beneath their lids. Only the slight rise and fall of her thin bed-cover betrayed that this was more than an exquisite marble statue lying before us, at least on par in craftsmanship with Zeus mounting a pelican. Peapoddy watched my jaw set as he touched her; he smiled as my eyes burnt with fury. He may have made some other expression too, but the lumpy mass of goop that was his face was a bit hard to read. I think he may have raised an eyebrow at some point? But it may also have been gas.

"The situation has turned dire," he said at last. "Thus the Chief Magistrate has endowed me with especial authority. As acting Solicitor-General, I can draw charges against whom-ever I please. And as my first official act, I can think of none more appropriate than demanding justice for the unfortunate demise of the previous Solicitor-General."

So that thin man had died. I felt something akin to remorse at the thought of the reedy fellow crisping in the flame of my late uncle's late Library, various vital juices bubbling through his skin—but I was hungry enough already without adding that savoury aroma to the mix. I craned my captive neck to regard the Ectologist, a doughy road-block filling the door-frame. "And what of your partner?" I asked.

"Succumbed this last hour to his injuries, just next door," came the sad reply, and I shook my head.

"And for what?" I asked. "You ectologists are scholars, accustomed to the hard facts of Science, are you not? You were brought in by the Head Inspector to take empirical measurements of spectral activity. But that whole time you were mis-led by *him!*" My hands still bound behind me, I gestured with my head towards Peapoddy. "He was the 'ghost' this entire time. It was a setup from the beginning! Your partner died for a lie," I managed, before a heavy hand from behind clapped o'er the lower part of my face. My breath caught in my throat, and clammy skin sealed my nostrils. I sucked in hand-sweat.

It was hard to read Peapoddy's expression, standing as he was with the sun-lit window to his back, but even in the dimness of his shadow I thought I caught a grimace. "That is quite enough of your rabble-rousing," he snapped. "There was no hidden passage in the Library. The Tome of the Cowering Sigil was never there. You've hidden it—secreted it away, haven't you? And look"—here he knelt at Lara's side, her smooth, white skin a stark contrast to the burbled meat of his scarred visage—"look at the good that book could do. She hovers here, between worlds, between life and death. The Tome holds between its covers the power to heal her." He stood. "And I have the lawful power to send you to death in an instant. What I want is what you want. You have but one play here."

I grunted from beneath the sweaty hand. Peapoddy gestured at the constable, and he let go; I gasped the sharp, antiseptic air. If my freedom would end before long anyway, I would make the fiend wait a moment as I heaved the breath of liberty while I could.

Before, he simply couldn't believe that I'd have torched the priceless Tome along with every other book in the building for no reason besides an abiding distrust of literacy. But the fact remained that I *had.* I felt no regret for burning the books (I'd do it again in a second, and in fact was severely tempted to set alight some of the paper-stacks here in the hospital room, if the result wouldn't have been such a commotion), but I was a bit sorry that I had no leverage to make this foppish bother simply *go away.* Would I ever be able to return to those happy-go-lucky days of bowl-the-artichoke in the parlour and stoke-the-munchkin in the bath? Or was that fey world gone forever?

I'd tried lying to Peapoddy before, and that had led most certainly to the ruinous state of affairs in which we now found ourselves. But the alternative that day would surely have been worse—I'd have been in irons, and all else to rot. He was right; I had only one play.

With a little embellishment to make it believable, of course. I took a breath and made it good.

"There was a passage underneath the Library—I'd found the servants diddling there once. Heard a noise in the night and thought it was oat-rats. Took me forever to find that cranny, so I figured on its being a secure hiding place for valuables. The Tome went in there at once, of course, along with many other priceless treasures from Uncle's travels—spiced ritual kerosene from Bangladesh; tins of Imperial celebration powder from Shanghai; a few oil-soaked rags the old man'd unwound from Cheops' sarcophagus.

See, I thought that chamber the most fire-proof room in the place."
I watched Peapoddy's face carefully. He'd only believe my account if
he drew the inevitable conclusion on his own. "It's possible that the
Tome survived the blaze, but it would require a careful survey—"

"There was nothing there," he said curtly. "It was not on the
grounds. Every constable on Waverly Hill sifted through those
embers. Several suffered from smoke inhalation; one had a stroke
and thinks he's a parakeet. They all looked like chimney-sweeps
by the end of it—black and beggarly. And oh, they found plenty of
amazing things within those gates—enough to hang you a dozen
times a day for a fortnight. But," he hissed, "no Tome."

"Then it is lost," I said plainly.

His retort cut me to the quick: "Then so is she."

30: A DESPERATE PLAN.

BEHIND ME, THE WRENCHING GRASP OF
the unseen constable threatened to rend my arms from
their sockets. "Let off me, Peapoddy," I called, but Peapoddy only
laughed, a terrifying chortle behind that mask of creamy, seared
flesh. It reminded me of custard, the way it sloshed about in pocked
waves. It reminded me of evil custard.

"You don't seem to understand," Peapoddy hissed, shifting his
weight such that his looming shadow covered Lara's face. "If that
book is gone, that means I have no use for you." If there was malice
in his voice, I certainly detected it. In fact, it would be safe to say
that malice crept from every corner of his sentence, wrapping its
slimy tendrils around the words and coating them with a dark,
bilious toxin. "As acting Solicitor-General, I hereby draw charges
against you for...Oh, where to start. Foul acts of vulgarity. Craven
acts of murder. Reckless assault and attempted injury to persons of
the Law..."

And thusly he went on at great length—he'd clearly read my file. Despite his wretched nature, I could tell that drawing charges against me was a concession, at best; he would have been much happier using me as a tool to retrieve his precious Tome of the Cowering Sigil.

But the book was gone! And so my bargaining chips were spent. I craned my ears for any sounds of conflict from the Hospital hallway—would, perhaps, the rough-shackle Kipper crew come bounding to my rescue with force of arms, o'er-powering Peapoddy and his constables to spirit me away to freedom? I enlisted the sum total of my telepathic powers towards this end; sadly, I had no telepathic powers. I'd suspected as much, but figured it good for a go despitewise.

"I will be conducting further investigations into your history," Peapoddy blathered on. He'd been talking now for the greater part of ten minutes, a grand oration on the depths of my depravity. The constable behind me began to nod off—I felt his grasp slip.

In an instant, I had my plan. "Do go on," I prodded, trying for that thin edge of sarcasm that would make him do exactly so just to spite me.

It worked—he redoubled his breath and launched into another volume of monologue. "Although normally I make a practise of nomadic mobility, offering my services hither and yon wherever I can be of most use to law enforcement—I have accepted the charge of acting Solicitor-General here precisely to see your foul deeds punished," he yammered. "How exactly did you come to assume ownership Wondermark Manor from your late Uncle M_____? Under what circumstances did the inheritance change hands? I intend to put this and other long-standing mysteries to rest." Vitriol fuelled his speech, splashing about the room with that noxious, blue-berry odour of hatred. Behind me, I felt the pressure on my wrists slacken entirely, and then slough off.

Like a felled timber, the constable fell heavily to one side. He tumbled head-long into the seated Ectologist, who'd also dipped into briefly into slumber, and into what was at first blush quite the compromising position.

I sprang for the door, vaulting the bodies still fumbling to disentangle one from t'other; in two seconds I was in the hall-way and stealing a last glance back into the room.

"Get him, seize him, you fools!" Peapoddy cried, but both the constable and the Ectologist were on the ground now, tumbling about like clumsy lovers, each trying to regain his balance while trying not to touch the other. They flapped their mighty bodies like girls in a school-yard; for once, their bulk was a hindrance. Peapoddy was blocked by the men and by the Head Inspector's bed from the door—I let my gaze linger on Lara, searing that chalk-white face into my memory, before I forced myself to look away.

In the hall, the sailors and the Kippers were enjoying a rousing bout of spin-the-drunkard, having rustled up some grog from the medicine-cabinets. They let out a wild cheer as I came tearing down the hall-way; clearly, they'd made fast friends since I'd left them at one another's throats. (I would learn later that they'd teamed up against some busy-body surgeons who "couldn't take a punch worth bean-hills," and become battle-fast allies.)

"Get out of here, you fools, there's nothing for us here," I called, but my shouts were drowned by the rousing cries of that age-old sailors' pastime. The drunk-o'-the-moment stumbled trembling from lap to lap, where the soldiers tickled him to the point of vomit; then the last with clean breeches would stand to chug some more. It was a fine game in most surroundings, such as pubs or church, but probably not best-suited for the lobby of a hostile Hospital—and as my own breeches were already heartily coated with most sorts of filth, I would probably be considered ineligible.

I rushed to Josiah and fumbled for words—"We need to leave Easthillshireborough-upon-Flats. Secure passage to Dublin. I have to find—"

Too late: Peapoddy and the constables had sorted their limbs out, apparently; they tore into the great hall at full speed. "You are all under arrest!" came the cry from those wobbly mounds of custardy face-meat.

The sailors stopped, mid-syllable if necessary, and turned as one hairy beast to Peapoddy.

Old Cap'n Narwhal, the leader of the scurvy crew, lifted the pipe from his teeth and squinted at Peapoddy. He held a chunky hand out to one side, and one of his mates placed in it a velvet bag festooned with gold embroidery. The Cap'n worked the satchel's leather tie, dumping an ivory eyeball into his wide palm—then screwed the white globe tightly into his socket.

"Is that Peapoddy I hear, then?" he rumbled, and the sailors murmured their murderous assent. "Peapoddy the mermaid, is it?"

Peapoddy's face drained of colour in an instant—his whole person took on the character of his crisp, white, foppy waist-coat.

"Yar, it be Peapoddy the mermaid, broke us for bilge-smugglin' back in the Straits o' Parcheesi," came a reedy voice from the depths of the crowd.

Cap'n Narwhal turned to me then, fixing me with that smooth white eye, an egg dipped in milk dipped into his head. "Peapoddy's givin' you trouble, then, lad, is he?"

I nodded. Cap'n Narwhal cracked a toothless grin. "Perfect," he said, and the sailors cracked their knuckles.

By the time Josiah, the Kippers and I stumbled outside, the sun was high in the Spring-time sky. We stretched our grime-caked clothes under the sun and basked nude in the park. Occasionally, various screams would resonate from the direction of the Hospital, but we paid them no mind; it was the Hospital, after all, where Modern Medicine was practised, and screams were the universal signal that techniques were having effect.

Josiah turned to me—"You mentioned Dublin earlier," he said. "I mainly blocked it out, because of my thing about Irishmen."

"There were two books," I replied. "The tome that Peapoddy was after, and its companion, its twin. The second book may still be out there. The Tome of the Precious Lore may hold the key to saving her life."

"But it'll involve dealing with Irishmen?" Josiah asked, his voice wavering with fear, his soft body echoing the motion.

I nodded slowly and seriously. This was not an expedition to take up lightly—we'd need fireproof gear at the least, and casks of Erin-repellent, and the requisite number of llamas would be expensive in the current economic climate. But I fixed my mind on that pale visage lying prone in my memory. For her, I would do anything, mostly.

"We'd better make quick about it, then," Josiah said, "before the Equinox. Before the loaming."

For the first time since the last time I'd killed a man, I felt myself smile. "So," I said, looking over at the tall pink sails of Cap'n Narwhal's jack-steamer, sitting low in the water with its cargo of beer-stones and clover-remover and leprechaun-traps—export items for Ireland, all—"where do you think we might find a crew?"

31: TAKING FLIGHT.

THE SAILORS CAROUSED OUT OF THE hospital, flush with victory. "A round for my men!" Cap'n Narwhal cried, apparently hoping a bar-keep was within earshot of the medical plaza. "Let's have a drink, what?"

"Cap'n," I shouted, forgetting my nudity in the haste to catch up. "Cap'n, please—I'd like to come with you on your voyage to Dublin."

"Welcome to't!" he cried merrily. "Many hands make f'r hardy swabbin'."

"Great!" I beamed. "Can we cast off now?"

At this, his face darkened. "I promised me men a drink, and I'd hate to deny that to 'em," he said. "Hate for you to be the one cooped up with'm after breakin' that news. Can't we wait till morning? Or two days, really—one t'chase the hangover an' one t'check the P.O. box, as we're not sure when we're back in this port."

"What's that rumbling?" I replied.

We looked up to see the street fill with carriages. Horses pounded the earth as if they were chasing God. Each carriage seemed stuffed to bursting with constables from neighbouring shires—Peapoddy and the magistrate had apparently called for reinforcements. The blue-coats began to indiscriminately seize any shabby-looking folks within reach of a billy-club; the Kippers weren't far from being next.

Nor the sailors. Cap'n Narwhal paused to weigh his options, but his crew, larcenous lots all I'm sure, made the decision for him. Before we could say 'jack-sprinkletoes' they'd made haste down the hill towards the harbour. "We'll see you down there," Narwhal said, "and from the looks o' that mob, me boys're fittin' to cast off with or without you."

I rushed back to where Josiah and the Kippers were gathering their clothes; we'd set them out to dry after washing ourselves in the Hospital's fountain. We'd found a fair bit of pocket-change in the fountain as well; the old man who'd spoken to the nurse in the Hospital was tying it up in a small purse. It looked awful with his shoes, but then the elderly never could accessorise. Also, his shoes were tin cans with twine tied 'round. I thought of my own favourite boots, still at the booter's, still held hostage by that loathsome chap who'd taken me to that bothersome political meeting some weeks back. At least I would have good reason to return to Easthillshire-borough-upon-Flats: to get my shoes back. Oh, and to save Lara, of course.

Suddenly a lunging figure in white filled my vision! At first I thought it was an angel, come to eat my soul with plum-jam and oyster-crackers. But I realised with alarm that it was Peapoddy—battered totally beyond recognition, save for a mad gleam in one remaining eye, and of course the torn but still-foppy clothes.

"You just won't die, will you?" I shouted as if I'd had anything to do with his latest beating, then catching his full weight as he fell. I strained to stop us both from tumbling down the long cliff-face towards the harbour. Down below, the ship was being readied for sail; it would have to raise anchor within minutes, before losing the advantage of the tide. Behind Peapoddy, constables fought with Kippers; street-whelps and the urchin-class were getting in on the act as well. Before the hour was done it would be full-out street-war. That ship was my last chance for escape.

"The *last* place you should try to kill somebody," Peapoddy sneered, "is at a hospital!"

He whipped his arms about like a Chinaman, working some bizarre fighting-style that made him look quite more daft than even he could normally manage. While I ridiculed his stance, he dealt me three smart blows to the clavicles. A deadly gleam crowned his clouded eye as I stumbled towards the cliff-edge.

Blow after fearsome blow, he battered down my defences, driving me from my feet. It didn't help that I was naked; it surely didn't help that I didn't really want to touch his gross, pus-oozing body. But even as droplets of his viscera flecked all over me, I managed one low strike that took his knees from under him—at this he fell heavily to the ground with a sour thump and the soft squelch of floppy flesh.

I rubbed mud into his wounds. He threw pollen at my face, trying to make me sneeze. I did. We fought as men did in the first days of the Earth.

He tore me up good, I'm ashamed to say. Oh, my fortune for a croquet-mallet! But none materialised. "Where's your tome now?" Peapoddy cried, over and over. "Where's your precious healing tome now?"

I was done for. His meaty fingers dragged me to the edge of the cliff and forced me to look down at the ship, where lines were being tossed with gusto, the poop deck was frantically being re-pooped, and nautical-type stuff was happening everywhere. "They're leaving you behind," he hissed. "Looks like I get you all to myself."

He stood tall above me and raised a huge stone over my head. I squeezed my eyes closed. "I'm sorry oh please I didn't mean it oh please I'm so sorry," I think I may have said.

But nothing happened.

"I'm really sorry," I added, just to be sure.

Still nothing. The only sound was a squeaky gull o'er the water.

I squeezed one eye back open just a small, apologetic crack.

He was gone.

I stood up. He was nowhere to be found.

And then—I smelled the cheese.

Abu Fromage's spiced blend. I'd know the smell in my grave. The first time it blessed me, I'd been in the Himalayas, outside Abu Fromage's monastery. I'd had but a wisp of a waft of a glimmer of a sniff. But it had been enough for a life-time.

The second time had been here, in the fœtid alleys of East-hillshireborough-upon-Flats. But that had just been a mouldy leper in a barrel, hadn't it?

Hadn't it?

I'd driven myself to vinegar-baths rather than entertain that notion. But I'd smelled it again, just this morning. It had led me to the Kippers.

To the old man with the coin-purse.

Abu Fromage was here.

He had saved me.

I didn't know where he'd gone, or what he'd done with Peapoddy. It was a mystery I would entertain another day—the ship, far below, was drawing anchor.

I scrambled down the narrow cliff-path, nudity flopping around as nudity tends to, and watched the ship slowly pull up gang-plank and drift away from the dock, picking up speed—too far to catch, now too far to even jump—

Josiah appeared at the stern. I surprised myself by feeling pleased that he'd made it aboard. "Wait!" he cried to the crew, seeing me. But they didn't; they couldn't.

I made it to the board-walk, bare feet slapping the wet wood, shoving through thick shouting mobs of cheese-twirlers and crab-smashers and rat-juicers and tourists, until my feet danced in open air—I was falling.

I hit the water full-on. The shock of the cold took my breath. The deep stole all light, and I felt nothing.

Then strong hands pulled me on board. I vomited o'er the railing as soon as I found my feet, praying that somehow, some of that floating offal might find its way into Peapoddy's bed-chamber and befoul his pillow-shams. But I knew this was a fool-hardy dream.

As the foul puddle crested the horizon and faded from view, I turned to my stupid nephew Josiah and placed a manly hand on his girlish shoulder. "Made it," I said. "Knew I could."

The wind caught the sails and we began to pick up speed, leaving Easthillshireborough-upon-Flats behind. I saw Waverly Hill in the distance, still capped by a red cloud of ash. I hoped I was doing the right thing. I knew I had no other choice. I also noted the breeze; I wondered if I could dig up some clothes somewhere.

"We'll be spending a lot of time together on this voyage, I reckon," Josiah said, and just as my spirit fell at the prospect, he added: "I hope you'll teach me all you know about being a true gentleman of class! For what a foolish ninny I've been!"

"The first thing you'll have to learn is how to kill a man carelessly," I said. "It's all part of growing up."

He broke out in a grin. Maybe the chap wasn't so bad after all. And if he annoyed me too much I could always just chuck him overboard—if the sailors didn't stick him on a peg 'fore we made open water.

Cap'n Narwhal came up behind the both of us. I hadn't noticed before, but he had hooks for both hands—and, looking down, I saw he had hooks for feet as well. I didn't comment on the roundish, pointy bulge in his pantaloons; not being familiar with the cut of his particular jib, it might have just been an odd wrinkle.

My mind worked unbidden, remembering how I'd taken over the Manor from my uncle by a shrewd combination of guile and what my analyst had labelled 'sociopathic tendency' (though I hadn't asked what that meant before shoving his cravat down his gullet). I idly wondered what the months at sea ahead would bring—if, somehow, through some unlikely happenstance or some (equally likely) boredom-spurred act of causeless malice—if I would, in fact, find myself in command of this sailing ship.

"Welcome to the sea, lads," the cap'n said.

I nodded meaningfully, to give the impression of considered thought.

But to myself, I appended: *Welcome to the good ship Wondermark.*

Three months pass.

DISPATCHES FROM
WONDERMARK MANOR

VOLUME II

Voyage from
Wondermark Manor

by
DAVID MALKI !

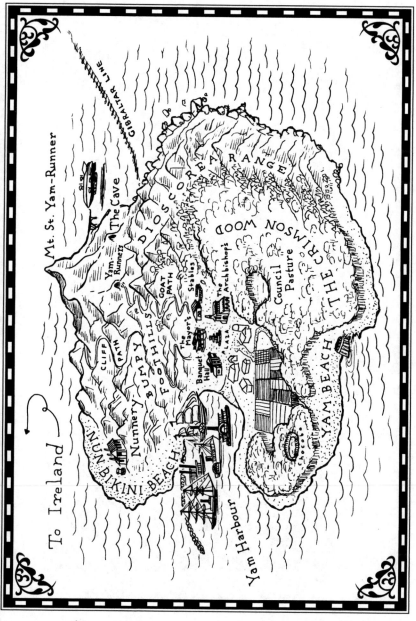

THE ISLE OF YAM-RUNNERS

"IT'S—IT'S THE GHOSTS OF OUR ANCESTORS!" MAURICE CRIED.
"URGING US TO LINE-DRY OUR LAUNDRY!"—[PAGE 617.]

32: LONG AT SEA.

I NEVER KNEW MY MOTHER," I TOLD the waves, leaning on the creaking railing of the H.M.S. *Flopsy Bunny*, staring at an unending sea, stretching farther and thinner than I imagined a sea could stretch without snapping.

I don't know why I spoke out loud. Perhaps I was tipsy from the breakfast-grog, salted with Cap'n Narwhal's own spice-mix, which some in the crew murmured was actually the leavings from his daily pumice-rub.

It may have been the gentle rocking of the merchant ship, which tended to lull me into a womb-like stupour; more than once on this voyage, I'd awoken in a fœtal position on the poop-deck, finding every hardy one of the crew—Narwhal called them "Nautonauts", without a hint of irony—with their peepers right on me, and staring at me too.

It could, however unlikely, have been a moment of genuine sentimentality—of which I'd been noting more and more since coming aboard those long weeks ago, and which I'd been assiduously policing out of my behaviour with a rigorous discipline-regimen below-decks.

Whatever the reason, my tongue continued to wag of its own accord. "I remember Papa telling me about her," I heard myself say. My idiot nephew Josiah turned to listen, shifting against the railing, no doubt waiting for a chance to interject with some stupid comment about himself.

I'd been certain that the feeble, motor-mouthed brat would be dropped on a peg by the crew within twenty minutes of making open water, but he'd actually shouldered a surprising bit of below-decks labour, having assigned himself head sock-darner and busying himself with a barrelful of the vessel's sweaty back-log. The Nautonauts had been quite happy with the arrangement,

having been without a suitable darner since their last had dashed
his skull against a bulk-head during a high swell and subsequently
proclaimed himself the Duchess of Vichy; at last account he'd been
holding court on the Continent and was apparently making quite
the rounds on the snooty circuit. Beneath all that French make-up
you couldn't hardly make out the beard anyway.

I recalled how Papa, the lout, had described my mother to me
as a means of making me fear him; for example, often he'd wield his
horse-whip high and thunder, "If I could bear to drive your mother
away, as perfect as she was—imagine what I could bear to do to
you."

Among the whits and drabs of his descriptions—things like,
"Your mother would swallow her pearlescent teeth if she saw your
room in such a state," or "If your mother saw these school-marks
she'd positively tear out her reddish-orange tresses," or "These
grapefruits remind me strangely of your mother"—I'd managed
to assemble a rough image of her in my mind. The figure who
beckoned me through the gauzy mists of my imagination was a
reddish-orange-tressed, grapefruit-skinned woman with teeth that
glowed in the dark. I wished I had known her.

"Some say she was a mermaid," I murmured to myself more
than to Josiah, staring at the sea foaming by below. "Perhaps we
will encounter her on this voyage yet."

"Oh, Grandmama wasn't a mermaid," Josiah said brightly.
"We used to go to her cottage for tea all the time, my mother and I.
I remember she always smelt thoroughly of menthol, even outdoors...
it put me off smoking all through university, because I couldn't bear
the thought of burning up my own grandmother and sucking in her
vapours, no matter what the chemical thrill. That's just the kind of
boy I was back then, and I won't apologise for it."

This was life on board ship with Josiah. Every day since we'd
first set off from Easthillshireborough-upon-Flats, I learnt a new
ridiculous detail about his neuroses. He was afraid of eggs. He
was leery of the Portuguese. He was unsure of his mittens' intentions; on cold nights he thought they might be trying to steal his

fingernails. And that was just Day 1. Day 2 had brought a litany of complaints about the hidden ingredients in corn-meal, as if the powder held *mysteries*—and it had been strictly down-hill from there. He had the frustrating tendency of being a fine help in a crisis, as we'd certainly been in back on land—but the unending boredom of weeks at sail set even the most amiable of room-mates at each others' throats, and each layer the sea peeled back from Josiah was proving more salty and bitter-tasting than the last.

A QUADRANGLE.

"How far do you suppose we are from Dublin?" I asked. Each day with the boy was one day closer to Dublin and the reason I had come aboard ship in the first place: the search for an ancient book, the Tome of the Precious Lore, which may hold the key to saving the life of the one I dearly loved...

Lara. Sweet Lara. Lying comatose back in that cursed Hospital, her skin white with pale blanchedness, struck into her prolonged slumber by my darkest foe, the venomous dandy Peapoddy. I would find that book, and restore her to the pink flush of life.

For I loved her deeply. And she had at least a solid professional relationship with me. At the *very* least.

THE OLD GAZEBO.

Josiah shook his head and shuddered at my question. "Not far enough," he groaned. "The closer we get, the worse my hives become. I think I'm allergic to the Irish. Or at least their representations in popular culture—my mother never let me have Lucky-Charms as a child, so I never developed an immunity. You should *know* that; I wrote that whole series of editorials for the ship's news-letter."

"I didn't read my copy," I replied through gritted teeth. I don't know where the boy had found a printing-press, but his sordid rag was always tucked into the hammocks when we awoke each morning. I'd actually made an effort to learn to read, back when I could afford the lad some favourable attention, but quickly abandoned the effort when I saw how decidedly one-sided the paper's official stance was on the hour that I commandeered in the ship's head each evening.

The *clink-clink-clink* of Cap'n Narwhal's hook-feet approaching precluded any further discussion. I whirled to face the craggy sot. "How long before we reach Dublin?"

"Oh, a good six months, with this wind," he replied cheerily, sucking on the stem of his pipe. "We'll have ourselves a nice Christmas in that old Irish port, then hit the sails for the return voyage when me men sober up right around Colonial-President's Day."

Six months! "Is the wind really that poor?"

He stared at me with his milky, ivory eye, gauging if I jested. "Dublin's our very last stop, after a whole tour o' the Baltics," he said slowly. "Ye didn't know that when ye made that big swim t'come aboard?"

This was most unfortunate news. Six more months with Josiah! At this rate I'd go mad and slaughter the crew after two, then eat them after four. "The leprechaun-traps in the hold," I said slowly. "The barrels of Shamrock Shakes. We're not taking them directly to Dublin?"

"Aye, bound for the Emerald Isle we are, 'tis true," the Cap'n replied. "But we can't sell leprechaun-traps without leprechaun-bait, can we? The best leprechaun-bait is from Prague. And we need bait-choppers to chop the bait; those come from Budapest, best in the world. Then we're on to three more similarly-ridiculous ports. *Then,* and only then, do we set sail for Dublin."

"That seems like a terribly inefficient route to take," I said with a scowl.

"Oh, *a terribly inefficient route?*" he mimicked, a bit too loud and high-pitched to be a reasonable imitation. He was terrible at impressions, as I'd learnt over weeks of tedious dinners. Still, deck-hands turned to watch the commotion—many of them were Nautonauts, but a few were Kipper stock, loyal to me. Tensions hadn't come yet to blows aboard ship, but trying as long days at sea might be on the best men's souls—for *these* chaps they were positively trying *and* succeeding.

Narwhal continued: *"Who's the Cap'n, eh? Who* sets the route? Who looks through the sextant and steers the wheel thing?" He was dancing, now, on his hooks, surprisingly nimble. *Clink-clink. Clink-clink.*

The jeers cut me to the quick, but I kept my anger tightly capped, like a jug of aardvark-nectar too precious to waste on the likes of seamen. For Lara, I had to get to Dublin. For Lara, I would suppress my simmering rage.

"You think you know a better route? You have some way to sell un-chopped, un-peppered, un-baited leprechaun-traps and expect to pay all these men?" Narwhal's hook-handed gesture indicated the growing crowd of swarthies—Kippers and Nautonauts both were beginning to gather. With his silvery hooks, he doffed his cap'n's-cap and fluttered it just out of my reach. "You want to be the Cap'n, is that it? You think you can steer this ship?"

The boat hit a swell. Brine-spray kicked the faint scent of far-off clover into the air. Josiah sneezed and doubled over, cursing his bloody allergies.

The sea had given me my chance. I had to take it. I stepped on the lad's bent back, pushed off into the air, and with an outstretched hand snatched the cap from Narwhal's smooth metal hook. Before my boots even hit the deck I was wearing the Cap'n's black velvet hat. It was warm and sweaty with cap'n-juice. It felt like Power.

It felt good.

"Throw him overboard," I shouted to the crew, indicating the Cap'n. When no one jumped to action, I tried "Do it!"

"The cap alone don't make you Cap'n," sneered Narwhal. "That cap I got at Target. It cost four an' tuppence on clearance after Hallowe'en."

Josiah sneezed again, gibbering snot all over the deck. I twisted my trunk, felt a satisfying *pop,* and gathered my strength—then I reached over, closed my hands around the boy's collar and his belt, and threw him over the side.

He didn't even shout as he fell. The sea swallowed him in a blink. The wind brought up the sound of one last burbling sneeze, and he was gone.

The sailors stared at me. It was still my move.

"If I'd do that to him, my own blood," I said, looking Narwhal straight in his unblinking ivory eye, "imagine what I'd do to you."

33: A FATEFUL SWELL.

O NE IN, ONE OUT," CAME THE LOW MURMUR from the gathered crowd. "One out, one in."

Cap'n Narwhal and his Nautonauts narrowed their eyes as one forty-eyed, forty-armed beast. The Kippers were chanting. Those men, old or young, dirty or dirtier—spoke in one voice, approaching the Cap'n and his mates, the resonance of their collective voice throbbing through the deck-planks and into my wobbling feet.

"One in, one out," they droned, save for one castrato who warbled a Latin refrain in high register over the rest. A nice counter-point, melodically, though mostly lost to the wind. The chant was what carried: *"One out, one in."*

The Kippers lived by a strict code of ethics, among them the mandate that no single member could wash his own trousers—all trousers were washed by all members, in a sort of communal bonding ritual that typically made for breezy evenings. Also, and more germane to the present situation, they enforced their rigid social order by maintaining a constant number of members at all times: should a new face join the gang, an old one would be ejected; likewise, should one individual be removed (say, hurled overboard), another must be drawn quickly in as a replacement, often-times without prejudice, predicated strictly on that person's proximity to the group. It made for startling diversity among the membership, if little else.

And so the Kippers advanced on Cap'n Narwhal. "One in, one out," they said, seizing the silver-hook'd meat-tubes of his limbs, drawing him into themselves, turning away and inward as a mass until the Cap'n's spotted coat was fully hidden by brown Kipper garment. Their backs to me & the crew, they worked the alchemy of indoctrination on him, right there on the fore-deck; as I recalled from my University days, it involved a lot of peeing on people.

"Oh, this indignity will not stand!" The Nautonaut first mate, a strapping Hindoo by name of Pranjit, stepped forward to wrestle the Cap'n free. He was quickly absorbed by the mass of Kipper flesh; he disappeared into the writhing mound like a snake devoured by a mongoose without even a muffled plea for Christian burial.

At this, the Nautonauts burst from their frozen shock; rally-cries echoing, they took up whatever weapons were handy—some found oars, others lengths of rope or chain, but most simply drew off their breeches and fashioned them quickly into nunchaku, using the traditional nunchaku knot that all sailors of the Empire are taught at christening. I had seen it many times, in my days working the wharf-front as a cheese-twirler; I must also admit to having felt the red welt of that vicious knot more than once after the rare cheese-transaction gone sour. Sailors under the flag of the Empire swear a solemn oath never to abuse the nunchaku-knot in service of a common tavern-brawl or fetish-ridden night at a pier-woman's; so here, the fact that so many mates had so quickly slipped their pants off, over, under, around, then tightly cinched them at the twain meant they were ready to do serious business.

More to my direct advantage, the Nautonauts now seemed more concerned with the Kippers and the Cap'n than with me. I still meant to take control of the ship, and head it for Dublin—and now, with the wheel-man tying his breeches into knots, seemed the ideal time to advance on the tiller. I kept to the railing, both to avoid the fighting Nautonauts as well as the moaning lump of Kippers who seemed to be assigning their ceremony a bit more gravity than may have been strictly necessary, and made for the helm.

The wheel was massive up close, with gnarled knobs worn smooth from years of stormy service. (I knew old wharf-hands who knew the feeling well.) It was heavy to my touch, and I could feel the pressure of the sea against its spinnish motion.

I squinted at the horizon, tasting the breeze, trying to pinpoint the source of the faint clover aroma that would direct me to the green shores of Ireland. I could almost sense a cadre of far-off lep-rechauns calling me with their sweet, telepathic siren song; I would have to steel myself against their psychic assault, if I cared to survive this journey with my moustache intact. I'd heard the buggers would lure unsuspecting men down to their fœtid warrens before tearing the saps' lips and cheeks from their skulls—then would wear the beards and moustaches of honest men as disguises to infiltrate the land of humans, wreaking havoc on live-stock or stealing chickens or getting with farmers' daughters or running for Parliament or whatever they did after that. I wasn't really up on the lore beyond the moustache thing. But that was bad enough! The wheel moved sluggishly, despite my weight leant into it; it seemed not to accept my direction, no matter how I rotated it, springing always back to a central position. And then I saw the reason—a lever-operated lock, no doubt to hold the helm steady should the operator be called away. A brass latch engaged the lock, and I thumbed it to the open position. It was tight, but it gave way with a squeak.

At once the whole of the vessel rocked as though struck by a wave. With vigour the wheel spun itself from my hands, the sea instantly assuming command of the ship's direction. The jib-arm snapped around to catch the wind, its boom swinging wide and fast

SPOOKY.

o'er the deck, ropes trailing like streamers. I struggled to control the wheel, but it snapped and spun too quickly for my hands to find a grip, its knobs, so smooth and inviting a moment ago, now tearing and biting at my finger-tips.

A mighty swell sent me sprawling from my feet and the Cap'n's cap sailing from my brow; I grasped after the headgear, but my fingers closed on empty air. Shouts filled the air around me, and the cries carried above the sound of crashing waves; I tumbled, feeling wet wood roll beneath me for ten long seconds before the ship found its balance again. My bones smashed against a bulk-head, yet I dared not open my eyes for thirty seconds following the tumult, and dared not un-clench myself for a full minute following that.

When I did free up one terrified eyeball for a tentative what's-the-story, I found the deck empty.

The Kippers were gone. The Nautonauts were gone. The Cap'n was mostly gone; one of his hooks was sunk into the main-mast, along with the most worthless parts of an arm. All that remained was three inches of foaming brine, sloshing o'er the swaying fore deck.

The sea had taken them all.

No! Not all! I glimpsed motion at the below-deck ladder—Marcello, the organ-boy! Woozy but alive yet, his pants loosely-done, clutching a copy of Josiah's news-letter! He must have been on the head during the commotion. His presence was quite a relief—should I come to need any new organs, after all that knocking about, it would be good to have him still around.

The hull creaked. With a horrific, rending screech, the main-mast leaned, curved, bent, and then *snapped,* spewing splinters airborne in a huge, dusty cloud. I glimpsed Marcello's eyes for one-half second before the free-falling tonnage made him the same height as the news-paper in his hand.

The boat shuddered, but settled. I was alone, on a suddenly still sea.

34: ADRIFT.

NO WIND RUFFLED THE TATTERED remains of the *Flopsy Bunny*'s sails. Not so much as a zephyr stirred the waves. The boat sat heavy in the water for weeks.

On the first day, I launched the vessel's sole life-boat, only to accidentally set fire to the oars, which alighted the dinghy itself. I watched helplessly from the *Bunny*'s stern as the smouldering row-boat bobbed in the current-less sea, slowly taking on water for an hour before finally slipping beneath the surface with a white hiss of steam.

With nothing else to do, I paced the deck a hundred times a day. I had no knowledge of rigging or helmsmanship or shipsmanprac-tise or even knottage, save for that bare amount I'd picked up in the back-alley sass-shops of Darkest Mudborough on prom-night. The poor organ-boy was now a brownish skeleton tossed into a corner; the gulls and I shared the sweet-meats he'd been cultivating.

Of Kippers and Nautonauts I saw no sign—not so much as a goop-stained kerchief bobbing up from the deep. It was just me, a dead vessel, and a hold filled with un-baited leprechaun-traps and barrels of Shamrock Shakes, vile, milky beverages made of sugar-syrup and hatred. After availing myself generously of the latter, I began to feel woozy and hallucinate, and at one point thought that a pirate ship was approaching—but realized, many hours later after trying unsuccessfully to hail them with a make-shift sema-phore of my own devising, that pirates do not, in fact, exist.

If I hadn't managed to pry the lid from a crate of leprechaun-traps, I might have tripped on Shamrock Shakes for days, until I starved or threw myself overboard or impaled myself on the splinters of the mast thinking I was diving through marshmal-lows chasing a scampering booze-pixie. But the traps' intricate mechanisms intrigued me; with so many bits and parts and pieces,

I thought there might be *something* in there of use to my present situation—and even if not, they were something to play with.

The leprechaun-traps were fashioned of flexible wire, the better to affix them around trees and branches and integrate them into surrounding foliage and terrain. A catch-and-trigger system attached to a powerful spring, which could be fitted with trap-cages, skull-piercing spikes, or the rather unpopular pillow-fight system, which pelted the little rascals with down-filled cushions. That last option was likely a ploy on the part of the manufacturers to claim that they offered humane alternatives to the poison-tipped bone-masher that came packaged with the unit—I'd overheard one Nautonaut mentioning that the pillow-fight attachment was listed in the manufacturer's catalogue but rarely, if ever, stocked in retail stores.

Not that there were even any leprechauns around here—they feared open ocean, or so I had been told, hence their chronic over-population of the Irish island. But I wondered if I might make any use of the spikes, or springs...or, in some sort of horrific worst-case scenario, the poison-tipp'd bone-masher.

I went on to ransack every room on board ship, searching aimlessly for anything useful towards any end. Cap'n Narwhal's quarters were full of gibberish charts and squiggly maps and stupid-looking sextants and the like; none of it was of any utility what-so-ever. I wondered, not for the first time, what the hook-handed old coot had been *doing* during the long days of our voyage. *Then* I wondered if he'd had a special attachment for use in the privy, or at least some sort of sheath to cover his hook for close-quarter work near the delicate bits. A quick peek into his mahogany-paneled soil-chamber proved my supposition correct—for hanging from loops in the wall were a whole line of gleaming silver attachments: a spork, for stews; a tuning-fork, for song-night; a tooth-brush, for who-knows-what; even a shoe-horn that looked like it hadn't seen much use since his feet had been swapped for hooks. Diabetes was a real beast.

Back on deck, I discovered while idly messing with everything I could touch that the helm's wheel now spun freely, as if it were no longer attached to anything. From this I surmised that the tiller had likely snapped. Which meant that should I even find some way to propel the ship, I wouldn't be able to steer it. With no land in sight in any direction—and, save for long-ago whiffs of clover that had since faded in the still air, no indication that land even still *existed*—I began to seriously doubt my chances of making it through the next week, much less on to Dublin or back to East-hillshireborough-upon-Flats. With the organ-boy totally consumed, my provisions were limited to the barrels of Shamrock Shakes; a crate labeled "Beer-Stones" that turned out to be, unfortunately, actual stones; and casks of clover-remover, which did me no good as I had no clover. I tried to huff the stuff to get high, but all that happened was that I suddenly grew a beard over-night, which was unexpected but rather dashing.

Clearly, my only options were to either leave the ship behind, or get blasted out of my gourd on Shamrock Shakes. After a shock-ingly-brief period of deliberation, I chose the latter, and headed straight-away to the hold.

I sucked on one of the green spigots for a while, and had a pleas-ant conversation with a French polar-bear on holiday from Calais until he started spouting republican nonsense about colonialism and I had to cram him into my coin-purse.

Then my barrel ran dry, and as I wobblingly rolled another into position, I began to notice my boots sloshing through an inch or so of standing water. The wood was soaked dark beneath my feet, as if it had been wet for some time. *A leaky barrel,* I thought to myself—and then I turned a corner and watched salt-foam seep through a crack between timbers. The ship was taking on water.

I staggered back against the row of barrels, dropping the one I'd been balancing onto its long side. It rolled along the lower deck, picking up speed as it wobbled, before finally smashing out the aft ladder and caroming thuddily into a bulk-head. The polar-bear in

my coin-purse struggled at the commotion—"*Qu'est-ce qu'il fait?*" it
cried. "*Dis-moi!*"

The barrel creaked as it came to rest. Then it yowled. A muffled,
human yowl.

I stared at that dark brown cylinder of staves and pitch, rocking
of its own accord—and accelerating.

Perhaps it was the burbling salt water filling the hold, or maybe
it was organ-boy sweet-meat and Shamrock Shakes corrupting
my decision-making from their perch deep within my bowel. But
I advanced on the barrel with a pry-bar, and with the shriek of old
nails and a splintering snap of wood giving up its secrets, I opened
the barrel. I held the nail-studded lid like a shield, peering over its
round, jagged edge.

The barrel was filled with salt. Coarse, white, clumpy table-
salt—a while mass of sand shifting and sinking as if bursting from
a shoddily-blown hour-glass like the ones my Aunt Maven used to
pick up for farthings at the flea-fair but which rarely survived the
trip home.

I poked at the swirling grains with the pry-bar. A few specks
came back on the metal, and I put them to the ol' tongue-test.
Definitely salt, fit for a nobleman's table. A hint of tallow in the
after-taste, similar to Uncle's old stock back at the Manor. A good
garnish for a meat dish, with hardy under-tones of labour. It tasted
like sweat.

I turned back to watch a heady mound of the stuff begin to rise
from the un-lidded barrel, pouring over the edge and avalanching
onto the deck with a sizzle like oil heralding the possible approach
of bacon.

And then a hand emerged, craggy and sallow, barely more than
a skin-wrapped skeleton. With a terrified shout I leapt backwards
and struck the barrel's side with the pry-bar—the bony fingers
flinched with the impact. The barrel began to rock from within,
and within a few seconds it was pounding back and forth, bouncing
and rolling on the deck until it fell onto its side with a crash. For

long seconds the only sound was the loud, high *shush* of salt spilling across the wooden beams.

My hands tightened around the hot metal of the pry-bar as I hid myself behind a bulk-head, watching a strange creature slowly pull itself from the barrel. The skeletal hand was joined by a bald skull, and then a shoulder, and then another hand, until inch by inch the torso of a man jutted from the barrel, salt pooled around him.

MY OLD DENTIST.

He lay back on the deck and drew great, heaving breaths into an impossibly wrinkled rib-cage flecked with sparse white hair. (*"Dis-moiiiiiiii,"* the polar-bear whined from the coin-purse.) After a moment of gathering his breath, the man—for it *was* a man, thin yellow skin drawn and stretched over the hundred points of a sharp, hairy skeleton—slowly brushed salt from his eyes, stretching the lids open with his fingers. Then he coughed, sending a dry spray of salt clattering across the hold. He looked around, curiously but deliberately, and it didn't take long for his gaze to fix on me.

"Abalasta watourapenishifa," he shouted, with a wheezing voice more creak and crinkle than speech—and then he shivered, and seemed to stand up straighter, a glimmer growing in his eye.

Demon-speak. My heart snap-drumming in my tightened chest, I rushed him with the pry-bar and made to spread his brains across the hold, crying and swinging the heavy metal at that bright yellow skull—

There was a flash of motion, and then a staccato popping as his thin fingers closed around the pry-bar. He wrenched the metal from my grip, then swiftly pulled his lower body free of the salt, standing on shaky legs and tossing the bar into the far corner of the hold all at once. The bar clattered heavily against a cask of clover-remover and came to rest before the echoes of its impact had fully faded.

The man's toes splashed into the pool of sea-water, and at once his eyes jerked down to examine it. He felt its wetness, slapping the surface with the sole of one yellow foot; he dipped curled brown toenails into the puddle, then looked up at me, cowering against the far bulk-head, searching vainly for another hand-held weapon.

"Looks like your boat's sinking," he said, in raspy but perfectly accented King's English. "At this rate, looks like you've got about three days."

I turned to stare at the shocking creature, searching for my breath, fumbling my tongue around the words. "Don't you think I know that?" I shot back, adding a glare for good measure. I didn't know who this guy was, but he'd gotten one thing right. This was *my* boat.

35: AN UNEASY ALLIANCE.

T HE AWFUL CREATURE FOLLOWED ME UP the sole remaining ladder and out onto the fore-deck, his wrinkled skin grasping the wooden rungs with a sureness that surprised me. Everything he touched came away with tiny particles of salt pressed into its surface; fine white dust still hid deep in every cranny of his pocked, jaundiced body. I found myself thankful that he was at least wearing a sort of soiled loin-cloth; who knew to what depths the salt had penetrated, and from exactly where the grains now scattered across the deck had originated.

Though his movements were deft as he ascended the rungs to the surface, crossing the threshold into noon-time sunlight nearly knocked him off the ladder. For a moment I thought he would topple backwards into the hold, strike his head on an iron railing, and solve my problem for me—though of course that would turn out to be just another foolish prayer. I had no idea who the man was, and could not entirely confirm that he wasn't a hallucination brought upon by too many Shamrock Shakes—the polar-bear in my coin-purse was certainly pleading for a look. But the man had been hidden away in what seemed to have been a perfectly physical barrel of salt, and he had easily defended himself against my prior attempt to murder him; thus I deemed him "real," and these were the same reasons that I would rather have him dead or vanished than clambering about my ship.

Regretfully, he did not perish in that first sun-lit instant—clearly, then, not a Draculan. He merely tightened his eye-lids for several long seconds, mustered his energy, then climbed sternly onto the deck.

He stood unmoving for a while, scraggly strands of his beard flitting about in the lightest of breezes, basking in the bright blue stillness all around.

I thought it perhaps best to divest myself of any Shamrock-Shake-related hallucinatory artifacts, the better to discern bitter reality from pleasantly deceptive fiction. Besides, once this inter-loper was dealt with, I could always retire below-decks and help myself to another heaping portion of that goopy, milky delight, and would enjoy the pleasure doubly for having earned it with begrudging minutes spent in the realm of this hot, dry truth. Thus I fought the coin-purse from my pocket and lobbed it quickly over the side of the ship, despite the bear's muffled Francophone cursing trailing an arc all the way to the lapping sea. I had no real need for the purse, as there was neither soda-machine nor laundromat nor self-service car-wash aboard ship; besides, all it contained (besides the bear) was a shiny button I'd found in the galley and my idiot nephew Josiah's spare dental-bridge, which he certainly wouldn't be needing any more. In fact, perhaps he would be reunited with it on the ocean floor.

As for the purse itself—well, whenever I found land I could always castrate another llama and make myself another satchel. It was one of the many skills I'd picked up by simply paying careful attention to Papa on our Sunday excursions.

The purse made a light splash, and the wrinkled man whirled. He snapped his eyes open, his pupils shrinking in the sun, shooting backwards, deep into his head. "Never toss anything overboard," he said sharply. "That's Rule Number One. You might need it later."

"Listen," I said, ensuring that the velvet bulk of the Cap'n's cap was seated firmly on my brow. *"I'm* the cap'n, here, and *I* make the rules. I've half a mind to toss you in the brig for stowing away. What's the idea, anyhow—suppose I'd wanted salt on my hard-tack tonight, but now you've sweated in it all?"

The man stared at me, slowly cocking his head as I spoke, until finally he appeared to be looking at me entirely sideways. "You're the cap'n, then," he said, turning to look around the deck. "And I suppose you're the first mate, too? And the head cook and the chaplain as well?"

Oh, it was going to be like *this*, was it? Lipping off to the Cap'n? I may not have been able to beat in his brains with a pry-bar, but I could certainly dole out a stout tongue-lashing—if only he wasn't so caked in salt! The act would dehydrate me.

I would have to settle for a purely verbal assault. "I'm whatever job needs to be done," I said, lowering my voice to what I hoped was an imposing growl. But the sea air had dried my throat, and the timbre of my words cracked embarrassingly. "I'm everything you're not," I squeaked at the end.

"Helmsman, then, too?" He asked, matching my growl and adding a much scarier one of his own.

I looked back to the helm, where the wheel was lazily spinning freely. "If there's a—"

The boat interrupted me by running aground.

The deck bucked, throwing me from my feet, and I slid a ways, coasting on the thousand grains of salt that coated the boards, including, perhaps, butt-salt; who can tell. The man never so much as wavered; his ancient old feet stood sure as rooted trees despite the vessel's fierce, shuddering motion.

The violence stopped as suddenly as it had begun. The man extended a thin hand to heft me up.

It was right there in my face. I had to take it.

His grip was perfectly strong, not at all the grip I would expect from someone pushing triple digits in age (as his copious body-wrinkles seemed to indicate). Once I'd found my balance, he strode purposefully to the railing and peered over the edge. "Sand-bar," he said. "Saw it coming a mile away. One degree to port or starboard and we'd have missed it by a mile." He turned back to look at me. "Tough steering the ship when you're busy down-hold sucking on juju-milk and assaulting old men, innit?"

My hands flapped to my brow, but I'd lost the cap'n's-cap in the tumble, and perhaps its associated charisma. "Now see here!" I managed, sputtering for a clever retort. I'd think of the perfect line an hour later, of course. "Shut up!" (That wasn't it, but perfect is the enemy of good.)

He wasn't listening, his attention captured by our surroundings. "Oh, I've been here before," he said with an air of recognition.

Then, with three long strides, he walked to the edge of the ship, vaulted the railing, and disappeared from view.

It was easily ten feet down to the water-line—would he break an ankle? Be caught in an under-tow? At this point I'd settle for sand in the pants, which could be pretty annoying. *Of all the nerve!* Making me out to be a bad pilot! On my own ship!

I climbed to the fo'c'sle and peered about. Sure enough, the ship's keel was ground firmly into a thin sand-bar, not ten yards long, crowning from the gentle green water.

WENT HERE ONCE ON HOLIDAY.

The old man tramped up and down the length of that tiny island, nodding and shouting with vigour and waving his arms furiously, having an argument with either himself or some invisible entity.

If I could cast off and maroon him there—! But how? I searched the battered deck for anything I could use to draw a sail, or a long pole I could use to push off from the sand, or even some discarded outboard-motor I hadn't noticed before...

No, that was stupid. This wasn't a dinghy at Aunt Lydia's lake-cottage, where she'd entertained agents of the underground anti-monarchist Revolution during my summer visits from primary-school. This was a multi-tonne merchant vessel, firmly run aground and stranded in the middle of the ocean, and taking on water to boot. There was nothing, absolutely nothing within a hundred miles, that could move this boat.

With a lurch, the boat moved. I stumbled but caught myself— I was getting better! I rushed back to the fo'c'sle, and of course, what did I see: the old man, feet planted firmly in the sand, shoving at the hull with his bare hands!

"Hey!" I shouted. "Don't be an idiot!"

His only reply was to just shove the boat off the sand-bar with a little grunt—then he scrambled up the side of the hull like a spider, clinging to tiny juts of wood with his impossibly sallow fingers. In three seconds he was back on the deck with me, watching the sand-bar gently drift towards the horizon.

"Happened to me once before," he said with a shrug. "If I'd been up here an hour ago I'd have remembered it's there. I think I buried something there once, actually. Figured nobody'd find it this far out." He laughed and clapped me on a sun-burnt shoulder. "I guess you're the lucky one!"

I turned to look at that crazy, bearded face, still flecked with salt, eyes sunken deep into a skull just barely wrapped with skin, stretched tight as a Sunday-morning apple picked late Saturday night. "You've...been to that sand-bar before? That very one?"

"Well, it's different now, you know, the tides and all mess with it a bit," he said. "But I'd recognize it anywhere." He looked over the utterly feature-less sea, blue sky and water stretching off in every direction, no trace of land visible at all save for that tiny sand-bar. "It's been a while, of course. But sure, I know right where we are." He pointed in a direction I couldn't tell was any different from any other. "France is that way, Morocco's that way—which puts Iceland way over there." He arched his finger as if pointing far over the horizon. "Iceland's nice this time of year. If you're going to Iceland, this is the time of year to do it." He stretched his arms and yawned. "Good to move around again. Nice day for it."

I could think of nothing to say, besides the meek admission: "I was headed for Dublin." Then I yawned as well—for his yawn-goblins had reached me and slid slimily down my throat. Not having been fed licorice as a child, I was vulnerable in this way.

He whipped around and laughed, spraying salt from his beard into my face, into my eyes. "Headed for Dublin? No, no. *Going* to Dublin, maybe, by a round-about route. But you're *headed*, at the moment, for Spain."

"The—the tiller's broken," I managed to stammer. "There's been no wind—"

"Only a lazy man needs wind to move a ship," he said, tossing the words over his shoulder as he loped to the stern, taking the steps to the helm two-at-a-go. I was alone on a boat with a crazy man—and worse, a crazy man I couldn't manage to murder.

The crazy man stopped at the helm, crouched, and came up with the cap'n's-cap in his hands. He looked at it for a few long seconds, tracing the cheap stitching with a finger-tip, then turned back to me.

"I'll take you to Dublin," he said.

He fit the cap to his own head, snugging it against that crazy old brow.

"But I'll have to wear this," he added, and when I could muster no response, he grinned. ✦

36: GRENADINE
AT THE HELM.

A BNER GRENADINE'S FIRST ACT AS
Cap'n of the *Flopsy Bunny* was to march me into the galley,
smash the night-locks with his thumbs in a way I'd been utterly
unable no matter how much I worked out my thumbs before-hand,
and empty the ship's entire store of grog into my gullet. That bitter
alcohol—intended for a full crew's six-month voyage—swept me far
from the realm of sense, and before long I was stumbling into cup-
boards, holding agitated discourse with the toaster, and answering
whatever questions the geezer posed without a hint of inhibition.

My memory of the whole affair is blurred at best, and I later
found many bruises, imprints, and tattoos on my person that
I couldn't account for fully, but I do recall recounting at full rambling speed my un-abridged life story—from hawking twirled
cheese on grimy wharves as a runaway urchin, to seeking out the
ancient cheese-monk Abu Fromage on a far Himalayan hill-top,
to eking out a fortune in tips by gamely belly-crawling through
Peru's Andean guano-mines, to finally burying a hatchet into
the top-bits of my dear Uncle M____ and assuming his estate in
Easthillshireborough-upon-Flats. I had quickly taken to that ostentatious life-style, the self-indulgent luxury of which I had been loath
to abandon—but that Manor was ashes now, burned to a cinder
by a hunch-back in a fight with hideous, man-sized bat-creatures,
dispossessing me in the most inconvenient fashion.

I told Grenadine, foolishly and slurringly, about my desperate quest for the Tome of the Precious Lore, and how I hoped it
could restore my beloved Lara to her full picture of health. I even
described the dastardly Peapoddy, the man who had smashed Lara
into my sitting-room wall and sent her into the coma from which
she had shown no hint of recovery—and the instant "Peapoddy"

slipped from my lips, I saw Grenadine's gnarled expression sour. I had the presence of mind to halt my account there, for it was clear that Grenadine had heard that name before.

"This Peapoddy," he said, a faraway contemplation beginning to work behind his eyes, "was he a tall fellow? Slim, with matching long scars down both left cheeks?"

"Tall and slim, yes, but no scars that I saw. I had occasion to examine him at close quarters, and saw only smooth skin, as if he had flayed a milk-bathed infant and laid the flesh upon his own bones."

Grenadine nodded. "Sounds like morning-tea for the Peapoddy clan," he muttered. "Perhaps you have encountered the younger Peapoddy, who was a mere babe when I tangled with the elder, so many years ago. The devious chap seems to have taught his spawn well; I wonder if that twisted patriarch even still draws breath. Peapoddy the elder was a far sight older than me when we first met, not to mention tougher than Me-Then-Times-Me-Now. Knowing I was no match for him at his peak, I packed myself into a salt-barrel and drew a breath of slumber-weed, hoping to emerge and find him an old man gasping on his death-bed, where I could drive the final nail through his skull myself. For that task I'd have to stand in line, I imagine, if some other wronged soul or even Fate herself hasn't beaten me to the strike."

I shuddered at the thought of *another* Peapoddy, my hands trembling with rage, my grip on the ship's railing slipping until I fell heavily onto my tail-bone. The sharp pain snapped Peapoddy's mocking face into my mind's eye, laughing at my discomfort. I hadn't thought about that foppish snake in the long weeks since the crew and the sea had taken his place as my primary enemies.

The villain had nearly finished me off, on a cliff-side back home, until I was saved at the last moment by agents unknown. As much as I wished the man dead, I also hoped I would still have the chance to take a croquet-mallet to his spine.

Grenadine took a long draught of water from the ship's water-pipe, swishing the murky liquid in his mouth. Now that

EARL TAUPE.

he'd been hydrating, his crinkled appearance had begun to soften some-what; apparently much of the parched-ness had been a side-effect of the salt he'd packed himself in, and the effect was beginning to fade. He now looked to be merely several hundred years old, instead of count-less thousands.

"How old *are* you?" I said, struggling to pull myself back to my feet, failing in the first seven attempts. It was an imper-tinent question I hoped I could play off as drunken foolishness, though in truth my high tolerance for spirits (earned in many a raucous overnight back at the Manor) meant that I was quickly regaining my senses. In my first few months of occupancy at the Manor, the constables would come 'round like clock-work at four o'clock in the morning, ready to clap irons on me for engaging in revelry past the revelry-curfew; however, my always-sober counte-nance and my frequently chicken-fat-stained attire lent credence to my claim that I was merely performing important offshore labour for a Chinese poultry magnate during the time of day in which that country regularly conducted business. Once I went to the trouble of printing bamboo business-cards, and insisted that the constables sit in on an all-Mandarin sales-presentation about the virtues of compartmentalised chicken farming, they seemed to take the hint, and their visits became less frequent after that. (However, I did have one of the constables stop back by looking for work after being laid off the force pending an investigation into misconduct, wonder-ing if I might be able to arrange a side-gig for him; it would have been an awkward call to my bluff, had I not strangled the fellow with a pair of trousers, thinking he was a salesman.)

Grenadine's ancient bearded face cocked to one side at my question, and he turned and ascended the ladder to the fore-deck with nary a word. Had I offended him? Did old people possess the faculties to take offence?

With deliberate care, I made my own way slowly up the ladder to find him squinting at the afternoon sun, holding his thin fingers at arm's length, counting softly to himself in a language I couldn't discern. I made to speak, but he shushed me without so much as glancing in my direction, which I thought rather rude.

After a full, boring minute of counting, measuring the sun's height from the horizon and position in the sky in increments of fingers and palms, then conducting intricate calculations on his knuckles, he seemed to arrive at an answer. "Eight hundred and fifty-nine, and my birthday is on Tuesday."

"Happy birthday," I said.

"Thanks," he said. "I think this year I'll try to keep things low-key."

"Probably for the best. I don't think we have that number of candles on board."

He stared at me for ten long seconds, and then his ancient face cracked open into a wide, yellow-toothed grin. "You're all right."

He looked again at the sky, then back towards the sand-bar still barely visible on the otherwise featureless sea. Then he dropped his gaze to the deck beneath his bare, salted feet, where he slowly shifted his weight back and forth, judging the minute movements that the ship made in response. I could feel nothing at all, as the vessel weighed many dozens of tonnes; but then I wasn't eight hundred fifty-nine, with a birthday on Tuesday.

Whatever he felt made Grenadine cluck in disapproval, like a duck discovering his credit card charging higher fees than he'd anticipated. "Not much time," the old man said. "She's sinking fast. But I think she can make it."

"To Dublin?" I sputtered. The sun had certainly baked salt
into his brain, if he thought this ship could make it to a shore not
even yet visible on the horizon, what with a broken mast, a leaking hull, and sails already torn into strips and commandeered for
toilet-tissue.

"No, just back to that sand-bar," he said, pointing to the tiny
island we'd grounded on this morning. He strode purposefully for
the stern, shedding his loincloth as he walked—with a cascade of
salt-grains and the weak slap of old rubber, he walked naked to the
back of the boat.

"How are we supposed to get to the sand-bar?" I cried, my first
step unsteady, but finding my strength by the second and third. He
climbed the steps to the poop-deck and I was afraid he was going
to make good on its name, the way he squatted and stretched.
"What current there is is drifting us in the other direction!"

VIEW FROM
LEUKEMIA ROCK.

He turned back to me, leaning one hand on the aft railing for balance as he stretched a leg out behind him. "It'll go a lot faster if you help me push," he said. He leaned forwards, bending his knee, then straightened, took a shallow breath, and without another word, dove over the side.

His slim, yellowish form pierced the water like an arrow. With two easy swims he reached the hull: then, leaning his back against the ship, he began to kick up a white froth.

The ship shifted. I stumbled. Within ten seconds we were drawing a wake. I stared in disbelief as the tiny old man began to push the ship towards the far sand-bar with nothing more than the power of his thin legs. I was *definitely* putting him on my fantasy cricket team.

"Well, *come* on," he cried from far below, tossing his wet beard and spitting out sea-water. "I'll need your help to land this thing before night-fall. We don't want to be in the water when the moon-sharks come out."

"Moon-sharks have been extinct for three hundred years," I shouted back to him, but my words were lost on the wind. *Oh well,* I thought, beginning to strip to swimming-nudity. *That's something I can hold over him later.*

The slight breeze the ship's movement sent scurrying past my skin was a welcome relief from days of stagnant doldrums. I had the most wicked farmer's-tan imaginable, my red-brown face and arms standing in stark contrast to soft, white under-flesh. I looked like a Polish flag flown in emergency conditions.

Bold, nude, terrified, I stood at the stern. The waves roiled far below my feet. My still-queasy stomach lurched at the thought of leaping that epic distance to the water. My toes curled away from the deck's edge, and my hands gripped the railing like the arms of an orphan-whelp caught befouling my favourite tea-kettle. I did not want to let go.

"The more you help, the faster we can both put our clothes back on," came a soft voice from below, and at that urging, I found myself free-falling toward the sea. ✦

37: ON THE SAND-BAR.

W E REACHED THE SAND-BAR AT SUNSET, our limbs aching and our lungs burning from the effort of pushing the ship across a hundred yards of open ocean. I wouldn't have thought such a task even remotely possible, especially considering that I'd begun to flail and choke on seawater almost immediately, and Grenadine had had to hold me in a life-guard's-carry almost the entire time. I tire quickly; it's an acquired condition of the upper class.

The ship safely shored on the thin ribbon of sand, Grenadine and I lay on the beach staring heaven-ward. The stars were beginning to pierce the growing darkness, and Grenadine sighed an ancient, wrinkled sigh.

"They change so much," he said.

"Have you really seen them move over your life-time?" I asked. I had always pegged the stars as pin-holes poked in the celestial big-top by the un-trimmed talons of wayward cloud-dragons, but I supposed the tent could flap a bit over the years.

"Not much, but enough to make me feel old." He turned to look at me, and it was light enough yet to still make out his craggy features. "It will be strange to see my family again."

"Your family lives in Dublin?" I hinted, hoping that Dublin was still our scheduled destination—for there, finally, I could perhaps pick up the trail of the Tome of the Precious Lore. I thought back to Lara, lying pale in her hospital bed, silently awaiting my return. I hoped she wasn't, you know, *dead*.

"My people live on the Isle of Yam-Runners, just offshore from the Irish main-land. That is, if the young'uns have kept up my estate, and Scottish freedom-fighters haven't annexed the place as a landing-base for their war-porpoises. So much can change in the world outside while you're lying asleep in a salt-barrel." In this last

WAVES BATTER INSOLENTLY.

I heard the first hint of bitterness the old man had expressed. Such vitality—and yet, such anger. And such wrinkliness—it was seriously hard on the stomach to look at him.

"How did you come to live such a long time?" I ventured, figuring that we were by now fast friends and bosom buddies, and that not to pry would be the rudest act of all. "Are all of your family similarly afflicted?"

"My family? Oh, no, no," he said. "No, they think I'm a bit crazy, I think, crazy old Great-Uncle Abner. I was an herbalist, back in the days of King Rufus of Roofie, and had a ritual of prescribing myself a daily tincture of double-potent long-wheat to keep the allergies at bay. Each day's dose, enough for a month on its own, apparently had a cumulative effect." He spread his hands out to either side, resting their sallow skin on the warm white sand. "Well. Here I am."

Eight-hundred-whatever years old from eating *wheat*? And *I* had had my pantry-lad flayed for imbibing oatmeal on the premises, in those Dark Ages before I had met Abner Grenadine, paragon of wisdom. "Tell me more," I told him and the stars.

"I have a hut on the isle, kept up by the family over the generations," he said, and then turned away from me for a moment—when he rolled back, I had to shield my eyes from a bright point of green light he held in his hands. It looked like jade, or perhaps a shard from a Sprite bottle. I had no idea where he had produced it from; he wasn't wearing pants at the moment.

The shard had a leather strand twined 'round one end, hanging in a wide loop about the old man's wrists and forearms. He lifted the loop over his head and brushed his beard to the side, so that the shard's green brilliance shone unencumbered by rangy chin-hair. "This is how we'll work at night," he explained. "This is how they know me, as I am often gone for long periods. When last I set foot on the Isle, my great-grandson had just passed on. I know not whether his descendants have kept my legend alive, or if they will even recognise me when we swim up to that fair shore."

Swim?

"I thought we were, uh, taking the ship," I ventured casually.

"Oh, no," he said. "We'll have to break her down for parts and build us a barrel-catapult. The springs in the leprechaun-traps'll provide the tension. With only our weight for payload, we should get pretty close to the Isle—I'd say twenty miles offshore. That's where the swimming will come in." He groaned, pushed himself up to a sitting position, and passed a palm over the green shard—instantly cloaking us in dusky dimness. The light went out. The green hung dull from its leather. "Still, that's a far sight better than swimming from here." He turned to me, and I only saw his silhouette, haloed by that crazy hair and beard. "What's your business in Dublin, again?"

I licked my lips nervously. "The Tome of the Precious Lore," I said.

A second of pause, and then the shadow nodded. "Ah," it said, and lay down again.

38: PARTING.

I COULD SCARCELY GET ANOTHER WORD from the old man after that, save for his intermittent muttering in a language I couldn't understand. We built the spring-catapult in twelve scorching days, drinking sea-water with the salt filtered out, somehow, by the old man's kidneys; we lashed leprechaun-traps to beer-stones with sail-ropes, and the catch from the helm's wheel became the release-trigger for the springs. Spring after spring I wrenched from those traps, setting them precisely in series to compound their energy. As hours spawned days, my skin ruddied under the sun, and my beard grew awesomely massive, tendrils of hair snaking in all known directions. After nearly a fort-night the H.M.S. *Flopsy Bunny* was no more, and in its place on the sand-bar sat a spring-powered catapult made of timbers and hawsers, with capacity for the simultaneous launch of two man-bearing barrels.

Also on the sand-bar was the ruined leftover hulk of about half a sailing ship. And barrels and barrels of abandoned Shamrock Shakes—I was off the juice for good. The hallucinatory polar-bears scratched to be freed from their wooden prisons, but I was a sober man, envigourated now only by Labour.

I tried to draw more from the old man about the Tome, in those long hours of monotonous work, constructing pulleys from kitchen-utensils or pulling nails from boards with our teeth. "In your many years and long travels," I said at one point, "have you ever encountered the Tome of the Precious Lore? Or its counter-part, now lost to the ages, the Tome of the Cowering Sigil?" I didn't mention that the latter Tome had been lost, in fact, to the stove in my manor one particularly chilly evening.

"Lost, is it?" he grunted, and then added, "Good. What's on those pages isn't for the likes of men to read."

How appropriate! I, it should be noted again, couldn't read. Couldn't so much as make out the telegram when Papa finally passed; I'd asked my Peruvian valet to read it to me, but he couldn't read either—he was a monkey, and not a particularly bright one, as it turned out. Singe and I didn't learn the news of Papa's passing until some years later, when we returned to Civilisation to find his inheritance disbursed among disreputable cousins and red-bearded relations. That night, I had eaten Singe in my grief. The following day I was hungry again. I learned an important lesson, about something.

Grenadine didn't speak of the Tome again until we were safely strapped into our barrels, awaiting a favourable shift in the wind.

"You have everything you need?" I asked.

He touched the green shard about his neck. "Seems that way," he said. "Got my birthday cake, my bright-jade, my senses." He sniffed the wind. "Getting close to time. Now listen—this is very important. We only have one shot with this rickety device. I tried to get you to work to more exacting tolerances, so we could test it, and so on, but you are like an oafish bull-pup with the wrench I made from that serving-spoon."

"It hurt my hands," I replied. "And besides, I'm saving my strength for this awful twenty-mile swim. I am pretty sure that's going to kill me anyhow, so go ahead, lay into me. You'll have eight hundred years of wandering the earth to regret being *mean*."

He ignored me, which I found rude, considering that *he* was the one who'd signed me up for a freaking *twenty-mile swim* after a rocketing barrel-ride into the ocean. "We must launch at the exact same time," he blathered. "If we don't, one of us will go shooting way too far; might even make it all the way to the Isle. But the other will be launched backwards into the ocean at blinding speed, and will surely be killed instantly."

"Exactly the same time," I nodded. "Oh, boy, I'd hate to overshoot and make it all the way to the Isle without having to swim."

Grenadine shot me a dark look. "When we land in the water, the barrels will break from the impact, but we'll be cushioned by the salt." He patted the chest-deep layer of salt that encased him in the barrel from torso to toes. I was similarly buried in my own barrel, and could feel my skin shriveling as we waited under the sun. "Grab a stave and use it to float. We'll link up together, and when we reach the Isle, the folk'll recognize the bright-jade and take us in. Or at least they should, if they've been taught correctly. My greatest fear is that public education may have been introduced in the last hundred years."

"What happens if they don't?"

Grenadine shrugged. "They will kill us. But don't worry—the bright-jade is *probably* a sacred diadem to them. And with the beard and the sun and the salt-wrinkles, you look almost like my twin, you handsome devil. We'll have no problem." He licked the breeze. "Almost ready. Let's count backwards from thirty-one."

"Hold on! In case we die," I said quickly, "in case, for some reason, something happens. I just want to know. The Tome of the Precious Lore. Can it heal my beloved Lara? Does it have that power?"

Grenadine took a deep, long breath. "When we get to the Isle, there is a cave set into a lonesome cliff. I won't direct you to it, because I'd rather it be forgotten, but if you happen to find it, you'll know it. There, you may find your answers." He scowled. "Now, for the love of Cramshackle, can we get going? Count backwards from five with me! Five, four, three—"

"One," I said, snatching the jade from his neck and slashing with one stroke the rope supporting his barrel. His eyes went wide for a split second as he tumbled from the launch-platform. I toggled the spring-catch, and with a deafening, metallic *crack*, I felt my own weight mount into a boulder pressed against my chest. The wind rushed by with blinding speed, and I saw nothing but the blur of the ocean far below. ✦

39: IMPACT !

THE WIND NIPPED AT MY FACE WITH tiny, teary bee-stings. I fought for a glimpse of the water drifting by a mile below. The sea was a smooth wash of colour, flat and spotted with specks of white, like my old porch-boy, Armand. I briefly wondered if the boy was happy with the Chief Magistrate, and allowed myself a secret pleasure at the thought that the mouth-breathing traitor was probably miserable with that corpulent man-mountain.

As I craned my neck for a better view, I disrupted the terrifying air-current, sending the barrel spinning wildly—my stomach lurched at the motion, my liver stopped making sense of the world, and the sun made a hundred rotations in a second; then my head mashed to the side, and I got a good, close-up look at my shoulder. The salt that encased my body began to agitate and swarm like tiny white bees. Again with the tiny bees! The granules stung my eyes, and I tried to scream, but the wind stole my voice—no doubt planning to sell it on eBay, the craven element.

In my periphery I sensed the approach of that great blue expanse, far below—and then rapidly, terrifyingly close—

Then, with a muffled *whump,* all became still, and dark, and boring. I felt nothing. I couldn't move, nor see, nor hear. I swam inkily in a sea of blackness. The demonoid stillness devoured my senses blah blah blah gothy clap-trap.

This was Death, I knew. Or else I had stumbled unawares into Professor MacGinnig's Sensory-Deprivation Chamber in the University basement after-hours—this last was unlikely, however, as I couldn't recall removing my trousers.

I briefly recalled the last time I had felt this detached from the physical world. It had been the morning (er, afternoon, by the time I'd awoken) after a raucous to-do at the Manor. I was in my pedagogical prime, flush with wealth and licentious energy. I had mutual agreements with the Police Bureau in effect, any unpleasantness with bat-creatures was still far-off and unknown, and I had not yet heard the accursed name of Special Investigator Peapoddy. True, I had not yet met Lara, the delectable Head Inspector who'd stolen my heart and spurred me upon this curious adventure—but my life was simpler for it, filled with nights of delightful waif-maiming, and afternoons of regretful hang-overs. It had been a blessed epoch.

As I lay suspended in darkness, a face squirmed beneath my eye-lids. A vaguely luminous sneer taunted me with haughty, fey disdain. *Peapoddy.* "You know I'll find you," the apparition said, with such assurance that I thought I felt my body shiver. Which was impossible, because shivering meant weakness, and I wasn't weak, because that would be ridiculous.

The face shimmered and shook, re-forming itself into the hideous, melted shape I recalled vividly, as if a wax taper had been smashed by a meat-ogre into the vague appellation of a visage: *this* was what the man had looked like the last time I had seen him, high on that lonely cliff by the Hospital back in Easthillshireborough-upon-Flats. Blazed to a crisp in the Manor, yet held alive by some dark alchemy, the wretch raised a stone with his deformed hands, ready to dash my brains out.

A stone? Nay, a human skull, a long, jagged gash gaping from the rear side of that scorched, blackened bone. *My uncle,* dead by my own hatchet-wielding hand.

I felt crawling tentacles of stinging hatred wrap themselves around my soul. More bees? No, this was a slimy feeling; more like a sadistic mould, or a jelly-fish of spite. Peapoddy rotated the skull, until those dark sockets were boring accusing holes in me, indicting me with their blank, be-sooted gaze. I tried to squeeze my eyes shut, but they were already shut. I couldn't hide.

For a brief moment I entertained the idea that I was still in the Manor, still asleep after that late night of wanton-ness, and that I would awake to find the entire terrible escapade but a rum-addled nightmare. I would find my sheets soaked with terror-sweat, and I would have Barnell, my sheet-wringer, hop to his task at once; then I would go down the stairs to the kitchen and have some brandy and old grapes. Then I would lounge about aimlessly, projecting an aloof sense of entitlement.

Peapoddy hammered the skull down at me, and I did not awake in my bed.

"Pull!"

I coughed on sea-water. Something, either a wave or a back-alley surgeon, injected a rasping gout of salt into my nose. I drowned in bitterness, thrashing my arms, finding them not pinned by the confines of the barrel, but free to smack the water gaily. Chattering cold enveloped me, and I rubbed at my stinging eyes. I tried to shout, but was unable with my lungs full of gross-ness and ocean.

"Hold his arms! Don't let him touch his face!"

Strong, brutal hands fumbled for my wrists, grabbing me powerfully, restraining me. I remembered those burly constables in Lara's hospital room, holding me hostage before Peapoddy's hateful, waxy inquisition. I smelled a powerful burst of sea-weed and clams, which did not exactly remind me of the Hospital, but that was okay, I could work it into my imagination somewhere.

I fought the hands. I lost. I struggled, but they were too strong. I tried weeping for sympathy, but it must have been too hard to see my tears among the salt-water, because they kept on dragging me along.

Rough stones slid past my back. I felt myself lofted weight-less for a moment—then I landed heavily on scratchy earth. My arms flopped free, and I poked myself on sharp blades of grass. Everything was uncomfortable.

My legs tingled with burning pain. I moved to feel them—and my fingers came away on fire with gelatinous goop.

It hadn't been hatred wrapping its stinging tentacles around me. It had indeed been jelly-fish.

What felt like sticks and branches and shards of bark scraped along my legs, ripping jelly-fish flesh from my skin with long bursts of blinding white pain. I tried to scream, but water drowned my breath in my chest.

With a powerful, body-folding spasm, I birthed a gout of vomit, trying to aim sideways so it wouldn't cascade back down into my face. I was only partially successful.

"He's breathing," came a far-off voice.

I was hit with a sharp finger of pressure, tracing itself over my legs, working in lines across my throbbing ankles. Then I felt another point, and another, and another, until a half-dozen wobbly nails pinned me to the ground. One traced its way across my face, and I realized it was a hot stream of liquid. Were they pouring tea on me?

No. No, they weren't.

I coughed, sputtered, and lurched my way upright. A shout rang out for someone to grab my hands, to keep my fingers away from my face. I fought blindly, desperate to rub my burning eyes, until strong muscles held me still. I was helpless as a crab on a crab-smasher's pummelling-stand. I wondered when the mallet would fall onto my carapace. Figuratively, I guess.

My fingers fell open, and Grenadine's shard of bright-jade tumbled from my hand. Then my skin tingled as warm breath encircled my ear.

"You need to keep still," came a woman's voice. "You've got jelly-fish poison on your hands. You mustn't touch your eyes."

I struggled to speak through broken, salty lips. I wanted to explain the blinding pain that seared its way through my eyeballs and augured its way deep into my brain. How could I possibly convey the wretched horror of that writhing, stinging agony? "Eyes...burny," I rasped.

"Lie back," she said, and a firm hand pressed me back down onto the grass. It had been some time since I'd heard those words from a woman, and I tingled with a vague sense of anticipation. This day might work out pretty well after all.

What felt like a bucket-ful of hot water smashed into my face, and I sputtered and coughed, finally forcing my eyes open. A slim figure swam into my vision, straightening himself upright and buckling his trousers, tossing long black hair over his shoulder.

Her shoulder. It was a *her*. But I could be forgiven for the momentary mis-judgement: for a *woman* was wearing *trousers?*

"Get the bright-jade," she told someone to her right, and I turned to see a husky, bearded man gingerly pluck the green shard from the grass by my hand. He reverently placed it back into my palm, and I wrapped my fingers around the shape. Then the man lifted my arms, and others my legs; they hoisted me atop their shoulders, and I saw the barrel, smashed into splinters in the shoals a dozen yards away, white salt spilled from its center like foaming, snowy guts.

I saw my own skin, wrinkled and parched from the salt, and felt my bushy beard scrape against my shoulders as I moved my head.

The woman turned to me, and I saw pea-green eyes sparkle in the bright sunlight. She was beautiful, ruddy and strong, with trousers that flattered her silhouette; all she lacked was a bustle, for her hips, oddly, were barely as wide as her shoulders. But despite that critical short-coming, when she smiled at me I felt my heart seize in my chest.

"Welcome home, Grandfather Grenadine," she said.

40: AN UNLIKELY CHARADE.

B Y THE TIME OUR ENTOURAGE REACHED the village in the centre of the island, word had inexplicably spread to every inhabitant. I could almost witness the frenzied rumours darting from lips to ear to stomach to lips to elbow: *Grandfather Grenadine's back! Hurrah!*

I gradually came to realise that old man Grenadine must have been absent for some decades or more, as it didn't seem that anybody had retained an actual, visual recollection of the man. Thus it was easy for them to assume from my bearded, salt-wrinkled, be-jade-necklaced appearance that I *must* be their long-awaited oldfather. And who was I to disabuse them of the notion? I ventured to myself that I should at least ride this tide of honour to see where it might beach me, and after some internal wrangling involving large gouts of questionable logic and not a few forays into possibly-improper syllogy, I convinced myself of the plan.

As we made for the village square, we were instantly set upon by chattering throngs of children, bothersome, wailing old mothers, and the high-craned necks of countless looky-loos. I perceived a general malaise in the place—this hamlet stunk of poverty, despair, and un-treated foot-odour. I seemed to be the sole attraction on the whole island; before we'd been clear of the forest two minutes, the mob had made our passage impossible. Held firmly aloft as I was, I couldn't even make a stab at my own way; wretchedly, I found myself passed from hand to grasping hand through the commotion, hundreds of greedy fingers exploring every crevice of my salt-encrusted form, scrabbling for loose granules as though those fine crystals were charged with some latent power. They wanted me. They *needed* me. They *loved* me, and it was a stinky, sweaty, grabby affair. I almost felt at home.

The pinpoint *crack* of a rifle-shot shattered the air, stunning all into silence at once. Loose words fell limply to the ground, trampled in the sudden confusion; half-formed thoughts melted feebly into gurgled moans of alarm. A fat man with his hand on my loin slipped in a wet puddle of burbled conversation and neatly deposited me into a muddy morass of abandoned speech, and I slid and fumbled through abandoned participles before coming to rest at a set of wide, shining boots.

A heavy wooden rifle-stock mashed the ground three inches from my skin. A calloused hand reached down from a meaty frame. It hovered at my nose-level, just sitting there, shaking a little bit, the fingers slowly reddening and plumping as Gravity sucked its blood greedily towards the Earth..

I looked up. The hand was attached to a bearish man, smiling widely from three feet above my face. I took the hand, and he bore my weight up, holding me steady as I found my wobbling balance. I hadn't stood upright since the sand-bar, and my limbs were still cramped from their long, speeding ride in the salt-barrel—to say nothing of the shocking impact with the sea, which I luckily scarcely recalled. It had probably hurt worse than the jelly-fish venom still coursing its way through my extremities, which now tingled, not unpleasantly, as if I had stood up too quickly, which I had, or briefly strangled myself with a cravat in the wash-room, which I had not yet had the chance to do.

"We are so pleased that you have, at long last, decided to return," the man boomed, in a deep voice that reminded me of a bear gargling cough-syrup. The sound had a throaty character, but wet around the edges, and it was a bit loopy, with a fake-cherry flavour.

"Happy to be here," I wheezed. To me, my voice had the rustling squeak of many days on a wind-less sea, followed by a sudden trip through terrible air in a salt-barrel, followed by a brutal sting from jealous jelly-fish. My utterance sounded pretty lame out of my throat and out there in the world. But the crowd loved it—they cheered as one, sharply and suddenly. I startled at the explosion of sound, but the big man clapped a hand around my shoulder and drew me tightly to his warm, dewy chest.

"You don't recollect, do you?" he said, softly, his breath hot at my ear, the whisper nearly drowned by the babel of the crowd.

"Er," I replied. A moment later, I figured I should add "Sorry."

"It's all crackerjack," he whispered. "We'll have plenty of time for reacquaintance." He squeezed my shoulder, powerfully and insistently, and I felt a tingly knob of fear begin to wrestle its way around my spine. The man was certainly attractive, as far as that sort of thing went, but *my word!* He would *crush* me, if it came to that!

"Citizens of the Isle," he boomed at the gathered crowd, and waited a few seconds for the collective voices to calm in anticipation.

"I have longed for the day I could make this happy proclamation. As your Mayor, it has rent my spleen in twain to watch poverty and hardship o'er-take this proud community. Decade after decade, we watched our children leave the Isle for the accursed Main-Land. We have bowed to plague, drought, and famine. We have, in dark moments, contemplated the consumption of each other's rangy flesh, and in the blackest of those times, given in." This last was met with murmurs of assent from the crowd. "And yet. And yet, we have held fast to the traditions of the Grenadians: prayed that the Bearer of the Bright-Jade might one day return to the land of his descendants. Friends, brothers, uncles—our fortunes have been rekindled this day."

He turned to me, smiling brightly, his skin ruddy and glowing with excitement. "Grandfather Grenadine, have you indeed returned to your anxious children?"

A hundred eyes fixed on me. Snotty kids watched my every move with quivering lips, gooey gravy pooling in juvenile philtra. Red-eyed widows peered through latticed veils at my cringing form. That really cute girl with the black hair—who'd saved me on the beach from rubbing jelly-fish venom into my precious, precious eyes—was hanging back with an aloof cool-ness, but still seemed kinda into me.

"Yes," I whispered.

"Speak up, now!" the Mayor boomed, all toothy grins. "Grandfather, will you heal your children and your island? Will you make the Isle of Yam-Runners once more the Lourdes of the Irish Sea?"

I didn't have any idea what he meant by that, so I hedged my bets with a firm "Yes."

"Grandfather!" the Mayor continued ecstatically, clutching me to his breast with a familiarity normally reserved for fast friends and not necessarily long-lost grandfathers, "will you use your mystical healing powers to give each of us perfect health forever, eliminate sickness and poverty, and bring droves of tourists flocking to our crockery-shoppes and post-card stalls?"

By now he was choking me in the folds of his neck, and I, still feeble from the barrel-ride and jelly-fish incident, could barely cough out a burbled "Yes, provisionally, however I should quite frankly inform you that—" before the entire crowd swept me up again in jubilation. I was tossed violently from weakling to weakling, banging about quite a bit along the way, and I finally ended up propped against a scratchy tree some hours later once everyone was too tired to bear my weight.

41: OPPORTUNISM.

MAYOR C____ ANNOUNCED THAT THE town would hold a lavish banquet to welcome me officially back to the Isle, and the entire populace was quickly swept up with banquet fever. Mr C____ originally set the date of the affair for the very night of my arrival, inviting the whole town to come over to his house and that his wife would "whip something up"—but the towns-folk raised objections at once, on the grounds that such an impromptu event would deprive others of their chance to contribute to the revelry. Thus, the town Council met in a standing-room-only special session in the middle of a pasture, and appointed all interested parties—that is, every man and woman in the town over the age of 12—to seats on the newly-formed Banquet Planning Committee. Then they convened a special Auxiliary Committee for the children.

By the time the moon rolled into the sky, as I was later informed at excruciating length, the town's carpenters had drawn up plans for a brand-new Banquet Hall, to be furnished by the craftsmen and the drapery-women, with the town's landscapers planning to cross-breed a special breed of flower in honour of the event. Nobody was left out—the town's chefs would prepare the meal; the shepherds would bring in sheep to corral; and the Auxiliary Committee began at once making nylon lanyards for the official souvenir keychains. Everyone had a part to play; for once their lives were driven through with purpose, and for the first time in many of their lives, they could while away their hours towards a productive pursuit, instead of huddling in stinking hovels waiting for death, as they were wont.

I had been instructed to keep away from the meeting (as it was to be in my honour, after all), so I spent my time ambling idly through the empty town, strolling through unlocked

THE MAYOR.

houses, rifling through bureau-drawers and trying on any robes and shawls that caught my fancy. I picked through waste-bins and took bites from ham-hocks; I kicked slippers through windows and piled laundry in larders. In short, I made myself at home.

As I wandered across roof-tops and relieved myself down rain-gutters, I began to note the appearance of the occasional ship-mast on the far, watery horizon. I was too engaged in my exploration of the town's domiciles to pay the phenomenon much mind, but later, as evidence mounted towards the revelation that people's houses were boring, I chanced to glance through a high-mounted window in the Mayor's dusty prison-tower and found the sky-line positively *littered* with sails, flags, and stalwarts.

It wasn't long before I began to hear voices and foot-falls on the packed dust of the town's main boulevard. Thinking that the town was returning from its convention, I hastened to remove the stockings and house-dress that I'd been scientifically experiment-ing with, and rushed out the back door of the Archbishop's home

so as to not make a spectacle of myself. But when I made my
roundabout way back to the centre of town, I found not the towns-
folk back from their meeting, but rather sailors, adventure-men,
and passengers debarked from ferries and steamers—all of them,
seemingly, infirm.

They lurched about like the walking death, gaping glassily
into shut-up store-fronts and empty fruit-stalls where flies picked
over mouldering tangeloupes. Word had spread of my return. These
pitiable fools had come to the Isle in pilgrimage. They had come
for healing.

So of course, sensing an opportunity to take advantage of the
sudden rush in tourist traffic, I broke into the swap-mall and set
up shop at some sap's basket-booth. All the town's establishments
were shuttered tight, from inns to taverns to the baby exchange—
so I did a thriving business, selling wicker baskets by the bushel.
The visitors paid me in the random and various currencies of their
native lands; I wasn't picky. I accepted them all; it was pure profit
for me—I hadn't paid for the baskets, after all. After an hour my
pockets were full to bursting with shillings, lira, piastres and at
least one goat.

As the sunlight faded, I began to parlay my success into
franchises, collecting fees from patrons who'd expressed an interest in relocating permanently to the Isle of Yam-Runners, and
installing them at nearby stalls selling whatever inventory the
stall's old owner happened to have sitting around. In just the first
hour, I must have broken dozens of latches and locks with a spade-
head—demand for commerce was climbing with each new wave
of spend-happy tourists. The sky was just turning from orange to
black as I handed over control of my very own basket-stall (for a
tidy profit, considering that I had invested exactly zero capital)
to an enthusiastic entrepreneur from Lapland, and with that,
I rested, satisfied; I had filled the entire swap-mall with thriving
independent businesses. Of course, as night was falling and there
were no lights in the swap-mall, I doubted that they would do very

well from here on out. I'd gotten out of the market just in time. It was my savvy way.

Just as a newly-installed kerosene-seller approached my young Lappish basket-merchant and began to outline a coöperative plan for selling torches, I felt a weak but insistent pressure on my hip. Thinking it was some insect, or perhaps the goat trying to be inappropriately assertive, I swatted it away—but it returned, stronger and more petulant, and I saw that it was a very ill-mannered young boy of about ten. "There you are, Grandfather!" he shouted, panting. "Who are all these people? Why is there a Gipsy woman at Papa's cell-phone cart?"

"You'll understand when you're older," I told him.

"Oh, you must come quickly," he said. "The Council's secretary has collapsed from exhaustion! Your healing is needed immediately! They dispatched me around mid-afternoon, but I couldn't find you until I decided to follow a long, winding trail of opened closets and discarded night-gowns. I fear it may already be too late!"

"Sounds like it probably is," I said, as sagely as possible. "No use rushing all the way out there."

"Oh, but you have to come, Grandfather Grenadine!" the boy wailed, and at that, the entire swap-mall fell silent.

Every head turned towards me. The word *Grenadine* echoed forever in the dark, enclosed swap-mall.

And then, with a terrible, ailing cry from a thousand sickly throats, I was mobbed by cripples. ✦

42: THE SURPRISING SAVIOUR.

THE INSIDE OF THE SWAP-MALL echoed fiercely with the shouts of the afflicted, each hoping their desperate yawp would reach my sympathetic ear. I turned to the urchin who'd given me up, lifting him easily by the wrists; with a single strong heave, I threw him deep into the assembled throng. "Here!" I cried. "This boy is enchanted! His flesh will heal your ailments!"

As the grasping crowd tore meat from the lad in great strips, I wheeled towards the nearest exit, only to find my path blocked by even more desperate shamblers. They were each leprous, or oozing, or ugly, or possessed of some unseen internal ailment or personality disorder. But despite their varied states of disfigurement, I knew I could count on one commonality: they would be, uniformly, physically weak. Thus, I could fight my way out.

I drew the saps close with a cooing tone, as I might have called a recalcitrant dog or a barn-yard idiot. When their pallid shuffling drew them within striking range, I seized a rake from a garden-supplies stall and took the face clean off the unfortunate chap at the head of the group.

At this, the crowd's enthusiasm dampened somewhat; taking my opening, I moved slowly towards the exit with large steps, swinging the rake with a deliberate fierceness that was mostly bravado but a small measure genuine malice.

Once I hit the cool night air, however, all bets were off; the sicklies could move faster, now, un-hindered by the crushing closeness of apple-carts and trinket-mongeries. They came at me from all sides, with surprising speed considering their infirmities; I dropped the rake and ran full-out, pausing only to grin as I heard the tell-

THE SHAMBLERS.

tale *spang* of someone stepping on the rake's tines and meeting the expected result with his forehead.

One after another, they *spang*ed past the rake, and I made the best of the head start their stupidity purchased me.

The flickering torches of the village filtered away behind trees and brush as I ran the other direction, but between my own heaving breaths I could still make out shouted pleas and viscous gouts of tuberculotic hacking. I made to lose them in the deep forest, stepping with care over protruding trip-roots and snap-happy branches, remembering the cautionary folk-tales of my childhood about travelers who've impersonated ancient healers being chased into a forest only to fall over a root and be torn limb from limb by gigantic wart-hogs.

I stopped in a dark alcove, resting my stinging hands on my knees, trying to shallow my breathing, hearing the rustle and crack of sickly searchers making their dreadful way towards my last known position. Here I was safe, from the sicklies and, presumably, from wart-hogs, nestled in a hollow beneath a craggy oak, feeling the tickle of old leaves and the night-time chirping of bugs that, if I could see them, I would be totally freaked out by. *Totally* freaked out by. But in the darkness I abided their invisible repulsiveness, careful not to touch anything.

In time the sounds of pursuit began to fade, as ailment replaced adrenaline and the last straggling searchers either retired their hunt or collapsed from the grief of defeated hope. My breathing returned to its normal whistling wheeze, and I stood, gingerly.

I felt a brief pin-point of cold on my chest and placed a hand over my necklace, that shard of jade that I had stolen from the real Grenadine.

At once my eyes were flooded with green light, as the bewitched jade illuminated everything within twenty yards; I yelped and covered my eyes, nearly falling back into the bug-warren. As colour danced beneath my eye-lids, I heard a far-off cry—in moments, shouts became footsteps became the thunderous approach of the entire phlegmy mob.

I turned and ran, but the brightness clouded my vision; I tried to cover the shard, extinguish it, tear it from my neck—all to no avail. Blocking the jade's light with my hand only filtered its rays into new and disorienting vectors, and I couldn't fit my fingers around the thing, either because of some enchantment, or else my fingers were still greasy from some long-forgotten fried-chicken purloined from a village larder.

I tripped over a root, caught myself on a scratchy, probably bug-laden tree, then staggered through a still-steaming mound of animal-leavings, wheeling frantically as the heavy thumping of footsteps approached from every direction.

I took two steps before I was met by a hot blast of stinking breath. Probably a particularly potent halitosis sufferer. Instinctively I shouted "Eat some stones! I've magicked them! They'll heal your gizzard! I swear—just give it a few weeks to take effect!"

"Get on," came a soft trill that I immediately placed as the black-haired woman from the beach. She sat astride a thick mass of horse-flesh, stamping the forest floor impatiently, and the approaching shouts left me no room for argument. I fumbled for the stirrups, she took hold of my collar, and after an awkward fumble or four I was nestled behind her, pressed against her back, sitting very sharply and awkwardly on the rear spur of her saddle.

"Th–thank you," I gasped. "They'd have torn me to pieces."

"We're not out of the woods yet," she said, a hint of some sly manner creeping into the edge of her voice, and she spurred the horse to action.

Within a minute we burst into a clearing filled with the wailing of the sicklies. I saw the green light of the bright-jade reflected as sharp points in their rheumy eyes as we blasted past. Their hands were too slow and shaky to catch us; their feet were too clubbed and behangnailed to keep pace. We left the lot of them behind.

Thusly the village and the forest both disappeared into the night.

The woman turned the horse onto a cliff-side road, and we threaded our way carefully along a narrow path suspended between tall rock walls and a sheer drop to the crashing sea.

After a rather long and bouncy ten minutes of this, I decided it best to ask where we were headed.

The wind whipped her hair into my face as she tossed words over her shoulder. "I know the truth," she said.

"The truth?" I tried my best to angle her statement away from my heart. "That I don't know where we're headed? That's the truth, all right. I really have no idea."

Her next words raced past my ears and dashed themselves on the rocks, and even the lurching warmth of her body couldn't stave off a sudden, piercing chill in my core.

"I know you're not the same man they taught us about in school," she said. ✦

43: MIDNIGHT
RENDEZ-VOUS.

S HE *KNEW.* THIS DARK WOMAN—RIKAH,
I later learned, a name that unfortunately meant "reeking"—
knew who I was.

"Even from the moment you arrived on the island, I could tell
something was off," Rikah continued, not looking back at me, but
continuing to direct the horse surely along the narrow, cliff-side
path. "We have prepared since birth for Grandfather Grenadine's
eventual return. The shape of the bright-jade has been imprinted
into our memories from the earliest days of kindergarten. We ran
flash-card quizzes until our eyes bled. We see it everywhere we look,
like it or not." She shook her head, as if trying to clear her mind;
the motion sent her hair spinning fluffily, like a terrier dropped into
a well. "We were told that Grandfather Grenadine would return
when the time was right, that age and the passage of years would
not affect him. We were told that he might return that very day, or
at the end of our life-times, or not at all while we still lived. So you
can understand the Mayor's jubilant reaction, and that of the town.
This morning was the culmination of their lives."

From my awkward perch in the saddle behind her, I stared
at the back of my hand, cast green from the jade—the wrinkles
brought on by time spent in the salt-barrel were beginning to fade,
and my skin was resuming its natural lustre. Oh, what a time for
my superiour genes to manifest their awesome greatness! What a
price I would pay for my body's healthful glow! Why couldn't I look
older? At this rate I would probably get carded at liquor-stores if
I ever made it out of here, and I'd have to settle for mop-barrel
Scotch again.

"Whenever we asked when Grenadine would return, we were
always told the same thing, whether by parents or teachers or back-

alley lovers," she sighed. "Those of us who cared to question were only ever given one answer. 'When he is assured of defeating our enemy.' By this they meant old man Peapoddy."

I sucked in my breath at the mention of the name. I knew she meant Peapoddy the Elder, who had apparently been a thorn in the side of the real Abner Grenadine—but I had my own beef with Peapoddy the Younger, the old man's son, who had nearly killed the love of my life, thus sending me on the quest that had so far led me to this lonely isle where there were no liquor-stores that I had found.

"Old man Peapoddy was the bogey-man of our childhoods," she mused into the night. "Our parents told us to go to sleep at night or old man Peapoddy would come from the closets and bite off our toes. Whenever we broke a tea-pot, we blamed it on old man Peapoddy, who'd rushed through the kitchen door and dashed the vessel from our tiny hands, laughing all the way—he loved the sound of breaking porcelain mingled with children's tears, if my stories were to be believed. Even in school, when we were caught canoodling in the locker-rooms the snide refrain was always 'In here with Peapoddy, then?' So of course, we as a society were eager for Peapoddy to be defeated, once and for all."

I wasn't entirely sure where this was going, but as long as it hadn't yet lead up to *Thus, you are not Grenadine,* I was content to keep my mouth shut and listen. Besides, the back of Rikah's head was awful pretty, and so long as she faced forward, I could stare all I liked.

"But the problem was, Peapoddy the *man* was never an actual threat to us. The *spectre* of his presence was all there was to the mythology. I never saw the old man in the flesh; I doubt my parents ever did either. And as soon as I became old enough to think—at my *quinceañera*—I began to doubt if there had ever even *been* a Peapoddy."

"Oh, Peapoddy's real," I muttered, but she didn't seem to hear me, or else was too enrapt with the sound of her voice to pause. I began to wonder if she could feel the pressure of my stare at the back of her head. With a shiver, I began to wonder if perhaps *everybody* could feel the pressure of lewd stares, and *I* was the only mutant who *couldn't!* The prospect suddenly seemed frighteningly possible—all these years, my servants and lovers and various victims had just been polite by not mentioning my handicap! Oh, the shame!

"So when we began to hear rumours from traders that old man Peapoddy had died—in the Dark Continent, as one early story went, or in an opium-den in Ceylon, covered in hogs-fat and in the company of the official body-double for the President of the American Confederacy, as most of the later ones agree—we had no reason to doubt the accounts. For when had we ever seen the man *alive?* Yet still our parents insisted that Peapoddy lived—if only because the almighty Grenadine had still not returned to us, and since our fortunes were still in tatters, clearly Peapoddy was to blame. Never *ourselves* for our fortune—always, for the Grenadians, *Peapoddy.* Here we are."

She didn't mention my head-staring. I was probably home free. She swung down from the horse and found her feet lightly on a thin outcropping of cliff-path, no wider than a child's torso, and about as firm to the foot. I followed her gingerly, the bright-jade piercing my eyes with its cringing rays. I could scarcely see one dog's-length ahead of me, so I concentrated on following the shimmer of Rikah's flowing black hair as she led the horse along the treacherous path on foot.

We rounded a corner of the cliff, and before us, a massive darkness blocked out the stars. Either a dense cloud, or a bizarrely uniform rock-formation, or a supremely massive Shamrock-Shake-fuelled-hallucination filled the eye-scape. I strained my eyes to discern its form, but at this distance, I could make out no more than a vague silhouette. To better see, I covered the bright-jade with both hands, and though green rays still crept through my fingers, a dark shadow descended over most of our path. What a relief from that incessant glare!

At the onset of darkness, the horse stopped. "Come along," Rikah cooed, and the horse took a single, tentative step into the darkness ahead. I stumbled, and leaned a heavy hand on horse-flesh for balance.

The animal was beside us one second, then off the edge the next, and after many long seconds we heard a thick splash far below.

One horse was a small price to pay for clarity of vision, but Rikah seemed a bit peeved. "That was my beloved horse that I'd raised since birth," she said flatly.

"He's fine," I ventured, playing the 'healer' card while it still perhaps worked. "I enchanted him as he fell. You'll soon find ol' Stallion-Man back at home, healthy as can be."

"*Her* name was Oat-Princess," she said, "and she had the horse-gout."

"Not anymore," I replied helpfully.

The woman's eyes narrowed even in the dark, and then she turned towards the dark mass ahead. I followed, because why not?

Rounding a curve in the cliff, we found gas-lamps flanking the path, and the flickering lights that marked the windows of some sort of ship-cabin—thought it would have to be a massively tall ship to have a cabin one hundred feet above the water-line. Perhaps it was one of the Emirati skyscraper-liners I had heard so much about?

Three yards closer and I could see guy-lines holding the massive shape to the cliff. Not an Emirates liner, nor a Filipino squid-trawler, nor any sort of impractical sea-vessel at all: it was a dirigible, floating gamely in the air, manned by dark shapes that heaved on the lines, with a gang-plank extending from the cabin to the cliff-side road.

"As I was saying," she said, as we navigated the dark path towards the air-ship, "after I reached a critical age, I simply refused to believe the stories."

Back to this? I said nothing, because she might retort with some comment about the horse again, and I had little faith in the promise of that avenue of conversation.

A dark figure ahead raised a hand in greeting, and Rikah called out: "I've got him." At these words, the figure plucked a gas-lamp from a nearby rock and started carefully down the path towards us.

Rikah went on, in low tones: "When you washed up on shore this morning, and you looked nothing like what we had imagined, I knew that I had been right to be suspicious of the 'official' canon. It was like my whole life of skepticism had been validated. I knew that it had been right for me to question the beliefs of the elders." She turned to the dirigible, and to the approaching man with the lamp.

Something was familiar about the man's gait, but nothing I could put a finger on, nor a nose, nor any part of the anatomy, which was a shame, because tactile feed-back might have helped my recognition. I've touched many more things in life than I've seen in the darkness along a cliff-side, after all.

"I saw this air-ship coming during my mountain-top meditation-luncheon," she said. "I ran to meet it, thinking it might be full of treasure, or knowledge, or perhaps celery, which we've not had on the island since the Celery Blight. But in that cabin it I found a poor soul, a pilgrim, more in need of your healing touch than any of those larking wretches back at the village. And I knew"—here she took my gnarled hand in two of her own, the yellow light from the approaching lantern playing across her smooth fingers, my heart beginning to rattle a tin cup loudly against my ribs—"I knew I could not believe the stories about your old grudges. I knew, that at the moment of truth, you would not shy from helping a soul in need simply because of his family name."

As my hand came away from my chest, the bright-jade fell dim and black, and I blinked. The world looked red to me now, with the green light gone. The cliff-side glowed crimson like a post-card from Hades.

The man with the lantern drew close and held the light high. "Hullo," he said, squinting at me. "Sure looks a wreck, don't he?"

I *did* know the man. He was an Ectologist. He had worked for the Head Inspector, back in Easthillshireborough-upon-Flats.

He had worked for Peapoddy.

"Let's go see the ol' boss, then," the Ectologist said, and Rikah leaned into me. I took a staggering step towards the air-ship, and then another, and then another, unable to stop or turn.

"*Who* are we going to see?" I croaked, my throat suddenly dry, the harsh salt spray of the sea below suddenly burning on my face.

Her voice was hot in my ear, burning all the way through my brain and out the other side. "Peapoddy, Grandfather. Peapoddy the Younger."

44: FACE TO FACE.

THE DIRIGIBLE LOOMED DARK AND menacing over the path as Rikah and the Ectologist led me towards the narrow gang-plank connecting the air-ship to the mountain, which rocked creakily and terrifyingly through the midnight nothing-ness. My hands shivered and fidgeted at my sides as I ran through my options—I would likely be able to hurl either Rikah *or* the burly man over the edge, to be dashed into meat on the sea-rocks below, but the other would likely object; the odds of my facing down both parties seemed grim, and worse still if Rikah decided, for some reason, to disrobe and use the weapon of her shapely form against me. This prospect seemed even less likely, despite my hind-brain's fiercest urgings, and after some internal wrestling I managed to discard the whole plan as an option, given the slim likelihood of that particular outcome.

Besides, as we slowly approached that thin, swaying platform, I found myself curious to see Peapoddy again. The closer I drew to him, I rationalised, the more likely I would have a chance to realise my greatest desire: to take a croquet-mallet to the man's spine,

CURING THALASSOPHOBIA.

and see him suffer for his many crimes against me, and also suffer in general.

As was typical when considering my abiding hatred for Peapoddy, I thought of the chalk-white Lara, lying comatose in her hospital bed, back in Easthillshireborough-upon-Flats—it was a quest for *her* salvation that had driven me to the sea months ago, and it was the man ahead, in the dirigible, that had lain her sadly and silently into that dreadful sleep. I shook my head, my cheeks waggling a little in the night. I couldn't forget my commitment to Lara. That was my whole purpose here.

I meant to recall the glow of noon-time sunlight on her soft, squishy-looking skin, but when I tried, all that filled my mind was Rikah, standing two feet away. I waggled my cheeks again to dislodge the impostor image. I waggled them with futility.

A burst of wind fluttered my beard and Rikah's cloak, and I saw that we were near the edge of the gang-plank. I glanced down in time to watch the Ectologist place in Rikah's delicate hands a purse that clanked of heavy coin. "Thank you, Mr Kelvin," she murmured, and let her gaze linger on the man a second or two longer than mere civility would dictate.

He cleared his throat, coughed weakly, looked over at me, then nervously hocked a loogie into the void off the cliff-edge.

Rikah raised her chin, and something crossed her eyes that I couldn't quite detect in the darkness. Perhaps a scorpion inside her skull? Who could tell? The thin pool of lamp-light from the Ectologist's—Mr Kelvin's—hand-held lantern swayed dizzyingly in a sudden gust, making shadows dance and lurch across this woman's proud expression. I felt a little nauseous, but I thought I could hold in any voidage at least until she got out of ear-shot. That would be *seriously* un-suave—and currently I was the only dude within arm's length who hadn't spit a gob of phlegm right past her off the cliff, placing me squarely in the lead for her favours. I wondered if I would get a good-bye kiss out of it.

Lara, I thought. *Remember Lara.*

I hadn't ridden behind *Lara* on a pointy saddle through miles of galloping forest, pressed against her throbbing back, though, *had* I? And I certainly hadn't done it within the last hour. In fact, I was ashamed to admit to myself, I had scarcely *touched* the woman I so claimed to adore—but I couldn't let my feelings cloud, at this critical juncture! I waggled my cheeks with vigourous fierceness.

Rikah turned to me, nodded curtly, and with a strange "We will expect to see you back in time for the banquet, Grandfather, but please avoid the stables" she turned and disappeared quickly into the night.

Without a lantern or a horse, I wondered how she would find her way back through the island's dense forest. I nearly called out to her to express concern; chicks liked that, right? But as I gathered my courage—and fought with my blasted, Lara-centric propriety—Mr Kelvin caught me by the arm and stepped heavily onto the gangplank. "Come along, Mr Grenadine, there isn't time to waste," he barked, and then added something else that the wind snatched and stole away. As it does. *Greedy.*

He walked quickly, and he had both my arm and the light, so I followed. Though I was nervous at crossing the expanse on such a treacherous bridge, the first step was fine, and by the second

I thought myself an old hand at this practise. But by the third I realised I was separated by just the thin plank from a hundred-foot drop to the foaming sea and black rocks below. My stomach lurched; I felt my knees begin to wobble—and there was still a good twenty feet yet to go, sloping gently upwards towards the bobbing air-ship, fading into the inky sky ahead.

Mr Kelvin's insistent pressure on my arm, however, left no quarter for contemplation. He made his way forward with haste and surety while I stumbled weakly, my innards churning and roiling with each step, feeling the vibrations that his foot-falls sent humming through the thin wood.

Against my best efforts, I took a terrible glance downwards, and that was it. I felt my center of gravity shift terminally askew.

I flailed and fumbled for Mr Kelvin, grasping his vest in a tight fistful, knowing for sure only that I would drag him to his demise with me, and also that Peapoddy would die as well, alone and un-healed, far above our mangled, never-to-be-found corpses—

My last thought before I fell was that I had never even been in a foursome. And then I tumbled, weight-less, for what seemed like an eternity.

But it *wasn't* an eternity; it was half a second. I thudded to the dirigible's deck, Mr Kelvin heaving me to one side, sending me tumbling across slick, lacquered wood. My fingers fought for purchase as my skin squealed against the floor like it was made of basket-ball shoes. I was still. I was sweaty. I was *alive.*

"This way, then," Mr Kelvin grunted, and I was left to scramble to my feet un-aided.

The interiour of the dirigible's cabin was a narrow affair, its central hall-way barely the width of the poor-aisle in an old Hindoo peasant-tram, and without even thinking hard I could name forty fat people who would have had trouble navigating its confines. Mr Kelvin strode confidently through the space, ducking 'neath bulk-heads and dodging 'round jutting spigots and sconces with a show-offy ease, though I hit every one of these protrusions with enough force for the both of us. With each collision I thought I felt the whole air-ship shudder, but that may have merely been the flicker of flames in the sconce-lamps, or else a delirious Shamrock-Shake flash-back.

The lantern-light ahead came to rest at the end of the hall-way, and Mr Kelvin opened a thin, squeaky door at the terminus. "Here you are," he said, and without further ceremony, stepped to one side.

I peered into the dark state-room and barely detected a thick, porky wheezing. A faint, bluish light seemed to tap at the boundaries of my perception. Also, something smelled like tanned chicken-leather, left to rot on an April afternoon. It was a distinctive aroma, and not one I encountered often—at least not since I'd hosted the Bacchanalia-Games back at the Manor last Spring.

"Is he there?" came a voice, heavy and slurred with afflictions I could scarcely surmise, but beneath it all, a foppish malice that plucked a basso chord of loathing deep in my bowel. It was, *indeed,* Peapoddy.

I leaned into the room—cramped on scale with the rest of it—and found a deeply shadowed hulk, buried in blankets and coverlets, poured onto an ornately-carved bed. His skin glowed unearthily with Aboriginal algae-dust, as it had when we'd first met—it gave him the appearance of a massive, sweating sea-slug, or some sort of vile, post-mortem Jedi, as if Jabba had learnt the ways of the Force late in life.

His face was twisted in a contorted mass of scarring. He sucked air from the room as if he was drowning. He was, a bit surprisingly, about a million pounds heavier than I recalled.

I stepped carefully over the polished wooden ridge marking the door-jamb, and turned back to Mr Kelvin with what I hoped was a haughty sniff. I hoped that in the dimness he would not detect my knees' violent quaking.

"I shall require a croquet-mallet and some privacy," I said, reaching out and swiftly snapping shut the state-room door. ✦

45: PEAPODDY'S
REVELATION.

I WAS ALONE WITH HIM NOW. Mr Kelvin's lantern no longer penetrated the state-room darkness. Only the eerie, bluish glow of Peapoddy's algae-dusted skin lit the chamber at all. The massive, heaving mound before me seemed to have no edges; the thick blankets covering his mass faded seamlessly into the black corners of the room. This was not the Peapoddy I remembered—this was a monster-man, the Peapoddy I feared in my deepest absinthian nightmares crossed with some gross infernal perversion of a glowing hippopotamus or something.

Fishy gasping from that revolting heap of wet meat surrounded me as I cast about for a lantern. "Is there no light in here?" I muttered.

"No light," came a voice from the direction of the sweaty blankets. "No lanterns. Keep it dark."

Of course—the algae-dust would shine brightest in utter darkness, and the brighter it shone, the more of its opiate it would leech into Peapoddy's sickly skin. The Aboriginal powder was narcotic. It had surely killed the nerves in his skin by now—and had probably, over the years that he'd been applying it as a fey cosmetic, leeched deeply into his brain. The cause of the man's madness? Or simply a convenient excuse for it?

If the croquet-mallet I'd requested ever materialised, I would have to make my blows deep and hard for this creature to even feel the pain.

"No light, then," I told Peapoddy, making sure to harden my tone and be-gravell my voice, the better to make good the illusion that I was indeed the old man Grenadine. "So are you going to tell me what's wrong with you? Or do I have to guess?"

Peapoddy cocked his massive, fleshy mound of a head, squinting at the darkness. "My father used to speak of you," he burbled. "He called you the most horrible, mean-spirited brute ever to float o'er the planet on waves of his own self-importance. He would rock me to sleep with tales of your sadism and cruelty. Your caprice, saving some while leaving others to wither and die, though you had the power in your hands to heal them all."

The algae cast my shadow on the wall across from the beastly figure, as I wondered how much of what he said was truth, and how much was the fabrication of his bitter, dead father, Grenadine's ancient enemy.

"Do you remember my mother?" Peapoddy said. "Do you remember that tear-spackled girl, coming to you with belly swollen with child, choking through her tears that she would be put out of her village, disowned by anyone that could detect her condition, and that it would really hurt to give birth, since she was only four-foot-seven? She came to you on this very island, old man—and you turned her away. You could have killed her and me both that day, Grenadine, and saved me and my family these past decades of heart-ache—but you *didn't*. You have made your opinion on the matter of my life clear, and all I ask today is that your position stay consistent. Allow me to keep the life *you* cursed me with."

Peapoddy's perfect logic suddenly made me feel like I'd stood up too fast. I was suddenly terribly, nauseously hungry; the last thing I'd eaten was stolen mangoes from the swap-mall back in the village, and that was hours ago, plus they'd been gross and wormy. It looked like Peapoddy had eaten plenty since I'd seen him last—in fact, a half-eaten chicken-carcass still rested on his massive chest, within easy gnawing-distance of his face. I delicately plucked the fowl from its perch and began to chew on its gristle, figuring that with my mouth full, perhaps Peapoddy would continue speaking— and shrill as his voice was to my revenge-starved ears, I would like to learn what had become of him in the months since he'd held a boulder over my head and threatened to dash my brains into the black dust of Easthillshireborough-upon-Flats.

"I thought," the beast gasped, sucking the air from the room and leaving me breathing a stale, coal-fired fug that settled dully over the both of us, "that if I found the Tome of the Cowering Sigil, I could become the healer you, in all your preternatural years, never were: fair, accepting, egalitarian. Taking all who came to me without prejudice, and sending them away cured of their ailments."

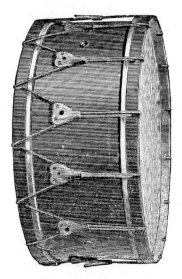

GENERAL SHERMAN'S BASS DRUM.

He sighed, and again a dusty, coalish aroma swirled around my chicken. "But I lost that Tome to a simpering fool, and we both know what became of the Tome of the Precious Lore. I am thus left with very few options."

I had nearly interrupted Peapoddy several times—firstly to speak up on Grenadine's behalf, indignant that Peapoddy apparently thought that a happy-go-lucky, everybody-gets-healed ethos wouldn't immediately degrade into slavering, grabby chaos (the likes of which had nearly torn me asunder back in the village); secondly, to protest the description of my true self as a 'simpering fool,' and to suggest that perhaps Peapoddy hadn't, you know, gotten to know me properly—but I finally *did* interject at this last mention of the Tome of the Precious Lore.

"Yes," I murmured, "we both know what became of the Tome." I paused to suck on a chicken-bone, in what I hoped was a dramatic fashion. "But, er—remind me, exactly?"

Peapoddy looked at me directly for the first time, now, his yellow eyes like hollow divots in the glowing brightness of his blue skin, barely visible beneath scarred rolls of burned and calloused flesh.

"My father told me you were cruel," he wheezed, "but I came here vainly hoping you would dredge a scoop of compassion from your black soul for a dying man. Whatever grudge you may have against my worm-et father, let it lie fallow today. I myself have never met you, never done ill to your ilk."

I bit my tongue on this last point.

"On his death-bed, my father pled with me to set fire to your Isle of Yam-Runners," Peapoddy said. "He spent the last dregs of his fortune equipping this dirigible with enough Chinese blast-powder to sink the entire island beneath the sea, its inhabitants with it."

My cheeks clenched involuntarily as I realised what he was threatening.

"You will heal me," he said, "or I will surely die. And when I die..."

He drew back the blankets covering his body, and black smoke billowed into the room.

I coughed in the sudden blight, wondering if the room was filling with Ninja while I stood gasping—but when the ash settled, I saw something far more terrifying.

Peapoddy was part of the dirigible.

A great, hissing piston worked his lungs. Thick brass pipes snaked from his chest down through the floor-boards and vanished into the deep, thrumming guts of the air-ship. His flesh-wadded legs were shrouded in twin, wrought-iron chimneys, pumping burning life from the vessel's furnace into his veins. He also seemed to have some sort of clock-work catheter, but I didn't investigate that too closely.

He cut off my musing with words smelling of charcoal and malice. An acrid tang of spite lingered deep in my throat no matter how much I swallowed. It was like a particularly bad night as a Kipper initiate.

"...When I die," Peapoddy said, "all of your descendants and family—and the thousands of sickly pilgrims that have come seeking your council and touch—will die with me."

He rubbed a thick finger along the wall, then ground his thumb into his finger-tip. Black dust crumbled from his hand.

Blast-powder.

"It's not the green stuff that Mamma uses," he smirked, "but it'll do the job—just ask the Mongols."

The entire air-ship was a single, massive explosive. I felt a bead of sweat roll down my spine into my trousers, and the chicken-bone fell from my fingers to clatter on the floor.

A knock at the state-room door startled me. It was Mr Kelvin, silhouetted in sudden, yellow light from the hall-way.

"I found you a croquet-mallet," he said, peering into the dark room and handing me the wooden instrument. It felt small and light in my hands, and not quite up to the task before it. But I had to try.

"Thank you," I told Mr Kelvin, shutting the door and turning back to Peapoddy.

I tried not to imagine the thousands upon thousands of decisions that Grenadine the Healer had made over his life, choosing who to heal, and who to let die. I tried not to imagine that Peapoddy had any sort of valid point, as it would make killing him some-what less enjoyable.

I tried instead to remember the exhilaration I had felt at up-ending Grenadine's salt-barrel, knowing it would drive the annoying old man into the earth at speeds approaching a cannon-ball. I tried to remember the life-affirming joy of homicide, of seeing irritating people's reign on this Earth come to a swift and sudden cease. I tried to work myself into the appropriate mood.

And I tried to remember Lara, and her pain at the hands of this monster I barely recognised. If we *did* die here together, at least she would be avenged.

"Let the healing begin," I said, and with a mighty heave, I slammed the mallet against Peapoddy's skull.

46: WHAT AILS HIM.

D ON'T WORRY," I GASPED, "THIS IS ALL part of the process." With that, I mashed the croquet-mallet into Peapoddy's flesh, over and over and over. I figured it would take about six hours to turn him into pulp, and I planned to enjoy every minute of it.

In an instant I had the whole scheme planned out. Knowing that Peapoddy's death would trigger the detonation of the dirigible, I planned to beat him to within an inch of his life, leaving him just enough awareness that I could watch him realise who it truly was that was beating his brains in with a mallet. Then I would sprint down the hall-way, bowl over Mr Kelvin if necessary, burst down the gang-plank, un-moor the air-ship, and let it blow into flaming smithereens safely out over the open sea. I would be dramatically silhouetted by both the blast and the rising sun, and Peapoddy's swollen, scorched head (or at least a goodly chunk of it) would spin gracefully from the fire-ball, trailing a wispy streamer of smoke before plopping, utterly defeated, at my feet. Then I would return to the village in time for the Mayor's banquet, and have a glorious dinner. It was an utterly fool-proof plan, and I set to its execution at once.

At first I thought I could just batter and bludgeon my way along until the matter was settled, as I'd battered and bludgeoned so many witless dolts in the past, but after the first few blows the croquet-mallet began to ring against Peapoddy's brain-case and spring, quivering, from my fingers. The flesh-mound that was my enemy simply peered at me as I heaved and struck his massive bulk; the algae-dust had evidently eaten clear through his skin's nerve-cells and destroyed his pain-receptors, and try as I might, I could not elicit so much as a grunt of discomfort from his twisted lips.

RIKAH.

"This is a bit of an un-orthodox method, from the lay-man's perspective at least," he muttered, squinting at me suspiciously as I struck the side of his face with the wooden weapon again, and again, and again. "I can't say that I entirely trust where this is leading."

"Fine!" I threw the mallet clattering into a corner with frustration and searched the state-room for a more potent instrument of murder. Something pointy, perhaps, or serrated? I found nothing good—chicken-bones, an avocado-pit, a single floppy boot bearing the ketchup-stained image of Hello Kitty—and nearly sobbed with rage like a nancy. My anger against Peapoddy was *justified*, for the love of Marvin, and yet I was receiving, as of yet, exactly *zero* satisfaction from my vengeance.

The problem was, besides his log-like tolerance for pain, that this wasn't the same creature as the man I hated. It might be the same *body*, after a fashion, but there was nothing here of the Peapoddy of my night-mares. These mounds of flesh feeding into clock-works and boiler-pipes and arcane, brass-valved man-juice pumps bore no resemblance to the hateful, smirking visage seared permanently into my memory.

"Something the matter?" he trilled, and for an instant that lilting tone wrapped around my shoulders and neck, gently reminding me that *yes, I could* hate this meat-mountain. I could maim him, even if my glee would be forced and mechanical. For Lara, I would make that sacrifice.

Maybe finding a way to hurt him would help me remember *her* face more clearly as well.

I took a soot-filled breath and assumed my best medical-professional tone. I'd played at Doctor many times, late nights back at the Manor. This would be no different. Well, a *little* different—this state-room was no hundred-seat surgery-theatre.

"My traditional holistic remedy is not proving as effective as I'd like," I mused, putting a finger to

RIKAH'S TWIN SISTER, TANEEKA.

pursed lips in what I thought might pass for smart-guy contempla-tion. "I'll need more background on your malady. You mentioned a fire—I see the scarring—but what happened after that? Please be detailed."

"Fire? Feh—it was a *personal attack*," Peapoddy spat, "and only through sheer cunning did I escape alive. I retired to the local Hospital, where my wounds were treated adequately, if a bit perfunctorily, and then I had a scuffle with some bilge-smuggling oar-jockeys." This I knew; I had been there, scooting quickly out the back. "They gave me a bit of a tossing, I don't mind saying, and I them as well; but I had Medicine on my side, and they had the cowardly nature common to sea-rats, so I came out ahead morally, as well as thumping them 'round the hook-ends in a manner, shall we say, a half-measure less than neighbourly."

I nodded sagely, knowing that this was a bit of an exaggeration; Cap'n Narwhal and his men had hated Peapoddy as much as I, and had laid into him severely. However, it was true that Peapoddy was pansy enough type to cry for help and aid and bandages or whatever, as the fight *had* happened within the confines of a hospital, while the Nautonauts had a certain bushy rough-neck pride about them; given a long enough skirmish under those conditions, of *course* Peapoddy would have escaped alive. As he, of course, *did*, chasing me onto that black-sand cliff-side high above the harbour.

"I had nearly laid my outstanding affairs in the crypt," Peapoddy growled, presumably alluding to his tussle with me, "when I was blind-sided by a terrible old man, all finger-nails and hissing, reeking terribly of cheese and old pork. Before I could react, he had laid his teeth into me with violence, right here where you can still see the mark." He craned his neck to reveal a pocked dimple in the blue-glowing flesh, a perfect half-circle of tooth-marks now bulbous and misshapen on all sides.

It *had* been Abu Fromage, as I had suspected. My heart swelled at the thought of that ancient body tackling Peapoddy as I lay vulnerable at the cliff's edge. My mentor, my teacher, and finally, at the moment of truth—my saviour. That had been *really* nice of him.

The reverent old cheese-monk had saved me by inflicting the gravest of all cheese-monk curses: The Camembert Under-Bite. I'd heard whispers of its existence on my long-ago pilgrimage to Abu Fromage's Himalayan hermitage on Tall-Mount, but had never given the rumours credence; here, however, was a soul actually afflicted with the Under-Bite, swollen from its ill effects, driven to algae-dust and coal-furnaces to keep his heart yet beating, and smelling like rancid old cheese to wit.

"I think he infected me with something," Peapoddy went on, sucking the room's sour air. "I haven't been able to eliminate, from that day till this, and"—here he spread his hands apart as far as they could move, which was about six inches—"you can see how it's affected my physique."

My throat closed. My stomach lurched. My sphincter sphincted. Peapoddy was bloated from the inside with *waste*.

How could I *conceive* of a worse fate to inflict on the man? Far from killing him, it would be cruellest to let him *live*—if I knew *how*.

In fact, it seemed likely, from the wheezing and gasping and oozing of fluids, that Peapoddy was fast closing in on death whether I bludgeoned him further or no—in which case the dirigible would explode, and I with it.

"I believe," I said carefully, "that the only known cure to your condition is contained in the pages of the Tome of the Precious Lore."

Peapoddy looked at me quizzically. *"You* were the one who told my father that you had hidden it safely away. If any man knows its location, it's you, and no other."

"Ah," I said, and then, after several long, awkward seconds, "Right."

Peapoddy sighed. "I guess we're boned, then."

Boned indeed. At that point I decided to simply truncate my earlier plan, and leap directly to the *bolt through the state-room door and run* portion. Perhaps I'd still get to find a flaming piece of his head. That would *have* to be satisfying.

I knelt to nervously re-lace my boots, preparing my escape. "Let me tell you one last thing," I said. "Let me tell you something about me."

"Wait! Perhaps you can check the old man who bit me," Peapoddy said hopefully. "Would it help to examine him? We kept him, after all."

I missed an eyelet with a boot-lace. *"Kept...*him?"

"Of course," Peapoddy said, his horrible mouth assuming the worst impression of a smile I've ever seen. "In shackles these many months, for just this occasion."

He must have read my expression, because his next words chilled my core like an ice-cream cone on Christmas in Siberia during a blizzard after chewing Dentyne Ice with teeth made of glaciers and a tongue made of penguins who had been rejected by their penguin-society for being too cold.

"Do you *know* him?" Peapoddy trilled, and his tone seemed to indicate that he knew the answer already.

47: THE CAVE IN QUESTION.

T HE MAD WHALE-MAN EYED ME IN
the blue-lit darkness. "You *do* know him, don't you?" he
wheezed, his breath laboured and sootish, each inhalation quivering the the brass pipes running from the dirigible's furnace into his
massive chest with a slight, hollow ring.

My mind raced. Would Grenadine have known Abu Fromage?
The *real* Grenadine was ancient, and seemed to know everybody of
note; but he'd also been boarded-up in a salt-barrel these last many
decades, and I had no idea where the boundary lay between what
I—as he—should and shouldn't be aware of. The many layers of
deception were boggling my mind! The only choice was to continue
to excellently weave my impenetrable web of deceit.

"Should I?" I answered dismissively, with a little wave. *Yes!
Nailed it!*

Peapoddy's eyes narrowed into meaty slits. "I may be misshapen from that creature's infection," he spat, "but I am still a
world-renowned Special Investigator." With a log-like limb he took
a fistful of my coat and dragged me into his seething aura of awful
musk and coal-black hatred. "Show me the bright-jade."

Of course! The bright-jade! That shard of jewel could instantly
illuminate the state-room, muting the numbing effects of the algae-
dust that coated Peapoddy's skin—perhaps I could find a way to
make the man feel pain, after all! I fumbled in my shirt-collar and
traced the cord of the necklace with trembling fingers...

...And *then* what? Peapoddy would die, and the dirigible would
explode, with Abu Fromage and myself aboard. Each second that
went by, Peapoddy seemed to be hacking up bigger and grosser gobs
of innard-juice from deep within his squishy gravity, and I had no

doubt that his end was approaching more hastily now than before. He was dying faster than I could ever kill him.

I needed to keep the man *alive*, at least until I could escape— but how?

Especially since I would now have to rescue Abu Fromage, as well.

Huge, rough hands snatched the green stone from my fingers, leaving a thin film of algae-dust on my skin, glowing blue in specks and spots. I felt a minty tingle stand the hairs of my hand on end. It felt a bit like rubbing tooth-paste into one's gums with a wooden spoon—hearty, without being exactly comfortable. Just for fun, I rubbed this little of the dust into my own gums, and got quite the buzzy rush—I could see how a man could become addicted to the stuff.

And then I realised that I had lost the bright-jade, and with it, my only claim to the identity of Grenadine. "Hand that back," I growled, trying to sound imposing. "I'm ready to heal you now. Congratulations, you've passed the test."

The huge man ignored me, examining the jade like a near-sighted jeweller with a staring problem, turning it over in the wan light.

I fought with my next words, but eventually forced them, pointy and misshapen, up through my throat and out into the air: "I forgive the slights that my family has held against yours," I croaked. "Hand that back, please." Then I added, for good deceptive measure: "S–so I can heal you now?"

I reassured myself that it was in the character of Grenadine that I was speaking, and that I, my true self, still clung tightly to the hatred that I felt for Peapoddy...

Didn't I? It had become less *fun*, somehow, and yet here I was, standing in his room, croquet-mallet tossed into a corner. I *had* to hate him. I was *here*.

He'd—he'd hurt Lara. He was a bad guy.

I wished, for the briefest moment before I shoved the emotion as deep down as I could manage without flinching, that I could just walk away from all this and go back to cheese-twirling on a wharf somewhere and live day-to-day without worrying about vengeance or the Tome or impersonating an ancient healer or even changing into clean under-pants. Life had been simpler, once.

But then I wouldn't have met Lara. That would—it would have been bad, right?

Right?

Peapoddy nodded, finally, with satisfaction and an effete charm I would have thought impossible in such a bulky creature. He produced a heavy black object from somewhere behind or beneath or within his floppy body, placing it delicately upon the side-table. It appeared to be a vise of sorts, with a clamp and a screw-handle. Peapoddy placed the bright-jade into the centre of the vice, and delicately began to tighten it into the clamp. "Thank you for returning my father's tooth," he said.

I leaned close—and indeed, sure enough, the bright-jade formed the exact shape of a human tooth. It was a slim incisor, not a molar with forked roots such as would be emblazoned on a dentist's shingle or a Badger-Scout's merit-badge, but a tooth all the same. I should have recognised that; I'd knocked out my share, and even replaced a few, as the situation had warranted.

"I was in the next room the day you wrenched this from his skull," Peapoddy continued, slowly turning the screw-handle. "You promised you would return it, and you have. You have held up your end of the bargain, forty years later—and so shall I."

I had the strange feeling that this conversation was going somewhere I didn't want to tag-along, but what could I say? 'I'm not Grenadine'? That would surely be suicide—as the only person Peapoddy hated more than Grenadine, I wagered, was my true self. Or perhaps Cap'n Narwhal, long lost to the sea by now; or, if he'd ever met him, my irritating nephew Josiah, just because *everyone* hated Josiah.

The handle stopped turning, the clamp screwed tight as Peapoddy could manage from his awkward position. "He gave this vise to me," Peapoddy said, "and told me how to use it, and why, and when."

With no further ceremony he rammed a fat finger at a recessed button on the side of the vise, and I flinched—but nothing happened. His digit was too thick to penetrate the recess.

"Would you mind terribly?" he asked, a bit sheepishly, adding a pathetic, phlegmy cough and what was either a fart or merely the wet shifting of his belly-folds.

What could I do? I pressed the button. It was cool, and felt like stone. It didn't give to my pressure at first—and then it *did*, terribly and violently.

There was a snapping crash and a brilliant flash of green as the heavy device flew spinning off the side-table. It bounced into Peapoddy's fleshy abdomen, caroming off a pipe-fitting, then smashed heavily and dustily into the wooden floor, gouging the finish. I dived into a huddle in the corner at the first sign of trouble and cowered beneath my arm for a good ten seconds before I even dared take another breath.

When finally I pried my eyes open and looked up, the room was bathed in soft green light. It was nicer than the harsh blue of the algae-dust. It was calm. It would have been almost peaceful, if the figure across the room hadn't been so horribly grotesque—but I guess I was getting used to that horrid sight, because I hadn't vomited with disgust in nearly an hour. In fact, Peapoddy looked downright beatific at the moment, a slight, putrid smile creasing his scarred and twisted lips, but a lightness and sanity taking residence in his eyes for the first time. "It worked," he whispered.

He had smashed the bright-jade. It was gone, pulverised into the brilliant green dust that coated the entire room.

"Wh–what have you done," I stammered, half from amazement, half from terror, half from confusion, half from irritation, and half again from idle curiosity.

"Now it's certain," Peapoddy said. "Now there can be no more healing. For if this is to be *my* end..."

He reached up and drew back the compartment's curtains with one, long swipe of his meaty arm. It wasn't yet light outside, but even the pre-dawn darkness was bright compared to the dimness of the state-room.

A panorama of the Isle of Yam-Runners spread itself before me like butter across my brain. The dawn sun only barely beneath the horizon, the island was a black silhouette on a black sea, only a vast sea of white stars outlining its heavy crags and hill-tops. I could have played connect-the-dots with that sky for aeons and never finished the activity. Already I saw a giraffe I could make, and idly I traced the pattern on the window with my finger.

A red spot on the land-mass made the tip of the giraffe's toe-nail. I looked closer—was that a mountain-top torch? A bon-fire?

No. I squinted as it glinted.

It was a cave, burning from within with other-worldly light.

Grenadine's own voice echoed in my memory. *There is a cave set into a lonesome cliff. I won't direct you to it, because I'd rather it be forgotten, but if you happen to find it, you'll know it. There, you may find your answers.*

I blinked, looked away and back, but the red spot still burned, tiny on the far-off mountain-side. That *had* to be it.

The Tome of the Precious Lore was in there.

I turned back to Peapoddy and froze. He was just lowering a phial from his lips.

He licked those chapped skin-flaps slowly, like an erotic snake, one that had been burned and mangled beyond recognition and then pumped full of its own waste and hooked into the furnace of a dirigible. He did it just like that. It was uncanny.

"Delicious," he said. "And now we wait. It won't be long—a minute, maybe, if even that. Could be any second, really—this is potent stuff. Pure mermaid-bilge; I've kept it for years for just such an occasion. Can't get this stuff on the street anymore. Thanks to me, of course."

"We wait for *what?*" I asked, although I think I knew.

He smiled, again, still at peace. "For us all to die."

48: A MAD DASH.

I BLASTED THROUGH THE STATE-ROOM DOOR and bolted down the hall-way as fast as my legs could carry me. The relative brightness of the lantern-lit passageway stung at my eyes, so I buried my face in the crook of my elbow and simply *ran*, caroming off walls and stumbling hither and yon, trusting that instinct would find me safely out of the corridor and that I would soon feel the cool night air and the dirigible's gang-plank beneath my feet.

"Ho, there, sir!" came Mr Kelvin's voice, and I looked up just in time to avoid crashing into the man, to say nothing of the massive tureen of soup he was balancing precariously on a silver tray. "How's Master Peapoddy doing?"

"Listen to me," I said, narrowing my eyes as a plan alighted in the plan-centre of my plan-brain. "He's in dire condition. You're just the man I need—get in there and start pressing on his chest with all your weight, over and over and over, anything to keep the blood pumping through his heart. *Over* and *over* and *over*, do you hear me? Keep his heart pumping! Break his ribs if you have to! I'll take this." I lifted the soup-tray from his hands, the warm aroma of broth enveloping me like a pleasant, nourishing swamp-gas. "And where do you keep the old man?"

Mr Kelvin faltered a step. "Old...man?"

"The old man who bit Peapoddy! Kept in shackles!" I was beginning to grow frantic, now—I really didn't have time to waste if Mr Kelvin didn't hasten on to Peapoddy's state-room. My voice slipped up an octave in alarm; I've found it to be a reliable method of communicating urgency, though it does make me seem a bit fey. "I need to find him! He's the only cure!"

Mr Kelvin stared cock-eyed at the ceiling like an imbecile, suddenly pale as a Finlander with a nervous tic. "I don't know the particular old man you mean."

I took a running start and shot-put the soup-tureen square at his widened eyes. "This tall! Looks old! He bit Peapoddy!" Soup scalded across Mr Kelvin's face, causing him to cry out, possibly prompting a wetting of his trousers if I was lucky, though it was hard to tell with the soup and all. I was running out of options—if my patented Soup-Interrogation didn't get the information out of him, I'd have no choice but to turn and bolt for the gang-plank. I might have already doomed myself by waiting this long.

But I would give him a last chance to speak. I couldn't just abandon Abu Fromage—not in this horrible place. Not even in a nice place. So I screamed one final time at Mr Kelvin: "Where do you keep him?!" Three-octave rise, with an audible slip in timbre; a sure-fire sign of agony if ever there was one. I should get some sort of trophy for that performance.

"I don't know the man you mean," Mr Kelvin spluttered, "but he's probably in the—er, in the engine room, with the rest of them."

The rest of *who?* "Which way?"

"Around the corner and down," he said, too slowly for my taste—but with the information in-ear I punched the wall, turned, and ran, calling back over my shoulder. "Back to Peapoddy! Pump his heart! Go! *Now!* Don't stop!"

The narrow, creaking stairs led down towards a red-glowing darkness that seemed somehow *squirming;* it was a solid-colour shadow that undulated in the gloom. A roiling sea of scariness. I hoped Mr Kelvin could keep Peapoddy's heart beating; I had no idea if it would even stave off the explosion if he could. I'd learnt that heart-compression technique from an old Cossack with a methadone problem, but he'd also told me that he'd ridden dino-saurs in the cavalry.

"Hello?" I cried into the engine-room, but the hissing crackle of the dirigible's burning furnace drowned out my words, and the sound only grew in intensity as I reached the lower steps. I shouted as loudly as my cracked throat could bear. "Abu Fromage?"

My front foot left the wooden stair and set upon something soft and moving. I jerked back, but it was too late—the surface buckled beneath me. I flailed for balance, but the surface twisted, solid but strangely pliant. My hands came down hard on that same churning lumpiness.

I heard a groan. They were *bodies*. Living bodies, warm and wet with sweat, their soft moans buried by the roar of the furnace. Hundreds of them covered every inch of the engine-room floor.

I recoiled, but there was nowhere to go—the stairs were lost now in the darkness, and every movement of my hands and feet put me in contact with more squishing flesh. It was as if the room had no true floor, just great piles of bodies stacked all the way up from Hades.

I heard groans and yelps as I shuffled my weight, but crammed so close together, nothing could give way. After a moment to regain my bearings I was able to stand once again, and now that I knew what I was dealing with, it was easy to walk confidently on the twisting masses of flesh. In fact, in a strange sort of way it almost made me feel at home.

"Abu Fromage!" I called out, taking large, confident strides across the room, making a wide circuit around the hissing iron furnace filling the air with flaming red light and the smell of charring beef. "Abu Fromage, can you hear me?"

By the time I reached the back-side of the furnace I was beginning to grow frantic. How much time did I want to spend hunting for Abu Fromage in this dark pit of misery? How few seconds did I have left before the entire air-ship blew itself apart? Each second was an eternity of terrible anticipation, imagining the dreadful, brilliant blast that could come at any moment. I realised with a start that I had barely breathed at all these last twenty steps.

Behind the furnace a tangled maze of belts, pulleys and sprockets clicked and hummed in the sweltering dimness, each swaying and spinning with clock-work movements. It was all a great, hot

tangle of machinery, lurching and blinking from the
jumping shadows cast by the
furnace's fire. My tummy
roiled with vertigo, and
I felt my constitution un-
ratify; my hands searched
for someplace to lean, but
the furnace itself was blis-
teringly hot, and the far
wall was yards away. My
blind fingertips found a
length of brass pipe, and
I set my weight tentatively
against it while I fought
for balance—but the pipe
creaked and bent and
I leapt back, flailing, surf-
ing atop lumpy, name-less
meat.

THE FOUNTAIN OF DECREPITUDE.

I set my eyes on the pipe. It snaked from a gear-box away and
up towards the ceiling, where I glimpsed some vicious and erratic
movement—I had the strange sensation of being a shark, all of a
sudden, or a beer-acuda or a duck-billed ninny-whale or some other
carnivorous under-sea creature, and for some reason at that instant
my pangs of hunger returned. Then the smell hit me—like a rancid,
maggot-filled out-house last used by the putrefied corpse of Judas
Iscariot—and I would never be hungry again.

I was staring at Peapoddy's under-side, his feet and legs
dangling through the floor of his state-room, kicking and twitching as he clung to the last dangling tentacles of life. I placed the
odour, too—Peapoddy had spoken truly in describing the source
of his bloat. His jelly-like legs rippled with each flapping movement—it would have been mesmerising in a circus, but here it
was nauseating.

But he yet lived, which meant that I had time. "Keep pumping his chest!" I screamed towards the ceiling, and as if in response, the feet kicked in a vigorous flurry, like a fat little dog trying not to drown.

Thus buoyed, I turned my attention to the bodies below. My eyes had adjusted enough that I could discern the faint outlines of faces in the churning mass—but none I recognised. "Abu Fromage!" I cried. "How can I find you?"

Suddenly the surface beneath my feet shifted, and I came down hard with my elbows on somebody's spine, rather hurting my elbows. The spine's owner let out a hoarse gasp, but I barely heard it: for two feet away, staring me in the face, was the unmistakeable pocked visage of the very man I sought.

"Oh good!" I chirped, figuring wrongly that the hardest part was over.

49: THE OLD MAN'S GIFT.

IT'S OKAY, ABU FROMAGE," I SHOUTED AT the wrinkled face, straining to speak over the blasting roar of the mighty coal-furnace. Abu Fromage twitched, his thin spine arching upwards until he resembled a Stegosaurus or perhaps my great-aunt Ingrid, back-bones spearing the air under a tissue-thin layer of skin. He may have been trying to look up, but his reedy neck couldn't begin to support the weight of his venerable cranium. He gathered himself, and then with a powerful exertion, the fine, ropy muscles in his neck strummed and bulged hopefully; with a sudden jerking movement, he whipped his head upward, and I met his gaze...

...Only for a moment, before inertia kept his head swinging around. He struggled to control his heavy skull, but it was like balancing a bowling-ball on a tooth-pick: a hopeless endeavour, if comical in its futility. The desiccated figure lurched this way and that with a birdish, tumbling clumsiness that was positively giggle-worthy in its pathos. He heaved a sick, wheezing breath— hilarious! "Oh, Abu Fromage!" I smiled. "Even in this horrid place, you delight in amusing me with your clownish antics. What an indomitable spirit!"

But I had no time to send a descriptive note recounting the event to The New World's Most Amusing Handwritten Accounts of Humourous Goings-On; nor did I have any paper, nor, come to consider it, e'en the necessary *literacy*. Instead, in the privacy of the dirigible's engine-room, surrounded by only the faceless, moaning figures supporting my weight with their miserable wretched-ness, I watched Abu Fromage struggle to sit upright, and everything about it should have been funny.

But I felt something peculiar inside me. It may have been gas, or else a tape-worm, or else perhaps the curious stirrings of new embryonic life deep within the womb that I had no reason to believe I did not have, but in fact it was none of these. It was something that an un-informed observer may have inaccurately labeled "com- passion"—though I will state for the record that I acted entirely in my own self-interest the entire time, as has always been my wont; any acts of mine that appeared in any way selfless were, in fact, obliquely contributing to my own ultimate benefit, and I'll never testify to any other interpretation.

That being said, I surprised myself by reaching out to the old man and steadying his freakish twitching with my own quivering palm.

It was as if Tesla himself had uppercut my teeth into my fore-brain. The touch of foreign skin to my own was electric. Abu Fromage's face felt like an old woman's hand-bag, leathery and dry with rhine-stones in unattractive places, swinging about heavily with too much junk crammed inside. Even as I stilled the frantic motion of his head, his eyes continued to fumble in every direc- tion. After stealing a glance towards the ceiling where Peapoddy's whalish feet still offered an occasional kick, I spit on my fingertips, rubbed them together in the Continental fashion, and manually stilled Abu Fromage's eyeballs.

"Abu Fromage," I said with what I hoped was a commanding tone, though my heart was fluttering like a flutter-snake digesting a Spanish vibradillo. "Let me take you out of here."

He didn't recognise me, I could tell. I was hardly surprised; my long, disgusting beard added years to my appearance, and my red, wrinkled skin stole precious points from my attractiveness-index; but all that besides, I would be surprised if Abu Fromage could recognise anything or anyone in his addled state—his expression suggested that, given the chance, he might stare quizzically at a glass of milk for an hour. I would get him out of this floating death-trap, and find the Tome of the Precious Lore, and using the ancient medical maths within, I would nurse him back to health; then he would thank me profusely, and impart on me the secrets of the cheese-trade, and I would become a cheese-monk like himself, and perhaps one day inherit his property in the Himalayas. I would become his protegé, and he my gruff father-figure, his brusque manner cloaking a deep and abiding love for my whelpish antics; together we would live on a cool mountain-top and train acolytes in the ancient art of cheese-twirling. The future looked happy for us, and with tears welling in my eyes I wrapped my arms around his thin, feather-weight torso and lifted him.

He didn't move—his legs were caught on something, stuck underneath some random body. I looked back up at Peapoddy's lower half, protruding through the ceiling; those fat flippers were only kicking about once per second now. I thought I almost heard a gurgling scream from the direction of the state-room, but it could have been wishful thinking, or my own stomach, or even maybe ghosts I guess.

Suddenly Abu Fromage spoke, a wheeze that sounded more like the wind through a barren canyon than human word-talking. I leaned close and bade him repeat the phonemes.

"Countess?" he breathed. "Have you returned?"

"No, Abu Fromage, it's me, your favourite son, your protegé-to-be," I told him, reassuring the scared li'l guy as best I could. "I'm getting you out of here, hold on—let me just free your limbs."

"Limbs?" Abu Fromage gasped, and lolled his head down to stare at the anonymous body weighing down his lower half. I released my grip on the old man's torso, and he fell back like a floating leaf, landing with a rustle on moaning flesh. I idly wondered who all these people were, and why Peapoddy would sand-bag his dirigible with their mass, but hey, what he did on his own time was his business.

I set a shoulder to the body covering Abu Fromage's legs and heaved it to one groaning side, exposing the engine-room floor for the first time, sending tiny bugs skittering to burrow God-knows-where; at this I leapt back in alarm, but hastily reassembled my courage—time was running out, and my heart was already working unpaid over-time as it was. Soon that moaning organ would be complaining to the Labour Board, and frankly, trouble with the Workies was the next-to-last thing I needed right now, after, of course, a collection of My Little Ponies in mint condition (NIB!! L@@K!!).

The old man's one visible foot was a tiny ball of black flesh, curled and misshapen like children's dreams held too long over a flame. What's more, a glistening, sucking mould seemed to infect the wood of the engine-room floor—vile tendrils of the slime encircled one leg entirely, only that awful foot protruding from the greenish gunk; the other leg was not visible at all, perhaps swallowed further by the fungus. I also glimpsed the corner of an iron shackle poking through the slime, pitted orange with rust and brown with mocking futility.

I stared in horror at the whole disgusting mess, not wanting to touch it, but wondering how I would extract Abu Fromage so that I could rescue him and we could go on to a perfect life together. My mind raced, and came in last by a length. My brain, exhausted, stalled. I turned the crank over and over. I tried to make myself think. My eye-lids suddenly felt a hundred pounds each.

The pointlessness of it all hit me like a gorilla-lobbed brown-bomb. What a dumb quest. What a *miserable* life. All of a sudden, all I wanted to do was lie down in the slime and fall forever to sleep. It would be *so much easier.*

A scream from up-stairs rattled the walls, and I snapped awake in an instant, calling on reserves I didn't know I had. Wouldn't *they* be surprised when they got their deployment orders! They kissed their wives good-by as I pulled myself to my feet and blew my nose violently. No South-American Sleep-Mould would plant its spores in *my* virile body! I had taken *vitamins*, once!

The scream became a horrible, gurgling death-rattle. I knew the sound. Mr Kelvin's frantic voice echoed from the state-room: "No, no, no! Master Grenadine! It's not wooooooorking!"

"Don't stop!" I screamed at a volume somewhere approaching a squeaky whisper, my throat suddenly burning from the soot-choked air, my voice-box blasted raw from fatigue and pain and gross little mould-spores with their gross little spore-hooks.

Peapoddy's feet gave a final, feeble flutter, and fell still.

I wrapped my arms around Abu Fromage, pulled with what was left of my might, and he came loose with a terrible, rending *rrrrip.* Mould-dust filled the air—I held my breath and powered through.

I clambered toward the stairs with the old man in my arms. "I've got you, don't worry, we'll make it out of here," I told him, or maybe myself, as I fought to find footing on the squirming, mould-infected masses of flesh.

All around me, clock-works clicked into new positions, and levers pushed pistons; the process was starting. I dashed at sprockets with knees and elbows and booted feet as I ran, anything to delay the blast, to weaken it, to buy more time. Copper and broze groaned under my blows. Steam hissed from split-open pipes, burning and fogging the air. Whatever I was doing, it was hurting the dirigible. I tripped on a lever—and kicked it as hard as I could.

The furnace-door flew open with a *bang* that shook the room, and a gout of oven-heat smacked me in the back of the head, along with the distinctive tangy smell of barbecue. *Ah,* I thought, *so that's what all these bodies are for. Fuel.*

The sounds behind me grew increasingly menacing—clicks, whirrs, electric hums. And then—finally and terribly—the sputtering, burning hiss of an explosive fuse.

My steps became solid as I found the stairs. I took them six at a time, bursting quickly from the air-ship's hall-way into the cool night air, everything green after the burning redness of the engine-room. In the pre-dawn glimmer outside I could just make out the gang-plank, the cliff-side, the sky—and, in the distance, atop a mountain far across the island, the orange flicker that was surely Grenadine's cave. I fixed its relative location in my memory as I dashed across the bouncing board.

And then my foot slipped, and with no fanfare or warning we were off the gang-plank and falling freely through the air.

I couldn't believe it. I watched the thin wooden bridge zip past my eyes. All that trouble to escape, and I fell off the gang-plank. What an *idiot!*

The whipping wind was refreshing, though. The ocean rushing up from below was a dark, roiling blue. It was pretty.

I looked at Abu Fromage, and time slowed.

"I'm sorry," I told him.

Sometime between the engine-room and now he seemed to have recognised me, because there was a twinkle in his be-cataracked eyes I hadn't seen before. It may also have been the star-light, but I prefer to think it was my charisma. "We all do our best," he said, and he reached his hand out.

His knobby fingers held a thin white rod. I took it. It was a cheese-twirling wand, as perfectly balanced as any I'd ever wielded. "Is this—is this for me?" I asked, my voice choking on something. Not emotion. Something else. Chicken or something. "Where did you get this?"

Abu Fromage looked down, and I followed his gaze. The cliff-side was approaching rapidly—but it was no tough feat to time it right and simply kick off the cliff-wall, sending us arching away from the crashing rocks where Rikah's stupid horse had landed, back towards the ocean, falling, ever falling.

But Abu Fromage had not been looking at the cliff-side. He had been looking at himself—or, more precisely, his lack of self.

His legs were gone. I had ripped the man in half.

"This," Abu Fromage told me, gently touching the ivory-colored wand in my hand, "is what kept me sane. Working every day, whittling it bit by bit." He grinned, revealing a mouthful of utterly-destroyed teeth.

"Is this..." I swallowed the words. Not because it was too awful to contemplate. But because it was the most awesome thing I could possibly conceive of. *This* was why Abu Fromage was the man. Dude had whittled the most perfect cheese-wand in existence from *his own femur*. With his *teeth*.

I knew then, as we both touched the wand, that this was it. Closure. It felt good.

"Thanks for giving Peapoddy the Camembert Under-Bite," I said. "Really messed that guy up."

"I was hoping it would," Abu Fromage said. "I'm glad it at least bought you some time."

"I'm sorry I ripped you in half," I added, as the sea beneath us loomed ever closer. "And I'm sorry I fell off the gang-plank."

He shrugged. "I'm not too worried about it," he said. "The way I figure it, when the air-ship explodes, the heat will instantly vapourise the top few feet of sea-water—effectively creating a cushion of steam that will arrest our fall."

"Huh," I said, furrowing my brow. "Really?"

Abu Fromage shrugged. "I have no idea." He looked down at the ocean, rapidly filling our vision, then up at the hovering air-ship, still floating silently against the night. "But since we seem to have a second, there's one other thing you should know about Peapoddy. The Countess—"

The dirigible erupted in a massive, orange fire-ball. I heard it for exactly one second before we hit the water at a hundred miles per hour. ✦

50: AWAKENING.

T HE WORDS OF GRENADINE HAD INFECTED me like a phlegm-beetle laying its eggs in my ear-canal, and now those tiny, earwax-eating word-larvae squirmed and wiggled and hatched into my consciousness.

There is a cave set into a lonesome cliff. I won't direct you to it, because I'd rather it be forgotten, but if you happen to find it, you'll know it. There, you may find your answers.

The orange dot of flame I had seen from the air-ship was a million billion times brighter up close. I shielded my eyes with my whole hands—and still I could see through the layers of skin and tissue as if they were...uh, *tissue*, but the *other* tissue. I peered between my finger-bones to make my way slowly along a rocky path.

Behind me, a steep cliff led to tiny waves, far below. That water stretched all the way to a land-mass on the distant horizon. Ireland, I knew—for in my dreams, I was smart.

I turned my head and found my idiot nephew Josiah by my side. He wore a green novelty leprechaun-cap adorned with a sparkly foam shamrock. "Been to Ireland, I see," I told the boy.

He nodded. "I found the Tome," he said. "I swam ashore, swallowed my revulsion, hiked up my socks and just started asking around. Three weeks later, here it is!" He held up a massive, leather-bound book looking like it belonged in a stuffy library somewhere. On the cover was a gilt engraving of a turtle struggling to climb atop a log. Behind the turtle, a mouse was laughing so hard that a little pellet was protruding from its bum. It reminded me exactly of all the books I had burned back at the Manor—so much so that I had to restrain my innate urge to set it alight at once.

"But this is the Cave," I protested. "Grenadine sent me here. He said *this* is where I'll find my answers."

Josiah shrugged. "Dunno about that," he said. "But I've got the Tome, so I'm heading back to Easthillshireborough-upon-Flats like we planned. See you there?" With this, the little sot turned and walked slowly down the path, one shoulder rubbing against sheer rock, his opposite toes trailing over the steep edge.

After about twenty feet of sure-footed striding, he turned back to me. "Come with me," he said. "Come back home. This is it. It's really the Tome. I really found it. It was actually pretty hard to get ahold of—I can't wait to tell you all about the hair-raising scrapes I got into!"

"But..." I stared at the impudent lad, the colour draining from my face to be replaced with a thin white whine. "But this is *my* quest! I've had all *sorts* of heart-break and distress and ter-rible, ultimately-rewarding adventures! *I* need to find the Tome!" I stamped my foot. "I'm at the freaking *Cave*, for crying out loud! Let me go *in*, at least!"

Josiah looked out over the sea. "All right," he said. "I'll wait, but only for a minute, because it'll be dark soon." His face glowed brightly orange in the reflected glare from the cave-mouth. Against the shadowed mountain-side, he looked like a torch, or a Q-tip™ brand cotton-swab set on fire.

I turned eagerly back towards that brightness, squeezing my eyes tightly shut against the light, taking one blind, tentative step before another, feeling the rock beneath my feet and rock on either side.

I stepped in something warm and wet. Dampness engulfed my foot, and then

THE WHELP I·FED TO THE MASSES.

my calf. I tried to step backwards, but couldn't—I was stuck. I shuddered: could it be *more slime-mould?* Knowing my crazy dream-mind, it would try to gross me out as much as possible. I covered my eyes with my hands and tried to peer through a tiny slit in my fingers.

It wasn't slime-mould. It was *magma*, and I was sinking in it.

My feet were already a trail of ash, drifting away on the slow-flowing current. My legs were next. In three seconds I was waist-deep in molten rock, and then I was twisting my elbows to keep them from touching the burning surface. I wondered briefly why I wasn't feeling any pain.

Oh. *There* it was. I screamed. My dream-mind slipped me a note: *Thanks for the reminder.* My dream-mind was being sarcastic. It was not actually grateful.

The orange light turned strangely green, and Grenadine's mocking tone echoed through the cave around me—or was it *within* me? It was hard to tell.

"Foolish, foolish fool," came that creaking, immortal voice. "You just *had* to go poking your nose where it doesn't belong."

This had been a *trap*—Grenadine's deadly go-away cave for people who asked too many questions! There were no clues here!

My last sight before the magma swallowed my eyes was Josiah, carrying the Tome, peering around the corner.

"No!" I tried to shout around the wet, hot rock filling my mouth and cracking my teeth into embers. "Take the Tome away! Don't let it get burned up! Take it back to Lara!"

But all that came out was a faint, gravelly burble. Lava filled my lungs, and then there were no lungs. *Man,* I thought, *this is one depressing dream.*

Wonder when I'm going to wake up.

Any time now.

Somehow the brightness became darkness without my noticing. A blue glow from my right caused me to whirl—only to find *Peapoddy* standing beside me. Natty, foppish Peapoddy, with two good eyes and a more common body-mass index—not the bloated, disgusting Peapoddy of the dirigible.

"Looks like it's just you and me now," he said.

I kept turning, and saw Mr Kelvin. "Oh, and me, sir," he said. Behind him, his fellow Ectologist—a chap who'd died in the Hospital back in Easthillshireborough-upon-Flats. "And me," added this second man.

I was afraid to keep turning, but I did, and they kept appearing, until they were *all* there—everyone I'd killed, from the training-urchins of a well-spent childhood to Rikah's clumsy horse just yesterday.

And behind them all: Lara.

"Why are *you* here?" I cried, rushing to her side, which was bizarre for a realm in which time and space had no meaning. "We're going to save you. We're going to come back with the Tome and save you. You'll be healed!"

She shook her head slowly. "I died a long time ago," she said, softly, in a voice that didn't sound quite right.

I realised then that I could not remember the true sound of her voice.

And so my mind had given her Rikah's voice.

"I died in the Hospital three days after you left," she said, enunciating each word clearly, as if speaking to a child. "You don't have to worry anymore. It's nice what you've done—but you don't have to bother. We're all fine, now. We're all here."

Grenadine stepped forward then, beard and all, as did my Uncle M_____, and his brother, my own father. Uncle M_____ still had the hatchet-wound on the back of his head where I'd laid him out cold when he'd given me audience without his hatchet-armour on (his over-sight!). I wasn't sure what to say, but he caught me in a sturdy polar-bear-hug, ruffling my hair agreeably—"Caught me by surprise, you did!" he said, miming his receipt of the killing blow, eyes bugging out comically.

We laughed. *Everybody* laughed. Everyone was *happy!* Everything was working out *great!*

Peapoddy stood with a man who could only be his father, and Grenadine, their sworn enemy, put his arms around both their shoulders. "Grudges don't *matter* anymore," he said. "I spent so many centuries trying to add meaning to my life—but the most meaningful thing of all was to simply let it all go. I'm *glad* you eventually took the initiative to do it for me—thank you."

"Thank you," they murmured, the whole crowd as one, and it was a little bit creepy. I wasn't sure if they were being sarcastic, or what.

I looked over that smiling crowd, an un-counted horde of my enemies, homicide victims, and the unnoticed collateral casualties to miscellaneous acts of violence, and I shrugged. "Okay, I guess!"

I *let it go,* and with that, an invisible anvil lifted from my ribs and floated into the æther like a balloon, its tether too gossamer-thin for me to clutch after even if I'd wanted to. But I *didn't* want to, because it felt *great*. I was liberated from guilt, from obligation, from pain and bitterness and hate and duty and *all* of it. It was just *gone*.

"You're right," I breathed, sucking in sweet, rose-hinted air, renewing my lungs, restoring those millions of tiny passageways that the lava had eaten away, building new ones from sugar and perfection and bliss. "This is *so* much better. And you guys don't hold any grudges at all? *Really?*"

Peapoddy and Grenadine and Uncle M_____ and all the rest of them smiled, all as one, all in the same instant, which was, again, a little creepy. "Grudge?" Peapoddy chuckled, spreading his arms, taking in the whole black nothing-ness on every side. "You gave us the gift of passage into this perfect, blessed land."

And then he leaned close, and the ice hidden behind his eyes jumped the gap to my spine. I felt its chill stab me in each of the four humours. His voice was flat, with none of the sing-song affect that had once grated on me so. "The least we can do is pay you back."

—And before I could say anything at all, everyone was gone, and I was staring directly into the blazing noon-time sun.

"*Aaaahhhhggkk!*" I shouted, sitting bolt upright, shaking sand and sea-weed from my cold, heavy body. I hurt all over. My head rung and my ears were filled with sea-water. My eyes burned from salt and light. All I could see was blinding whiteness. Was I back in the cave? Was I still dreaming?

The anvil-balloon suddenly screeched back from the heavens with all its weight, knocking me so be-sillied I fell back in the water. It *all* came rushing back at once—the guilt, the pain, the hatred, the fear, the terrible, terrible crush of life's many and conflicting demands. I was definitely *not* still dreaming—which meant I wasn't in the cave, either.

I was on a rocky beach, piled among a hundred massed bodies fallen from Peapoddy's engine-room. All dead now, simply more of the dirigible debris that also littered the area—canvas, wood, bits of twisted metal, bone fragments scattered over miles of shore and ocean.

Not three yards from me, half a skull was buried to its nasal bone in the sand, one wide, hollow eye staring at me. Mocking me. Peapoddy, probably. Why not.

"Look—one's alive!" came a cry from far to my right, and as I clamped gritty, wet hands over my eyes, I heard voices shouting and foot-falls on sand and stone. I coughed, and my lungs burned with soot and ash from the engine-room; no sugar or bliss here. Everything I had was in agony. Some new stuff I didn't know I had was also inventing new forms of pain. Each second, each movement, each breath brought new discoveries of novel types of misery.

Over here, guys. I'm alive.

Hooray. ✦

51: A SURFEIT
OF THINKS.

I THOUGHT I MIGHT DIG FOR HOURS AMONG the mounds of beached corpses without ever finding the remains of Abu Fromage. It was heroic to think of him as one so pure of spirit that his passing would leave no heap of jerkied meat behind for ravenous earth-worms—perhaps, at the moment that the dirigible had exploded, he'd vanished into an æthereal dimension; or else perhaps he had sublimated whole-sale into angel-dust. Or, even if he had left a meat-heap, it might now be lost among the nameless bodies and dirigible-wreckage choking the island's shore-line—the old man's small stature, and, er, *lack of legs* (which, I admit, was my bad), seemed to make this prospect down-right inevitable.

But in fact I located his body after a brief search of about four seconds. Turns out, I was standing on it.

I fished it out of the water and held aloft that droopy mess of floppy skin and liver-spots. There was none of Abu Fromage in this sad-looking bone-bag; none of his majesty, or his carriage, or even a hint of that signature cheese-musk. In this, at least, I was glad—for I could return it violently to the sea guiltlessly, which I did at once because it was slimy and kelpy and gross. I didn't want that under my finger-nails.

With the splash came a creeping certainty, a jagged fact sinking slowly and steadily to the sea-floor of my awareness until it came to rest half-buried in the silt. Something I *knew* was true; perhaps the *only* thing. *Abu Fromage was dead.* There was no arguing the fact. He would not speak to me again, except, perhaps, in dreams.

The dream haunted me and depressed me in equal measure— for unlike most normal dreams, of hat-making or candy-races or gleeful, sensual outhouse-arson—there was nothing obvious I could point to upon waking to discredit its twisted somnambulous logic.

For instance, in my hat-making dreams I always had trouble with thread because I had lobster-claws for some reason. Upon waking, I could always breathlessly tap my clammy palms together if I needed to verify their non-crusta-ceanity. Likewise with the candy-racing dreams: no

ARE ANGELS REAL? UNFORTUNATELY.

matter what I might believe in the night, come dawn I could easily prove that I wasn't really an Italian simply by making a quick visit to the water-closet.

But for all I knew, Josiah *had* survived being thrown (by me) from the deck of the *Flopsy Bunny*, made his way to Ireland, and found the Tome—who could say? And if *that* was within the realm of possibility...then what about the *rest* of it? *Was* Grenadine's cave merely a volcanic death-trap?

Was my sweet Lara already dead?

Whether Peapoddy, in death, really had *cursed* me to stay among the living (thus chaining me to the myriad pains inherent to mortality, and depriving me of the animus-free delight that was apparently gifted to the departed like a complimentary sewing-kit for the soul) or whether that was an invention of my fevered, dirigible-fleeing imagination, it mattered not, for the result was the same. With every motion, I was now conscious of the anvil-weight sitting heavily and metaphorically atop my still-living frame. I per-ceived, for the first time, how my hastily-embarked-upon quest had always been fuelled more by hazy optimism than by any legitimate sense of, say, *what to do* or *how to go about it properly*. I'd seen no fault to this approach, for just such a slap-dash approach had served me well thus far in life, whether on the cheese-wharves or the jungles of the Americas or in the Manor upon Waverly Hill.

But like everything in life, from livers to crêpe-paper rain-umbrellas to one-legged bar-stools, it only worked until it didn't. And *now,* every path before me seemed doubtful and silly.

By the time the villagers' corpse-waggon deposited me back at the out-skirts of the town, the only course of action that appealed to me even remotely would be to shave what was left of my scorched and be-seaweeded beard, track down a proper velour vest-coat, and present myself to Rikah as *myself*—not Grenadine, nor a Siamese spice-merchant with a speech-impediment, nor anyone else. Merely a dashing stranger with a sassy grin and murky past, who nonetheless somehow commanded remarkable insight into the issues that troubled her. (After all, she'd blabbed for hours about herself during that long ride from the forest to the air-ship, thinking she was speaking to her kindly ancestor, and I could have a keen memory for chick-blather when I needed to.)

Or, I realised, I could *also* earn her devoted love by black-mailing her with knowledge of her cahoot with the Peapoddy clan: the villagers' enemy as much as my own. Either this plan or the other seemed honourable as well as probably fun; I would let circumstance decide my specifics of my tactic. I liked to stay adaptable. It made me feel competent.

Besides, it was probably about that time again. Time to start over with a new life—I'd done it before; I could easily leave everything behind again. It might be the only way to dislodge the dream-anvil from my metaphorical chest—weighed down, as it was, by obligations, doubt, and the spectre of having made as many foolish choices as possible under the circumstances.

(It seemed to me that a large dog, or perhaps a small ogre-

MR KELVIN.

pottamus, might weigh exactly the same as an anvil, and yet the dream's metaphor had featured an object that could not be lured away with old meat [as could the dog] or compelled into hibernation by extended oral discourse about the relative merits of oaken cart-wheels vs. maple [the ogre-pottamus had a renowned and severe physiological reaction to the odour emitted by humans engaged in pedantry]. But an anvil could only be hammered upon, an act which would drive it, metaphorically, even deeper into my metaphorical chest.)

But though everything I had been working towards now seemed insufferably silly, I couldn't just *forget* it all—not because of a *dream*, for Jehu's sake. Cor, *two* nights ago I'd dreamt that I was slapping a baby with a fish, but it didn't mean I went out and *did* it. (I'd found the village's orphan-foundry closed at that hour.)

No. Despite how easy it would be to just forget all about everything and start over, in a new place with a new life—the doubts lingered. Maybe Lara *was* alive. Maybe Josiah *wasn't*.

Clang! The metaphorical hammer fell heavily upon that black iron, and I faltered a step from the blow. The anvil was sunken deep.

I had been walking now for some time, and as was my habit while suffering from bouts of deep, melancholy self-pity I had been holding my hands firmly over my ears and eyes, the better to concentrate on my own miserableness. But as the air about me seemed changed, somehow, I lowered my hands—and found myself in the town's central square.

It was a bustling hub-bub of activity. Busy-looking folk hurried to and fro; shop-keepers hawked tourist-wares from a hundred shabbily-built stalls while leprous pilgrims begged for alms or opiates under-foot. Thousands of visitors, most of them gravely ill and disgusting, crowded the eye-scape. The village had become a *city*.

A sickly goat wearing half a cable sweater staggered across my path, and I nearly tripped over a sicklier child chasing it with what appeared to be blood-stained knitting-needles. A shambling, be-goitered woman behind me *did* trip o'er the caprine and fell to the ground with a clatter of weak bones. Within seconds, I watched a dozen scabby hands strip her of anything resembling value: her shoes went to a scowling man for an early supper; her finger-nails to an urchin to re-sell for dirt money; her hair to a Saxon for dental-floss.

These disgusting people had all come to the Isle of Yam-Runners to be healed by Grenadine—and the locals, the villagers, had built an economy on them. I saw stalls selling second-hand kitten-gut next to stalls hawking "replacement kidneys" clearly made of orange-peel (and doing a brisk business). One creaking shack leased various miserable steed-animals either for tours or soups, it was unclear which; another, next door, rented chewing-gum. It was truly Enlightenment capitalism at work.

And then I stopped. I *had* it—an idea so brilliant that I didn't even care when a fat man stumbled into me from behind: I didn't budge an inch. A passer-by even tipped his hat at me for my perfect performance. I was a man possessed.

I couldn't know if my dream had been real. If it *had* been, I should give up now—for I had already lost. It was time to start a new life.

But if it *wasn't* real, there was still a chance I could prevail. I should persist in my search for the Tome.

I had no way to get word back to Easthillshireborough-upon-Flats; I couldn't learn if Lara lived or not. I didn't know if Josiah was digesting in a whale-belly this very moment, or if he was in Ireland clutching the Tome in his idiot fingers. There was nothing I could put to the test, to pit the dream against verifiable reality, as I had with the lobster-claws or the Italian thing...

Except the cave. It was here, on the island. I could rent a steed from the soup-shack and make haste for that far mountain-top. Then I would see with my waking eyes whether it truly burned bright from molten rock—or if it was something else entirely.

52: PROBLEMS
WITH GOATS.

I'D LIKE TO RENT A HORSE, PLEASE," I told the stall-keeper at the leasing booth, waving away buzzing flies and trying to look like I *hadn't* just ridden a waggon full of corpses from the site of a dirigible explosion.

To his credit, the squat, hairy stall-keeper seemed not to notice my dreadful appearance—he simply began ticking off his rental options on squat, hairy fingers. "Half-crown for one hour with small dog. Full-crown for big dog, one hour. Three crowns for pygmy-goat. Six crowns for big goat, one hour."

Six crowns for a goat! What madness! The shabby-looking animals tethered behind the stall looked barely worth pennies. The single pygmy-goat resembled a sad old man with his massive pot-belly and tufted tail, just like my great-uncle Yancy. The few larger goats looked more robust, but still possessed a deep, intractable sadness. Clearly, this fellow was delusional to charge so much for an animal that would likely struggle to bear my weight up those treacherous mountain-paths; there was no way I could rent a dog, or a goat. I needed some sort of equine, if for no other reason than who in the world rode *dogs?*

"Where *else* can I rent a steed?" I asked the man. "Something bigger, perhaps? A donkey, or a horse, even? Something a normal person would ride?"

He scowled at me, then turned to yell at a young boy galloping by on what appeared to be a wheezing dachshund. So many different languages these pilgrims and immigrants spoke! I considered myself worldlier than most, and yet I couldn't begin to place this squat fellow's consonant-heavy intonation. "Half-crown, small dog, yes?" he said, holding out a grubby hand, palm up, as if I was just going to drop money into it, which I wasn't. "One hour, small dog, very good for children."

"No, I need a horse," I said, "or a donkey? You know, donkey?" I made a gesture cleverly indicating a donkey, though if you asked me to repeat the motion I couldn't describe what I did. It was a purely instinctual act. My family line was heavy with donkey-breeders, all the way back to Charlemagne, I'd been told, and before him, the famed Donkey-Hoti of the Nile, Chieftain of the Donkey-Tribe. They said I had his tenacity. "I need something bigger than a dog."

"Ah, big dog! Yes, big dog, one crown, one hour," he said, nodding. "For you, best price." He barked something at the dog-riding boy, who disappeared behind the stall only to emerge towing a glumly skeletal Great Dane. "Look, teeth are excellent," the man said, pulling back the dog's lips to reveal black, glistening gums.

"No, no. I need something that can carry me up the mountain! Something bigger!" This was beginning to become a challenge, and not the fun kind, like Uncle's collection of puzzles made from ribald daguerreotypes. At least those had been in the universal language: of *love*.

"Mountain? No, no. Nothing goes up mountain. Only for beach, forest. No mountain." The stall-keeper frowned at me, as if suspecting me of illicit intent. I was getting nowhere, and to make things worse, a line had grown behind me. A red-faced man in a bowler cap tapped his foot impatiently. "Look, some of us are trying to rent goats," he said. "You want a donkey, go to the stables. This is dog and goat rentals, can't you read the sign?"

I stared at the man, and at the stall's sign with its unfamiliar squiggles and curlicues, and at the dogs and goats roaming around the area. "Terribly sorry," I murmured, and wandered back into the crowded square. This illiteracy thing was really putting me in a bind, I hated to admit.

I knew where the town's stables were; I'd wandered this place when it was deserted, not two days ago, and knew all its crannies, save for the hasty structures erected by merchants, supplicants and Gipsies in the interim. Everywhere I went I heard the name "Grenadine" whispered in wheezy, dying voices; as busy villagers bustled past, I also caught scraps of conversation about the Mayor's massive banquet planned to honour the healer, set for this very night, and rumours flew that Grenadine was expected to make his grand re-appearance there. By now, my salt-induced wrinkles had largely faded, and of course the signature bright-jade was gone from my neck, smashed to dust by Peapoddy; I was in no danger of being mistaken for the old man any longer. I admitted a certain morbid curiosity: what would *happen* at the banquet, when Grenadine failed to appear? Would there be riots? Would the sicklies rise up in anger and take over the island? Stranger things had happened; after all, look at Malta.

The stables were a series of long, low buildings set back from the main road. A few thin horses trotted around a pasture behind the structures. I made for the nearest door—then froze, my hand an inch from the knob, as a voice echoed through the thin wooden walls. My heart caught in my throat—for it was Rikah inside.

"I absolutely did *not* leave the gate open! That's something I'd expect from *you*—and besides, Oat-Princess is smart enough to stay inside the pasture!" A pause; a low voice replied in murmurs too faint to discern. Then Rikah rejoindered, much closer and louder: "I *can't!* I don't trust *anybody* anymore! Who *are* all these people?"

The murmuring voice spoke again, then Rikah: "Well, when Grenadine shows up and starts healing people, *then* you can talk to me. But *until* then—" She shoved the door open wide, and the handle struck me in the forehead. I staggered.

"Oh! I'm so sorry! I didn't see you!" She rushed to my side, and then her eyes went wide—I can only imagine the sight I must have seemed: half-burnt-off beard, corpse-reek aplenty, topped with a generally dazed expression that even on my best days hasn't served me too well in the wooing dep't. But did she *recognise* me? Without the bright-jade? I couldn't tell. There were so many shabby ne'er-do-wells around the village that I must have looked like just some other of that low class.

"That's quite all right," I croaked, straightening and attempting to brush some dust from my filthy coat. "I was just looking for a horse to lease, or a donkey perhaps, for a sightseeing journey up the mountain."

She cocked her head and searched my face, but no spark of recognition set in behind her eyes. "We've had one horse disappear," she said, "and until we track her down, we're not letting any others out, sorry." Behind her, a barrel-chested man folded his arms and leaned on a beam, facing back into the stable, showing the two of us his massive back. Rikah turned, then sighed. "There's a dog-and-goat stall in the square. I'd check with them."

Before I could reply, she stood, turned back into the stable, and in the split-second before the door slammed closed I saw her slip her thin white fingers into the big man's hand.

The slam of that shutting door may as well have been on my heart.

As I walked back towards the square, I caught my runaway thoughts with a butterfly-net and made myself think about what

I was thinking about. *Why* was I so upset that Rikah had a man-friend? She was in no way "mine," nor did she even know me; she only knew my impersonation of Grenadine, her ancestor, and even that, only barely. She had never expressed any romantic interest in me. And besides, I had Lara.

My sweet Lara, waiting for me, back in Easthillshireborough-upon-Flats. Maybe dead.

No! Wait! Not "maybe dead"! That was no way to think! She was fine! Everything would be fine!

When I returned to the stall in the square, the dog-and-goat-monger stared at me accusingly. "No go up mountain," he said, unprompted. "Not my animals."

"I, uh, don't want to go up the mountain," I said. "I want to go sight-seeing on the beach."

The stall-man narrowed his eyes and jabbed at me with a thick, hairy finger. "You think you can just take this dog up this mountain? This goat? This goat is not made for mountain. You don't know anything about goat. This goat cannot take this mountain. You will be stuck on mountain with no goat. You will be in trouble."

"I heard the beach was nice," I persisted, forcing a smile, wondering if I even had any money. Had I stolen any crowns from unattended night-stands and jewelry-boxes, during my late-night survey of the village's many residences? Had I secreted them away deeply enough that they might potentially still be on my person? How would I get an animal out of this man?

"You want my dog, my goat, you must leave deposit," the stall-man growled. "You must sign waiver. No mountain. Beach only. Dog is good for beach. Goat is so-so, but for you is okay. What you want? Dog or goat?"

I licked my lips, suddenly chapped from the heat of my lies. "Goat," I said. "That dog didn't really look strong enough to carry me—I thought I might snap its spine."

"You snap spine, I keep deposit!" the man bellowed, pounding his thin wooden counter-top.

With the creak and snap of hasty, non-union construction, the stall collapsed. Boards turned to splinters; dust billowed up in a cloud. Dirty children rushed to seize anything of value, snatching away paper, bent nails, dachshunds. A short gray pygmy-goat bolted away from the debris, but its tether caught it short—so I quickly worked the knot with fumbling fingers, and before the stall-man could shove his stubby arms out from under the fallen boards, I was galloping away on the goat, headed for the mountain.

53: THE PITIABLE ASCENT.

MOUNT ST. YAM-RUNNER WAS STEEPER than it looked. Its paths were winding and narrow; its tall, looming silhouette never seemed to draw closer, even as the goat and I made our treacherous way toward that far-off peak.

The pygmy-goat's tread was slow and plodding, despite the most spirited flank-spurring I could muster. Its gallop had given out after thirty seconds of sprinting, and the hour since that initial burst had taken two tedious hours to pass. Riding the low, pot-bellied animal was surely slower than subjecting my own tender feet to the mountain, but I remained astride nonetheless; perhaps it was loyalty that bound me to the beast, or else a deep-seated sense of man-to-steed honour. It also could have been simple curiosity at how long the creature's legs could bear my mass.

The answer, it turned out, was slightly less than three hours. By then, the goat had slowed to a quivering creep, and we were barely making two inches per minute forward progress.

All of a sudden its knees popped, one after the other in quick succession, and the animal deflated beneath me like a rank, furry balloon, exhaling a final feeble goatish breath and expiring limply without so much as a bleat of apology.

I felt my knees slowly descend onto the hard earth as my own body once again assumed a peasant's task of supporting my weight. It sucked; there were little rocks, and they were pointy.

The stall-man had been right. My goat had given out on me, and now I was stuck on the mountain with a sad, decomposing hulk of furry, uncooked *chevon,* with night fast approaching.

I creakingly stood and stretched my body, weary from the arduous trek. The trail was barely discernible against the rocky ground—I'd been largely trusting the goat to stick to the path, but upon examination, I wasn't entirely sure that there was a path to follow. The thin line of broken brush ahead could just as easily have been the aftermath of a bear's violent charge as a trail to the peak, and I wasn't eager to rush head-long into a bear's den, or warren, or whatever, especially so soon after the Day of Bear Atonement. The bears would be especially ravenous as their ritual fast came to an end. (Though I wasn't entirely sure if the bears on this island were even Jewish, or if that was just a cruel stereotype I'd heard in passing.)

I paced in circles for a while about my goat-corpse, straining my eyes to find the trail, ready to dash behind a tree at the first sign of anything that growled, trying to remember my bear-calls from school. I thought I might whittle a quick lady-bear decoy from leaves and twigs, to distract any man-bears that might appear, but a quick pat-down confirmed that I had neither any sort of pocket-knife nor the necessary honey-flavoured tar. Besides, I wasn't quite sure that I would be able to construct a convincing bear-replica without any sort of visual reference; though loath to admit it, I was *not totally confident* that I knew what an appealing lady-bear might look like. I imagined it would have an abundance of hibernation-fat, and probably a decent day-job in a solicitor's office, but I had no idea how to fashion an appropriate business-formal pant-suit from the leaves in this area.

What I *did* have, however, was Abu Fromage's femur-crafted cheese-wand—truly the most perfectly-balanced twirling-wand ever fashioned by a human. (I didn't want to speak for bears, in

case there were any nearby who might be offended by the insinu-
ation.) The wand positively danced across my finger-tips without
the knuckle-friction common to cheaper, shop-bought wands,
typically carved in bundles by orphan-children in tangled-sounding
countries for pence on the pound. *This* specimen, however, was a
marvel of cheese-twirling engineering and as it sparkled brightly
in the reddening dusk-light I wished, in that moment, for nothing
more than a properly-steamed fondue-pot. *Then,* I knew, I could
let muscle-memory and reflex take over; I could clear my mind,
and focus solely on maintaining dextrous command over a narrow,
cheese-focused micro-universe. *Then,* if only for a handful of fleeting seconds, I could be in *total control.*

But alas, there was no cheese to be found, and I discarded a
hasty plan for making mud with spit and dust and fluids to try and
approximate the consistency of a week-old Fromunda. What would
be the point? Even if it scraped, it wouldn't twirl, and if by some
miracle I could get some slobbery mess to lift on the wand, why
would I be-soil this sacred gift with such a vulgar offering?

My fingers twitched, and I knew I would have to fight the urge.
I *had* the wand. I wanted to twirl *something.* And before I could
stop it, my mind began to run through the many viscous and
appropriately-goopy substances to be found in the body of a not-yet-
putrescent pygmy-goat.

But when I returned to the site of the animal's collapse, *someone was there.*

It was a big woman, the size of a man the size of a big woman.
She was dressed in denim trousers and a sailor's tunic, with long
hair pulled into orange braids. She moved heavily, like an oak tree
given life. She stood by the goat. And she was real—for, given the
chance, I'd like to think that my imagination would surely have
conjured up someone a bit comelier, a bit more, say, Rikah's shape.
No! Lara's shape! Okay, compromise—Lara in trousers.

"Hullo," she said. I couldn't say from whence she appeared, but
her deep voice rumbled the ground beneath my feet—or was I just
quaking in fear?

"Hello—I'm trying to reach the cave at the top of the mountain, but as you can see, my goat has given out on me."

"No wonder," she said, lifting the goat-carcass with one big hand and slinging the whole creature over one thick shoulder. "Goats aren't good for much on this mountain. We never see 'em much—so this'll be a nice treat for supper. Obliged to you."

She turned and walked away, taking my goat with her, while I worked my jaw up and down, trying to force words from my mouth.

After a few steps, she turned back to me. The movement struck a chord in my distant memory, but I couldn't place it... "Well?" she called. "Aren't you hungry?"

"Starved," I croaked.

"Then come on," she said. "Let's get you washed, shaved, and fill that stomach."

"Wait!" I shouted, stumbling to follow the woman through the under-brush, fearful that I might lose sight of her in the twilight and not find her again, too afraid even to blink even when I stumbled through a mini-cyclone of gnats. One got in my ear and it was weird. "Who are you? What about the deposit on the goat?"

"I can't help you with that," she laughed, a booming sound that scared the gnats away, except for one glued by tears to the surface of my eyeball, its wings fluttering feebly and futilely. "But I'll gladly answer the other. Step up here and take a look, will you?"

She took a mighty step up onto a boulder, and with her non-goat-encumbered hand helped me to clamber up next to her. Her hand was rough, and wrinkled, and red, and strong. She did not let the touch linger but gestured outwards, at the island spread before us—and beyond it, the ocean.

From a trouser-pocket she produced an squat cylinder of light blue crystal. She peered through it as if it were the world's thickest spectacle-lens, before offering it to me between two meaty fingers. "Look through."

I did, and the oceans vanished: the island itself became a mountain among valleys and canyons of dark, dry rock. Through the crystal, the sea-bed was bare as a canyon: what might have been whales and sea-serpents slithered through empty air. I caught my breath and moved my eye closer, making out the barest traces of flashing lights, glowing red and orange trails of smoke and flame, streaking in long lines between the island and the far-off mainland of Ireland. The impression was of lightning-fast railroad lines, embedded in the ocean floor.

But that was crazy! I knew crazy, and that was just plain crazy.

She dropped the lens back into her pocket, and the water was back, as if it had never left. I thought I saw a flicker of orange beneath the waves ten miles away, but it might have been the reflection of a twinkling star. She was smiling when I finally tore my eyes away from the water.

"I am of the Yam-Runners," she said.

54: IN THE RAZOR-CHAIR.

I'D NEVER HAVE FOUND THE CAVE entrance on my own, had I had a detailed map and searched for a week. It was a scrub of prickly booger-bushes one second, and a marble-carved hollow in the rock the next; the woman gestured for me to enter, and I did, slowly and tentatively, a bit apprehensive about caves in general—even before my recent dream had plunged me into a cavern of deadly magma, I'd slipped on seal-fat in a subterranean city populated with misshapen freak-creatures; before *that*, however, I'd had a very nice birthday-party in a cave once, but before *that* it had been problems inside the Earth all the way back to childhood. My relationship with caves was a tortured one, and the frightful woman hauling a dead goat ahead of me wasn't making it any less scary.

I needn't have worried. The tunnel soon gave way to a sprawling, rock-hewn chamber, in which lines of marble and brick snaked up interiour walls in spindly columns, creating the impression that we were inside an egg being embraced by a giant spider who was holding very still and whose legs were for some reason made from building materials. Airy, spiraling stair-cases bore dim figures towards far-off hall-ways; a series of crystal sky-lights amplified and refracted the late-evening sun. The entire room glowed an orange that seemed to hang in the air like floating dust-motes. It was lovely and surreal, until I sneezed and everyone turned to glare at me.

The woman handed the goat-carcass to a man in a spattered apron, which replaced the rude stares with overt lip-licking and tummy-rubbing. Everyone within view was of hardy build like the woman, and possessed of the same poor fashion sense. I saw old men wearing riding-chaps and young girls in over-coats; comely wives in gigantic ruffled collars drew water from a burbling spring while a scampish lad the size of my old serving-dwarf toddled about in what looked to be the remains of a potato-sack to which huge brass buttons had been affixed. The overall impression was of a traveling troupe of entertainers who specialised in being the 'before' subjects in beauty-product make-over exhibitions. The whole lot of them cried out for the touch of a campily-flamboyant fashion expert.

I was shown to a small room, where I was provided with fruit and a steaming copper wash-tub; the former was sweeter than God's own tears to my famished gut and the latter was like the searing brand of Hephaestus upon my mud-blood-and-brine-soaked carcass.

I must have dozed off for hours, because when I sat up suddenly I noticed that the water had become tepid, to say nothing of filmy and disgusting; also, I had a half-eaten apple-wedge jammed in my teeth and a crusty line of apple-drool down my scraggly beard.

But it was nice, nonetheless, to finally taste a small measure of the luxury I had once been accustomed to. Months at sea had made me wonder if I would ever smell scented soaps again, and though the wire-stitched squirrel-bladder seeping with juicy washing-fat that I had been provided with was a full yard-and-a-bit afield from lavender, honey-suckle and opium, it was at least a nod in the right direction and I hoped the trend would continue.

As I towelled off from the bath, I found that an ugly (but warm) yak's-wool robe had been laid out for me, and I wondered where in the world they had obtained such an Asiatic item on this tiny island in the Irish Sea. Trinkets in the room only deepened the mystery: here were South African bum-beads sitting beside a Canadian beaver-tooth bottle-opener, both nestled within a dish carved from an Aztec brain-pan. Who *were* the Yam-Runners, anyway?

Letting my robe fall open, I turned to find a tall, thin man leaning nonchalantly in the stony corner. "Enjoy the bath?" he drawled with a raspy rumble.

I yelped and snatched the yak-skin about me once again. "Just standing there, are you? Didn't feel like speaking up?"

"Come along," he said, and ducked through the door behind him, never taking his hands from his vest-coat pockets.

He led me to a room lit brightly by ten gas-lamps set in a wide circle. I sat as indicated on a tall chair in the centre of the lanterns, listening to the man splash gaily in a wash-basin. The ringing chime of leather against metal was a soothing lullaby: I was about to get a shave! This scratchy Grenadine-beard business had gone on long enough, thank you.

"So, what's your name?" I asked, as he tilted my chin back and snipped prissily at the longest scraggles with long, thin scissors.

"Paco," he murmured, "and don't move your chin."

The tufts cut away, his thick fingers wrapped my face in soapy foam. His straight-razor glinted in the lamp-light, and my heart stopped for a moment as he touched the blade to my throat. But Paco was deft, and soon I felt the delightful tingle of newly-shorn skin gradually spread across my neck. This was nice.

"Be heading to the banquet, then, I assume?" came a voice from behind the row of lamps, and I startled—Paco clucked his tongue at my sudden movement, and when he drew his blade back, I saw a tiny spot of blood.

The oaken-built woman from earlier stepped into the ring of illumination. She wore a wide smile in addition to her ridiculous sailor's shirt. "We haven't been properly introduced. You can call me Ursula. Because it's my name! Ha, ha!" She slapped her thighs, a gesture I had thought reserved for vaudevillians and sarcastics— but she genuinely seemed to have amused herself.

"Hello, Ursula," I said through a clenched jaw and lips piled with shaving-foam. "Quite a set-up you folks've got going on, here."

"We used to rule this rock! We gave this island its name! But now we're stuck underground like voles," she snapped, beginning to pace around my chair, disappearing behind Paco then re-appearing on the other side. It was a creepy effect, her voice circling around, surrounding me. "Generations have lived and died in this mountain, and generations live and die down on the Shorelands. The difference is—we can see them. But they can't see us."

"So you've seen all the people coming to the village, these last few days?" I asked.

"Terrible," Ursula nodded. "Drowning the island with that trash. Oh, there's not much that escapes our notice, no sir. We keep a close eye on affairs down in the village, all around the island, yes we do."

Paco scraped my cheek delicately. Had a hint of something dark crept into Ursula's voice? It was probably just the blade dancing around my face making me nervous; that, or the fear that my junk was hanging out of my yak-robe.

"We saw *you,* even," she added slowly. "Quite an entrance you made. One of Narwhal's old barrels, was that? Thought I recognized the trade-stamp. Distinctive wanger on that whale-stencil."

My mind lurched inside my skull. She *knew!* How should I respond? So many lies and double-truths and negative-half-insinuations had tumbled from my lips lately that I didn't know which would be most credible. Could I claim to be Grenadine, again? Or else a simple traveller who'd happened to crash on the shore in a salt-barrel?

"I am a wandering kelp-merchant who fell in with some bad hands in Reykjavik," I said with what I hoped was an indifferent certainty. "My crew was trying to toss Cap'n Narwhal into a steam-geyser over some old debts. I saved the man, and asked only for a barrel of his salt in return. The rest you know." *Whew.* That was a pretty great story—I'd have to remember it for the grand-kids. Oh, I'd embellish it, of course, with daring sword-fights at the geyser's rim, and graphic tales of Narwhal's attempted sexual assault of the local marine-life (which would be sure to earn me rounds at the tavern commensurate to the level of detail I could stomach describing), but at the moment, for skin-saving, it would do just fine.

"You are a patrician from Easthillshireborough-upon-Flats who has killed Narwhal and his crew," Ursula said flatly, and I became vaguely aware in my periphery of Paco's blade at my throat. "You have killed Grenadine, and now Peapoddy the Younger in his dirigible." She tilted her head to a sinister angle, and narrowed her eyes in the lamp-light. "You are an odd agent, to have killed both Peapoddy and his enemies."

I wasn't sure if I should speak, with the blade so close to my wind-pipe, but when she didn't press on I managed to form a few sentences. Should I add the bit about the marine-life? "Peapoddy was my enemy as well," I squeaked. "Because of him, my manor was lost to flames, and my love to probable death. Because of that snake, I have been left with nothing." *What! Truth! Come on, brain, get with the program.*

"Your love, you say?" Ursula arched an eye-brow. She retreated beyond the circle of lamps, and I heard the clinking of thick glass against wicker; then she returned with a stubby cylinder of crystal. It resembled a clear wine-bottle, except solid through and heavy to the hands.

"Put it to your eye," she said, and after a bit of fumbling I managed to look through the end of the cylinder. I saw a flicker of shadow, but not much else. "Look at the light—it helps," Ursula added, and I moved to point the glass at the brightest lamp.

It was a blurry image of me and Rikah, riding Rikah's late horse along that narrow, twisting mountain path at midnight. I watched myself cling to her like a man on an uncomfortable saddle. She wasn't doing much to object; we were close, the two of us. Frankly, it was kind of arousing, and the yak-robe was doing me no favours in the modesty department.

"Our array of telescopes are pointed at every corner of the island at all times," Ursula explained, "and are fitted with these light-jars of different thicknesses. It is an ancient design; we temper them in the earth's crust, deep beneath the ocean. You are holding the core of the world in your hands." She said it simply, as if were obvious. "Light cannot pass through it but slowly—so when you gaze at the light-jar, you are seeing yesterday."

I turned the heavy glass over. It was utterly unremarkable from every side but one—but when I looked into that one side, I saw my own past. Light from yesterday, trapped in this cell's core, moving sluggishly as a slug. Incredible.

"So you see, there is nothing that is hidden from us," Ursula continued. "I could take you up to the observatory and show you light-jars from yesterday, last week, last year. I could show you yourself, landing on the beach; I could show you the woman you were with spending yesterday afternoon in the forest glade with the Mayor's son. I could show you the Mayor praising 'Grenadine' in the town square. And if we went deep into the library, I could show you a light-jar ten feet long and a yard across—and within it I could show you Grenadine himself, leaving this island on Narwhal's ship, vowing revenge on Peapoddy."

"I *would* like to see the forest glade thing, if it's not a lot of trouble."

"Later," Ursula said, and nodded to Paco; a moment later, a warm wash-cloth swabbed the shaving-foam from my smooth, beautiful face. "But first, do me a favour and cover your privy-dangles with the yak-fur we've provided. Tonight, you're going to the Mayor's banquet." ✦

55: COMMISSIONED.

"Y OU LOOK REALLY GREAT," URSULA said, brushing dust from my hideous tail-coat. Paco had given me a terrific shave, but the Yam-Runners' wardrobe collection seemed scavenged from a second-rate circus-tent pitched behind a thrift-shop at the leanest time of year. The paisley-and-spots number I'd found was the least eye-bleeding of the lot; still, perhaps I could pass myself off at the banquet as a colour-blind eccentric, or perhaps a visiting dandy from another universe, here to learn about The Ladies.

Still, the clothes were clean and starched, and I felt recognisably human for the first time in some months. Tugging smartly at my lapels, I ducked through the cave-mouth out into the night-time air.

The moon hung low and fat-faced in front of me; Ursula filled my periphery with her massive sailor's blouse. "We're grateful for your willingness to carry our message to the Mayor," she went on. "Our folk can't pass the tree-line; it's in the Yam-Runners' code. So it's not often we get word down to the village."

"Really?" I turned to see her pig-tails outlined sharply in the moon-light. "Is there some reason why you can't go down the mountain?"

She stared at the twinkling torches of the town far below, then took a heavy step and started down the trail, her ruck-sack swinging as she walked. "It's just the code, is all," she said. "All we know is what we're told, right? So there might be a dead-vicious reason going back a thousand years, or it might just be a boogy-tale me mum made up to scare me." She glanced over as I caught up to her, her hair bouncing as we skittered down a steep portion of rocky slope. "Either way, this is where I leave you."

She fished in her ruck-sack and produced a lens of clear glass, which she handed to me. It was thin, like a monocle, and fit snugly between my cheek and brow. I set it to my eye, and the ground was suddenly aglow with a line of faint greenish light, tracing a thin, meandering trail stretching from my feet down towards the village.

"Quite the dapper look," Ursula smiled. "The opticle will take you straight to the town, though it'll fade as you get near fire-light. Daylight too—it's no use after dawn, though you'll be down far before then."

I looked back up at the mountain. The whole rock pulsed with bright green veins of paths and trails and tunnels. "You guys have a lens for everything, I guess."

"That's what happens when you live in a mountain," Ursula said. "You figure out things to do

"LET THE LITTLE CHILDREN COME UNTO ME—SO LONG AS THEY'VE WASHED THEIR HANDS FIRST."

with rock. Grind it into sand and tap the fire of Hades to blast it into glass. It fills the days pretty nicely."

I strained on tip-toes to try and glimpse the ocean from here— though this wasn't the same lens she'd shown me earlier, the one that had revealed flickering orange rail-lines dug beneath the sea-floor. "Say, do those trains actually run under water?"

Ursula took a step down the slope and considered the trees beginning to dot the mountain-side, as if gauging how closely she dared approach, I was curious about her people's code—were the Yam-Runners cursed? Would she burst into flame if she touched a tree? Would stuff get on my new suit if she did? Most critically, would it be awesome to watch?

"No, and I don't think so, and probably, and probably," she murmured without looking at me, and I realised with a blush that I had voiced my questions aloud. She grinned, though, and shrugged. "Just always figured, why take the chance. As for the trains, they run in the old crust-worm tunnels; my grandfather laid the first tracks from this island—met a Scotsman mid-way and never looked back, if you know what I mean. From then, our fortunes were locked to the global yam-market. These days the trains run just after sunset and just after dawn—tonight's will hit Dublin, then London, Calais by noon, and Gibraltar by sun-down tomorrow. It should be leaving pretty soon now—you'll hear it, if you know what to listen for."

Dublin. Then London. Calais by noon. Gibraltar by sun-down. Any of those places could give me a new start, a new opportunity to build my fortune, a new freedom from, well, everything. "Can a person just—ride the train?" I asked.

"Oh, sure, if you've got a load of yams, you just get right on. Good way to travel, down in the Earth—you'll sweat off ten pounds on the ride, but on the plus side you'll never go hungry." Her eyes seemed to narrow in the moon-light. "But that's idle curiosity speaking, right? Mere wondering at the ingenuity of modern industry, and all that? You're not—thinking of—"

In my coat-pocket I felt the folded and wax-sealed parchment that she'd pressed into my hands just minutes ago. "An important message from the Yam-Runners to the Mayor," she'd said. *And a chance for me to see Rikah again,* I'd added silently to myself.

"Hah! Good luck, sport, she's the Mayor's son's girl, and he's a bruiser," Ursula had rejoindered, as I'd apparently said that bit aloud as well.

But the dream of Grenadine's cave still shook me. I might be throwing my life away on a fool's errand, chasing a hope that I just couldn't admit had died a long time ago. *I should make a clean breast of it,* I thought, and then *No! Stop thinking about Rikah!*

"Forget about her," Ursula said. "Just deliver the message. At this rate, if you *do* talk to her, you'll end up thinking something untoward, accidentally saying it out loud (like you just did again), and then having the Mayor's son's fist full in your face before you can blink hopscotch."

A low, haunting whisper suddenly vibrated my bones, and I felt my ear-drums crackle. Ursula canted her head towards the mountain-top. "Aaaand there's tonight's train," she said. "So it's too late for you anyhow."

A wave of heat rolled along the ground and wrapped around my feet. The greenish lines in my opticle turned a searing shade of yellow. A light flickered in the night sky, and far off at the top of the mountain, a burning red plume of smoke burst thickly into the atmosphere in clumps.

"That's the Cave," I said. "That's what I saw from the airship."

"Exhaust vent for the trains," Ursula shrugged, and turned back towards the village. "You'd better get a move on; that Banquet's already started, I'll wager, and you've got a stiff walk ahead of you."

I stared at the dissipating cloud of red-orange smoke, wondering at the sight that had been so remarkable from a slightly different angle. "Exhaust vent," I murmured. "The place that Grenadine told me to look for?"

Ursula narrowed her eyes. "What did he tell you?"

"I had asked him about the Tome of the Precious Lore, and he replied, 'There is a cave set into a lonesome cliff,' " I recited from memory. " 'I won't direct you to it, because I'd rather it be forgotten, but if you find it, you'll know. There, you will find your answers.' "

I don't know what response I was expecting from Ursula, but explosive laughter wasn't it. "Crazy old man," she cackled. "Flair for the dramatic. Don't know what he meant, but that's as good an answer as any. Tell you what, when you come back from the

Banquet, I'll tell you everything you need to know about the Tome of the Precious Lore. All right? We'll go up to the observatory, I'll pull the light-jars and I'll even show it to you in person, let you have a look at the thing."

I stared at her. She *knew!* She knew where the Tome was! "Where is it?!" I croaked, suddenly hoarse, feeling my face flush with hot blood, my gizzard pumping fiercely in my ears. "Do you have it? Show it to me!"

I must have taken a step towards her, because she stopped me with a solid, calloused hand. My nimble cheese-twirling fingers were no match for her mannish grip. "Listen," she said. "All anybody knows is what their parents, their teachers tell them. Right? Nobody down there"—she jerked an angry finger towards the town below—"knows the real Grenadine from some dirty old crook with a stolen necklace. But things are different in the mountain. We're not Shorelanders and cripples up here." She shoved me backwards onto the rock, sending gravel and dust into the air and pain shooting up my hip, scuffing my paisley trousers. "Abner Grenadine was a Yam-Runner. A long time ago we lived in peace with the Shorelanders—until he rebelled against our king, Larcenic the Lithe. *That's* why there's a code. *That's* why we don't go down to the Shorelands."

She scowled at the flickering light of the town as if trying to snuff their lamps with a glare. "At first he lived as one of them. But when you *outlive* people you can start making yourself into something *more,* can't you? You can get to people when they're kids, and make yourself some sort of *god* to them. And when you do it *that* way—you never have to prove yourself. You never have to heal *anyone.* Not when you can make everyone in the village—in the *world!*—think *they're* the only one who doesn't believe."

She was coming at me now, step after heavy step, sure-footed on the slope, and I scrambled to my feet, ducking quickly behind a stand of trees. She stopped, looking up at the gently-swaying branches, then down at me.

"Put that letter in the Mayor's hand straight-away, and we're square," she growled. "You can talk to your lady-friend if you want, or find yourself a whole harem of fresh Shorelander strumpets, I don't care—but the first thing you do when you walk through that door is you put that letter in the Mayor's hand."

She stared me down for a second, then turned, and through the opticle I could see that she followed the invisible green trail perfectly in the night.

If what I thought had been Grenadine's cave wasn't really it at all, that meant my dream hadn't been real—which meant that Lara might still be alive.

"And the Tome?" I called after the retreating figure. "Will you show it to me?"

"When you return," came the reply, as Ursula disappeared into the darkness.

I watched the space where she vanished. And then with nowhere else to go, I turned back towards the village and started my descent.

56: STRATAGEM !

EACH STEP DOWN THE MOUNTAIN was a hammer-blow driving home the task before me. I would enter the room, locate the Mayor, and press the Yam-Runners' letter directly into his fat hand. Then, before ten seconds had passed, I would pivot on my heel and climb the mountain once again, returning to those caves to confront Ursula and learn what she knew about the Tome of the Precious Lore. If I had a chance, I would snap off a whuppin'-sized tree-branch on my way back up the mountain, so I might make my argument as convincing as necessary.

Ursula's opticle, fitted to my eye, guided me clearly through the unsteady hills directly down to the village. Even when a slow-moving cloud obscured the bright moon, a coloured line pulsed on the ground through that lens—closer to the mountain a sharp green, fading into a dull grey across the furlongs. Before long, shadows of lantern-light danced between the trees, and music and voices ruffled the dangling leaves—I had made it.

It wasn't hard to see where the banquet was being held; everybody in the village was crowded around one tall building bedecked with banners and bobbin-bunting. The mob was relatively quiet, for a mob, probably because it was largely comprised of sick individuals dangling o'er the precipice of death. Fistfuls of the ill and infirm lay heaped upon the dusty earth; others milled about, peeking occasionally through the hall's brightly gas-lit windows, muttering foreign oaths to themselves or (presumably) cursing their sorry lot in life. The ground was thick with mucous-coughing brats and wobbling cripples, and I had to pick my way carefully through their moaning masses.

Closer to the banquet-hall door, I could clearly hear lively music from within; the crowd was thicker here and a constant press of smelly bodies pestered the entrance. A single gibbering door-man fought to keep everybody outside, and was surprisingly successful despite his flop-sweated sheen of frustration.

"Come on, now, let us in," one shabby-capped soot-monger crowed at the sputterer. "Just ten seconds with old-man Grenadine's all I need, just one touch to clear up me rheumatis', and I'll be on my way quick as you please, Jack's-your-baby—I'll even nick you a mug from that beer-barrel I see they've got, and none'll be the wiser."

"We'll be the wiser!" a shrill harpy of a scum-woman snapped back, pushing her own way in front of the be-hatted man. "I need to see Grenadine right away, else I'll die of angst-poisoning within the fort-night! The stuff's seeping out from every stinking pore—just look at these diary pages!" She fluttered a stack of purple-penned journal-leafs at the door-man, sending misery-soaked paper-pellets spewing in a white cloud. I coughed on an emo-poem and staggered back against the wall.

The door-man raised his palms to the gathered, a gesture that was probably an insult in some of their home nations. "Look, I've told you! Grenadine's not even here! We don't know when he'll show up," he insisted in the plain tone of someone repeating what he's been told even if he's not quite sure of it himself. Evidently the mob believed the healer to be inside the hall—a rousing cry of protest went up at the door-man's every other syllable.

It was clear I'd have a tough time elbowing my way inside. Perhaps if I explained my urgent business with the Mayor himself? Then I could leave my yam-tainted letter in this smelly place and make haste back up the mountain.

I fought my way through the press of thread-bare coats towards the door-man, only to be interrupted by a gruff voice. "Look, let me through, I've got an important message for the Mayor," said a homely chap with a scruffy moustache, raising a hand beside me. "It's critical that I see him right away."

"What's the message?" the door-man replied, resting his hands on his hips dubiously.

"That Grenadine can rot in Gehenna!" Scruff-stache bellowed, flicking his fingers at the door-man in a horribly obscene gesture I'd previously only seen attempted by die-hard fjord-pirates in ice-braving Norway, where the wind could grow so bitter at sea that deck-hands had to keep their extremities in constant, frantic motion or else risk losing fingers to frost-leprosy (or as we called it in the taverns, "snow-stubbies").

Scruff-stache kept up the abuse on the door-man: "It's *sick* how these people wait at the edge of death for some *miracle saviour* none of us have even ever *seen!* You people with your *mythology* are giving them nothing but *false hope* in some 'Grenadine' that you probably *invented* so you could sell *souvenirs!* I hope you all *rot!"*

A few scattered cheers drifted from the furious chorus rising to condemn Scruff-stache's assertion. Shouts of "Get him out of here!" and "Kill 'im before Grenadine can heal 'im!" burbled to the surface of the chaos, but the door-man admirably held his ground, even lifting his hands to quell the tumult. He offered no defence of the healer or his own island-folk, content to merely stand steadfast in the entrance. "Regardless, you're not getting to the crab-puffs," he said simply, and the mob, as one, moaned in sorrow.

From what I could tell, this was the only open entrance to the hall. Behind the door-man's silhouette I could make out a lively collection of well-dressed islanders; surely the Mayor was among them.

I searched the pockets of the awful suit the Yam-Runners had given me. Its cut

GENERAL SHERMAN'S DOG-HOUSE.

was old-fashioned to say the least, and its colour and design were well into and back out of the so-ugly-it's-ironic realm. To make matters worse, the coat and trousers were dusty and scuffed from my long, panting hike down the mountain, but at least their contents were intact. The Mayor's letter had its own pocket, and I also found a thimble and a small copper spring in the trousers—probably left here by the last wearer of this suit, back when it was in style during the days of Oliver Cromwell.

And of course—there was my cheese-wand.

I drew the long, perfect rod from my trousers, then tucked it back in and pulled out the cheese-wand instead. As soon as I saw its ivory colour glisten in the gas-light I knew I had my plan. I ducked back into the darkness, away from the mob and towards the abandoned village square.

It didn't take long to round up a lantern, a kettle and a few mounds of old cheese—the owners of the shanty-stalls in the square's make-shift flea-mongery had thoughtfully left me exactly what I needed, poorly locked within their inventory-crates. A few smashed latches later I had assembled a crude fondue-pot.

The wand felt light and delightful in my hands, and I was pleased to make its first introduction to the medium it was made for. Cheese burbled in the kettle, and with a sharp intake of breath,

I drew out its soft orangeness with practised fluidity. The oily liquid balanced on the tip of the wand like a dew-drop on a rose-petal. I had forgotten nothing of my old craft, and it was exhilarating.

When the door-man looked up two minutes later, he gave no second thought to the wackily-dressed cheese-twirler making his way through the crowd. "Entertainment for the banquet," I said nonchalantly, spinning the wand between two fingers. The mob hushed instantly, every eye on that perfect, mesmerising twirl.

57: MEETING THE OAF.

OUTSIDE THE HALL, THE STREET teemed with the ill and the reeking—but inside, the very same sweaty funk of fever and mashed-together bodies was heavily masked beneath clouds of imported body-cologne and rarely-aired show-clothes. The Grenadians of the village had gone all-out to welcome their ancestor back to these shores, and I wondered how they would react if I told them what Ursula had told me.

The dancing cheese-blob at the tip of my twirling-wand cut a path for me through the pressing crowd. I flipped and spun the wand deftly to keep the cheese pliable, as it would likely set up in an instant were I to slow my motion. Nonetheless, images of Grenadine kept creeping un-bidden through the sluice-grate of my mind—the crazy old man from the salt-barrel, speaking languages I'd never heard, discerning our location from a glance at the sun, diving overboard to move a loaded merchant-ship with just steady kicks of his strong legs in the sea. If that was Yam-Runner stock, I'd better stay on Ursula's good side.

I paid dearly for the distraction. My fingers fumbled the wand and an orange drab of cheese-goo settled wetly onto the back of a large woman's silk shawl. I recovered quickly and managed to prevent another glop from escaping the central mass—but it took all I could muster to keep it flowing and lively, and the errant wad was beyond rescue. I vaguely sensed a murmur growing in the crowd around me, but all I saw was flopping orange and the tip of the wand; the art filled my vision, and my periphery blurred to nothingness. It was me and the cheese fighting for control, wrestling with gravity and momentum and Sir Newton's damnable bodies-physic, and it was glorious.

"Oi, Twirly, up in back, flop on!" came a call from behind, vague and dim in my perception, and instinctually I whirled and globbed a neat row of orange onto an outstretched bratwurst—then a stripe on a pickle-spear, a full drip-blop on a nacho-plate, and finally a triumphant half-smear on a twice-bitten bruschetta as on-lookers roared their approval. Finally the wand spun clean, free of cheesy load, and my job was done. A crush of applause returned to me my full spectrum of senses.

This was what I loved to do. I had forgotten it, over the years of lazy indulgence, servant-branding and whippery-sport. I heaved with breath and wiped my brow, exulting in the triumph of craft and labour. They were eating *my* cheese, and they were *enjoying* it.

Suddenly stifling, I shrugged out of my coat. The Yam-Runners' letter brushed my fingers as I did. My mission returned in a crush of weighty responsibility that darkened my brow and rooster-blocked my glory. I scanned the crowd for the Mayor, searching out that boisterous fat face, but didn't find him.

Folk were rushing to me now, clapping me gaily about the top-quarters and proclaiming my wizardry to each other, but I had eyes only for a pair of deep-set eyes in a ruddy round visage. I found many ugly, gap-toothed features in the masses, some gleefully spittling effusive praises in my general direction, but not the *precise* ugly gap-toothed features I sought.

For an instant I thought I'd found him—a large figure, half-hid in gloom, leaning against a service-exit and wearing a sour expression—but I corrected myself after half an instant. This shadow was shaped like the Mayor but younger, busy cultivating a fashionable apathy. It was Rikah's beau—the Mayor's son.

Perhaps he would do for my purposes, however, and I set through the crowd towards him, laughing along with hearty congratulations from strangers and accepting the occasional honour-fig, sweet to the throat after my exhausting performance.

As I broke through the crowd at the far end of the room, I realised that the bulky not-Mayor wasn't alone: he had with him the raven-haired beauty whose horse I'd knocked off a cliff not twenty-four hours previous. Rikah was splendiferous in chiffon with fine beeswax adornments, possibly bedecked in saucy *trousers* underneath, but *definitely* aglow with the sly demeanour of a woman who knows more than she's telling. She slanted her head an inch as I slipped casually into conversation-range.

"When she puts the shawl back on, she'll be surprised to find her special gift," Rikah smiled, and it took me a second to catch that she meant the large woman with un-ordered bonus-cheese still resting in her silken accessory.

"I've not met a lady yet who wouldn't delight at a free sample," I sparkled right back, and she smiled politely. With a jolt of beautiful energy I realised that she still didn't recognise me at all.

This was perfect. Here, where nobody knew me, I could be whom-ever I wanted; all I had to do was choose a persona. Who should I be? The rakish cheese-twirler from Beloochistan? The cheese-twirling rogue from Darkest Sandwich Isles? Perhaps a duke or baron from the New World, moon-lighting with a cheese-wand to hob-nob with the locals?

"Go on, we're not in the habit of socialising with the help," Mayor Jr snorted, and I deflated. But Rikah shot him a glare, which did much to pump brightness back into my teeth.

"Actually," I said, sidling up to the big man and drawing the Yam-Runner's folded letter from the coat draped o'er my arm, "I have an urgent missive for the Mayor himself. Will he be making an appearance tonight?"

Mayor Jr traded what might have been a meaningful glance with Rikah, then scowled at me impassively. "Not here yet."

"I'm afraid it's terribly urgent," I said. "It's—it's about Grenadine." Anything that would get this oaf to take the letter to his
equally-oafy sire. Or just take the letter, full stop—perhaps that
would count for my obligation, and how would the Yam-Runners
know, anyhow?

"Let me see that," Jr said, snapping the letter crisply from my
fingers, squinting at it, then holding it up to a gas-lamp to attempt
to read the inside. The letter's circle of green signet-wax began to
glisten from the heat, and I caught the man's arm—best not to take
chances.

"It's for the Mayor's eyes immediately," I told him, putting on
my gravest of grave voices, and in my sideways-vision I saw Rikah
stand a little straighter; likely she was batting at my wicket with
a little Woman-Stare Action, which just goes to show how much
credit a little cheese-twirling and Authority can earn you with the
finer sex.

Jr looked caught between his natural haughty aloofness and a
genuine sense of obligation, staring at the folded parchment as if he
could divine its contents and they would tell him what to do, anything to absolve him of Making a Decision. I wondered if he would
leave me alone with Rikah, and if he did, if it meant that I should
probably go on and leave her as well, to go climb that tall, lonely
mountain alone, to re-shoulder my heavy burden of obligation to my
Quest, or whatever.

Or, I supposed, I could just stay here, the rakish cheese-twirler
from Beloochistan, for all she knew, and simply have a go at another
new life.

Jr fixed me with a Meaningful Stare, then scarpered, and
Rikah and I watched him go. His back looked exactly as it had the
first time I'd seen him—at the stables, arguing with Rikah about
Oat-Princess. She'd told Jr that Oat-Princess was missing, when
she well knew that the horse was dead. Why had she lied?

Peapoddy. *That's* why. She had welcomed to the island a Peapoddy, a sworn enemy, unthinkable in this town loyal to Grenadine.

My mouth must have been open, or my stare must have graduated to a leer, or maybe I had said something else out loud, because Rikah's smile, so winning a moment ago, slowly sank into drawishness and headed quickly for losing-dom. I rakishly assumed my rakish persona once more. I wondered if I should even find a rake, to seal the deal.

"So," I said with a charming smile, "I hear you're a fan of Peapoddy?"

Her face fell. *Whoops.* Whatever I had meant to say, *that* wasn't it. "What are you talking about?" she hissed. "I don't know what you're talking about! Seriously, what do you mean? Ha ha ha!"

She must have taken my stunned lack of response for a serious stop-this-frontin' impassiveness, for she then took my arm fiercely and dragged me out the small service exit into a dark alley-way. We stepped quickly but commandingly over moaning heaps of ailing supplicants until after several minutes of tromping in the dark we reached a spot on a hill completely out of ear-shot of anyone remotely near-by.

After a moment to catch her breath, she turned to stare down at the banquet-hall, its fiery windows lit brightly from within. The flatness of her voice surprised me.

"What exactly do you know," she asked.

My first instinct was to say "Nothing," in the hope that she would think this was all a deep and tragic misunderstanding. *I don't have any evidence that would make you an outcast among your peers! It's not like I would use that to gain your favour! Honest! I just—uh—like make joke! In Beloochistan this is good joke!* It was a pretty good plan, but by the time I'd come up with a an Beloochistani joke to follow up with that didn't include an insult about her mother's yak-herd, I realised that my mouth was already talking.

"The dirigible," my fool mouth said. "I know you were there."

She looked up sadly at me then, and if a dark cloud hadn't been blocking the moon-light I would surely have seen her eyes shimmer. "And Grenadine?"

She didn't know that the man she thought was Grenadine had actually been me in disguise. But if she was hoping that Grenadine might still show up at the banquet, well—best to put this to rest as cleanly as possible.

"Grenadine's dead," I said.

She looked back down at the banquet-hall and nodded. "I'm— I mean, I'd hoped," she said, almost too softly for me to hear. "But I'm not really surprised."

She looked like she might start to sob over the old man at any second. Time to change the subject, then. "Mayor sure threw a swell banquet," I said. "Were those crab-puffs in there? I heard there were crab-puffs, but I don't know if what I saw were eclairs, or what. Did you get any crab-puffs?"

"The Mayor was waiting for Grenadine," she said flatly. "He's in his house, now, dying of a shrapnel wound sustained from the dirigible explosion." She turned and pointed across the way, to where a shadowy figure—Jr, presumably—trundled down a deserted avenue. "That'll be Morty, taking your letter to him now."

Morty? Dumb name. My mouth wanted to mention that, but luckily I intervened in time and our team said nothing, I think.

"He was waiting for Grenadine to heal him," Rikah shrugged. "But I killed them both. I brought Peapoddy to our shores. I killed my people's saviour and also the father of my dearest love. We call that a 'twofer.' It hurts worse than a twofache."

Dearest love. That stung, a bit. But what did I expect, really?

"Well," I said in what I hoped was a helpful, I'm-solving-all-your-problems voice, "I don't know if Grenadine could have done a whole lot for him, anyway."

She whirled, and even in the cloud-blocked dimness I could see the flash of indignation in her eyes. "Why's that?" she said. "What else do you know that you're not telling? Don't tell me you're one of those Anti-Grenadine protesters—because Morty went out on a limb for you, delivering that letter, and I don't appreciate you using his kindness to make some sort of political statement at the worst possible time for our family!"

"That's not quite it," I said. "I just wanted to give the Mayor a—"

Whatever else I might have said was drowned out by the Mayor's house deafeningly erupting into a blinding pillar of green flame.

58: DARK CLOUDS GATHER.

WHAT HAVE YOU DONE?" RIKAH shrieked, once the shock of the blast had passed. She battered me with her fists, but I scarcely noticed the blows—I was too mesmerised by the dancing pillar of fire. The Mayor's house was gone, pulverised into sparkling embers and wood-dust; the Mayor presumably with it, and perhaps his oafish son too. One could only hope: it was an unexpected development to be sure, but I wasn't one to look a gift explosion in the blazing mouth. (Not without a pinhole camera—bad for the retinas, you know, and I needed my retinas in tip-top for much of what was to come.)

Earning no response from her assault, Rikah abandoned an impact-based strategy and instead seized me by the collar of my flouncy blouse. "What did you give him?" she cried. "You monster! What was in that letter?"

"It was just...paper," I mumbled. "It weighed an ounce and lay flat as a ghost. It was just paper."

"Paper coated in triple-processed Burmese jade-powder, obviously!" she screamed. "Which explodes when it touches open air! You must have paid a pretty penny for so much of that deadly dust—whatever did the Mayor do to deserve this? And my Morty— oh, you've killed him!"

"I was just the messenger," I said, grasping her wrists and shaking her violently as an ill-behaved infant. "From the Yam-Runners! They bade me bring the Mayor that letter in person..."

My bones locked together in alarm. "They asked me to hand it to him myself. *I* was intended for that blast too!"

"The Yam-Runners are a myth," Rikah spat, and flounced down the hill towards the flaming debris. "Oh, Morty!"

If Ursula had never intended for me to return, then what about everything she'd said about the Tome...? "Wait!" I cried, scrambling to bound after Rikah. "They're not a myth! Where do you think I got such ridiculous clothes?"

As I chased her down the hill-side the night-time air felt suddenly very bright. The moon had emerged from the ominous cloud that had sheathed it for much of the evening.

"What's that buzzing?" I asked the back of Rikah's head. A low drone had settled into my ear-drums—I feared for a moment that my deafness would return. Had it had lain latent these past months, waiting for the most inopportune time to re-surface? What a cheeky bloke, that abstract concept of deafness—if I could get fingers 'round its throat it would have hell to pay.

Something moved above me. I caught a floating sort of motion in my periphery, and obligingly looked towards the sky.

The darkness was no cloud. *It was an armada of air-ships,* hundreds of them, floating slowly Earth-ward beneath pendulous gas-sacs, belching thick black coal-smoke from airscrew-turning engines.

"Huh," I said, which is probably what the nerds call an "under-statement."

The lowest ship in the flock belched lightning, an instant of brilliant, crackling energy darting from its hull to the town, splitting the sky with a shattering green bolt. A half-second later the ground at its target erupted in a furious geyser of mud, wood, and flesh.

Rikah skidded to a halt and recoiled, staggering backwards into me. I caught her elbows to steady her.

"The Countess," Rikah breathed. "She's returned."

Then, in the span of one second, the night filled entirely with green lightning, millions of forks combining into one crackling panorama.

The village disappeared in a flash—reappearing only as a cloud of burning, settling ashes.

Every building was leveled. Every sales-cart was vapourised. Every living creature turned instantly to charcoal. Rikah and I watched the town before us become the remains of a camp-fire.

"We have to get out of here," I said, pulling Rikah away without protest—perhaps she would compliment me later on my creative use of the "under-statement."

The mountain loomed ahead of us, high and forbidding in the shadow of the armada. The sky was black with drifting hulls and billowing smoke; the paths on the ground were un-lit, treacherous, and filled with lots of roots and stuff to trip us. We moved quickly as we dared through the forest, putting distance between us and the smouldering ruins without giving thought to direction; but soon we found ourselves turned-about and facing the devastation again.

"It's no use," Rikah gasped, folding and clutching her side; I nearly agreed with her but for fear of seeming poufy. I surreptitiously held my own side where a stitch had suddenly bound my intestines together, and my fingers found the shape of a disk in my vest-coat pocket. *Of course!* I retrieved Ursula's opticle, and fit the slim glass against my eye.

Instantly, the ground was alight with branching, shimmering path-ways, and I took Rikah by the wrist at once. "This way," I cried, and we pounded the earth with sure-footed shoe-slaps. We didn't stop till we broke the tree-line, fearful that the air-ships were sensing our movement; but the heavy cover of leaves protected us, and also shaded and nourished a thriving ground-level eco-system of mosses.

"I have to rest," Rikah gulped, leaning against a tall trunk; I thought she was going to lose her supper right there onto the ground, the way she sucked air and paced and dry-heaved and prodded at her tonsils with a thin finger. Behind her, the valley was alight with a solid bed of burning green flame—it seemed a roiling ocean in its evenness and agitation, and if I listened carefully enough I thought I might have heard echoes of wandering screams on the breeze. I wondered idly if the ashes of those scores of sick and dying pilgrims might infect my lungs from the inside, and just in case resolved to hold my breath whenever possible from here on out.

For a splitting moment the sky lit again, far across the island, and two seconds later we heard the smashing, rumbling crack of snapping masts and splintering hulls. Then the harbour went up in one massive blast, and I whirled to shield my precious eyes from a searing blaze of green light.

Every ship in the harbour had become kindling within seconds. "No getting off the island now," Rikah wailed.

I turned my glance back towards the sea and imagined the long, blinking rail-lines nestled deep beneath the ocean floor. I squinted at the mountain through the opticle and traced the web of bright trails farther up-hill and deeper into Yam-Runner domain, trying to discern which to follow, which would lead us to safety—and which led back into the maw of the people who had tried to kill me.

One trail branched from the others, and glowed a duller shade of yellow; it led towards a cliff-side path overlooking the ocean, and out of curiosity more than anything I took a few steps in that direction.

"Hey—don't get too far," Rikah called, and I heard her scramble to follow. It was dark out here, and clearly she, like I, hadn't put the thought of bears entirely out of her mind.

We followed the yellow trail to a narrow ledge crumbling against a sheer rock-face. From here I could see where Peapoddy's dirigible had been moored, a half-mile down the coast and lower on the cliff. The occasional blink of green lightning from afar illuminated the debris still littering the shore-line far below. I wondered about the bodies crammed up against those stones, and if the tide had swept them away. I wondered if they would wash up on some far Irish beach-head, and thought to myself that I would like to see the reactions of the local beach-Irishmen if they did. Perhaps I could inquire after any humourous accounts, once this whole business with the Tome of the Precious Lore was done and settled.

I fumbled with both hands against the rock-face and found myself abruptly gaping into emptiness. Wet air tickled my skin as I took a shaky step deeper into the black. My shoes crunched on gravel, no longer the soft dirt of the trail. The yellow line in the opticle was hard to see, now; it seemed to jump out of view when I set my focus on it, and only shone brightly as I glanced away.

"Where'd you go?" came Rikah's voice from behind. Her words echoed back from wet rock walls.

My hands suddenly met a smooth glassy surface, round and as large as myself. I moved my fingers across the coolness and a sudden flare of sharp green light over-loaded my vision. With my touch the cave had suddenly become bright as a summer's day in a deodorant advert. I staggered backwards, nearly falling into Rikah; I'd caught her before, and now she re-paid the favour. The touch of her hands on my arms made my hair tingle, and with my eyes rammed firmly shut against the light, the pressure of her warm grip filled my senses.

Then she let go, and I tumbled against the cavern wall. My eyes didn't like the brightness, but they just had to deal; bright light was the score in here, and Rikah was walking towards the source.

After a few seconds I was better able to see that it was a massive egg—no, an egg-shaped stone—no, a fossilized egg-shaped coprolite—no, I was right the second time. It was a stone the height of a man, smooth as glass but veined with fine cracks and chips.

Rikah stared at the stone, then slowly held up one hand to almost touch it. Her fingers hovered a half-inch from its smooth surface. "Come look at this," she said softly, and I would have done anything for that voice. (In service of it, that is, not 'I would have done anything to have it myself.' Just to be clear.)

I joined her at the stone. She stared at a depression in its surface, a jagged, triangular hollow the shape of a tooth, where a piece had been chipped out.

"Grenadine's bright-jade," she breathed. "I'd know that shape anywhere."

"What's that buzzing?" I said.

With a thrumming roar, two small air-ships descended over the mouth of the cavern, their air-screws thrashing the darkness with a frightful clatter. These were tiny compared to the lightning-ships; two-seater jobs, just a basket-like pilot's cabin suspended beneath pulsing, round gas-sacs. It was clear they had seen us.

One ship drifted closer to the cliff-side. A leathery figure in black wriggled out from the second seat behind the pilot, leaping nimbly onto the mountain. Hand on his head to keep his cap from flying off, he crossed the distance from the cave's mouth in five long strides. When he spoke, it was with a voice hoarsened by the practise of shouting over those fearsome engines.

"Countess Peapoddy sends her regards to the Yam-Runners, reports the initial bombardment as successful, and awaits further instructions," he said.

59: SKY-WARD !

THE WIND FROM THE AIR-SHIPS WHIPPED dust about the green-lit cavern, scrambling my thoughts like so many ostrich-eggs over-easy. The leather-clad aviator seemed to be expecting a response to his greeting, but what could I say? "Countess Peapoddy" was presumably some relation to the late corpulent beast whose waste-engorged entrails I'd splattered about the wave-pounded shore within sight of this very spot. Grenadine had hated Peapoddy the Elder, and I his son; but how many more of this brine-swilling rat-clan still dug worm-holes through this blasted planet?

Three observations fought for primacy in my fore-brain, and gamely I allowed each its say, so long as it did not exceed a pre-determined syllable count:

Firstly, Rikah had pledged alliance—or, at the least, clemency, which to the villagers was synonymous with fealty—to Peapoddy the Younger, a great enemy of her people, in the name of mercy and compassion. This facet of her character I noted, for possible exploitation anon.

Secondly, the aviator and his hovering noise-ships were expecting to have met an emissary from the Yam-Runners, with whom the Countess Peapoddy was presumably in accord. The Yam-Runners' long-standing animus against the Shorelanders married well with Peapoddy rancor against the same folk. It was not a stretch to imagine their confederacy.

And, finally, of course, none of these people knew who I was.

"Welcome, friend!" I called to the aviator, stepping forward both to offer a hearty hand-shake with reach-around and also to put distance (and background noise) between us and any objection Rikah might mount. She would have to catch up quickly—having just watched her entire village be atomised, she might not be in the most stable of mind-states, but I hoped she would trust me and match my lead.

Too late, I considered that she had no reason to trust me, the man who had (in her eyes) certainly triggered the attack, and nothing I was doing now gave any indication of subterfuge. For all she knew, everything was going perfectly according to my plan. This might hurt later, when I told her the truth and she inevitably didn't believe me.

But I had already spoken. Now the aviator leaned close, and I could smell brandy and Cologne on his stubbly neck. A man's man he was, rugged down to the silk scarf flapping gaily in the air-ships' furious flurry. "Shall we take the Lady aboard to see the Countess?" he asked, peeking back at Rikah.

"Of course," I smiled—perhaps a bit too toothily, but there it was. I turned back to Rikah, prepared at any moment for a fist in the nose, or a boot in the groin, or a knuckle-jab to the right kidney followed by a teat-twist to detachment (a.k.a. the Stockholm Surprise), or at the very least a blistering stare to take the skin from the inside-rear of my skull.

Instead I found nothing—a somber blankness far more unsettling than any show of violence.

I was not familiar with the sublimation of rage. I did not own
the proper tongs to handle it.

"He wants to take you to see the Countess," I whispered to her,
a tender breath that she totally couldn't hear over the din. I had
to ratchet the voice up all the way to "harsh snarl" just to reach
minimum audibility. "The Countess!" I snapped, altogether too
menacingly. "Trust me! I'm just playing along—I've nothing to do
with it—but let's not pass this opportunity to face the monster in
person, what say?"

I gather that she heard about every fourth word, but to my
amazement she clutched my wrist and allowed me to lead her to the
mouth of the cave. Her fingers were tight and cold and I apologised
to them silently, sending magical thought-messages down through
my wrist and into her palm. I gather she got the less decorous ones,
as she tensed; I felt bad, but she hadn't responded to the mental
images not involving copious amounts of butter.

The night was suddenly red as we left the cavern and its
oppressive fire-hose of furious green light. Illumination from the
jade-stone penetrated the sky like a finger picking a pimple on the
face of God, casting a faint emerald kiss onto a bank of billowing
fog a mile away.

Suddenly an air-ship rumbled into the light-beam, barely a
hundred feet above our heads, and the green leapt into sharp, close
focus: it drew a fine out-line of a distinctive, tooth-shaped triangle.
The light traced Grenadine's sigil on the craft's billowing gas-sac.

Then the air-ship was past, and the light was diffuse and distant again; I blinked, and turned to where the leather-clad aviator
was gesturing to the pair of smaller aero-skiffs that hovered near
us, barely an arm's grasp away. Their racket was extraordinary, the
wind they cast up as they manoeuvred an assault to every sense;
but in truth embarking was like stepping into a gently swaying
boat, and soon I was nestled tightly into a passenger's-cage with
Rikah, seated in close quarters behind a fresh-faced pilot.

"Hullo," the man said blandly, and I nodded like a big-shot.

"Take them back to the Countess!" the aviator instructed our pilot, as he himself headed for the passenger's-cage on the second craft. Before the words were whole out of his mouth he had already begun to diminish in our vision—my stomach tumbled somewhere north of my eyeballs as our aero-skiff rose briskly and steeply through the cool evening.

The mountain dropped away, and the horizon glimmered with green flame in the direction of the village.

RIKAH'S AUSTRALIAN COUSIN, ELSIE.

Rikah's eyes never left that sorry landscape no matter the gyrations our craft suffered as it rose, and I feared the prospect of wearing her half-digested crab-puffs as corsage before the ride was through.

"Lucky thing we read your signal," the pilot called back to me. "Bright as day, and thanks for that. We'd been told to watch for a green flare on the mountain to meet the Yam-Runner emissary and her valet—and sure 'nough, there's that green light, and here you two are. Couldn't have gone smoother, if y'ask me mum's son."

"Ah," I responded importantly, as we drew ever closer to the menacing shadow of a monstrous air-ship, barely visible in silhouette through a layer of mist that wrapped the mountain's peak. A throaty drone signaled both its proximity and its weight; we would be breaking through that fog soon, and apparently the Countess Peapoddy's chariot awaited us beyond.

I wondered idly what clouds were like to touch—would it be marshmallowy, perhaps? Would we have to gather momentum to penetrate the threshold? Would my services with a shiv be required to gain entry to that nephotic nether-realm?

Suddenly a new green speck flared on the mountain-side below, a goodly distance from where our jade-light still spat from the cavern like the post from a particularly stony lolly. Tiny at first, then flickering and brighter by the second, the spot could only be the Yam-Runners' true signal-flare. The pilot seemed not to have noticed, and I leaned forward as far as I could to try and block his view should he turn about.

Our aero-skiff, already groaning as it bore our weight sky-ward, rocked with the shift of balance, and the pilot in fact turned about instantly—"Hold still back there, we've got a hundred fathoms to climb, yet," he scolded, before trailing off into silence...and I saw the pin-prick reflection of green light in his eyes as they clouded over with confusion.

I whirled and pretended to see the flare for the first time. "Imposters! They've penetrated the camp!" I shouted. "Quickly—we must press on!"

I grasped Rikah for emphasis and she vomited explosively through the cage, soaking the pilot, baptising a passing sea-gull, and spraying a bit on me as well. She was positively pale with vertigo, and secretly I wondered if she had another blast left in her—we might turn this whole affair around yet.

"Ho, there!" the pilot cried, spasming in horror and nearly up-ending the craft. I threw my weight around the cage, adding to the tumble, ignoring my own innards' protest—*Daddy's working now,* I admonished them; there would be time for proper nausea later. Grasping the twisted brass of the pilot's entry-latch with blistered fingers, I leaned my weight as far backwards as I could.

The whole aero-skiff swayed horizontal as a ship facing the water-fall at Old Benson's Bligh, the stop-all of the Earth.

My heart stopped for a weight-less second as Old Benson sucked its crimson nectar through a bamboo straw to test my cour-age. Rikah, to her credit, performed admirably on cue, heaving up another helping of *hors d'whatever* right into the pilot's terror-stricken rictus.

He recoiled backwards, against the latch I had helpfully disengaged, and three clumsy seconds of struggling preceded a sudden and violent surge of vertical motion. We had been freed of twelve stone of dead-weight, and in an instant we were surrounded by the pure, freezing blackness of midnight fog.

60: PLUNGED TO EARTH.

D ON'T WORRY!" I CRIED TO MY SUDDENLY invisible companion, seated not six inches away but cloaked, utterly cloaked in dense, dark mist. "I have a thousand hours' experience flying these contraptions. I once chased an entire yurt-ful of yak-poachers across the Mongol steppes for six sleepless weeks, using my own waste for coal. That last detail may not have been strictly necessary," I asserted with what I hoped sounded acceptably like confidence. I couldn't tell if she was reassured by my claim or what, but I figured probably.

Visibility ahead extended to the end of my nose and little further; by leaning forward I could make out most of the brass grate separating our passenger's compartment from the now-empty pilot's cage. I wondered absently if I should be concerned about the lack of occupant in said cage—the wind whistled through that vacant space as our aero-skiff continued its heedless ascent, buoyed by our sudden dumping of dead-weight in the form of the aforementioned aviator.

The fog-bank was colder, wetter and less marshmallowy than I'd anticipated; I began to wonder what horrors might await us should we break through the top of the cloud-layer. The Countess' massive flag-ship dwelt at that altitude, but what of the danger of sky-dragons and star-whales? It would do us no good to burst from the clouds only to be impaled on the massive horn of a galloping nighticorn.I had no idea what monsters abided in the far-off heavens, and suddenly realised with a shiver that I was about to find out.

I reached my arm as far through the bars of the passenger's-cage as I could, straining to reach the control-tiller in the pilot's-cage. I fumbled blindly in the damp dark, scraping my fingers against indistinct levers and wheels along the way, some of them having definite ramifications on the skiff's velocity. We were still climbing at a rapid clip (so far as I could tell; with no visual reference, I relied only on my gut for my sense of direction, though unfortunately my gut had failed the Brighamptonshire Young Dragoons' Trail-Seeking Examination more times than I'd like to admit, to the tune of a half-shilling per go), and the engine still belched coal-smoke behind us.

I squinted and bugged my eyes and peered as vigorously as I could through the night-ness, and wouldn't you know, I *did* seem to see a bit better—perhaps the cloud was thinning, or perhaps I suddenly grew adept at nocturnal vision. It was a talent I'd long attempted to cultivate, practising in furtive midnight moments off-and-on since early childhood while other youngsters busied themselves with furtive torch-reading and self-abuse.

Aha! Yes! All at once, something changed in my eyeballs—and I achieved perfect night-time eye-sight! I could make out every detail on the pilot's control-panel. I grasped the tiller firmly with a shivering hand and turned to Rikah. "I can see in this darkness now!" I shrieked over the raging wind. "It's going to be fine!"

She didn't look at me, poor blind lass; she was instead focused on some far-off point. I turned my cat-like eyes to see what she might have vaguely discerned in the darkness—

And realised that I wasn't really seeing in the dark. It was actually really bright above the cloud-bank.

The source of the brightness, glowing brilliantly from within like a cool bluish moon, was Countess Peapoddy's aero-galleon. Larger by a factor of ten than Peapoddy the Younger's dirigible, the Countess's vessel sported what must have been a hundred churning

air-screws mounted at every juncture along its architecture, straining to keep the beast aloft and leaving a thick, black cloud of
coal-soot in its rumbling wake.

And it had a face.

A wide, angry face splashed across the luminous gas-sac,
projected from the vessel's core like a grotesque kinetoscope-show,
painting the sky with the gruesome, bloated countenance of what
could only have been the Countess herself. Her features bespoke
malice without conscience; her withering glare could only have been
described as "awfulleeringghastlyloathesscary." (The Cherokee
tongue, I believe.)

Sparks of greenish electricity danced about the Countess' ship
like sea-leeches around dolphin-corpses, lighting the night sky with
flashes too bright to stare at—though I tried, futilely. "Well, there
she is," I breathed to Rikah, with what breath remained after cursing the abhorrent apparition at lungs-emptying length.

The poor lass was still mute, and looking a bit blue herself;
I wasn't sure if it was the light or if her nausea was returning.
Either was unflattering.

I suddenly became aware of a harsh coalish odor, and noted that
the engine behind us was now blasting its exhaust directly towards
us. I took a moment to process this turn of events, and then, with
the help of handy visual cues, landed upon the cause.

We had stopped climbing, and were now drifting back to the
Earth. The smooth, from-this-height-unbroken fog-layer crept
towards us again like a deceptively placid sea, though I knew that
lurking just below were jagged rocks, enemy air-ships armed with
lightning-bolts, and a harsh, unforgiving ocean. This was no time
for half-measures; it was time to leap full-bore into the heart of that
moon-ish madness, with the thunderous roar of aero-thrust and
the whip of speed in our hair. I fixed my gaze on that evil, floating
Countess-head and growled in my most adventurey growl:

"Let's *do* this."

I rammed the tiller full to the stop.

It wasn't the tiller. With a sharp *spang*, our gas-sac popped free and began to float merrily towards Heaven.

Suddenly entirely non-buoyant, we plummeted like a not-very-aerodynamic anvil and were enveloped in the cold cloud immediately.

It was actually a not-unpleasant feeling. I felt weight lift from my body in waves, and turned to Rikah long enough to say, "I suppose we should enjoy this sensation while we can."

Her only reply was a hacking retch-heave. This one sounded dry, at least; she seemed to have been emptied of her more volumetric gastric ammunition.

We descended through the cloud-bank much faster than we had ascended. The night below us swarmed with aero-skiffs like wasps about a mud-nest, zipping to and fro and crackling with bright green lightning. A faint, sparking glow across the island below us betrayed the ruins of the village, and a thin, emerald finger pointing at the clouds the cave in the mountain we'd just departed. Elsewhere in the mountain, Yam-Runner signal-flares burnt in isolated specks of yellow and green flame. The attack had certainly been coördinated splendidly.

I tried working the tiller again when I noticed I had been clutching it hard enough to embed splinters in my palm. I found that slight lateral movements sent us careening into wild, cork-screwing spins; we screamed directly for the deep water one moment, then the village fire-scape the next, then narrowly missed punching through the bulging gas-sac of a passing air-ship.

Quickly getting the hang of the control, I managed to stablise our flight somewhat, but still we sank at an alarming rate. Rikah mashed her eyes closed and muttered something I couldn't quite hear. A prayer? A liturgy? A comforting poem from childhood? Conveniently, a poem from her childhood that was also a curse upon my house and descendants. It was hard to be sure.

Something about the falling sensation brought Abu Fromage's last words tickling at the corners of my memory...

The way I figure it, when the air-ship explodes, the heat will instantly vapourise the top few feet of sea-water—effectively creating a cushion of steam that will arrest our fall.

"We have to blow up an air-ship," I told Rikah, and she nearly vomited into my face.

I turned around and began to un-fasten our engine from its moorings. These aero-skiffs were remarkably cheaply made—probably by Icelandic beggar-children with no firm grasp of modern industrial quality-control—and I was surprised at how easily the churning motor came un-lashed from its mounts. Once it was down to one thin

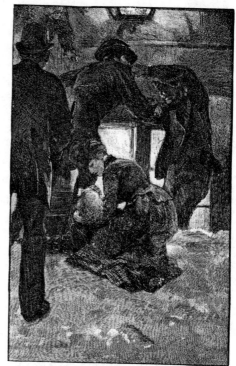

"KICK ME IN THE STOMACH AS HARD AS YOU CAN." —[PAGE 670.]

bolt the engine thrashed itself loose, shearing brass fittings in twain like bright orange leaves; then all I could do was watch it fall, its air-screws clawing futilely at loose molecules of sky, falling toward that thick knot of so many air-ships that they blotted out the night—

I saw a brief shadow cross a single ship's gas-sac before the engine tore through that inflated canvas. The air-ship shuddered, and began to sway, then staggered Earth-ward.

But it did not explode.

The crippled craft began to tumble along-side us on a double-date with Gravity, its punctured gas-sac collapsing slowly like the world's second-most inebriated jelly-fish, looming closer by the second.

The mountain grew huge and dark before us, and I do not recall making any sort of conscious decision on the subject before clambering into the narrow doorway of the passenger's-cage, Rikah's wrist grasped firmly in one hand. The gas-sac was just yards away now.

My feet left the cage. I whipped Rikah ahead of me, towards the billowing blanket of canvas threatening to engulf us. She shrieked as she fell, and then I followed her, our mangled, destroyed aero-skiff falling away and floating for two solid seconds before dashing itself into brass-dust and splinters on hard rock.

We entered the gas-sac's pillow-like depths, and felt it begin to smother us as it met the ground and began to slide down. Ropes and nets and supports tore at us, but we stayed floating in the centre of the squishy mass, like a thrashing two-headed yolk in a scrambling egg of Science, until it finally came to rest, still partially inflated. But we'd not even a moment to rest—for voices echoed across the hill, deep and thrummy-sounding through the canvas. The Yam-Runners were coming for us.

61: A SHORT CHAPTER.

I DUCKED BACK INTO THE STILL-BILLOWING cover of the deflating gas-sac, not especially wanting to encounter the Yam-Runners who'd just used me as their unwitting instrument to annihilate the entire village—but Rikah, apparently, had other, rather more stupid plans.

She leapt to her feet in a flash, moving with more confidence and surety than I'd seen since before she watched her family and everyone she loved get incinerated in a single brilliant instant. With a yank on my collar, her sudden strength pulled me heavily to my feet despite my vehement struggling. "What madness has you?" I hissed, angling back towards the relative safety of the gas-sac. "They'll see you!"

"Exactly," she said, and turned to point at the green light-beam of Grenadine's sigil, that thin, perfect finger spearing the night-time clouds and shining its sharp triangle onto passing air-ships. "The villagers will heed the call—any who escaped," she added, silencing my impending rejoinder. "I'm sure there must be *some-one*. They couldn't have...have...well, not *all* of them, anyway," she trailed off, unable to wrap her voice around the horror that we had both watched befall, indeed, *all* of them.

I struggled to pull her back towards the gas-sac, but she resisted, and I'm a bit ashamed to admit that her obstinate resolve bested my quite-exhausted straining. Realising how difficult this situation was for her, I put on my most sympathetic voice to reason with her. "There's nobody left! They're all melted to cinders—those are the Yam-Runners coming, and unless you want to join your boy-friend in Hell then let's get out of the road!" Not for the first time, I mentally polished my Perfect Attendance trophy from the German National Correspondence-Course in Tactfulness.

She shook her head. "It's the *sign*," she said, calmly, clearly, a bit sing-songy, a bit creepily. "You don't know what it's like to live *your entire life* waiting for something to happen, being told that things will go a certain way, never really believing it—and then, in one terrifying, beautiful moment, watching it all come together in a way you never could have imagined." She turned to me, and the breeze blowing slowly through her hair made her seem to be floating under water. "They told us Grenadine would die. And then his sign would lead his people into the womb of the earth for their salvation. It is how it has been written for centuries."

"Grenadine lied to your people," I snapped, trying hard to keep my voice below a shout. The green torches were bobbing closer, and I could hear foot-falls now on stone. "He told you he was a healer so you'd worship him. He was a Yam-Runner! Exiled from the moun-tain to live among the Shorelanders!"

"The Yam-Runners are a myth," Rikah said calmly, as the Yam-Runners came around the bend and found us.

There were three of them, burly men I hadn't seen before, but definitely Yam-Runners: their size and awful fashion-sense gave them away instantly. "So glad you're here," I said to the first man, playing the we're-all-pals card, which earned me a smash in the face with his torch. Instantly the night disappeared, and I saw green, then red, then, slowly, black. And it wasn't even Christmas.

62: THE OBSERVATORY.

A BLINDING STAB OF PAIN WOKE ME. My face felt like a rail-way spike had been rammed through my cheek and stirred around in my humours. I reached a hand to touch my face—but couldn't move. My hands were bound. I couldn't see. I could only shiver in a cold, damp stillness.

"You've done us quite the favour," came a voice from what sounded like the other side of an enclosed room—the words echoed about a bit, and swished about my face like honey-bees around a flower before alighting on my skin and stinging. "Thank you for delivering our letter."

"Got the wrong guy," I mumbled, though my teeth felt like they might tumble from my aching jaw any second. "I'm just a simple, ordinary rakish Beloochistani cheese-twirler."

"Don't be so modest," the voice chuckled. "You did well. Pity you couldn't hand-deliver the letter, however, like we asked."

"You wanted to blow me up too," I snarled. "Sorry to disappoint."

The voice seemed to shrug, though I couldn't see it. "It would have been nice. But so much for regrets." I heard a clink as the figure picked up a piece of ceramic, or glass—one of the Yam-Runners' mystical lenses, perhaps? "Grenadine. Dead on that sand-bar, I take it? We knew he lived when our people started keeling over."

"I don't know what you mean," I said, for no good reason other than to be contrary. I'd killed the old man on that sand-bar, sure; but that didn't mean I wanted to brag about it. Okay, I did, a little. But more than that, right now I wanted to be rude. "Butt-head," I added.

"So much we could do with you," the voice sighed. "Send you out in a row-boat to retrieve the old man's skull—now *that* would be a prize, wouldn't it? Pecked to the bone by sea-gulls by now, no doubt. And you'd *do* it, too. Take you a month, but you'd bring it back to me, I'm sure of it." The voice moved closer as it spoke, until I felt hot breath on my face, foul and stale, like old biscuits gone soft. "Or you'd take a hammer to that jade-stone, in Grenadine's cubby-cave. Wouldn't *that* be fun—knocking the old man's jewel to pieces, watching it fragment, watching all those flickering images trapped inside, learning everything about my brother Grenadine that you never wanted to know." The voice was so close now I could hear teeth clicking against teeth. "You do present an embarrassment of opportunity."

"Let up my hands, and we'll settle this," I barked. "If you're Grenadine's brother, even half the age he was, I could take you in a fair fight. Or do you not care to fight fair?" I dimly seemed to recall Grenadine being a handy sort, hardy and strong, but this fellow sounded a bit more rickety of the lungs. I dare say a good sympathy-fist to that smug voice-box might ease the stabbing pain in my face.

"Oh, it's not a matter of fighting," the voice trilled. "Not a matter at all." A sudden light burned my eyes as the shadowy figure lit a lantern, then carefully trimmed the wick like one last split-end before the big moustache-contest.

Light blinked and glimmered and refracted from dozens of tiny surfaces all around the room, until the whole chamber was softly twinkling with lamp-flame—revealing tubes of glass jutting from the walls in such density that I couldn't even see if there *were* walls. Huge rods of glass, a foot in diameter or more, descended from the ceiling; smaller cylinders filled every cranny where the larger ones left gaps. It felt like being inside a salt-crystal, except I was alive.

In the faint light, I got my first glimpse at the figure who had spoken. A Yam-Runner, all right—his courduroy blazer told me that much. He looked old, but not as wizened as Grenadine; he had a full shock of hair, carefully braided in a terrible style. I couldn't see his face; he was holding the light up to the walls, as if searching for something among the glass tubes. *Light-jars,* Ursula had called them.

He held his lamp up to one identical tube among many, then peered into its end with squinted eye. "You'll like this one," he said softly. "This one sees all the way back to Easthillshireborough-upon-Flats." He clicked his tongue, a parent disapproving of a mischievous child. "Made a mess of that place, they have. Shame, really. Hope that fire doesn't reach the Hospital."

I felt my heart seize in my chest. Lies? Horrible, manipulative lies? *How would I ever know?*

"Like I said before, you'll do what I wish," he went on, "because I have in my possession the Tome of the Precious Lore."

My mind ground to a halt, not daring to compose a single thought until he said something else, or did something, or *something*.

I could have stood there for an hour in permanent stand-by—but luckily he turned to me after a moment, holding a book in his hands. It was smaller than I might have expected, but clearly heavy, and so musty-smelling it *must* be important. (Get it?)

On its cover was a well-worn engraving of a worm falling in love with a plate of spaghetti. Surely this was the real Tome.

"So what do you need me to do?" I asked. "Kill Countess Peapoddy? Because I can do that—just bring her fat face down to me, and I'll take care of that for you right away, no problem."

He laughed, a cackle that sounded some-what like two cats wrestling in a bed of dry leaves. "Capital! *That* would be a sight. No, sadly my alliance with the Countess runs deeper than the affairs in which you currently wade. It's much simpler than that—there's a train that leaves here at dawn, and you can take that on to Dublin or London, and from there catch whatever transport you like back to Easthillshireborough-upon-Flats, or wherever you like," he said. "And really, you're surprisingly close with your suggestion."

With great strides he crossed the room, and shone his lantern into a far corner—where Rikah lay bound and unconscious upon the floor.

"All you have to do is kill her for me," he said, "and the Tome is yours."

63: A STRUGGLE.

R IKAH'S HANDS WERE BOUND WITH rough rope, the same sort that encircled my own wrists like unshaven humus-worms, except inert, not eating away at decomposing flesh the way humus-worms love to do. (Great pets, those, and handy in my avocation.)

With the quick stroke of some sort of glassy blade, the man cut my arms free—then, before I could so much as rub my scuffed skin, he pressed the hilt of the blade into my hands.

But it was no blade at all—rather a long, thin piece of light-green glass, cloudier than the jade I'd seen in the cavern outside, but *similar* to that stone in some niggling respect I couldn't quite identify—I was no vibrologist (three credits short of a vocational certificate), so I couldn't tell if it resonated at the same ætherial frequency or some other such malarkey nonsense, but it still struck me as somehow the *same.*

The shard was also sharp, and it was this property that inspired me to aim its narrow edge at the man with the lantern.

He made no sign of fear. "Go ahead, all you like," the man said. "Yam-Runners are immune to jade-stabs. Eugenic predisposition— and you can't argue with Nature, now, can you?"

Drat it all! My plan—namely, stab the man and run—was unraveling faster than it had raveled itself brilliantly just a moment ago. I looked over at Rikah, sprawled on the rock-hewn floor in what was likely an uncomfortable position. She'd have a crick in her neck when she awoke. *If* she awoke.

"What happened to her?" I asked, walking over and taking the liberty to kneel by her side, noting a gash on her forehead, another on her rosy cheek. My own cheek pulsed with pulverised flesh— she and I were cheek-wound buddies, at least. For whatever *that* was worth (tuppence at the fair-grounds, back before the labour-inspectors moved in and bolloxed the whole operation).

The man sighed, fingering the rows of glass cylinders set—nay, *crammed*—into the cavern walls like so many giant drinking-straws. "She tried to run for it—you can see for yourself if you like," he said, drawing a thin bar of glass—a light-jar—from its sconce and handing it to me, even obligingly lifting his lantern to illuminate the scene within.

I stood, set my eye to one end of the bar, and dared not wonder what dreadful scene might unfold: had she but fallen? Had they struck her? Had they struck *me,* knocked me out, then used my fists to batter her senseless?

Flickering images within the glass told the tale: I watched a devilishly-handsome figure crumple, smote by the e'er-unfashionable Yam-Runners—then saw Rikah turn and run, abandoning what could only have been *my* body to the fiends. They left me and gave chase, and though the figures grew smaller, their silhouettes were clearly described against that bright green finger of light, reaching to the clouds from Grenadine's cave.

In a shadow reflected on the clouds, I saw her driven against that brilliant stone by a cruel Yam-Runner blow. The green beam shuddered and faded, and all within the light-jar turned to darkness.

I lowered the glass.

"Where she sought to find sanctuary, she found only pain," the man explained. "Such is the lot of the Shorelanders. They threw in their lot with my brother Grenadine, and his false teachings have led them blindly, gropingly to their doom. You have seen the consequence of their sad belief, made manifest this evening."

"You mean the destruction of their village."

"We are indebted to you for the part you have played in our victory," he smiled. "Even now, the Countess' air-ships scour the ash-heaps of the Shorelands to finish off any survivors. It will not be long before *she*"—a jab at Rikah—"is the last of their kind entirely. A problem we can solve right here, right now, with the shard from Grenadine's jade, there in your hands."

He might have said more, but I was fixed on the idea of *survivors* in the ash-heaps—surely it couldn't be! Rikah and I had watched the lightning-barrage reduce the entire village to charcoal! Still, a well-spring of hope sprouted deep in my rib-meat: perhaps there *were* some Shorelanders remaining, and perhaps they had seen the jade beacon-light—and perhaps they would mount a resistance. The jade beacon itself was shattered—I held the proof in my hand—but perhaps those brave, remaining few were nonetheless clambering up the mountain as we spoke, organising themselves into a rough-shod militia, carving spears and the like from branches and mud-logs, possibly even now constructing make-shift trebuchets and wind-gliders to fight for their noble lives against the Countess' vile aero-machines. Hardy people, and pure of spirit all; I swelled my breast with the decision that I would stand by their cause to the end.

Then the man opened the front cover of the Tome of the Precious Lore, and I caught a whiff of old book-dust: it was the sort of odour that in past years had made me gag, or enraged me, or thrown me into hair-trigger fits of unconscionable violence with dire consequences for all within flame-thrower range. At the first nose of that stuff, I felt ancient chords of homicide begin to thrum within me, and heard a voice in my head plead in harmony with that building melody: *What do you care about these people? Take the Tome and run back home—or at the very least, get on that train. Get away from here while you yet breathe.*

It wasn't a voice inside me—it was the man, speaking aloud.

"I could kill you easily," he said with a shrug. "I could kill *her* easily. But I have no quarrel with you—you have played an instrumental part in our war-fare this evening, and we are, as I've said, indebted for your service.

"Thus, I make the offer once more: you must kill the last Shorelander. In return, you may have the Tome, and passage on our yam-train safely away from this place of grim death. For there are grimmer times to come here, I promise you."

The cavern rumbled and the thousand light-jars tinkled softly, like wind-chimes in the barest zephyr of spring-time, or a baby just learning to make bad-water. "There's the dawn-train arriving," the man added, his voice echoing across the chamber. "It leaves the station once the sun crests the horizon—and when it goes, it takes with it my offer."

I searched the shard in my hands. Its corners pierced my palms; beads of dark red appeared where jade met skin—but I felt nothing except a sinking, cold sensation in my feet and a bit of itchiness about the collar where I'd been sweating. Even the pain in my face had dulled to a background throb as I contemplated the instrument.

I had murdered before; it had even been my hobby. And it had always been so easy.

Besides, came a voice that I triple-checked to ensure was actually coming from within my skull, *you can heal her. With the Tome. You don't have to kill her—just draw blood. Proclaim her dead. Secure the Tome—then you can find a way to heal her.*

The argument was apparently convincing enough to my feet that they made their way to Rikah; I watched my hands carefully turn her over. In my stupour I barely registered the velvet softness of her shoulders beneath her tunic. I watched from outside my body, as my fingers fished Ursula's opticle from my vest-pocket and tucked it secretly into Rikah's clenched palm.

"Use this to go back home," my mouth whispered to her. "Find your way back to the village. Before the sunlight erases the paths."

Her eye-lids stirred, and I froze: she was awakening. "Did you hear me?" I hissed. "The opticle. It shows you the path back home. I can get you out of here—but for now you'll have to trust me." I raised the jade to draw her blood, and her eyes went wide.

"I *knew* it!" she said. "From the moment I first saw you at the banquet—I sensed the presence of evil on this island. You've done nothing but bring misery to me and my people. So *go ahead,* you horrible beast. May you rot forever in the Hell reserved for... for people as bad as you."

"No!" I whispered. "I'm doing this to *help* you!" I snuck a glance back at the man, across the chamber. Was it my imagination, or was it growing lighter in here? The dawn was approaching!

"I don't want any more of your *help*," she spat.

"You have to trust me," I whispered, lifting the jade slowly.

"Send me to my Morty," those beautiful lips snarled at me.

I drove the dagger into her throat.

Blood burbled rapidly from the wound. I quickly pulled up my sleeves, to avoid any unsightly stains on my upcoming train-voyage. I wondered if Paco would have time to give me a shampoo before I left. My hair was getting greasy.

I looked down as something tickled my fore-arm: Rikah's finger-tip. She gasped for breath, spitting blood and sucking deeply at nothing at all, and it seemed that she had something to say—so I pulled the jade from her throat and allowed her a moment to gargle. "Je...jellah..." she croaked.

"Jealous?" I said. "Of *Morty? Me?* The man's an *oaf*—don't be *absurd*," I shrieked perhaps louder than necessary, and my voice cracked, which was a little embarrassing in itself.

"Jelly...fish," she sighed.

Her finger touched the scars on my arm from the jelly-fish stings I'd suffered my first day on the island.

"Gren...Grenadine," she whispered. "It's you. I'm sorry. I...I failed your test."

She recognised me—rather, she recognised the person I had pretended to be. "No, you, ah, passed," I said lamely. "You did smashingly okay."

She shook her head. "I am failing this test as well," she breathed, as the muscles in her neck softened and her head fell with a solid-sounding *crack* onto the stone floor.

A burst of orange sunlight spilled through the million tiny cracks between the thousand light-jars, the dawn splashing rainbows of prismatic color across the brown cavern floor, over Rikah, and over my blood-soaked hands.

We...cannot...READ! my mind reminded my body, speaking slowly so it would be understood. *How could we* possibly *have used the Tome to heal her?*

"Is the Tome mostly pictures?" I ventured, calling across the room.

The man shook his head as he offered me a towel. "Sorry."

I stood, slowly, and wiped my hands with the towel. The blood streaked and smeared, but didn't come entirely off. I blotted my skin as best I could, then handed the towel back

"Keep it," he said.

Then he handed me a wicker basket containing two more things: The Tome. And one single yam. My train-ticket.

I placed the dagger in the basket —why not?—and looked at the brightening sky through the cracks in the cavern walls. Countess Peapoddy still hovered up there, I knew. But I had the Tome now, and a way home. This was no longer my fight.

I extended a hand to the man to shake. He wouldn't get out of this affair without some blood on his hands.

He hesitated, but did shake my hand. His grip was terribly strong. He probably would have kicked my arse so bad my great-aunt Lindy would have crapped boot-laces for a week. I was doing the right thing by going peaceably.

"Oop," he yelped, yanking his hand back as a bead of his own bright red blood seeped from his finger-tip. He picked at the cut with a finger-nail—and flicked off a tiny triangle of green. A chip from the jade—it must have flaked off in my hands.

He *wasn't* immune, after all. I could have stabbed him.

I could *still* stab him.

He looked up at me for a single moment, utterly frantic, as if he were afraid I might already have the dagger in my hand. "You'd better run," he said. "Right now. Out this door, then straight down the stairs. All the way down to the bottom. Can't miss it. Go! This second!"

He wasn't lying—the train's whistle rang faintly, far-off, echoing inside the mountain. I had no time.

But at the doorway, I turned back, just for a second. "I don't even know your name," I said.

"That's okay," he replied. "Trust me. If your destiny lay here, on the Isle of Yam-Runners—you would."

"Sissy answer," I said.

He smiled. "Larcenic," he said. "They call me Larcenic the Lithe."

64: BOUND FOR ELSE-WHERE.

ANY CONSTABLE WORTH HIS PEPPER would have been able to glean my identity from the deep, anxious finger-prints gouged into my ticket-yam, so hard did I squeeze that starchy tuber. I wondered: *would* I have to answer to constables anytime soon? *Were* there any survivors of the Countess' fearsome bombardment? And perhaps most importantly in the present moment: was the train itself susceptible to aquatic merman attacks?

The train-whistle seemed far-off—as if the engine were a hundred cars ahead, instead of merely three-and-a-coal-car-staffed-by-surly-munchkins-with-grimy-sneers-and-a-bad-union. With a shuddering lurch, the car began to move.

I expected the train to burst into dawning sunlight, I suppose, but the blackness through the windows remained unchanged even as the sound of dense rock around us gave way to a hollower gurgle, accompanied by a sudden pressure-shift about the ear-drums. I had heard of this phenomenon before—the Peruvians called it 'gnome-bobbing,' and it was supposedly caused by tiny men swimming back and forth in the ear-canal. It was a constant problem in the heights of the Andes, where apparently they had quite an infestation of tiny

ear-men, though I couldn't explain its occurrence at this severe
depth. Regardless, I plugged my ears with my fingers and began to
softly sing in Ancient Andean, as I had been instructed by gauchos
those many years ago.

A shadow fell heavily onto my lap, and I looked up to see Ursula
mouthing something. I let her speak for a while, then removed my
fingers from my ears: "What?"

"I said, it's a lovely song, 'tis," Ursula said, folding her tall
frame into the seat opposite and in front of mine, so she faced the
back of the rocking car. I looked away, paying great attention to the
featureless blackness perhaps passing by at great speed through
the window—it was impossible to tell, so I naturally assumed we
were moving at near the speed of smell.

In the seat next to me rested the wicker basket Larcenic had
given me. I saw Ursula craning her neck discreetly, trying to discern its contents—but I gave her no satisfaction, and said nothing
about it. She'd used me, and tried to kill me; I could let her peer
without volunteering what was in my basket.

"Headed back to Easthillshireborough-upon-Flats, then?" she
ventured, her voice high and trilling in what probably passed for a
pleasant conversational tone when you lived inside a mountain with
a bunch of anti-social vegetable-smugglers. "Shame what's become
of the place, since the violence broke out."

I shrugged, still staring at the darkness outside.

"We'll be in Dublin soon," she continued, "and from there you
can find over-water passage, I'm sure."

GENERAL SHERMAN'S BEES. [NATURAL SIZE.]
A, DRONE ; B, WORKER ; C, QUEEN.

"What*ever,*" I said to the window.

"Ah," she said. "So I take it you've seen the jade, then?"

I bristled at the word *jade*. My eyes flashed to the dagger—safe in the basket next to the Tome of the Precious Lore. An instrument of murder and an instrument of healing, bumping gently together in this jostling passenger-car. The worm on the Tome's cover seemed so happy that a burning rage begin to fester in my gut.

Presumed instrument of healing, I reminded myself. I hoped I would be able to somehow use it to heal Lara, back in her hospital bed. Given the chance, minutes ago, I had not used it to heal Rikah. It would be no good to that worm, either, no matter *how* much he loved that spaghetti.

Just like Grenadine never healed anyone, I thought. Slowly, I picked up the frail book and opened the cover. The text looked strange to my eye—swooshy, hand-written, with delicate line-work clearly laid down painstakingly by someone with too much time on their hands—and I wondered how anyone could possibly remember what all those letters were supposed to *mean*.

"You're holding it upside-down," Ursula said softly.

I glared at her. "I know."

"It's a great read," she shrugged. "Inventive, subversive. Pity, really—Grenadine could have made a lot of money. But the series never really caught on, once the Church got wind, naturally. Those kill-joys really know how to destroy a franchise."

She must have read my baffled expression, because she added: "You *haven't* seen the jade, have you?"

A buzzing electric lantern ensconced on the car's wall provided a good light-source for me to examine the shard. It was milky white along the side where it had sheared from the massive stone in Grenadine's cave, but its rounded edge was smooth and glossy green. "Just hold it to my eye?" I asked.

"Jade holds light far longer than glass," Ursula nodded. "You're looking back decades, at least—who *knows* how long?"

After a few seconds of adjusting the jade to the light, a faint, ghost-like picture began to appear—a figure moving within the

stone as if sluggishly trapped in amber. The image was fragmented
and blurry, but soon I was able to discern a cave-like environment.
The figure's features were indistinct, but something about the way
he moved seemed familiar to me—sinewy, determined. Annoyed.
"Is it Grenadine?" I breathed.

"Of course."

"He's writing," I said. "He's...he's placing a book on a shelf.
Stretching. Now...going to sleep?"

"Let me just spell it out for you," Ursula said. "Grenadine wrote
the Tome of the Precious Lore. In an afternoon. As *fiction*."

No—that wasn't right at all. Public education on the island
really *was* awful. I racked my brain for the names of the authors
Peapoddy had described to me, those many months ago..."Rubidarch
and Mouseketeer? And Plaxus the Unwise? *They* wrote the books,
I thought. *Ages* ago. *Centuries.*"

"Inventions and pen names," Ursula said. "Grenadine actually
wrote ten books in the series. He figured they'd sell better labeled
as non-fiction. The Tome of the Cowering Sigil was first, then Precious Lore, of course. Back in the mountain we've got a few of the
others—Tome of the Jealous Rainbow; Tome of the Slippery Sandwich; Tome of the Dried-Up Turkey-Leg; Tome of the Intractable
Grass-Stain. He, ah, started to run out of steam after the first
couple."

My mouth was suddenly dry, and I tried to lick my lips but my
tongue felt like a snail reluctant to emerge from its fragile shell.
Afraid of salt, perhaps? Metaphorically?

"And Peapoddy?" I croaked. "He believed...?"

Ursula shook her head sadly. "Old Man P fell for the whole
thing hook, line and sinker," she said. "All you know is what you've
been told, remember? His wife—the Countess—never did believe
it, and managed to convince her kin to hate Grenadine as much as
she does, which is probably why we Yam-Runners get on with her
so well. But Peapoddy the Younger—well, when you're raised with
a belief, especially by your old man, you can never really shake it
from your deep-down."

"Like you, and the tree-line," I said. "There's nothing enchanted about the tree-line on the island. You could go past it any time, if you wanted to."

She frowned. "That seems unlikely, or we'd have killed the Mayor and the towns-folk years ago," she said. When she saw my sour expression she laughed. "Look at you! So sad! You're a hero, don't you realise? You killed Grenadine. The fraud! The faker! You set that right! And then—you drew all those sick people to the island, kept them all in one place, and delivered the signal so we could exterminate them all. You *have* healed them, in a way! You've healed the *island*, at least. A far better sight than Grenadine could ever have done, or ever did."

I suddenly felt ill. I had no love for the miserable, ailing whiners that had flocked to the Isle in search of a get-out-of-sickness-free card from Old Man Grenadine—but to be *lauded* for the horrible act of mass murder from above?

There was no joy, no *sport* about that at all! No rascally *rebellion!*

And, of course, Rikah. I had thought I would, at worst, trade her life for my sweet Lara's. I told myself that she welcomed death, pining as she was for that oafy Morty. But now...

Perhaps she could have loved me, in time. I would never know.

"So, are you still going back home?" Ursula asked. "To Easthillshireborough-upon-Flats?"

"Not really interested in talking right now," I told the roof of the passenger-car.

I'd felt this sort of energy before, back in Peru, or in rakish Beloochistan, or at a restaurant trying to figure if I could make it home to the water-closet or if I should use the nasty facilities there. It was a cross-roads time. With my manor in ashes, there was little point in returning to Waverly Hill now—if the Tome was a story-book, it meant my Lara was as good as dead, if not already dead months ago.

My yam bought me passage all the way through the end of the rail-line—Gibraltar was the last stop—and what would stop me from just riding all the way there? Further, what business was it of Ursula's? Further, why talk when we could sit in stony silence just as easily?

"I happen to be heading to Easthillshireborough-upon-Flats, myself," she said. "At Countess Peapoddy's personal request."

That got my attention. "What business has she there?" I snapped. "Going to burn the place to the ground?"

"She's going to quell the riots. You shouldn't be so judgmental," Ursula said. She fished in her pocket and retrieved a glass lens the size and shape of a hockey-puck, even etched with the official NHL logo. I'd seen it before, back on the mountain-side—it was the light-filter that made the ocean disappear.

"If you were to take this on a boat," she said, "and peer over the side—it's like you're flying. You can see all the way to the bottom. Nothing's in-between."

A faint shaft of light zipped past the blackness outside the window—suddenly I was reminded that we were actually moving forward at blinding speed.

"You see everything underneath you," Ursula went on. "You see dolphins, and fish. Canyons, and ship-wrecks. Bodies, sometimes. Skeletons of sailors, taken by the sea. With the sea removed, they lie there, un-buried, sunlight striking their bones."

She leaned close, and placed her hands on both my knees. She didn't speak until I looked her directly in the eye.

"There are more skeletons in the world than breathing men," she said. "None of us will ever be a worse killer than Time herself."

My heart was suddenly obnoxiously loud. Ursula had found the volume control somewhere, and cranked it up to 12.

"Come with me," she said. "Come back home. We can bring order to your city. I can help you. We can make it over the way you would want it to be."

Ursula's fingers pinched my knees. My hands clapped over hers, and she twisted her wrists to inter-twine her fingers with my own. Our palms were slick together with sweat.

I had been so taken with her size and odd clothing that I had never noticed how attractive Ursula really was, up close.

This was a bad idea. I should get up, shake it off, leave. I should keep the Tome, learn to read, maybe, see for myself if anything she said was even true. Otherwise, all we know is what we're told, right?

But I could rebuild. I could have servants again. I could be in control of everything, just the way I liked it. I could be happy again, and she would help me do it.

And then, when I was powerful enough, I would get rid of her, and Countess Peapoddy, and everyone else who had crossed me. I just had to play along for a little while, and I could clamber right back on top.

She leaned closer, and her lips brushed my ear as she whispered: "I can make you King of that place."

"I get a man-servant," I said. "As soon as we get off the train. A proper estate as soon as practicable. And *I* do all the clothes-shopping."

"Done," she breathed.

I don't even remember telling my body to kiss her.

Nine months pass.

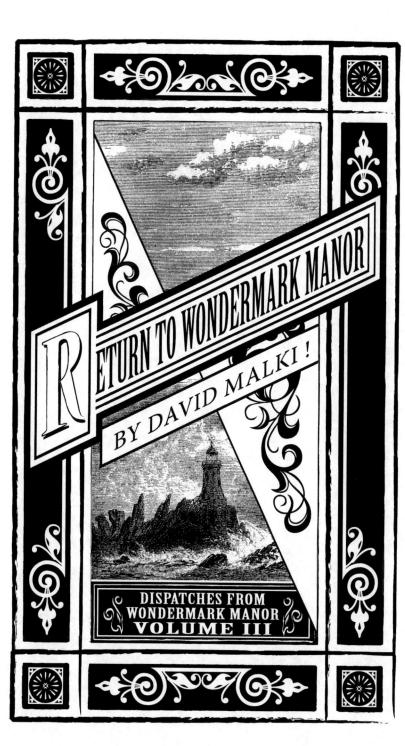

RETURN TO WONDERMARK MANOR

BY DAVID MALKI !

DISPATCHES FROM WONDERMARK MANOR
VOLUME III

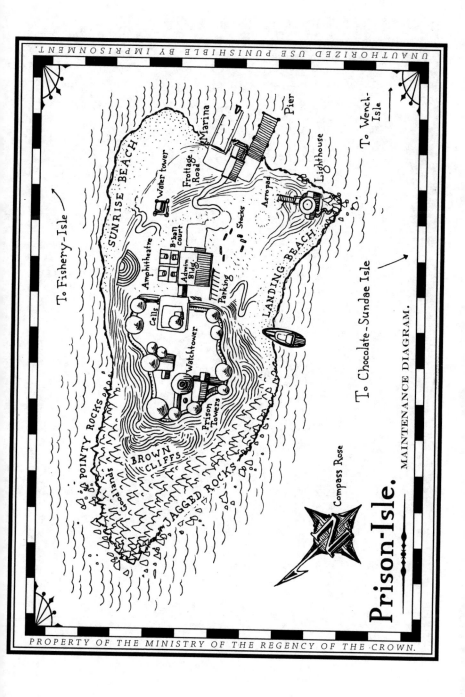

AS MAURICIO HEAVED HIS FINAL BREATH, THE
SPIRIT LEAPT FOR HIS JUNK.—[PAGE 917.]

65: THE BON-MOT GALA.

WE MOVED QUICKLY THROUGH LONDON'S crowded boulevards and cramped alley-ways, the clatter of our chariot's wheels on filth-encrusted cobblestones like a thrumping rumba beat from a Casio key-board's 'demonstration mode'. I had owned one of those enchanted Oriental music-pianos once, long ago in another life—now its tonnes of pipes and pulleys and coal-fired synthesizer-sprockets reduced, like the rest of my past, to a muddy mixture of figurative and literal ashes.

The beat stumbled—I whipped Thigton by reflex.

"Faster!" I cried to the imp-man who threaded our rick-shaw 'twixt poor-folk dung-heaps and the dung-heaps of the nobler class. Thigton suffered the blow with a dignified moan—any yelping squeal would no better communicate his pain, and would merely embarrass us both—and redoubled his pace. He was a competent valet in most respects (if a bit squeamish before the branding-iron) but at this—running through London's stinking streets, pulling Ursula and me in a two-wheeled cart made of birch-wood and lead—he was without living peer. His predecessor, a thick-waisted stevedore named Bumbercraps, had been equally fleet of foot but had proven to have a rather pitiful pain-tolerance. Thigton took the blows I dealt with dignity; in fact I suspected the man to be a fetishist, which, if it made him more competent at his becharged duties, I was fine with. I was open-minded like that.

Ursula took my hand in her bear-like paw. She was a tall woman, stout of limb and poor of fashion-sense in the Yam-Runner way, who seemed to choose her day's wardrobe with eyes closed tightly shut against the distant chance of finding any article of clothing that remotely matched any other that she owned. It was *this* characteristic that drew the most stares and whispers from London's street-sooted gawkers, but she was self-conscious about her size as well. If I cared, I would tell her that the card-gallery and opium-den nick-names for her were "Steam-Sheet" (after the billowing character of one particular dress) and "Shoe-Bomber" (after a particularly ill-chosen pair of flamingo-skin loafers), *not* "Giraffe-Wench" or "Crazy-Mac-Crane-Head" or "Yo That Is One Massive Frickin' Mama" or any other common slur heard spat from the gruel-blasted throats of school-yard punks and their mud-flecked orphan contemporaries. Usually when they said that they were referring to the jolly orange statue the French had just pranked the big-britched colonials with, or HM the Queen.

Ursula's sweaty grip dwarfed my delicate, manicured fingers. Her skin was coarse and labour-thick'd, while I had recently gone to considerable expense to have my hands de-roughed and restored to the natural, buttery-silk texture of God's own meat-hooks. (Assuming, of course, that the Father hadn't done all that "sculpting Man from dust and clay" business *manually*.) Ursula's touch reminded me of a life of less comfort than I currently enjoyed: a mean one of hard-ship and loss, where every selfish act had blasted *consequences*. It was a life I had been happy to leave behind, but if Thigton didn't get a *move* on, it would be one I would have to return to all too soon.

We rounded a corner and there, across Cobbling-Balls Square, was the theatre—I could make out the shapes of expensive carriages and at least one peanut-oil auto-car. This was a Society event, to be sure—but I detected neither top-hatted fuss-budgets nor preening man-servants alighting the famed steps of the Puddingpop Theatre. The ceremony must have already started—I feared we were already too late.

Without needing to be told, Thigton drew upon some still-deeper well of rick-shaw-pulling energy and powered us across the rabble-strewn square. I felt his gait transition from a run to a gallop, and knew his intentions instantly.

"Smashing idea!" I cooed, and made myself ready for the coming manoeuvre—first extricating my hand from Ursula's, then doing everything else I needed to do to get ready.

Ursula shook her head, bracing herself against the sides of the rick-shaw. "No, no, no, no, no, no," she said—but her meaning wasn't clear. Was she opposing the technique to come (after seriously injuring herself the last three times Thigton had pulled this manoeuvre off, she was *due* for a success), or simply rejecting some series of objections she might have? I reached up to the chariot's cloth roof and folded the frame down and away, bringing the harsh moon-light into direct contact with our tender faces. Or *my* tender face anyhow—Ursula's somewhat resembled a de-tenderised strip of buffalo-beef, salted and cured in a meat-bin behind a slaughter-farm. (That is to say, hearty and nourishing.)

Thigton's shoulders twitched in a deliberate sequence: five tenses of those ropy muscles, then three, then two...the count-down was a rather new development I'd taught the lad, after his prior tendency to simply launch into the manoeuvre *sans* warning had left a certain *success* to be desired. I set my hat on the seat, flexed my knees, and Thigton kicked backward and flattened.

The rick-shaw lurched, and Thigton pressed his whole impish weight into the pull-bar, laying the seat-bits' fore-edge across his arched back and pulling forwards and down. The rear part of the chariot thusly launched upwards, and I shoved off powerfully as Ursula and I were propelled into the cool night air.

For a moment we were flying, the Theatre's steps drawing closer each second, and then we were *there*—I tucked in my chin and rolled smoothly across the marble portico, springing to my feet and assuming a most dignified expression for the benefit of on-lookers. Ursula smashed into the floor and careened across the porch wildly, bowling over two ushers and the Duchess of Corn-Hash, whose tedious garden-functions we'd presumably be spared from attending now.

"Dear me, sir, may I enquire..." The head usher was a gelatinous man with what seemed to be a permanently aghast expression; at least so far that's all I'd seen out of the chap. I cut him off with a stern wave and my usual air of awesomicity.

"No time to lose," I growled. He gulped down his protest—I was *that* good. "Has the awards ceremony started yet? The Bon-Mot gala?"

"I—er, that is to say, we've—er, yes, the, ah, the first presenters are just going on now," he burbled, clearly no contender for a trophy himself. The Bon-Mot gala was an aristocratic tradition honouring the year's best quips, snide asides, and clever turns-of-phrase uttered by the snooty set during the previous year. I was surely in the running for next year's prizes—reference previously-heralded awesomicity—but Ursula and I'd only arrived in London a scant three months ago; not enough time to be eligible, but more than enough to learn of a dastardly murder plot to unfold here, this very night.

"It's an emergency," I barked at the usher. "A *killer* lurks within!" This elicited only more stammers from the usher—evidently this sort of thing hadn't been covered in the employee primer. I pushed him aside and made for the doors to the theatre.

"You can't go in there!" he finally huffed, having found his tongue beneath a quivering mass of jellied cowardice, striding to

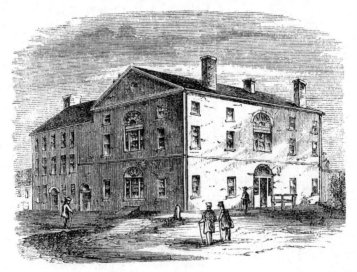

A TRACT MANOR.

intercept me. Applause was beginning to grow from behind the doors—there was no time to lose.

Ursula intercepted *him*, laying massive hands on his shoulders, his feet suddenly swishing along the marble without bearing him forward. "Go on," she nodded. "He'll stay here."

"So I shall," the usher squeaked, which wasn't a bad rejoinder on short notice. I turned and pushed through the theatre doors, a murder-plot to stifle—or, if I failed, a murder to watch.

I entered amid a standing ovation. Despite (probably) not being its intended honoree, I was glad of't—the bumptious whooping served nicely to mask my impertinent ingress. I had to exercise a certain measure of discretion with my investigation; if I simply announced that there was a murderer in the building, chaos would result and the vile plotter could easily escape. Thus I decided against making any loud cries of alarm or shrieks of "Fire"—but don't think I wasn't tempted, just for the adrenaline rush.

I surveyed the roomography of the room: above and to each side were balconies and private viewing-boxes; presumably the target—one Field-Admiral Richey, of considerable esteem and renown from his exploits in the Crown's African colonies—was in one of them. But which? I had no way of knowing. I could yell "Zulu attack!" and listen for a disturbed yelp, but that still had the potential to cause more problems than it would solve.

As the applause died down and the audience groped for their seats, exhausted from the exertion of lavishing one another with praise, I spied Police Detective Amoson not far down the aisle. He'd chosen a seat near the back with easy access to the exit, presumably in case of trouble—and, well, there was going to be trouble. He was a gawker, though, always interested in gossip and tabloid trivia; I knew how keenly he yearned to be a part of the capital-S Society goings-on, so it would be no easy task to divert his attention from the ceremony.

Added to this challenge was a creeping dread that seized me as I approached a man of the law. Amoson had never wronged me personally, or at least not yet—too eager to fit in with the noble classes, he turned a convenient blind eye to some of our more, er, *storied* excesses. But his acquiescence did nothing to erase the mis-treatment I had suffered at the hands of that villain Peapoddy, now thankfully dead but once a deputized, handcuff-toting Special Investigator in Easthillshireborough-upon-Flats—the riot-besieged city to which I would certainly have to return if tonight's assassin succeeded in dis-aliving old Field-Admiral Richey.

"Our next presenter was last year's honoree for Best Quip or Zinger in the Context of Church," someone announced from the stage—a quick glance confirmed that they'd hired that tiresome suck-up Carlton Rube to host the event again this year. Never at a loss for a chewy pun or groanish riddle, he was the sort of nuisance that everyone though they *themselves* were too sophisticated for but that surely their less-cultured peers would simply *love*. This pluralistic ignorance had sustained Carlton's career for some decades now—any moment, he was going to whip out his shop-worn impression of George III, whom our grand-parents may have barely remembered.

And *there* it was! The audience tittered politely and conde-scendingly. Police Detective Amoson laughed, probably because he thought he should. On this very sentiment of obligation had Carl-ton's many grubby children long been fed.

"Detective, would you come with me please?" Amoson looked surprised, then put-out, then reluctant, then guilty, but finally agreed. Soon we were whispering in a secluded alcove near a rear door.

"There is a murderer in the theatre tonight," I hissed. "His target is Field-Admiral Richey. Do you know where the admiral is seated?"

"I, er..." Amoson stammered, clearly feeling pressured to rise to the level of repartée expected of attendants of tonight's occasion. "I don't know the admiral, I'm afraid. Haven't had the pleasure of shaking his sailing-hand." Amoson was bad at banter.

I let it pass. "We've got to find him, or flush the murderer out some-how. What if you search the East wing of view-boxes, and I'll start on the West—"

"Better yet," Amoson beamed, face lighting like a waif who's been told he'll be entered into a lottery for the chance to eat unspoilt food one night this week. "I'll make an announcement to the crowd. Something witty—asking the Field Admiral to take a bow, or something. Get it? *Bow?* Like a ship? With such attention focused on the admiral, there's no way the killer would strike."

It was a dumb plan, but it was one he was already aboard, and we were running out of time. "Fine. I'll wait on the mezzanine— maybe the killer will beat a hasty retreat from the balcony and I'll be able to catch him."

"Capital," Amoson nodded, already clearly running through all the clever remarks he could bring to bear. As I headed up the stairs to the mezzanine, I hoped that he would simply say whatever he'd landed on by the time he reached the stage, and not dally about in the wings, trying to come up with the perfect clever phrase. If he did, I'd be waiting here all night.

I located the doors leading to each private balcony-box—behind one of which lurked the Field-Admiral and, potentially, his would-be killer. Were I to enter any one, I might miss a fleeting figure across the way—so I found a position in view of all, held my position, and waited for Amoson to make his announcement.

Ten minutes passed, and still the ceremony had yet to be interrupted. I cursed my decision to stay put, cursed my enlistment of a dilettante like Amoson in the first place, and fierily cursed my fiber-rich supper.

Finally, I could take no more waiting and simply entered the nearest balcony-box, opening the door softly and only wide enough to make out the figures within.

It was Lord Dunburton, Earl of Tostada, and his wife the Lady Tostada. On stage beyond them, Carlton was riffing on how peasants walked like *this,* but the bourgeoisie walked like *this.*

"THIS PLACE SMELLS LIKE SPITTLE."—[PAGE 740.]

"Someone really should get rid of that Carlton Rube," the Lady Tostada sighed. "What a tiresome bore."

"A canker on the crust of the Earth," her husband agreed. "Simply intolerable. The man should be put to death at once." Peering closer, I was just able to make out Amoson down by the stage steps, pacing and muttering to himself. *Come on, man!*

And then—the terrible explosion of a pistol-shot. Lady Tostada sat upright and craned her neck to see what was happening, fumbling with a pair of ornate opera glasses, while the Earl dove under his chair in an instant—"It's the Boers come for revenge," he choked. "Why did no one listen to my many rambling warnings?" The audience shrieked. Carlton stopped mid-joke to dive for cover. Amoson was lost from view, absorbed into a mob at once.

I ducked back from the balcony-box and out onto the mezzanine, running toward where the shot had originated—only to catch the barest glimpse of a shadow disappearing down a far-off stair-well. I made to give chase, but suddenly the Lady Richey was full in my path, covered in blood—

"He's dead," she sobbed, "he's dead."

My stomach sank. It was small consolation, but my first thought was that she certainly wouldn't be winning any Bon-Mots next year with *that* one.

66: THE TANGLE
YET TO COME.

RICHEY WAS MEAT, A HOLE IN HIS brain-case the size of a pygmy-apple, victim of a burst-ball to the back-hook of his neck-head. This was bad news for me. Oh, I didn't care for the man personally, nor for his politics, least of all for his self-important grand-standing at every blasted Dog Show and Farmers' Pretty-Pony Exhibition; the man took every opportunity to sell himself to on-lookers as the greatest military mind since Richard the Lion-heart, to what end I wasn't entirely sure—he *had* a post over-looking an entire city as a Crown's Regent, and could scarcely take on further responsibilities what with the trouble that had brewed under his watch. Always thinking of the next great post and looking for something better, I suppose he was; now he was looking at the carpet, his eyes mashed into red-soaked pile with heaps of squishy cognition-burger in great smears and mounds to every side, and I daresay he wasn't thinking about much anymore at all.

The Field-Admiral had been in London to attend the Bon-Mot gala, but he was actually stationed in Easthillshireborough-upon-Flats, the city from whence I had fled some months of adventure ago. Each afternoon as Ursula and I took in the city air for our constitutional (pulled along in the chariot by Thigton, of course), we heard rumours and fragmented reports from that city under siege. The reports were bad enough, but the *rumours* were down-right salacious—for who would have guessed that the long-suffering Viscount of Easthillshireborough-upon-Flats was actually a chimera, and that his homely grand-son would be our next pope?

After a while, such rumours began to contradict one another—the boy-who-would-be-pope could surely not simultaneously be the father of the half-buffalo, half-human infant discovered in a schoolteacher's chalk-cupboard—but I had been able to piece together a thin grain of truth in between the sensationalism. It seemed that the day I'd fled aboard Cap'n Narwhal's Dublin-bound *Flopsy Bunny* was the day that the oppressed classes had arisen to take the city by force. While I had been off on gallivanting escapades hunting for the Tome of the Precious Lore, rampaging mobs had laid the city half-way to ruin, three-quarters of the way to chaos, and a full fifth of the way to Life-Ending Apocalypse. The Crown's military brigades sent to restore order seemed, by the accounts that reached our plummy ears at least, to be the only tenuous thread lashing the city to anything resembling not-anarchy.

But now Richey, who had been the one fiercely grasping that tenuous thread 'twixt knotted thumb and fore-finger, was stiff and stinking. The perpetrator was unknown, but I knew what the response would be from whichever starched-shirt crony the Crown would appoint as Richey's successor: pull out the troops, seal the borders, and bomb the city into flat, steaming, barbecue-smelling rubble.

I had seen such things happen before.

Ursula came up behind me, stopping short when she saw the splash of crimson on the wall, not even wasting a glance for the man himself. "Oh," she said, cooing sadly as she was expected to, but I knew how she really felt. I briefly wondered if she or her Yam-Runners had ordered the murder themselves—but no, she would have told me of that.

Wouldn't she have?

She kept many secrets from me, and the few I had uncovered had been kind of gross (mucous-heavy genetic conditions and the like), so I didn't really pry much anymore.

What she *did* tell me was about matters such as

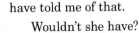
LOST MY KEYS SOMEWHERE AROUND HERE.

these—machinations, plots, conspiracies plotted and executed. She thought I was on her side. Hers, and that vile Peapoddy clan—I still treasured the memory of Peapoddy himself falling from the sky in great, burning gobs of fat and flesh. No matter how weak-willed this London life-style made me, I would never regret killing him, for I would never forgive him for the violence he did to my first and dearest love, Lara.

Poor, ankle-flashing Lara, of the Police Bureau back in East-hillshireborough-upon-Flats, of the chalk-white skin and the kind, dancing eyes. She was dead: between the terror in the city, and her serious injury, and the fact that I never returned to her comatose bed-side with the "mystical healing power" of the wretched Tome of the Precious Lore as I had hoped—it was too much. Ursula had sent discreet enquiries on my behalf, and the news that returned was sad but not altogether surprising. I had failed her.

Besides, there had been that maddening dream.

On the Isle of Yam-Runners, I had been visited by the spectres of many souls I had committed to the Hereafter. My uncle, whose manor in Easthillshireborough-upon-Flats I had gleefully resided in for several years after burying a hatchet in his skull, was there; so too was Peapoddy, a murder I will gladly take credit for no matter who shall ask; and so too, among that cadre, most disturbingly of all, was Lara—among the g-g-g-ghosts of the passed.

A dream! Nothing more, perhaps...but I then helped Peapoddy's mother, the equally-vile Countess, rain green sulphuric death onto a village of thousands of sickly pilgrims, and the acrid taste of that flesh-smoke had not yet washed itself from my sinuses. The bitter tang of mass-death welled up periodically in my throat on windy days, and I think I can almost smell the awfulness—invariably it turns out to be a bratwurst-seller or something, but still, it's plenty disturbing, and sometimes, in the small of the night, with every house on Sixpenny Row deeply asleep, I carefully consider almost learning to weep.

Whatever—Easthillshireborough-upon-Flats was a hell-hole, and the smouldering ashes of Uncle's old manor had already been razed and looted by scoundrels, I was sure. With Lara dead, there was no reason for me to ever return to that place. Right?

I was bad at convincing even myself.

A stabbingly-cold evening greeted us outside the theatre. Thigton waited patiently in the valet-lane with the chariot, while Ursula helped me down the front steps.

"Good show in there," she whispered into my ear. "Convincing performance, a nice touch with Amoson and that. I could have done without the tumble through the foyer, but all in all, you looked noble." Her wide hand on my elbow nestled closer into my side. "Commanding, even."

Her grip on my arm was firm, leading. Was I really so unsteady? "A shame he's dead," I said, trying to keep my voice even. Ursula had some strange allegiances, and she tended to assume my own matched hers, not always correctly.

She shrugged as Thigton helped her into the rick-shaw. "Paving the way," she said. "I expect to send the Countess the order before the week is out." She turned to me. "Well, come on, then, it's cold as a Komodo's hoohoo out here."

Indeed. My feet felt frozen to the cobblestones. The execrable Countess Peapoddy commanded a fearsome armada of air-ships armed with the most horrible, city-leveling weapons known—and she worked for cash on the barrel-head. In the past, in East-hillshireborough-upon-Flats and before, I'd kept my distance from authorities, royalists, and those with sabres clattering their medal-bedecked breasts; my kind were the affluent un-allied, whose money bought freedom from such authority. We flew no flags but our own, and that was fun because we got to design our own flags! Sadly, I was bad at it: my standard was a square of yellow flannel with my coat-of-arms represented by a glued-on mound of sequins. At least they were genuine Zanzibar blood sequins—I'd spared no expense.

But in three months of entertaining London's insufferable élite, I'd learned that they often spent their money as freely but much more deviously than my type—the same thrill afforded me

A RELATIVE OF THE MONARCHY.

by commissioning a marble statue of, say, Zeus mounting a pelican, would be afforded a Duke or a Count by hiring a gang of cut-throats to do mayhem to foreigners. These were people I could relate to, but only at a distance, from the far side of some type of jewelled sword, because they were dangerous and usually unstable. Worst of all, they always thought they were bloody brilliant.

"And where does the plan go from there?" I asked, falling heavily into the seat beside Ursula. "The Countess turns the city to an ash-heap. What happens then, once the place is uninhabitable?"

"Oh, my little cabbage. Sometimes I wonder about you." Ursula smiled as Thigton began to pick up speed. The cold evening breeze pulled red into her cheeks, and her eyes sparkled dark and orange in the passing gas-lights. "What the Crown wants destroyed, the Crown will want re-built. That's the whole point—to wash the filth off into the sea and build a new city, cleaner and better. One for ourselves." She leaned into me. "Keep my blood flowing, it's deathly chill out."

I had no fire within to keep myself warm, much less her. "Is that how Lord Dunburton got to where he is?" I asked. The Earl of Tostada lived in Bakersfieldshire, up the coast, and seemed to rule the place as a hybrid Emperor-King, by all reputable accounts.

"It's not hard to become a Crown's Regent," Ursula smiled. "It just takes being in the right place with the right tools at the right time, for the right reasons and in the right manner. And for us—Countess Peapoddy's armada happens to be the right tool."

"For you and the Yam-Runners," I reminded her. "You were coming to Easthillshireborough-upon-Flats before I even boarded that train."

"We're all in this together," she said, her head bowed and her voice muffled by the collar of my coat. "You keep trying to forget that."

As she leaned her weight into me and fell silent, I thought about Richey. Whatever party had wanted him dead must have known that his successor would simply turn the whole of Easthillshire-borough-upon-Flats to ashes; anyone who traveled in royalist circles knew that the admiral was a steadfast conservative among a council of belligerents. The finger of accusation pointed squarely at Ursula or one of her Yam-Runner, Peapoddy-allied cohorts, all   . of whom left a dreadful, coppery taste in my mouth that copious amounts of birch-rum had never been able to fully wash away, no matter how frequently and deliciously I tried.

The worst of it was that I knew from the moment I learned of the murder plot that these dominoes had long since been arranged to fall. As much as I hated the thought of returning to East-hillshireborough-upon-Flats—descending into the Third Circle, as it were—I had *known* that, should Richey die, I would find myself coming forward in the city's defence. There would be no other voice piping up to save the town from utter destruction.

What I couldn't quite pin-point in my mind was *why I cared* about the city. With Lara dead and my manor in ruins, and my vagrant friends the Kippers all dead at sea, the only occupants left were villains like the Chief Magistrate and strangers. I should welcome their destruction. In fact, in the case of the strangers, I'd in past put many of them to death myself; the Countess's method would simply be a more efficient way to the same end.

I'd had this argument with myself before, back on the Isle of Yam-Runners, running along dark mountain paths with the village-girl Rikah, watching her family and friends annihilated by a searing column of jade-green fire. I cared little for the citizens, and in fact held open contempt for the weeping and wailing sick-folk that had overrun the island in search of the healer I was impersonating at the time. (And what a time it had been.) Yet I'd felt *bad,* in that moment of flame. Perhaps there was some personal connexion at play: Rikah had been anguish-ificated beyond all sense, as women are wont in such circumstances—and finding her highly attractive, it had been hard to avoid the meagrest stirrings of something approaching empathy.

Then, in that cold night speeding through London, I finally hit on it: I didn't want a Peapoddy to *win.*

I *didn't* care for the people of Easthillshireborough-upon-Flats. I'd lived there for a few years, had a few laughs, and then left under horrible circumstances. The place could be swept away in a deluge, for all I cared—I'd even long since given up hope of getting my favourite boots back from Josiah's old crypt. *Those* tears were dry.

But the Peapoddys of the world—and their friends, the Yam-Runners, of which Ursula was one, I was constantly being reminded—had taken Lara from me. Then they had taken away Rikah. (Technically, she had died by my own hand. But a Yam-Runner had basically made me do it.) At every turn, they had played me for a tool. Ursula was probably trying to do so again—her Yammy bosses had put us up in a draughty old mansion on Sixpenny Row, and so I was sure they considered me on their pay-roll.

But I resolved only to play their game insofar as I could reach my own ends. I just hoped the rules of the game allowed it; there was nothing printed on the under-side of the box lid, because it was all a big metaphor.

Ursula was sleeping on my shoulder, or perhaps pretending to, as women are wont in such circumstances. I turned away from her, careful as always to play my true allegiances close to the vest, which was silken and felt nice to keep close to. It was a quiet assurance that I was doing this all right.

I spoke into the wind, knowing my words would be whipped away into oblivion at once.

"I won't let it happen," I told the air, and Ursula, at my side, shivered. ✦

67: A ROYAL COMMISSION.

THE NEXT FEW DAYS WENT MUCH AS I had anticipated, with a few key exceptions. The Crown's Regents held an emergency settee, ostensibly to settle the Richey issue but in truth to waggle their prodigious moustaches at one another in the third-fanciest dining room in London (the second-fanciest being previously engaged by a meeting of the Cossack Under-Sea Ballet Academy, and we wouldn't want to disturb *that*; the first-fanciest being the King's own water-closet, to which access was tightly restricted). It seemed that haughty, poorly-veiled moustache-comparisons always took up the first few hours of these types of meetings; a typical exchange between some-Baron-or-other and some-Duke-or-other would tend to go thusly:

Baron: "Dreadfully sorry for the late entrance—had quite the fright when it seemed my specialty whisker-pomade was exhausted. I tend to go through those tins so quickly, you know, as it's no use scrimping when I've gone to the trouble of procuring the finest Indian wax-creams."

Duke: "Indian? Oh, you do mean *Americas* Indian, don't you—I *did* think you were sporting quite the warrior-fashion, that clean-shaven look that's such a savage trend, I hear, across the Atlantic. Tell me, do you find the breeze much cooler in the evening, with such a bare lip as you have?"

Baron: "Bare? Why, this is six weeks' full growth, Sir, in the style passed along by the Barons of my line since the days of Charlemagne, a fine Dundrearies man himself," &c., &c., &c. Such arguments and comparisons could easily stretch for decades if not stopped by a firm hand on the gavel; it was this instrument that I found myself wielding at the gathering in question. In truth, it took every ounce of self-control within my straining muscles not to bury the little mallet in the fore-brains of all assembled.

But I had to think of the bigger picture: the portrait of Lord Keystroke above the dining-room's blazing hearth, stern as ever, looming over us mortals quite disapprovingly, that lazy eye following one everywhere throughout the chamber.

It was a bit of a marvel that I was allowed into the meeting at all—as a rather recent addition to London's Society gatherings, I had not yet finagled a massively over-paid Crown's Regent assignment to any minor village, nor any royal appointment at all if one discounted my brief stint as a bunion-grinder to a three-generations-removed Crown Prince. (We had had a few days to fend for ourselves in London before the first of the Yam-Runner money crossed the wire—Ursula spent the time picking dandelions in far-off meadows and extorting asthmatics for coins; I spent it with rasp and file, burnishing the crow-like claws of an inbred blue-blooded troglodyte. He tipped better than he thought, though—considering that he dozed off during our sessions and kept his purse within easy reach.)

In any event, the meeting of the Crown's Regents, like most of the Society gatherings that Ursula and I would deftly insert ourselves into, was not so much *attended* as *infiltrated.* So far as the door-man knew, I was an invited guest; Lord Such-and-Such presumed me a relative of some minor earl, while that same Earl took me for the valet of a foreign general. By turns I introduced myself as an Irish colonel, a last-minute replacement for a Welshman stuck in a bog, the last surviving son of William Wallace, and, in one memorable exchange, a rakish cheese-twirler from Beloochistan. Given my illustrious pedigree, then, no soul was surprised to see me take the podium and call the meeting to a brutish semblance of order.

"With Richey dead," I said plainly, "and his iron hand fallen from the lid of the simmering stew-pot of Easthillshireborough-upon-Flats, that town will surely be over-run by mobs within days, if it hasn't fallen already."

LORD OF THE REALM.

"Where *is* Eastellshaborough?" the Earl of G＿＿ interrupted, pudgy fingers raised as if tickling the under-belly of a soap-bubble. "Is it in the North at all? Anywhere near my peaceful village of Hamletshire? Need I be frightened that marauders might do violence to my prize-nominated livestock?"

"It's a port along the coast," I said. "A key importing depot that we must not allow—"

"Ah, then the Naval Brigades can clean up that mess," Count L＿＿ harrumphed. "Richey was always brooding and asking for hand-outs from the Treasury's coffers, yammering without end about more soldiers, more cannons, more this and that. It'll be nice to have that bothersome Eastellsha-whatever-it-is struck from the balance-books this year, what?" This was met with jowly nods and a chorus of murmured assent.

"The city is near collapse," I insisted. Whatever happened, I couldn't let them decide to write off the town and destroy it—for they'd hire the Peapoddy crew to do it, and I was determined to keep that vile family as far from these shores as possible. "Thousands of lives. Richey was tenuously maintaining order—we can seize the reins from his still-charging steed before it flies from the rails." Mixing metaphors would make me sound desperate. "In bed."

"Nonsense," said a new voice—a powerful tenor that could only be General Hap "Happy" Happydie of the infamous Happydie Infantry, the maddeningly-brave squad that had pushed back the front in every Imperial military engagement of the past twenty years. "Easthillshireborough-upon-Flats is a lost cause. Field-Admiral Richey was a determined fool, but a fool nonetheless. The insurgents in that devastated burg have cut through his defences like hot wire through a Turk, and the fact that he's dead today is no accident. If it weren't as bad as it is, he'd be alive to tell you so himself."

Sensing his opening, Happydie continued: "Here, as in the Congo, our only tactic remaining is to contain the damage—with a simple, targeted strike. Come, this is plain to all of us with battle-field experience and who aren't—like Richey—simply seeking hand-outs from the Treasury. How many sad stories did he plague us with? How many tear-speckled expense reports did he submit? Need more imported Champagne for the bunkers, Admiral?" The masses tittered.

"There are *monsters* in Easthillshireborough-upon-Flats!" I blurted. "Bat-creatures! Half man, half animal, half dragon of Hades. Half evil, half malice—bursting at the seams with ever-multiplying halves of terror." Finally, their attention! "They kill indiscriminately—men of avarice, men of God, it matters not to them." I pushed my sleeve up my arm, searching for a scar, any scar. "See here? Their claws rent my flesh. And here? Rug-burn from a buggering. *This* mark? Scaly-skin noogie. These beasts are *real,* and they must be stopped. Richey never mentioned them to you. And see how Richey died for his silence! I shall stay silent no longer!"

"If the halves are multiplying," ventured the Earl, "shouldn't they be down to quarters?"

"Silence, nerd," I bellowed. "I'm no man of maths, 'tis true. But I know my enemy—beasts of fire, borne from Judas' steaming offal itself. If you bathe that city in flame, you will marinate a bigger, larger, more horrifying creature than even those that roam the Easthillshireborough-upon-Flats country-side today!"

"Here now," Happydie interrupted. "The insurrection—"

"The dragons are *behind* the insurrection!" I shrieked. This was going well, now—I could see eyes white with terror all round. "They are provoking you to act. They *want* that fire from the heavens! For then they will rise up *stronger* than ever before, their veins running thick with white-hot hate, and they will take over this country *town* by *town*." I made sure to point to each Regent around the table as I dredged their territories from a roiling sea of adrenaline-drenched memory. "They will devour Hamletshire. They will move on to Grousington and Fresnoshire and Farting. They will lay waste to Bloopington and Wanker-on-Thames and Spittingford and Prang. Finally, they will come for *London*—and fat with the blood of you gits, there will be no stopping them. *Forever!*"

Thus, I secured my commission as Crown's Regent to Easthillshireborough-upon-Flats.

Within a day, Ursula and I had set off with Thigton and a few other effects to the harbour, her dark mood in tow. As our ferry began to progressively empty, shedding passengers in port after distant port, a hazy smudge on the horizon began to define itself into a cloud of sooty ash, and Ursula began to resemble it in disposition. "This is all backwards," she hissed. "You've made more work for us all."

"There's still some of Uncle's treasure hidden beneath the old Manor—and I couldn't bloody well tell that to the Regents, could I?" I hissed back. There was really no reason to be secretive; we were alone on the deck now, choking in the brownish air. No other passengers were foolhardy enough to travel this close to the damned city of dragons, or chimeræ, or half-buffalo-men, or whatever.

And lies were compounding on lies. The bat-creatures *were* a menace, to be certain; but they were *weak* against fire in truth, and a death-blast from Countess Peapoddy's air-ship would surely turn their colony to dust. The ruins of my Manor *did* sit on treasure, so long as 'treasure' was defined as great, wet gobs of seal-fat; the underground tunnels were surely slick with the stuff still.

And, of course, we had told Thigton that we loved him. Not true, and awkward besides.

My choices had been few. Deceit ran through my veins like alcohol, thinning my blood and numbing my fingertips. I blew into my hands. Ursula glared at me. I was doing something she didn't understand. She hated that.

"This's as far as I go, lads"—a cry echoed from below-decks as the ferry creaked to a slushing halt. Through the choking haze it was obvious why: the Easthillshireborough-upon-Flats harbour was thick with jutting wreckage: the shattered, rotting skeletons of a hundred half-sunken vessels, and probably more scary stuff beneath the surface as well. Before I could decide to press on, I saw that Thigton was already readying a dinghy—hey, maybe I *did* love that guy after all. A champ, he was.

And, of course, this meant that there was no turning back. The imp-man had lowered the dinghy. We were committed.

The water sat still and red. Thigton held the craft steady while Ursula made her shaky way down the ladder and settled heavily into its hollow. The awful town awaited us all.

Up top, I paid the ferry-man in pennies. On the day we oared our way into the city of death and weeping, it seemed only appropriate.

68: ASCENT TO WAVERLY.

THE HARBOUR REEKED OF CHAMBER-WASTE. As Thigton's strong, hobbity arms pulled oars through the foul sea, I kept watch for ship-wreck dangers and hidden under-sea obstacles; who knew if the water had been mined, or laced with psychedelics, or stocked for cod season, or what. We saw what was once a hopeful merchant-ship, listing and smelly, its optimistic, once-new wares ruined by the mere thought of this accursed place and also by millions of gallons of nasty water. We passed a poop-barge lashed to a rotting pier, its fly-infested cargo left to bake in the sun for lack of a crew to take it properly out to dumping-depth. We passed *sadness.*

As we neared the shore, smoke stung my throat; visible even from our low, dinghy-centric vantage point were trailing, smoky tendrils from a thousand barrel-fires and vandal-torches. Occasionally a far-off scream and the sounds of stabbing would punctuate the damp heat that settled like a muggy Welsh bull-frog atop the lungs; through the hazy air I could almost make out gangs roaming the street dressed as New York Yankees. The place was rough indeed.

We moored the dinghy without incident. Admiralty Way, once the thriving home to buskers and fraud-hustlers, peddlers and trash-vendors, crab-smashers and cheese-twirlers, sailors, sirens and those simply lost, was now a desolate ruin. It looked like a fire-brigade's burned-out training-course, or images I had seen of America—empty, charred, and decrepit. There seemed to be a weight in the air; the echoes of our footsteps died quickly, as if terrified and hiding, or else murdered as they ventured out too far—which it was I could not say, for anthropomorphizing *echoes* was a bit twee even for *my* rambling taste.

I glanced at a card in my hand, embossed with the ostentatious gold-foil crest of the Ministry of the Crown's Regents. Some engraver had slaved for weeks on the detail in that emblem, and the Regents used the cards typically for market-lists and the like, making sure everyone else in the greengrocer's saw the fancy *Crown's Regent* stationery. *Whoo,* aren't I a *special* fat little toadie to the King's second assistant's fourth squire's bum-wiper.

I'd been told that I would be met at the harbour by the Vice-Regent, someone named Major-Leftenant Tapiorca—but the wharf was empty, save for the sad, wisful wailing of the city's ten thousand whinging ghosts and an old dog.

"I wonder if he got the message to meet us," I mused aloud, not to anyone in particular except for Major-Leftenant Tapiorca, if for some reason he happened to be around and hiding.

"I think that *is* the message," Ursula answered, indicating the card. Typical Regency behaviour—sending a man to meet someone to give him the instructions for the initial meeting in the first place! It smacked of wackiness, which always (in my view) had a whiff of the sour-bottle about it any-haps, as no sober being would stoop to such very tommish of fooleries.

With no one to tell us different, we took possession of a wheel-cart once used for hauling bodies to the dumping-pier, spread a mostly-mild-smelling burlap over the most questionable of its lumpy stains, and Thigton pulled us into the city.

Aside from the constant, smoky burning, and brief glimpses of rats or children scurrying into rat-holes or children-holes respectively, the city was spookily quiet. It was as if a sand-castle had been abandoned by its sculptor and was now sliding slowly back into the tide, disintegrating parapet by parapet as it caught fire. I recognised certain shop-fronts and mercantiles, now brown-tinged with neglect and damage, their occupants likely dead or driven mad, their sale-coupons and gift-cards never to be honoured again.

Thigton pulled our cart steadily up the rutted road to Waverly Hill without being directed, never questioning where to aim our minor trolley of sadness. The truth was, I didn't know where the Regency headquarters even *was*, and if we would not make for the Manor, then wherefore should we make?

"Do you know where we're going?" Ursula asked after several dense minutes of cart-wheel crunching and perspiration-inducing proximity. Her voice had a snap in it that I knew from arguments past; she wasn't getting her way, she wasn't allowed to tell me what to do, and it made her twitchy and mean. It was her Yam-Runner temperament, a culture crafted by long centuries of pulling men's puppet-strings. "I don't see anyone around here. We should go back to the harbour."

"I know exactly where we're going," was my rejoinder, even affecting the great sighing patience of a correcting parent. "If the Major-whomever will be anywhere, he'll be on the high-ground. That's Waverly Hill." We passed underneath a bridge, and I pointed ahead for emphasis as we emerged into the light.

But any view of the hill was blocked by heaped wreckage of carts not unlike our own. Thigton stepped carefully to a halt and looked round tentatively—but our path was barricaded on all sides by splintered wood.

It was a constructed road-block, and it was manned.

At first they seemed like more wisps of smoke, moving softly and billowingly between the cart-carcasses. They were dressed in brown, like the air and the wood and the ground and everything, and they carried long sabres—Royal Battalion sabres, from the looks. But these were no Crown troops. They were the enemy, and they were mean-looking and dumb.

"Ho there," I called, and Ursula nearly soiled herself yanking down my hand as I hailed them with bold waving.

"What are you *doing,* get us *out* of here," she hissed. "We need to find the Major—we need to get back to the harbour—tell Thigton to turn us around!"

Rather, I stood on the shaky cart and spread my arms open. "What a nice welcoming committee. Tell me, who is the leader of your school? Bring him word that I have returned to Easthillshire-borough-upon-Flats." I would address them as Kippers, members of the ancient, shabby brother-hood of vagrants—should I be wrong, and they be foes of that clan, we would be no worse off than we were before, I reckoned, possibly in error.

The swordsmen passed weak looks to and fro, then retreated to converse in a patois of grunts and gurgles. Finally, one stepped forward, coughed up and spat a wad of quavering inside-juice, and pointed his sabre at us.

"The Crown sends a friend of the Kippers?" he growled. "You poesy-waisted tuna-humpers have always struck me as eager to snuggle to a Royal teat. We could do with a few less AWWWWGGHH—"

He stopped abruptly as a paving-stone struck him in the ankle—Thigston's blow, to take his eyes from me. I leapt from the cart and with a cobblestone chunk clutched tightly in my fist, carefully and precisely collapsed his face into marmalade. His untended sabre clattered to my feet, and before I could even bend to retrieve it, the others were gone—vanished into the rubble—fled.

The man gurgled as I pulled the scabbard from his belt, so I stepped on his wind-pipe to kink off the annoyance. Ursula, still in the cart, sat quaking, white as a North fog with fright.

"See?" I said, brandishing the blade fiercely in the smoky air, cutting the billowing soot into swirling banners of victory. "Cowards all. And you thought this assignment would be dangerous."

69: RUINS ON
THE OLD HILL.

FOR BEING A HEART-RENDING WAR-SCAPE of horrific tragedy from which no man was said to escape with his skin un-flayed, Easthillshireborough-upon-Flats was surprisingly calm.

Thigton pulled us slowly and steadily up Waverly Hill as the sun slogged ever-higher through the swampy sky. The sides of the roads were more littered with orphans than usual, husks baking pungently in the mid-day, ensuring that the miserable blight of the town touched *all* our senses. (Thigton had shared a bit of salt-jerky with us earlier without disclosing its provenance, and I was beginning to think better of having gleefully wolfed down a double portion.) We were among mansions now, palatial estates once tended and kept by poorly-paid house-staff and garble-tongued immigrants, their deeds held by creamy Society wagglers too vapourous of spirit to ever rise even this early in the afternoon. That milky set was vanished now; the manors of Waverly had gone ramshackle, torn to pieces and looted for valuables ages ago, and what remained were akin to what the Romans had left behind—stark skeletons of once-mighty structures, picked over by poor people who thought that the crap that rich people owned was better than the crap they themselves owned. Rightly, of course.

Watching Thigton exert himself in our service, I began to grow weary. The smoke in the air was torturing my throat with every breath. The heat made my mind light, and I imagined shadows leaping about the shuttered shells of the ruins we passed; spectres danced in my imagination, watching from abandoned eaves and darting behind hedge-rows as we trudged through the silent city.

Then the shadows were all around us, circling with the intensity of ghouls collecting on debts, or coal-hearted children scheming to maraud some wandering parson. The world spun in my vision—the wheel-cart upturned, and I was suddenly tumbling—

A cracking pain jolted me full awake. *We were under attack*—it seemed the vagrants from before had summoned reinforcements. We were surrounded.

The wheel-cart lay on its side, Ursula and I spilled beside it. Of us all, only Thigton was ready for action, crouching fiercely, backing against me and helping me to my feet with his shockingly-prehensile toes. He and I steadied Ursula against the cart while she regained her senses—the heat had taken a beggar's ride on her as well. "Awake?" I asked, my voice weak and surprisingly raspy from a morning of breathing ashes.

"A bit," she growled, her own voice harsh and horrible. I watched the attackers' eyes widen as she raised herself to her full height, clenching and un-clenching huge, meaty fists. She brushed brown dust from her ugly clothing, the billowing mass of mis-matched colour adding to the whole fearsome effect. She wasn't much of a fighter, but she certainly *looked* terrifying—moreso when she was trying to.

I glanced about for bearings—and found us right on the grounds of old Wondermark Manor. The garden-shed, to be precise; though there was nothing left of it. Not a wall still standing, not a dry bone to mark the plot. I only knew the spot because I recognised the view to the South—the old red light-house (hardly visible through the haze) at the whale-juicing depot, its narrow shape framed by the chimneys of ne'er-do-well nosey neighbours Mr C_____ and Dr W_____ of the Garden Society. Those chimneys still remained, less a brick or fifty perhaps, but not much of the walls surrounding them. I was *finally* able to see what was so important in Dr W_____'s bed-chamber that he always kept his North-facing curtains drawn: an copper bath-tub. Well *lah de dah*. The shackles were a nice touch, though; they looked prescription-strength.

A vicious assault from the vagrants precluded further pondering of the premises. I fished about for any hand-held weapon—a branch? a stone? a soot-blackened skull from a massacre that had taken place here, either since my tenure or during?—but found naught but charcoal and loose sand. The Royal Battalion sabre must have been lost in the tumble of the cart. Thigton leapt at the first attacker, but his slight stature prevented him from being terribly effective; Ursula was scrambling to reach high ground on top of the cart, at a cost of exposing her back to the mob.

With no alternative, I lunged for the nearest snarling tramp, recalling wistfully that my favourite sturdy boots had been left here in Easthillshireborough-upon-Flats when I made my hasty escape months ago— these London digs were poseur-grade at best, crafted for showiness and no good for real jaw-cracking action. One must, however, make do. As heel met head and the first man fell, I heard more shouts echoing from afar—more crazies to join the fray, no doubt, and as good as it felt to get my punchin' mojo back, I began to reluctantly worry. My muscles were warming now, and with one man down I'd struck a bolt of fear into the others that I was cashing in for injury as best I could, but too many of them could simply smother us, and I'd been too close to too many sweaty men in my life to quite welcome the sensation again.

In my periphery I made out a large shadow bearing slowly closer; as it grew, the ground shook with each step. With a start I realised that we were being approached by a row of shambling elephants.

I'd never seen such beasts in person, only lurid reproductions in penny-pulps which probably painted an altogether unrealistic portrait of the fearsome creatures' marital practises. In the flesh they were impossibly stern-looking, not hardly in the mood for any conjugal delights at all; but this was a battle-field, and such a chastity of emotions was to be expected, I supposed, if one was not me.

Yet the greatest surprise was to come: atop each elephant was mounted a great, dark shape that, as they lumbered closer, resolved terribly into *cannons*. Our road-side attackers seemed as shocked by this development as we were—and I knew why the instant I heard a crisp, aristocratic accent call "Fire!"

The lead elephant's cannon cracked open the air with an echoing *snap*, spitting a blast of orange flame and white smoke in the general direction of the mêlée. The elephant itself stumbled back a step, steadied by a dozen soldiers on foot, its ancient eyes widening for a moment in fear, or blood-lust, or possibly fearful blood-lust.

Then, after a heavy, whistling second of nothing, there was everything. Stone, flesh, dirt and bone erupted, and my feet suddenly felt no weight. Then my back struck the ground violently some yards away. I skidded through charcoal and came to rest looking like a chimney-sweep before the Clean-Sweep Act regulated their swabbing with moist-towlettes every quarter-hour to prevent racism. I heard nothing but a soft buzzing, and for an instant I feared I had lost my hearing again, as I had the last time I met violence at this ruined Manor. I should never have returned! I should have listened to that Gipsy's rubbish about ley-lines.

A peevish annoyance at the jumbled sound of twenty men shouting over one another suddenly reassured me that I *could,* indeed, hear—then gloved hands were pulling me upright. White-leather dusted charcoal from my coat, with a net result of the white leather turning black; I shrugged an apology to the smart-moustached soldier who'd tried his best.

Looking around, the vagrants seemed to have vanished again, which only frightened me anew—they had run off once, only to return with substantial force; how might they respond to *this* ridiculous display of violence? Would they start throwing scorpions?

I hobbled over to where several red-suited soldiers were helping Ursula down from where the cannon-blast had knocked her clear into a tree. I noted with pride that her knuckles were skinned; she'd either caught some damage in the fracas, or had had a knitting-accident earlier that I hadn't noticed. If it were the former, she was coming round to my way of doing business; if the latter, well, whatever. She met the ground heavily, then stooped. I thought she was going to draw something in the sooty earth until she straightened up with a gleaming blade in her hand—the Battalion sabre I'd reclaimed earlier.

Instantly ten clanking rifles rose at her, and as many voices shouted conflicting commands. She froze, and I could see a fight slowly brewing behind her eyes—there was terror in there, of course, but also ire, at being told what to do, and I think she might have had to pee as well. First she'd been bossed around by me, and now by strangers with overly-coiffed moustaches? The indignity!

But there was no argument to be made. These were Royal Battalion troops. Smart red uniforms, with swords at their sides; pith helmets protecting furrowed eye-brows from the noon-time sun. Flared breeches fed into soot-scuffed boots—of decent manufacture beneath the soilage, it seemed. It was a nice look, if you were into that whole uniform-fetishism.

"Where did you come by this?" The voice was bold, and smacked of blue-blood; it was the same that had given the *Fire* command earlier. A figure crossed in front of me to snatch the blade from her hand. "This is full property of the Crown. Where did you come by it?"

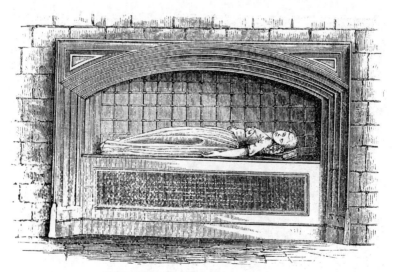

FINALLY, SOME PEACE AND FREAKING QUIET.

"We found it," I called out, knowing she would sooner spite the man than answer swiftly, and the sun and my throat and my ears and the whole mess were quickly grumpifying my mood. It was time to get inside and find some chilled water, perhaps a Fresca if one could be had in such a hell-hole, and I had an inkling of who I might be speaking to. "We were attacked on the road, and I recovered this from a man I...detained."

The figure—a ranking officer, by his gaudily-embroidered epaulets be-decked with ludicrous insignia perfectly suited for battle-field attire—shifted his chin to stare at the meat-spattered dirt where several homely men had once stood before being obliterated by elephantine cannon-fire.

"We don't make a practise of *detaining* men in Easthillshireborough-upon-Flats. Especially not on the Dead Waverly. This sad place is hallowed to them—and here, there can never be quarter. Only blood-shed." He turned further, to stare at the ruins of the Manor. I well noted the sternly jutting angles of his face, his skirmish-weary eyes, and of course his voluminous moustache. He had the look of a man who'd make a grand show of trudging wearily

LOADED DOWN FOR THE CRAP-MARKET.

through a corpse-laden war-zone, but who secretly, inside, was in love with every minute of destruction. He was possibly my sort of fellow, if he wasn't a whack-job.

"Major-Leftenant Tapiorca, I presume?"

He looked at me for the first time. I fished the wrinkled Regency stationery from my coat-pocket and he plucked it without taking his eyes from me; suddenly it was a merciless staring-contest, and it lasted for three full minutes until one of the elephants shifted uncomfortably and let out a wee little trumpet.

At the startlement he blinked a few times, shook off his fugue and scanned the paper, giving both sides his nod. "Reads that I'm to pop you up at the harbour."

"I think you were supposed to," I replied.

Tapiorca glanced around, then gestured for his soldiers to make ready the elephants. "It's a bit out of the way," he said, crumpling the message in a powerful fist and grinding it into dirt beneath his boot. "And I don't reckon you're there now."

To him, that was the end of it.

Watching him recede, I ventured, "Richey's dead." I didn't know if he'd gotten the message already. "I've been appointed by the Regents' Committee in London."

"Dead," Tapiorca laughed, swinging himself up and over the back of a cannon-laden elephant. "Welcome to Easthillshireborough-upon-Flats, lad." He whipped the reins, and the elephant wheeled, sending a mighty trumpet echoing through the hollows of old Waverly Hill. "Everything here is dead." ✦

70: AN AWKWARD TEA.

FIELD-ADMIRAL RICHEY HAD SET UP his headquarters in the old Police Bureau, back presumably when its brick façade had still consisted mainly of bricks and not sand-bags lazily buttressed with corpse-logs. The centre of town was ostensibly a refuge from the violence, a sharp-wire fence having been erected to circumscribe old Pool-Party Plaza and the municipal buildings therein, but I found the inside of the wire no less awful than Waverly and the rest of the city—except that here, the filth stacked into every crevice and corner was product of the Crown troops, and in these environs it would be impractical if not outright redonkulous to simply dispatch the more annoying examples of the former.

I tensed as we followed Tapiorca's elephant brigade across the thin steel boundary-line and into the Plaza proper. Tapiorca dismounted from his elephant nimbly, without seeming to stop moving at all; one moment he was riding, the next he was striding along the ground in seemingly the same action, and I got jealous. He was an elegant man in motion, I'd grant him that; promoted quickly through the ranks, I'd wager, with all the Crown's best interests at heart and an effortless sort of charisma that drew all his soldier's eyes like a magnet as he passed, and all their choicest ham-cuts like a ham-magnet come Christmas-time.

I wondered how much of the appeal was the snappily-pressed uniform, and whether there'd be one like it waiting for me in the field headquarters; Field-Admiral Richey, whom I was replacing, had been a larger man than I, but Thigton was a passable seamster and could surely have me looking suitably commanding in no time. The sour-ball looks the soldiers lobbed my direction were already growing tiresome, and it would be fun to whip them into shape a little—a perk of the position I'd not considered till now. I could yell at slackers with the best of 'em.

We tracked through a labyrinth of ransacked brick-walled rooms, till Tapiorca stooped through a half-collapsed doorway, ducked under a flap of mud-specked canvas, and lit a tobaccy-pipe with the wick from an oil-lantern. "Step in," he snarled through the half of his mouth not clutching the pipe-stem, "but alone. This is Royal Command."

Thigton and Ursula stopped in their tracks. Ursula narrowed her eyes. "I'm not unloading our belongings," she said flatly. "Since we're not staying. Thigton can row us out at least to the ferry-lanes tonight." She glanced at Thigton for confirmation, but the little man just shrugged. Of course he could do whatever we asked of him.

Tapiorca grunted, and with the slightest of gestures he summoned two pith-helmeted soldiers to flank Thigton and Ursula. "Round back for now, lads. Settle in after tea. You'll see Tip an' Birdie again soon," he added to me, and disappeared behind the tent-flap of the Royal Command room.

I debated for a moment whether to look back at Ursula and Thigton—would it be a show of weakness in front of the soldiers to appear to care about them?—then followed Tapiorca under the flap.

My boots clicked on scuffed mahogany—it was the Head Inspector's old office. Soot-marked and conflict-nicked, for sure, but *there* was the overstuffed chair the Solicitor-General had collapsed into; *there* was Lara's old desk, where she'd first unfurled the fist-thick stack of onion-skin pages detailing my deviances in that mansion atop Waverly. It felt rude to be in here without her; surely we were trespassing, tracking the grime of war into her boudoir, rubbing dust into her yellow, long-dead hair.

I stopped one step in from the door-flap, letting my eyes pick out increasing details in the dimness, finding her outline dancing in every ill-defined shadow, her scent in every breath not filled with rot. Was *this* why I had made myself come back to Easthillshireborough-upon-Flats? To revisit the loss of Lara, my greatest failure?

Tapiorca settled heavily into the chair—Lara's chair—behind the wide desk, spreading maps and battle-charts before him, rolling schematics into tight scrolls and binding them deftly with string before setting them neatly into a corner. "This here's the view of it all," he grimaced through pipe-clamped teeth, running knotty fingers swiftly across a crinkled expanse of curling parchment. "But let me quicken you up as to how the days roll by here. Given your lack of any military bearing and your apparent total ignorance of our circumstance, my reckon is you're a blue-blood nance with e'er too many shillings or too little sense. Either way it's lights-on for me—we're mid-campaign presently, and as you can read on this man's face, I'm so bubbling ecstatic that your merry jaunt this afternoon didn't muck us up irreparably that I'll allow you to watch the grown-ups play war if you promise to keep it all shut, all times, mouth to mittens, sun to slumber. We're quiet now for tea-time, but once we've cucumbered we're runabout till dark, so find a corner out of the paths, hunker back and sign out your sovereigns from the Treasury fort-nightly. There! Settled, what? Cream or sugar? Reckon you take sugar, you've the look of it within you, a deep sort of sadness you prolly mask with cane-root." He poured a cup of tea and held it out to me, the porcelain clinking in his hand, and I could think of no other action but to take it.

"Look," I said, after a moment taken to wet my wheedle and gather the shards of my thoughts from the ash-swept mahogany below, "Richey was killed. Shot by an assassin in the theatre—and the Council's next move would have been to order the air-ships to burn this place clean. Correct me, but I doubt you want that to happen. We both agree there are battles to be fought here—so let's not take up more arms than we need." The words came from me unbidden. Conciliatory, almost? It was shocking—the power of his bold, moustached personality had steam-rolled me flat. I could summon no assertiveness to my own defence; instead, the rusty wheels of logical argument fought to gain traction within my oil-slippery vocal-cords.

Tapiorca stared at me, brow all scowled, bright cinders of eyes fixing me to the wall, one hand resting easily on his pipe, and he did not move for some time.

I wondered if it was another unannounced staring contest—I'd been blinking all along like a dunce. I'd have to get better at reading these soldiery signals; I'd already picked up one from an elephant-driver that I think meant "you've got a little some-thing over here, no, here, other side, there you've got

CHAIR-SITTIN'.

it" and felt quite pleased at having established such a manly camaraderie with a man who rode an animal bigger than even the largest oxen I had ever eaten over the course of weeks.

"Richey was good for one thing," Tapiorca finally said, standing and tapping his pipe into his tea-cup, then taking a long sip. "He could sit quietly in a room and let me fight my war."

"I'm making it *my* war now," I said, because I thought it sounded pretty good, and also I'd thought of it quickly, it being a variant on what he had said. "And I'm staying right here, in this room. I'll brook no argument. So let's just start there and move forward." To emphasize my rootedness to the Royal Command, I sank slowly into the chair opposite the war-desk.

Like a bath-tub, I recalled thinking as I'd watched the old Solicitor-General take this position long ago—and it *was* nice. Soft, warm even, as if it had been recently occupied. *That* thought was a little creepy, but it was comfortable—*so* comfortable—that I didn't even care who the mystery warmer might have been.

"Fine," I thought I heard Tapiorca say, far-off somewhere, but it might as well have been the beginning of something else..."*Find...*"

Then I was yanking myself awake. It was night-time. A terrible chill blew through the room, and I shuddered with fright.

The tent was gone. The canvas that had been erected inside the shell of the old building had been taken away, along with the desk, maps, and all of Tapiorca's effects—I was left now in a room with four crumbling walls and a distinct lack of a ceiling, exposed fully to all and chilly. *Fine,* indeed.

The camp was dark; only a few flickering torches marked other tents, far-off but still inside the wire-fence. I wondered where Ursula and Thigton had been taken, and if it might be a place with a stove, or perhaps a roof, which would be nice.

I briefly puzzled over where all the soldiers had gotten off to, but a rumble of cannon-fire in the distance seemed to answer that concern. An orange flash briefly lit up the horizon, and in the momentary illumination I saw that the night sky was thick with smoke—as always seemed to be the case, anymore.

A floor-board creaked beneath my foot and I startled a bit, turning to stare at nothing, darkness in a corner, a shadow. But of what? Something moved, barely, in the blackness of the room—then it scurried again, distinctly now, a hobbling gait, not-quite human, but upright. For a moment I thought it was Thigton, but *his* nearly person-like shape moved with more of a cruel sort of elegance borne from vicious instruction. This was *feral.*

I fished for the oil-lamp in the silver sconce and lit it with my mind. The thin flame near blinded me, but did worse on the animal. It cowered in a corner, shuffling for an escape, but I had it, dashing the lamp at it and spattering the far wall with angry, defensive fire. The creature hid behind familiar-looking hands, then stared at me in the sudden brightness...

"Master?" came its thin voice. It was Sandy, my old hunch-back—covered totally in blood.

71: DASH THROUGH DARKNESS.

F LICKERING LICKS OF OIL-FLAME LIT
the corner of the room with a dim orange glow, enough to
make out the creature's face. Sandy, indeed; I was surprised I even
remembered the brute's name, except that I had in past employed
a mnemonic device: "Sand," like beach sand, plus "Eee," the sound
a hunch-back makes when beach-sand is poured in its eye. The
hunch-back—Sandy—gleamed red in the darkness, slick with
blood, jam, or some combination of those condiments.

"Master, you've returned to save us, as we've prayed you would,"
the figure croaked, taking a halting step toward me—I back-ped-
aled into the relative safety of the centre of the room and touched
the chair-arm behind me. If need be, I could cower behind it; it was
barely a fear-addled leap away, in a direction I could picture easily.
At the slightest provocation I would spring for it, and hope that in
the commotion Sandy would forget I was there.

He'd (she'd?) saved my life once, that day the Manor had burned
to the ground, but he'd (she'd?) then gone on to spirit me away not
to freedom but to face trial in a vomit-inducing theatre of misshapen underground monsters, all of them angry at me for various
trumped-up offences I never quite understood, having been quite
deaf at the time. Suffice it to say, this was a familiar squashed-up
face indeed—but this chance meeting could all too easily lead to
more trouble.

"I save nobody but myself, at the moment," I called into the
corner. "In fact I am making ready even now to abandon this city
to the Crown and to Countess Peapoddy's armada. You and your
wretched cadre are as good as flame-broiled even now—so take
heed, flee with your hideous gang while you still can!" If I was to
have any chance of rehabilitating Easthillshireborough-upon-Flats,

a nice first step would be to scare off the vole-like vermin that lived beneath the streets.

Sandy took two loping steps closer, crushing the last of the oil-flames beneath a wickedly-clubbed foot wrapped with black rags and super-market coupons from the broadsheets. "You don't understand, Master, you don't realize what this means, that you've returned! Finally, an ambassador who speaks both languages fluently—the silver tongue of the aristocrats in the calloused mouth of the beggar. Underground, we heard about you and the Kippers—in fact, it was your revolt against the Police that gave us the courage to rise up at all! Come, come, we have much to discuss. I have saved many of your effects for your return; you must come with me at once." With this he was gone, a cloud of mal-odour left in his wake, and despite my better judgement I found myself a half-step behind him. He had my *stuff?*

We crossed through a low door into the old Bureau's small kitchen and I learned why the hobbling beast was covered in blood—for in here lay the remains of two Royal soldiers, their brains dashed out against the brick, punished for guarding the meagre rations of turnips and millet allotted by the Crown. Sandy went on to make quick work of the soldiers' larder, stuffing loaves into a burlap sack ingeniously marked with an icon for *contaminated needles*—"to prevent suspicion," Sandy explained—before prying up a floor-sluice. A faint greenish light emanated from a deep-looking tunnel below, and for a frightening moment I was reminded of old man Grenadine's brilliant bright-jade. I clutched at my throat dramatically before remembering that I no longer wore that totem.

When I had, I had been mistaken for a saviour, and had in that role only brought ruin—would the same happen here? In general, I seemed to accomplish much more with my sights set on doing ill.

The green light was coming, predictably, from a swamp-frog, lying dully in a wicker cage held at the end of a pole. Its sad light illuminated a few feet of tunnel ahead, the walls cross-hatched by shadows from its cage in a manner eerily familiar. Dark lines bobbed on the earthen-ness as Sandy scampered ahead, calling back to me, telling his story in bursts and burbles, his voice caroming and distorting off the stone as if the very Earth was telling him to shut up.

"So long did we live in fear of the top-folk!" I think he yelped. "Subsisting on dog-leavings and growing our population in dribs whene'er a well-to-do matron would toss a mal-formed baby into a rubbish-heap. We thought you were no different, of course; you treated us poorly, failing to maintain the caves as your Uncle did, with his seal-fat obsession and peculiar disposition for yodeling in Gaelic. But we wronged you when we aided that duplicitous Peapoddy in his overly-elaborate plan to deceive you, for he never paid us what he pledged, which was eight hundred bushels of week-old sheep-meat. Not a single ounce did we receive of our promised mutton! Yet he continually claimed the whole lot was but a waggon-ride away, down at the harbour! The *fiend!*"

I glanced nervously overhead, wondering if some soldier on patrol might hear the rantings of a lunatic hunch-back beneath his feet and decide to shoot his rifle into the paving-stones.

Oblivious to this particular danger, Sandy went on—"We did not know you had a bond with the Kippers," he said. "We did not know you were once a man of the streets, fighting like we do for scraps, for stray pennies to use to buy scraps, for the raw materials used to make scraps, and for the luxury to scrap things ourselves at times. Yet despite your humble station, you stood up to Peapoddy and fought! And we knew that we could do the same." He consulted a fork in the tunnel by frog-light, then ventured on, beckoning me to follow. I wondered how far afield we were now from the Royal encampment; it was impossible to tell.

"When you left on that ship," Sandy blathered on, "we took control and *seized* the city from those who had denied us everything for so very long."

I squirmed. It was nice that Sandy's people apparently didn't want to kill me, as they had tried their doggedest to do the last time I'd come over to play, but being hailed as a hero might not actually be better—I had already declared an allegiance of sorts to the Crown troops, though they seemed douches through and through. I decided to keep my mouth shut (an advisable practise in the tunnel anyhow, because of mine-flies) and see where Sandy's story would lead.

"We made sure to save everything we could from your estate," Sandy said. "So it would be here, just as you left it." He set the frog-cage into a hook on the wall, and stepped forward into an open space. Cool air hit my skin as I followed him into a cavernous atrium, where tunnels branched off in every direction. Lanterns half-lit the area, and several people—shabby poor folks mostly, with the occasional hideous underground monster—milled about officiously.

WHAT'S THIS GUY'S PROBLEM?

"Right through here." Sandy loped to where several grimy fellows were unloading scraps of meat from dented metal buckets. "Care for a bite first? You must be famished!" The hunch-back took a delicate finger-pinch of bright red flesh from a bucket and downed it in one slimy gulp. "Oh, deliciously fresh. New today, this is?"

No response from the men. Sandy looked up, then realized they were staring at me—and I knew why.

These were kin to the men we had fought this afternoon, and these scraps of meat were the leavings from Tapiorca's cannon-fire.

"I'd like to introduce you fellows," Sandy said brightly, the instant before the men pounced upon me with furious screams of murderous, vengeful, nail-bared rage.

72: THE BARON OF THE ALLEY-WAYS.

B LACK DOTS SPOTTED ONTO BRIGHT green stones. *Drip, drip.*

For the longest time I made no sense of what I saw. Bright green stones, speckled with black spots—first a few dots, then more, many more, dripping darkly, sounding like a far-off underground leaky spigot. *Drip, drip.* Was an O-ring leaking somewhere in my skull? It echoed so!

Then, in waves like a dark tide rushing to the shore, I felt the pain. My shoulders hurt, and then my hands, my face, my body.

I was suspended by something scratchy—ropes? Entrail-jerky? Who could say—around my shoulders, my frame hanging limply from a cavern wall. The floor was paved in glimmering green; the black spots were blood, dripping from my face. *And,* I noted proudly, *from my knuckles*—I'd apparently given the fight a fair bit of my own what-for. It would hurt to tighten a fist for a while, but that was a fair price for being a bad-arse.

Gradually I remembered the brawl: the meat-hoarding pair had lit into me, recognising me from the morning's skirmish in which I'd taken a paving-stone to their leader's smile-hole. They'd rejoindered that day with an ambush on our carriage, which had been countered by Tapiorca's elephant-cannons; at this rate they must be planning an assault on the harbour with dynamited barges, to which the Crown troops would retaliate with a cruise-missile, and then things would have to get *really* creative. Tricky business, war; I reminded myself that the smart man avoids the bloody mess of it all and instead profits from the fighting.

With painful effort, I looked around as best I could manage. Polished green paving-stones lined the floor of a rock-hewn cavern littered with the detritus of the city—old bits of furniture, twisted masses of metal that had begun life as shopping-trolleys, tins of turpentine, the odd sausage-casing. Nothing, I noted, outright rubbish—that had all been left above-ground.

"Awake, then? Good." A voice startled me, thick with the accent of the below-folk and dense from a life breathing sulphur-fumes and seal-fat vapours. I turned round to watch a squat man twist a curled ribbon of parchment-paper 'twixt talon-like fingertips. "You'll pardon the Callowag boys their fighting-vigour, but they're understandably upset. Aren't we all on edge, these days."

He moved a lever, and the cords binding me to the wall suddenly released. I fell splattingly to the ground; my chest hit hard, but I kept my chin high to avoid taking the impact on my jaw. Bright green light filled my vision till I found stiff hands to push myself up.

The stones were warm and soothing to the touch; they reminded me of eggs just-stolen from a wailing-crane's nest and scrambled in the shell, except without the incessant pecking about the head and neck from an irate mama-crane. Instead I had this gnome-man to deal with, who bore no resemblance to the crane besides a certain brazen gawkiness.

"The hunch-back said he'd kept my effects," I growled, my voice hoarse. Managing to stand on wobbly feet, I discovered myself a full two heads taller than the man, yet still he held a commanding presence in the room—perhaps it was the voluminous black beard? I'd never quite managed *that* impressive a display myself, which was too bad. Back in Peru I'd put the natives to shame in an afternoon, but underground was clearly where the professionals dwelt. I brushed my hands to clear them of dust, and a fine, glowing powder clouded off to settle at my feet.

"Your voice sounds so raw. Scraped to blazes by the ash, hmm?" With a branch-like finger the man pointed above his head. "A shame, this conflict. We used to gather so much that you top-landers would simply toss away, in richer times. My people would come to me and say, 'O Baron, I have lost a leg to leprosy', and I could fit them with a waggon-wheel to the hip, and they'd be rolling around, beaming. Or 'O Baron, my daughter has not eaten this month', and I could stir up a bucket of kitchen-grease and hand it over with a kindly, benevolent smile." He smiled, neither kindly nor benevolent. "For better or no, those days have gone."

"My belongings," I said again, sucking moist cavern air past tonsils that felt exfoliated by a bruin's pine-cone scrub-brush. I drew myself up to as imposing a height as possible—the last time I'd been at the mercy of these subterranian trolls, I'd been able to simply wade through their weak blows to freedom. *Today's was different, though,* I reminded myself, for today they had the alliance of rangy brawlers like the Callowag boys, whose gnawing, champing vitriol had apparently trumped my clearly-superiour fighting technique.

After a long pause, the Baron nodded. "Sandy has shielded them for you." Tucking the thin ribbon of paper into a pocket of his stained trousers, he turned to the cavern's doorway. Lifting a swamp-frog bindle from a sconce on the wall, he extended the pole to me but did not release it himself, even after I had set both hands to its shaft and clearly meant to take hold of it.

"Sandy has spoken very well of you," the Baron growled. "I have granted him a boon today. He is idealistic, and more than a bit stupid, but he is hard-working and that horrible back of his is wretchedly strong. He is like a son to me, the terrible but annoyingly-happy son that I thankfully never had, and I cannot turn down a moaning request from his mangled lips." Pulling on the pole with a jerk, he brought my face level to his own. Light from below cast bright green reflections across his eyes. I could not see through them to his soul. "Be mindful of his delicate spirit. He sees some virtue in you that I do not—but he also sees ghosts in shadows, and religious icons in the patterns of his waste. When he looks at you, he may perceive a saint. But I think I know what is really there."

Up close, this fellow's skin was as pocked as cliff-side rock. The black wires of his beard cork-screwed ominously at me like a thousand twisty daggers at my throat. I was struck with the feeling that this Baron was the type to order men killed to suit his purposes. "What can you say about the death of Field-Admiral Richey?" I asked, perhaps a bit boldly. "Since I'm here."

The Baron shrugged. "Royal troops are all the same hate-filled man to me, Admiral this, Leftenant that, no matter. They have come to take our city away from us. We had one brief moment after you left—thirty glorious seconds or so in which to collect our fair share of the sun that shines freely on every creature." He let go of the pole, and I stumbled back a step, the cage at the end of the bindle swaying, casting weird, nauseating shadows. "We drove out our oppressors, patricians like yourself, and they called the Police. We drove out the Police, and they called the Royal Regiments. And here we are today." He spread his gross hands. "We will drive out the Regiments as well, with a tidal wave of blood if we have to. And we will have our city to ourselves when there is no one left to call."

I looked at the swamp-frog in the cage. It was a sickly creature, too dry, too weak without exposure to its native climate, the marsh. It shone a weak blue-green, not brighter than any stone beneath my feet, and I felt for its captivity. "You *do* know," I told the Baron, "that when the Regiments leave, they will be replaced by Countess Peapoddy and her air-ships. They would be above us even now, if it wasn't for *me* fighting to keep this city alive."

"Oho! Always putting yourself in the centre of the story, of course," the Baron chuckled. "Well, we thank you for your boldness. Heavens, whatever would we have done without you?" The words were sticky with sarcasm-syrup crammed deep in every vowel. The swamp-frog sensed it too, pulsing slightly amber in protest, that species' equivalent to a roll of the eyes. "It was people like you always putting yourself in the centre of the story, never caring a whit for the needs of the disadvantaged, that drove us underground!"

He dove at me, driving me backwards against the wall, his eyes flashing angrily in the cavern's eerie glow. "Do you think I was not there for the trial? We orchestrated that for *months*, planning every detail, while you frittered away above us, making our lives worse day by agonizing day with your carelessness. You arrived and killed our entire prosecutorial team with one buffoonish blow, in the middle of a speech they had worked on for *weeks!* So do not tell me of all the wonderful things you have done for us. *You*, and your comrades in the uniforms up there, are our *enemies*. Sandy will get you your effects, and then you will leave us and never return. Pray you do not meet the Callowags above ground."

He shoved me bodily out of his cavern and somehow slammed a door that seemed to be carved from a boulder. I was left in the antechamber, alone with the sad-looking frog casting a faint, dying pool of light at my feet.

Looking back, I saw glittering foot-prints where the dust from the green paving-stones had clung to my boots; looking forward again, Sandy's horrible, lumpy grin was suddenly right in my face and I about crapped my pants in alarm. I fumbled the frog-pole with a shriek—Sandy caught it deftly with one hand, his other holding a cloth-wrapped package.

"Are you ready for your belongings? I've kept them safe for you all this time, knowing that you'd want to come right back home and have things just as you left them. Maybe you can be like your Uncle, and work on getting us some seal-fat again?" A wistful tremor crept in, like a mouse unsure if there was a cat in the house, or if said cat was a maniac. "It's so *cold* at night, and a little insulation—"

"Those days are *gone*," I said, echoing the Baron's words, figuring if Sandy would listen to anyone, it would be his Baron. I was beginning to foresee a bad end to this relationship—the last thing I needed was another weepy, clingy side-kick trailing me around everywhere. There'd already been my idiot nephew Josiah, and I'd ended up throwing him overboard when he became too much to bear; before him, I'd been hounded at various points by Peruvian mining-children, cheese-hungry wharf-urchins, and in one memorable instance a particularly tenacious manta-ray, all of whom had met similarly unpleasant ends by my hand. I just wasn't *good* at mentorship.

"I *know* they're gone, but *still,*" Sandy sighed. I wondered what effects of mine he'd saved—I hadn't expected there'd been much left after the fire, and in fact when I'd returned to that ash-heap the following day, I'd been able to make out the statue of Zeus mounting a pelican and not much else. Still, that statue would be a coup to recoup, and the confidence its presence would endow me with could be a nice asset in other arenas. And of course there was always the chance that some of the silver had survived, or bits of antique brassery, or my branding-iron kit, or my codpiece, or any of Uncle's accessories I could don to look fancier than Major-Leftenant Tapiorca.

Sandy carefully set the swamp-frog on the ground, then knelt and unwrapped the bundle. "Saved a bit of old shirt to keep it all safe," he said. "More than once they've tried to commandeer it for a bum-rag or such, but I've always said no, it's for the Master." He lifted the threadbare sleeves of the shirt to reveal three items—a curio-sized picture-frame, complete with silhouette of Uncle; a single, brass skeleton key; and a glass dram-sized phial of a viscous purple liquid, a bit grayish in the frog-light. That was all.

"I hope this is useful," Sandy chirped. "Figured you'd want the portrait of old Master, being your Uncle and all. The key I found after a long search through rubble and burned-out timbers; thought it might be handy for locked doors an' such, or at least the door that it goes to. And this, I believe, is blackcurrant jam." He held up the phial proudly, swishing it around. "Many's the night when I've had to fight off the deepest, most cramp-inducing hunger-pangs imaginable, and thought fondly of this jam—but I've saved it for you, since it was yours, and you deserve to have it back."

A portrait of a man I murdered. A key to some door long since burned to the ground. And *old jam.* "This is everything? These are all my effects that you saved for me?"

"Well, yes, of course," Sandy said, standing, a hint of a pout creeping in. The Baron had warned that the lad was slow, and it was clear now that his mind worked at an amble rather than a run. I'd followed him down here with no gain other than some new enemies, and I'd been beaten soundly to boot. This was not a good reward for the night I'd had.

In that moment it became clear that there was nothing left of the home I had fled. Lara was long dead. This town meant nothing anymore; its warring factions could mulch each other into compost for all I cared.

Faced with what would surely be an intractable conflict before me, only one choice made any sense. "Sandy," I said, "it's time for me to walk away."

His grotesque face sank, I think. It was hard to tell, what with its misshapen-ness. "But...but you're our *champion!* I kept all this stuff for you. I had to *fight* to keep it all safe! You don't know *how many* people *really* wanted that jam!"

I took the jam from Sandy, cracked it open, and downed it in a swallow. It was overly tart and probably mouldy, but it was gone soon enough. Without even a glance down, I ground Uncle's portrait beneath my heel, then knelt, picked up the brass key, and shoved it into Sandy's eye.

He shrieked, flopping around like an idiot, but I held him tightly as I could, wrapping one arm around his horrible hump and with the other hand pressing the key deeper and deeper into his skull till it hit the stop.

It felt good, this act of pure caprice, even knowing that the Baron could surely hear screaming behind his impassive boulder-door, even as I pictured the painful process of fighting my way free from this place.

I *knew* I was making life harder for myself, but *I did it anyway,* because *that is the kind of man I am,* and sometimes it was worth suffering to make others suffer.

Sandy's weight sagged against me, and I dropped the body to the ground. The swamp-frog began to turn slightly blue in fear, and I knew there were people coming—muffled voices echoed down the halls; commotion approached from several sides. This would

A GOOD WAY TO CATCH CRABS.

be a tedious slog, punching and kicking my way back aboveground. I racked my mind to contrive some manner of easier escape...

Of course! These people were likely dumb-nuts. I knelt and hefted the body of Sandy to my shoulders, knees trembling with the strain—he was light, but I was weak; I gathered my strength, steadied my stance, and hoped for the best just as a babbling knot of shouting creatures swarmed into the room, rifles, swords, cudgels, bone-clubs and opinions of self held high.

"Help!" I cried. "He slipped and fell—oh, I think he's badly hurt! He needs air, and light—where's the nearest path to the surface?"

Suspicious but concerned, they ushered me to a steep, narrow path, one considerate monster holding the frog before me to light my steps. Even they realised that living underground was anathema to health. The uphill trail was torturous, and the body in my arms grew more weighty with each step, but I managed, squeezing the corpse from time to time to simulate the rise and fall of breath, crying "His breathing is getting shallow! Quickly!" at intervals, and finally, at long last, feeling the hot, ashy breeze of the Toplands stir the air in the passage.

One step away from freedom, dreading discovery every instant, my fear crystallised in my chest. The Baron's voice echoed through the cavern: "Stop! You fools! What's he done with my boy?"

I took two great steps into the bright world, knowing they'd all be too momentarily blinded to follow. Then, because I couldn't think of anything particularly bold to say, I turned, threw Sandy at them, and ran.

73: THE CRITICAL PRICK.

CROWN SOLDIERS COVERED POOL-PARTY Plaza like ants on a honey-comb, bristling with rifles and sabres and great, wooden manliness full of all the vigourous activity that spells War. I was pleased to discover that the gate-guards and their floppy attendants seemed to have gotten the memorandum regarding my promotion to Crown's Regent, for despite my soilish, blood-caked countenance and the fact that I could barely croak a double-word when hulloed at, I was quickly identified, ushered to a posh suite behind the Royal Command (né the old Police Bureau headquarters), and left alone with a glorious copper pot of steaming bath-water. I tried to impress upon the page who showed me the room the importance of staying to help scrub down my hard-to-reaches, but perhaps my voice was more torn than I sensed, or else the authority of the Crown's Regent extended somewhat less far than I had hoped. The lad did not, in fact, stay.

The immersion was delightful, a fine harkening to the days I had loved in Easthillshireborough-upon-Flats and had only had middling luck re-creating in fussy London. Uncle's massive, late fortune dwarfed the pittance that Ursula's Yam-Runner kin had been sending our way, and even on rare days when those coins proved sufficient to maintain my life-style, I still harboured a measure of reluctance to take their slick, sweet-potato money—for what would they, in return, require of me in days to come? And what role was I already accidentally playing in their schemes? Would I, one day, in crossing the street, inadvertently explode the House of Parliament? Would their devious double-plans find me accidentally dropping the London Bridge into the Thames whilst tying a boot-lace? I was aiming to stay one step ahead of the slimy Yam-Runner schemes Ursula weaved not-so-subtly about me, but whatever wiliness she lacked personally was made up for in full measure by her masters back on that island. I felt their hot, prickly gaze on my neck even in this tub, and I wondered how long and magnificent would a telescope have to be to convey to them my rude gesturing from this far away.

Bathed, I was pleased to find a selection of weird—fancy!—fruits and salt-meats awaiting me in the Field-Admiral's old quarters, as well as a smart military uniform well-befitting a Crown's Regent—tailored to just my measurements. My shoulders held no rank, Field-Admiral or otherwise, but the crisp linen coat and khaki battle-jodhpurs nonetheless injected a rush of role-playing confidence into my quavering loins. Perhaps I was, in fact, a superb military tactician after all; I'd been known to have other latent talents, as Ursula could attest.

The one shortcoming to the new uniform was the footwear. The boots provided were far too small, so reluctantly I stuffed my feet into the splitting seams of my own pair. *There must be a cobbler here in the Regiment,* I reasoned, and resolved to seek him out before my next dashing adventure or execution of naturally-brilliant battle-field strategy; it would only be fair for the Crown's Regent to have a nice new pair of well-fitting boots, all the better for bum-kicking the enemy. Flush with boot-citement, I sent for an attendant, asking for the cobbler to be located at once.

The errand-chap paused at the door, all eagerness and fawning grins. "Will there be anything else, Your Excellency?"

Excellency. I liked that. "Find me some more fruit, even weirder this time," I said, because I could, and because he would.

Having donned the garb and eaten the meats of the Crown's Regent, there was left only the matter of a wooden curio-box, sitting plainly on the Field-Admiral's old bed. I knew the casket well; it had been in Thigton's hand when last I'd laid eyes on't, and to see it here jabbed a slight thorn of worry into my otherwise quite bejollied demeanour. Its presence meant that Thigton and Ursula had departed—most probably back to London, but potentially anywhere.

She had some plan, I was sure. I didn't know its details nor its step-by-steps, but I knew its terminus: air-ships in the sky sending green flame to the ground. Ursula meant to take over this city in the name of the Yam-Runners, and I was only useful to her so long as I aided her toward that goal.

With Ursula already in action, my only chance to stay the approach of the Countess's armada would be to end the war myself.

I called the page back in. "There *will* be something else," I said. "Send for Major-Leftenant Tapiorca. Tell him I have his orders."

The weak-willed responded well to assertiveness; the lad darted out of the suite as if his heels were alight, leaving me alone with the curio-box. Simply to verify the integrity of its contents, I slid open its lacquered lid and lifted out each object within.

First came a human femur-bone, carved and whittled into a wand designed for twirling melted cheese. This had been the late Abu Fromage's dying gift to me, and I would treasure it always; with a peculiar pang of sentimentality, I fitted the wand into a belt-ring of my uniform where a sabre would normally sit, and with pleasure noted that it rested perfectly, even snapped securely into its rest.

Next came a dusty book with frayed covers—the Tome of the Precious Lore. Its arcane secrets, Ursula had revealed to me, were merely fiction, the lunatic ravings of a mad-man named Abner Grenadine, now dead by my hand. Another mad-man, the Countess's son Peapoddy the Younger, had quested his whole life after a book like to this one, and had killed my dearest love Lara—and later, Abu Fromage as well—in his crazed hunt for power. Now Peapoddy too was dead, by my own hand. The only pleasing thing about the book was its cover-illustration: a worm hopelessly in love with a plate of spaghetti. On sad days I sometimes felt as if *I* were that worm.

Finally came a shard of cloudy green jade, sharp as a knife and deadly as the truth. I turned its weight in my hand until I found its one smooth, deep-coloured facet, then lifted the stone to my eye and turned to a window, directing the jade at mid-day sunlight. In the heart of the artefact I saw the ghostly figure of Grenadine, setting down the reams and reams of worthless text that would become the Tome of the Precious Lore. An image from the past, trapped to haunt my present. The whole drama a noisome farce that so many had died over.

The door to the suite slammed open and I jolted in surprise, pricking myself in the eyeball with the jade. I screamed and dropped to one knee, clasping my hands to my face. Booted figures rushed to my side, and I was given a wet cloth to apply pressure; but the tiny cut burned, racing electric bolts of pain about the inside of my skull, and I grit my teeth nearly to powder.

"Buck up, then," came Tapiorca's voice, and a heavy hand pushed me backwards onto the bed. I curled there atop the duvet, remembering how the body of Sandy had fallen heavily to the rocky ground with a key through his eye-socket, remembering other men and creatures that I had stabbed through eyes at other times, in far-off lands, for offences as trivial as a nudge, or an insult, or the inequal division of a ham sandwich. *This was what it felt like,* I realised—*and somehow, I am not immune.* Father had lied, when he said I was special.

Tapiorca sat next to me on the bed, his weight on the mattress tipping me slowly toward him until I lay twisted against his hot, musky side. He brushed my boot-dust off the duvet with a disapproving cluck, then slowly righted me with his hands.

"I've—I've got your orders," I managed, after some sniffling.

"That so."

I was unable to open the pricked eye, but did manage to pry open the other and fix him with a glare that I hoped would approximate sternness despite my afflicted state. "The enemy lives underground. A tunnel leads into their camp from this very building. I even know where dwells their Baron. I can lead a garrison to them directly—we can put an end to this ceaseless bloodshed at once, simply by exterminating every one of them."

Tapiorca slowly nodded. "Been cavorting with the Baron of the Alley-Ways, have you?" He looked up at the soldiers who'd come in with him—then back to me with a shrug. "Quite an admission to make."

"I was led against my will," I snarled. "I fought my way out. I killed one of their deputies!"

"Against your will?" Tapiorca stood from the bed, bouncing me a little. "We have witnesses to hold-an'-swear that one o' *them* chirped you as 'Master', and that you clicked your ankle-bones and scarpered after him."

"What witnesses?" I shouted, bounding from the bed, ignoring the pain that spiked through my eye. The jade knife skittered across the floor, stilling at the feet of the soldier nearest the door. He picked it up, his brow curling downward in a hateful sneer.

"That man, for aces," said Tapiorca. "His brother was sentryin' the pantry last in-the-dark. Care to explain what went flippers on your watch?"

I remembered two soldiers, dead in a kiddy-pool's-worth of blood on the kitchen floor. "What kind of Royal Command isn't secure against intruders coming up the sluice-grate? Might as well put your headquarters in the enemy's own bed-chamber!"

"Easy there, no need to get up in twitchers," said Tapiorca, extending his hands. "Let's keep it calm, let's talk like gentle-bobs. First thing's sure—you're full appointed Crown's Regent, true? We've got the orders from London, you're up-tight and official, Council's signed off and the whole bit, clean?"

"Of course I am," I spat. "Why do you think I cut such a striking figure in this uniform?"

"Right, just wanted to verify first. See, if a citizen blazes out a soldier, it's mere murder; but if it's the Crown's Regent lays out two in a pantry, well, then it's proper treason. Boys, if you'd take up His Excellency?"

The soldiers stepped forward and seized my arms, dragging me bodily through the door, almost bowling down a stooped-over man with a pair of boots in his hands, waiting patiently for his turn to enter. I kicked, I screamed, I wriggled and floundered and Indian-burned and bit—but I was a prisoner of the Crown now. ✦

74: A LONG DAY
AS BEAST-CARGO.

I STRUGGLED AGAINST THE CLAMPING grips on my arms, but it was no use—these were battle-tested war-men, thoroughly professional and drilled in just this manner of brutality; they were not weak against my whinging like the men of lesser uniforms (dog-catchers, postmen, the odd orphan-hunter) might have been. Completely unable to resist being dragged bodily across the Plaza, I decided to postpone my daring escape for the moment and focus instead on planning my eventual revenge-filled return. Through one blurry, tear-filled eye (irritated by the dust, nothing more!) I registered as much detail of the layout of the place as I could manage, instantly pin-pointing defensive vulnerabilities, weak-looking bits of border-fence, and particularly sparrow-chested guards. Soon, I decided, I would come back here, and I would wreak *havoc.*

The same soldiers that had earlier welcomed me into the Plaza and ushered me carefully to the Regent's quarters now stared harshly as we all passed, spearing me in particular with glares that could splinter wood and flexing solemn, down-turned mouths over too-strongly-set jaws. Some of these were genuine bad-arse soldiers, heroes of African or Bengal campaigns, or simply men born sociopathic who had gone on to encounter sharply well-designed career-guidance quizzes—but many were clearly dolts and luggards playing the roles of bad-arse soldiers because it was expected of them. Even with my afflicted vision I could tell that one in every four moustaches in the ranks was desperately over-waxed, lest their fellows detect a tell-tale drooping of uncertainty or, Heaven forfend, the wholesale mange that would signify an out-right ninny unfit for the Crown's uniform. The P.R. drubbing the military had taken after the quagmire of the Alaskan conflict was bad enough, but droopy or shedding moustaches in a theatre so close to home would be cause for, at the *very* least, an unflattering editorial cartoon in *Punch*. The Crown did not need another 'boar's-bristle and mucilage' incident.

"You've a bit of a choice," growled the soldier holding my right arm, the same who'd picked up the jade in the bed-chamber and, according to Tapiorca, whose brother'd been one of the victims in the pantry last night. The edge in his voice threatened to prick my ears to match my eyeball. "Front-ways, or back-ways. Which'll it be?"

So it had come to this. A sophomoric semantic taunt, the type common to track-suit-clad street-toughs and the more-mammon-than-manners frat-lads prowling some of Oxford's lesser colleges who'd go on to the type of career in Parliament that would be dignified in history only by its eventual end in embarrassing scandal. If I answered 'front-ways,' no doubt he'd lay fists into my ventrals every way he could justify; whereas 'back-ways' was obviously an act that could only begin by being dropped onto a work-bench behind a tool-shed when nobody was around. And, of course, any snappy third answer of the type I was usually wont would serve to only accelerate one punishment or the other.

My master-tactician brain raced through a thousand awful options in an instant, but when his hand curled into a fist the size of a grapefruit—fingers still wrapped around my upper arm—I found myself squeaking "Front-ways, front-ways, ahh ahh aggghh."

I did not anticipate being lashed to an elephant.

'Front-ways' apparently meant being bound spread-eagle across the wide grey trunk-bridge of one of the Regiment's massive combat-o-phants, my arms wrapped about its prickly head, tender thighs spread against its cheek-

GENERAL SHERMAN'S MOTHS.

bones, knees dangling over its fearsome, possibly poison-tipp't tusks. As the beast began to take great, swaying steps away from the Plaza, my body tied to its face, I *was* momentarily grateful that I hadn't said 'back-ways'.

One major disadvantage to this mode of travel was the inability to know if we were about to be ambushed by roving hordes of blood-hungry paupers. All I could see from my vantage-point, pressed into the rough skin of the monster, was what I could make out from the reflection in the elephant's massive right eye. Indistinct shapes and highlights passed across that mucousy surface like the long-ago refractions caught in the jade-shard. It was hard to know what to make of those twisting, ambiguous plays of light and shadow—whether a splash of colour glimpsed for a brief half-instant was a passing bird, an in-bound murderer, or simply just a deep-vein thrombosis in the animal's retina.

I thought back to the shadows in the jade. I knew the Tome of the Precious Lore was a fiction because Ursula had told me it was. She had confirmed it by showing me Grenadine, in the jade, at the

ANDREA SOBBED INTO HER SEWING-TRESTLE.
"BUT WHATEVER SHALL I TELL THE VICAR?"—[PAGE 531.]

moment of its cockamamie concoction. *He,* not the ancient scribe Plaxus the Unwise, had written it.

Or he had written *something.*

But what did it matter if the text was true or not? The book was of no use to me—for my beloved Lara was dead; Ursula had told me so.

And all we know is what we're told.

The elephant stopped walking. We had arrived at the Harbour. No gulls cried overhead; the stink of rot from the water was at high reek. The tide lapped the wharf-front weakly, full of skeletons and ship-wrecks and death and poop-barge cargo. There would be no joy-dipping on *this* hot summer day; the sea looked like it would make you sad.

"From here the ship'll take you to the prison, till Major-Left-enant can get word out to London and have a tribunal convened," the brother-less soldier told me. "I've got to stay with you till it arrives, so I've a mind to make it easy on myself and leave you be for the being."

And leave me he did, lashed to that foul beast for long, uncounted hours.

By the time I fell to the grime-encrusted board-walk in the twilight, my knees stiff, my wrists torn, my brand new jodhpurs soiled probably un-launderably, I knew that *I had to destroy everyone in this entire town.*

A once-casual indifference, nurtured into a dislike, then fanned to an intolerance, had now blazed up into a full-bore, flesh-searing, Hades-devouring *hatred.* Everyone within the borders of this accursed city—soldier or beggar, hunch-back or hero—would have to die before I would be satisfied.

I would not be deterred from this plan; eight hours tied to the face of an elephant had granted me a clarity-of-purpose rarely seen in life. *I would raze this place and everyone in it.*

My clarity lasted until the prison-ferry gently bumped up against the wharf and I saw the grease-smudged face of its driver. It was, unmistakeably, Lara. ❖

75: GRIM VOYAGE
TO DESTINY.

I SAW HER FOR BUT A BRIEF MOMENT in the wheel-house, before the ferry turned to dock and her face was lost from view—but it was her, I was positive. She wore a fierceness in her eyes, and her skin was red and hearty, so much changed from the white pallor I remembered from her hospital bed. She wore a ferry-bloke's cap, which ill-suited her delicate features and cast an odd-shaped shadow across her face, such that for a moment I thought she had grown a massive goiter. As the shadow changed with her movement, at first I thought the goiter was pulsing. And yet—I had never *seen* a goiter so lovely.

"Guh," I said, as my voice caught up with my roiling thoughts and burbled forth a noise. Then "Gawah-hah," as my arms were caught up behind me and I was dragged like a sack of mouldy turnips across the gang-plank, my shoulders and wrists crying out in pain, their shrill screams apparently audible only to me— though I *did* see the elephant wince and turn, shufflingly, away. Apparently *he* hadn't cherished our time together either.

The soldiers dragged me on board across the ferry's length and into an iron-barred cage bolted securely to the deck. "We'll leave you in care of Viktor," the brother-less (and, it should be stated, humour-less) soldier whispered fiercely into my ear. I could feel his hot breath envelop my neck like blood-marsh stank-water eddying past a rotting log or sleeping crocodile. (I, of course, would be the latter.) "He'll see you as far as Prison-Isle, and *we'll* see you in London for tribunal—if you ever make it off the island." His hand clapped my shoulder and squeezed, and I buckled in pain—a day spent tied to an elephant's face left one feeling a bit disjointed.

I sagged against the cold, black bars of the cage as the soldiers locked me in, the door creaking like an old woman's ankle-bones before a thunder-storm, or like Carlton Rube's awful awards-show jokes. The ferry-boat belched steam and trembled, and then the vessel was moving.

The soldiers and their sad-looking elephant shrank on the distant dock until swirling gray mist enveloped them and the shore entirely. The ferry drifted on a ghost-scape of formless fog and ashy smoke; the only sound was the throaty thrum of the ship's deep engine. It was as if we'd been swallowed by some massive steam-whale and were now cruising through that spectral creature's insubstantial bowel; I half-expected to cross paths with the shades of old mariners long dead, Cap'n Narwhal perhaps among them; Cap'n Crunch likely not, as I'd heard that salty old scag had finally ascended into breakfast-buttressed immortality—surely the ultimate goal of any corvair-driver of the modern age.

"Wot's we got here, then?" A hearty voice rolled over me like a storm-wave, sluicing through the cage-bars and sliding like salt-water across the deck. I turned to see a tall figure dressed in a Crown uniform (a salt-stained once-black, instead of the conspicuous red favoured by the Regiment), crowned with a bald pate that would make Otto von Bismarck jealous, his wide lip topped by the single bushiest moustache I'd ever seen outside of slaver-smeared fetish-pulps. This must be Viktor.

He worked the latch to the cage-door with fingers surprisingly nimble for their calloused thickness, beckoning me to approach. "You've got legs, then, 'aven'tcha? Aw, don't give us no ol' boo-hoo about hurtin' or what's-yer-sob; ain't no malady made what one cain't put some strengf in it wif a bit o' brisk perambulation. On up it is, then," he championed, and with the support of the cage's bars I made my way over to the door, and through it onto the ferry's deck.

The air was the same, these five feet away, but life outside the cage felt freer, more mannish somehow, as if I were riding the ferry simply jauntily, instead of being borne to certain doom.

"Now, I know it's a bad scene comin' up, the Prison is," Viktor said, supporting my elbow as I hobbled over to rest on the ferry's railing. "But ol' Viktor's always said, not a bit of 'arm in giving a man a last drink o' freedom afore that big clangin'-shut, as you don't know which men's gonna see the light out of it again, s'truth."

"I didn't do it," I croaked, finding my throat still burned from the ash of Easthillshireborough-upon-Flats. "They...they arrested me for something I didn't do."

"Ain't it always the way," Viktor clucked disapprovingly. "Always seems to be the case wif all the ones we pick from that dock. I don't doubt there's a bit of veracity in it all—but e'en if it ain't, and you's the fiercest murderer this side of the Ripper's stocks? Well, ain't no man yet bested V.R. in a bit o' the ol' hand-ta-hand, so I ain't afear'd." He pounded his solid chest with a fist the size of the most massive fist in existence. "Go on, take up a lungful—you's a free man on this boat, says Viktor, 'e does, an' for the next twenty minutes, that's the whole score, so eat it."

The cool sea-mist *did* feel good going down my soot-ravaged gullet, but I couldn't help feel the weighty presence of the wheelhouse on the second-deck, above me. I longed to climb the thin set of stairs I espied at the far end of the ferry—to lope up three steps to a pace, and face the figure who had weighed so powerfully in the dreams and ambitions of my recent life, imaginary goiter or no.

But what if it wasn't her? What if I was mistaken? What if she really was dead, and that figure in the cabin above was visiting from the mean capital of Hades?

Or what if it *was* her, alive and well? Whatever would I *say?*

"So," I said to Viktor with what was probably a detectable measure of forced nonchalance, "tell me about yourself, won't you? What's the name of this ship? What's its home port? And," I added almost as an afterhought, "who's the cap'n?"

"Oh! A wild-cat she be," Viktor grinned. "Strong under pressure, yet yielding to a firm man's touch. Oh, she'll buck you onto yer seat on the roughest nights, she will—but a man's never loved a lass like I've loved her. Yer in good hands with her."

"Ah," I squeaked, blushing a bit.

"Aye, she's the finest ferry in the Royal Navy. *Sea-Section*'s her name," Viktor went on. "Like a section right out of the sea herself, ridin' a wave as if it's part of her being. We dock at Prison-Isle for the time, but this ship is an Easthillshireborough-upon-Flats ship, commissioned by the Crown Regiments for their...porpoises. Purposes. Porpoises? Purposes." He spat over the railing, into the waves. "I get 'em a-mixed."

"I've spent many a day in the past working the wharves of Easthillshireborough-upon-Flats," I nodded. "Mayhaps I've seen your ship before, on some cheese-filled day long forgotten."

"Them were the finest days," Viktor nodded, "when a ferry could go to *all* the isles of this fine slice o' the world, instead o' just the Prison. I miss them day-trips to Lighthouse-Isle, an' Fishery-Isle, an' Wench-Isle, an' Chocolate-Sundae-Isle. E'en Poisonous-Cactus-Covered-With-Rancid-Beetles-Isle was nice now an' again, just so you'd appreciate the uvvers more. But now it's just Prison-Isle, Prison-Isle, day in, day out, Prison-Isle, Prison-Isle! Enough to make a man mad." At this his eyes twinkled, but he smiled. "Maybe."

"Well, you know," I shrugged, "we don't necessarily *have* to go to Prison-Isle to-day."

Viktor looked at me with a knowing smirk, searching my face for any hint of jest. Finally he laughed, holding a hand to his powerful belly. *"You!* Don't have to go to...aw, we get a jokester on this voyage! Be a shame to turn *you* over to the wardens, it will. Be a real shame."

I smiled weakly. I turned to look behind me and upward, but I couldn't see the wheel-house from here. "Is your cap'n also from Easthillshireborough-upon-Flats?" I asked innocently.

"The cap'n...watch yerself aroun' her, son," Viktor growled, suddenly serious, his voice startlingly deep. "She used to be the Head Inspector o' the Police Bureau, 'fore this bout of...*unpleasantness*, what wif the goings-on, an' such affairs, an' all."

It *was* her! My breath groped about for hand-holds within my chest. "The Head Inspector? You don't say!"

"An' a hard-arse she was," Viktor nodded. "She'd 'ad some run-in wif the leaders o' the fightin' early on, it's rumoured, an' they'd laid her under, drat-near curtains for 'er." He drew a finger across his throat. "It was a bad time, then; I'd sent me family on to the nana's, an' I was packin' the ferry to join 'em meself, o'er on Ancient-Nana's-Isle, out in the Straits o' Yer Grandparents. But Tapiorca? That soldier's put you in this cage? 'E brings his regiment in, takes o'er the place, sets soldiers on every corner, sets the Crown's control over every ship still in harbour, an' sets his medicine to her, on through till today."

"And she woke up?"

"Woke up? She *leapt* up, sonny, right as rain with just a bit of a foggy-cobweb up top for a bit, an' right into his service. Turned over the Police Bureau to him an' his ilk, and went on doin' her part, helpin' out the effort. It's what she can manage," he added, his voice lowering for the last bit. "Not entirely still there, from the, you know." He pointed to his ample noggin. "Had it rough, she has."

"I think I know her. From before," I said carefully. "We were friends. I did some work for the Police Bureau."

"Aw, I bet you did!" Viktor guffawed. "An' a smart mess o' yerself you've made of things now, eh? Headed to Prison-Isle in your nice new red-coat. Oop, and 'ere we are, then, look at that, ain't that a daisy bit of light now?" The fog was lifting as we approached Prison-Isle, as dreadfully forbidding as its gothic name implied, a black-cliff'd mess of crags and stony abutments from which no soul likely ever emerged. A lump settled in my stomach. It wasn't the salt-meats I'd had earlier, but rather (I gathered) my body ingesting my own organs.

"Do I *have* to go?" I asked Viktor. "Aren't we *friends* now?"

"I hope you've enjoyed it, lad," he said. "Ain't never regretted lettin' a murderer loose on the deck for a bit, 'cept for the one time o'course, but wouldn't do ol' Viktor no good to get too attached. Off you go, now, let's move it." He shuffled me toward the gang-plank as the island loomed closer. I craned my neck in gymnastic-grade contortions, but still couldn't get a good view of the wheel-house.

"Oh! I forgot something back in the cage," I said, snapping my fingers. "Do you mind if I take a quick look? Before I get off the ferry. It's a pencil-stub—so I can write to my Ma. She'll be terribly disappointed if she doesn't hear from me from Prison."

"Don't see the harm," Viktor shrugged, opening the cage-door for me to return.

I hobbled into the cage, holding onto the bars for support, making an awkward time of looking for the pencil-stub. "I think I left it around here...or was it that corner over there?"

Viktor turned to watch the island grow ever-closer. "I'll give you another stub, lad," he said, fishing in his pockets.

"This was my dear Pa's," I coughed, hunching over to examine the sea-soaked wood. "It was his favourite colour."

"Let me lend a rubber, then," Viktor said, entering the cage and peering into the corners. "'Bout how big was it?"

With a supreme burst of strength I leapt across the cage, dove through the opening and whirled to swing the door shut again. Viktor saw me move and darted for the door himself—I made it first, but he got a finger through just as the heavy iron creaked to its massive stop, the latch clicking into place with satisfying certainty, or perhaps the crunch of crushing finger-bones—the sounds were very similar.

Viktor howled as he withdrew his finger. "Oooh, you're a lying rat, y'are! May the Prison hold ye for all an' eternity, an' may the rats feast heavily on yer grand-children's grand-children!" A similarly colourful litany of curses followed me, but I diverted all effort away from listening and toward sprinting. With adrenaline-burning steps, I made my way for the stair-case. Before this ship saw dock, I would see Lara again. ✦

76: STEP BY BLOODY STEP.

OOT-PRINTS OF UNDERGROUND-CAVERN dust tracked across the ferry's deck as I ran for the narrow stairs leading to the ship's wheel-house. Each step that I pounded the wood was like a new nail into a barn-frame, adding strength and load-bearing power to my weary skeleton, envigourating it with new energy, hope, fervour, and if I wasn't careful with the nails, tetanus. It was a risk I was willing to take.

I reached the first step. Metal-topp'd. *Fine.* I leapt it with ease, landing on its higher brother, which held my weight with a sharp *tang.* I skipped the third and fourth steps, pressing right to the fifth with all my weight, green cavern-powder dancing as I slammed my boots onto that rusted plate. With just a few steps still ahead, I pulled on the railing with my peeling hands, yanking my legs along even as my knees threatened to buckle, and with a mighty *heave* set my old, dusty boots defiantly onto the top step. I was *there.* I had conquered *stairs.*

I shifted my weight firmly—and all erupted around me in roaring, brilliant flames, searing white-green light against my eyeballs, enveloping my feet, legs, then trunk, then arms and the pointy bit at the top all in swirling, rushing blaze. The steps disintegrated beneath me and I fell, burning, terribly, at once upside-down and disoriented, descending into a scalding, groping mass of filthy hands and writhing meat that was certainly the grasping clutch of the Devil come to pull me into the eternal Lake of Fire, or at least the Swimming-Pool of Hot Tea, which, for the first few centuries before I built up the appropriate callousing, would surely be nearly as bad considering the Prince of Darkness would probably not have even the decency to provide lemon.

Then I hit something hard—a below-deck of the ship: cold wood with heavy, bulbous rivets set in. Fire crackled above, tracing a hole in two consecutive decks that I stared all the way up through—the edge was just embers now, fading and flashing into sparks that drifted off into drunken fire-flies of slow-dying ash. Burned-out timbers creaked perilously

GENERAL SHERMAN'S SWEET RIDE.

where they'd been blown half-apart, and splinters showered onto my prone form; it was like being indoctrinated into the Canadian Society for Wood-Choppers' Side-Kicks, where the entire ceremony was intended to get one used to being rained-upon by saw-dust from your senior lumberjack's careless choppery above you. I'd skipped that particular Society in my comprehensive survey of every professional society offering matching retirement-plan funds during my first foray into the world of Fiscal Adult-hood; it had seemed rather silly to spend days at a time supporting the endeavours of crass and vulgar Canadian lumberjacks what with the vicious maple-syrup shortage back home at the time. Now, at a loss in this situation, I regretted not having that professional expertise, as I was gradually coming to regret everything I had ever done in life.

"Watch it," came a soft voice, and I managed to roll aside just as a particularly jagged-looking piece of deck-wood came thundering down, missing me narrowly. I could only see it barely as a throbbing out-line, my eyes still swimming purple and red from the fierce green light a moment ago. I could see nothing down where-ever I was, in some lower hold perhaps—no light reached my seeing-brain at all, perhaps because I'd fallen on my back, and I'd heard that's where the seeing-centre was, somewhere in the spine or pelvis

or something. Another Society I'd skipped: the Fraternal Order of
Eye-Sight-Centre Locators, as at the initial meeting it'd seemed
like just a bunch of pikers with lousy taste in the grape.

I came to rest with breath ragged, skin curled and blistering from the intense heat, praying that all toes were still where
they ought to be, nursing a horrible suspicion that I may have
inadvertently left them where I first lay. I made out neither shape
nor gesture around me, only a vague sort of brightness from the
blasted-out hole and a flit of shadows that meant the eruption
had caught the attention of others above: perhaps Lara; perhaps
others; perhaps tigers or something—I didn't know what all was
on this boat.

But the voice down here had come from *someone.* I patted the
space around me until my hands met tattered cloth and filth-soiled
skin, which I'd recognise by touch anyplace. My first thought was
that, like the vile Peapoddy's old dirigible, this ferry was powered
by human combustion—the moonish eyes of the captives in that
dreadful air-borne boiler-room, waiting to be turned to fuel by that
villain's churning death-engine of tears, haunted me still whenever
I wanted to creep myself out. But the same *couldn't* be true, here—
for this was a *Crown* vessel, for the love of Jonah! Commanded by
Lara, no less! And she was pretty nice, I'd thought!

"Are you," I stammered, licking my lips, "down here waiting to
be fed into a steam-engine? Tell me obliquely, if so—as I doubt I can
handle the unvarnished right now."

"Oh, no, sir," came a wispy reply. "We're veterans of the good
fight against the Trinket, held out six weeks in the siege of Ports-
Awful across the cape, till we couldn't take no more of eatin'
worm-tripe and makin' digestives from mouse-pellets. Four hundred of us there were, entrenched in Ports-Awful and shoring up
for a good push inland, when those blamed *elephants* set up on the
cliff opposite and just *bam! bam! bam!* day in, out, and in-between.
There's no man can take that bombardment and survive it—four
hundred of us down to six, here, plus this straggler picked up along
the way, and Stanley's not bound to make it to next dock, I don't

believe." The voice dropped off. "Stanley? No. No, Stanley's bound for a different shore, now—four hundred down to five men, thanks to the Trinket, and I only hope I see Prison-Isle soon, as I've been promised a proper biscuit and a porridge, and that's the finest thing I've e'er been promised since childhood Christmas when Pops found a chair-back bent like a sled-rail in the rubbish, and brought it back for us young-'uns to ice-fish on-toppa."

Lord, my heart rent in many with each new word. *Trinket* was a new term—it must be a disparaging term for the Crown. "Are there many more of you? Pockets of fighters, hidden in enclaves? Or is this war soon to be over?"

"Heaven take us if we know. Might be five, might be five thousand, but I'm sure there's some, meagre chaps like myself and these down here, simple conscripts at the full. Out there in the thick, each report comes that the final day's approaching, or there's a quiet on the front that gets us hopeful—but it's a lure, each time, to draw us out for more slaughter. It seems the Trinket's gaming with us, holding back now and again, sending a few cats in for us to get some protein and recover a bit of strength, tying radishes about the odd neck so we'd scare off the scurvies as well. And then—massacre." A groan. "Oh, bring us to Prison-Isle, please, I can't wait another minute for that biscuit! I haven't craved a biscuit this fierce since they stopped makin' the hashish flavour."

Further reply was cut off by the sound of shuffling feet from the deck above. I suddenly noticed that the ferry's engine had been cut; I could feel lapping waves through the hull, vibrating subtly through the wood at my back. Footsteps grew closer, and muffled voices; then shadows, figures, too faint for me to make out. I could still see hardly anything at all, and my eyes stung terribly; the scratch in my right, where the jade had cut me earlier, throbbed meanly, fiercely sharp in the momentary silence. I wondered if these sad folk would think less of me if I bawled a little.

Then I felt hands rustling at my wrists, pulling me up. Were there wardens down here? No, it was a figure from the hold, one of the prisoners—urging me, possessed with strength I wouldn't have guessed from a man fed the last six weeks on mouse-pellets. In fact, the fingers' shrunken shapes were familiar to my hands...

"Thigton!" I cried, to the sounds of scuffling above. "What're you doing here? You've not fallen in with the rebels...!"

"That's the lad they plucked from the sea," came the soft voice from before. "Found him making strokes for open water. Hasn't said a word, though."

"That's his way when he's frightened," I replied. "His cords get all swollen. Freakish disorder." With the imp's help I sat up, though I didn't know where he was leading me. I felt his hands work around me, as well as the gentle touch of his worn-down teeth, like a lion moving its cub; and with a start, I realised exactly *how* worn those teeth were. More worn than before, for sure.

"Thigton—you were off swimming for London, weren't you?" I cried. "And you were able to reach the undersea telegraph-cable! You chewed on it and got out a telegraph-message! Oh, it's done, it's done, it's all done!" Thigton managed a croaking moan in assent, and in that moment I knew. Ursula had sent Thigton to call in the Armada. She had used my authority to order the strike. It had all been orchestrated—her objections carefully measured to

"ALL THESE AND SO MANY, MANY MORE."—[PAGE 622.]

derive my reactions. I had been played! And now, she had gotten me installed as Crown's Regent, and in *my* voice, had called in the Countess! It would only be a matter of time, now. The whole town would be ablaze, and us with it, along with Tapiorca and the Baron of the Alley-Ways and the elephants and everyone.

And the conscripts, peasants like these sad captives. Every pocket of resistance would be wiped away as well.

I knew Thigton's gentle nudges like a shrieky twin-language. He was saying *We need to get out of here.*

"Careful," came a faint voice from above. A light voice, female, yet stern, hardened. Lara. "Don't know how much more powder's down there. Could be a whole cask, and we don't need to set *that* off."

That golden voice! Scorched a bit by war and the sea, but whose wasn't, now-a-days. "It's her," I told Thigton, but he pulled me along. "I have to see her!" He rounded behind me to push me on with his shoulder. He was having none of it. He was my man, too well.

"There's no cask," came Viktor's growling voice, above. Lara must have released him from the cage! Oh no—and he probably told her how he'd gotten there! I was probably not making a sterling first re-impression on her. I had to see her!

She had to see my face—to know it was me! All this foolishness would disappear in that marvellous instant!

I struggled against Thigton, but he pulled me fully to my feet— which were torn apart and bleeding, and which did not bear my weight. I collapsed with a cry, landing squarely on a wheezing, dirty shape. The mystery figure gasped, then seemed to shrivel.

"Well, by Jiminy, four hundred down to four, look at that," said the soft-spoken prisoner from before. I paid his sentimental squawking no heed, unable to conceive of anything past the pain in my feet. My boots had been completely blasted away, save for a strip of leather ringing my ankles. My toes were black bits of charcoal. I would look awful for Lara.

The world swam—Thigton lifted me. We were moving whether I wanted to or not.

"Look—there's a trace o' the powder," came Viktor's voice, far-ther now as he inspected the deck above my and Thigton's heads. "From 'is bleedin' boots. Jade-powder must have been in the cracks of 'is *boots!*"

"And when he hit the zinc on the steps..." Lara replied. "Of course. But why on his *boots?* That's like having...I don't even know. *Mayonnaise* on your *ears!*"

"Right, and how could he 'ave spooned it out of an artillery-shell?" Viktor said. "He'd 'ave to—"

I didn't hear the rest, because with a horrible rending and shrieking of wood, Thigton splintered open the hull of the boat with his two, bare, powerful hands.

77: ASHORE ON PRISON-ISLE.

DEXTROUS DESPITE HIS DIMINUTIVENESS, Thigton's powerful fingers sought out tiny cracks between planks and tore them apart like an ourang-outang at a crate of rum-soaked cantaloupes. I could feel the imp's powerful muscles rippling across his back as he worked, shifting his feet as needed to keep me perfectly balanced across his shoulder-blades, never falter-ing for an instant.

I wondered where the Yam-Runners had *found* this specimen— a few days after I'd angrily fired old Bumbercraps (in our small wood-furnace on Sixpenny Row) Thigton'd arrived unannounced in a trunk sent post-paid from their Isle, and had been a handy labour-mill without pause e'er since.

I was mid-way through the composition of a ballad lauding his hardiness, intending to croon encouragement as he worked, when a great, deep blow reverberated through the hull. Another explosion? Had the ship run aground? Thigton stumbled as the deck beneath us heaved and began to incline, lifting us, threatening to deposit us tumbling back toward the prisoners. A mechanical *grinding* echoed from outside—we were being *winched.*

"They're pulling us onto the island!" I cried. Thigton redoubled his efforts on the hull, twisting a long, curved board free of its pitch with an ear-splitting *crack.* At this rate, we would escape the ship directly onto the beach of Prison-Isle, and likely into the waiting bayonets of the guards there-upon.

As escapes go, ours would be only slightly more effective than the oft-recounted attempt of Bembadier Snoodlander, a noted felon incarcerated in Australia for some years who managed to spoon-dig his way out of an underground coffin after successfully playing dead with the aid of some bum-smuggled Borneo snooze-grass—only to stow away in the dead of night on a scow-barge promptly destroyed by Crown cruisers for gunnery-practise.

(In Snoodlander's defence, the scow *had* been flying the colours of a Tanganyikan pleasure-trawler [a bit of dark humour on the part of the sea-addled Navy men], but still, I was glad I wasn't within angry-fist-shot at the moment Snoodlander snuck through a cabin-door labelled "free opium" only to find cask upon cask of combustible taint-oil with cannon-fire crossing his bow.)

Thigton and I were probably one-up on ol' Bembadier, but our situation still had the potential to spiral abysmally into the pooper. "Faster!" I shouted, to help.

Sea-water sprayed through cracks in the boards, and I thought to

"I HAD MY SLEEVE TO SHARE
SECRETS WITH." —[SEE PAGE 519.]

wonder how far we were below the water-line. I glanced back at
the five—no, four—no, three, now, wasn't it?—prisoners-of-war,
huddled in blurry masses across the hold. Would we all be swept up
and drowned by the merciless ocean? "Are you sure this is going to
work?" I asked Thigton. "Not that I don't have faith in you, but—"

A pistol-shot silenced my doubts. Lantern-light bobbed through
the void in the hold's ceiling, and even through eyes swimming with
(strictly mannish) tears I could make out the cold glint of a fire-arm.
"Don't let them escape!" came Lara's cry, and I wondered if she was
the one manning the gun's likely-pearl handle. Our reunion was
getting off to a rockier start by the minute.

"This has all been simply a terrible misunderstanding!"
I shouted back to Lara with as much force as my weakened form
could muster. Another pistol-shot caroming off the hull by my ear-
lobe shut me up in a hurry. This would certainly be a funny story to
recount at our hundredth wedding-anniversary!

With a mighty heave, Thigton wrenched a final board free of
its home, and the sea did the rest. Water blasted into the hold like
great bursting barrels of pressurised seltzer-whisky during the
rather disastrous first (and what proved to be final) operating day
of the Greater Beetlesburg Seltzer-Spirits & Dynamite-Testing Co.
Ltd. The rushing ocean tore boards from their moors like heirloom
tooth-picks from the slack jaws of trolley-jumping tramps, and we,
like those tramps more often than not, were immediately flooded
to our appendices. My mouth filled with water before I could shout
in alarm, which was probably for the best, as I didn't want to seem
like a ninny in front of the guys.

Thigton pulled me close in a side-snuggler's-carry, grasping
the shattered edges of the hull with his other hand. Despite the
powerful current filling the hold like half-penny moon-shine down
the gullet of a disgraced beekeeping-gear-magnate's penniless heir,
we were soon free of the ferry entirely in a way that the heir would
never be free of his family's soiled heritage. Submerged for several
ear-choking seconds, we finally split the surface and gasped at the

cold air of Freedom, sweeter than any abandoned ware-house of honey-strainers could ever *possibly* be.

But danger's fangs still gleamed in the late-evening light—for Prison-Isle itself loomed before us, tall and foreboding as it'd seemed from the ship, but a good sight closer and a full eighty percent craggier in all the worst ways. Waves pounded against jagged black rocks that dreadful giants had probably used for bone-mashing dentures, and despite my vociferous protestations, the current carried us lurchingly toward them. It was as if the sea wasn't even *listening.*

To make matters worse, Thigton released me and dove away. When I did not feel his reassuring touch for several cold seconds I began to feel abandoned, stranded pitifully in an unforgiving world—I suddenly became terrified of the prospect of otters, and of the water splashing chillily about my ears and mouth with completely unknown quantities of otter-offal diluted within. Each taste of salt was like otter-sweat on my tongue. Left to myself in the water, it seemed that treacherous fire-ants of pain were running sprint-trials through my veins, and when my face emerged, spluttering, from some crashing wave or other, my eyes composed elegies in honour of the million new meanings of the word "owwie."

So complete was my misery that I did not even notice the shouting voices of soldiers in an approaching row-boat until they were hauling me aboard with rough, inconsiderate man-handling, and I slumped into the bottom of their craft a resident of a horrible Other-Zone beyond imagining, awash with self-pity of the totally-justified type. I didn't *like* pain. *Rich guys were not supposed to have to deal with things like this!* We were supposed to be able to *pay* people to feel our pain *for* us!

"Easy now, let's get him handled easy," someone said, and with a wet *thump*, another shivering body joined mine in the bottom of the row-boat. A splash of freezing shock heralded another, and then more; soon the boat was creaking with an over-load of flesh, and shouting voices instructed each other to make for the shore.

Ten seconds or one hundred years later—who could tell—the craft beached, and scratchy hands fished about for crannies to drag me out by.

In some moment before the setting orange sun-ball shot a parting fusillade of pain-daggers into my eyes, I glimpsed the *Sea-Section*, half-sunken, winch-rope hooked to its bow, hauled partly ashore like a rotting prize of the world's most disappointed fly-fisherman. From this distance I could not make out a hole torn in the hull, but the sky around the ship hung gray with smoke and it was clear that the craft had sustained grave injury. A handful of black-garbed soldiers scrambled to bring a ladder to bear against the vessel; I thought—but could not be certain—that I saw the agitated figure of Lara (or perhaps Viktor) on the boat's highest deck.

And that was all the light my tortured eyes could stand. I collapsed in a heap on the shore, and would have sunk into oblivion had not a cry gone up from a near-by soldier. "It's the Crown's Regent!" he yelped. "Look! Look at the uniform!"

A gravelly and considerably more spite-laced voice joined the first. "That ain't Richey," it spat. "The Field-Admiral's an older bloke, looks worn-down, a bit roundy, with a buggery-scar on his forehead. What's this is a brigand's stolen the Regent's uniform, the sly git. It's disrespect like this makes it so hard to do warfare properly." Next I heard the sharp *snap* of a rifle's bolt. "Let's fix this up tidy—stand back, mates, else it's laundry-day come early, eh?"

"No! Wait!" I struggled to sit up, but a thousand amperes of pain stopped me; I fought to open my eyes, but the world was still far too pokingly bright. My throat would have to do the work. "I *am* the Crown's Regent. Richey's dead! Assassinated—and I'm sent in his place!"

A gasp erupted from the collected crowd. How many soldiers stood over me now I had no idea, but it was probably at least half a grip. Scrapes of boots on gravel preceded a snort from the gruff one.

"Nice story. First I've heard that detail—but then a chap last week went about claiming to be Napoleon. The underlying deceit's ultimately unconvincing." Even with eyes tightly shut, I sensed a shadow fall over my face—the rifle, perhaps, or something equally-deadly: a boulder, brick, or, at this rate, a simple lack of attention to my severe wounds, apparently given corporeal form in the shape of wise-cracking prison-guards.

"It's true," I croaked. "I was confirmed by the Council last week. Memoranda are due to you within the month; you know how slowly that paper-work travels. But surely you've heard about Richey—shot through the head at a ridiculous award-ceremony in London. His wife was right there! Poor thing had to watch the act unfold!"

*Tsk*ing from the assembled. "That's a shame, for a man's wife to see that with eyes cain't never wind it back," muttered the sour one. "And the culprit? Apprehended, lynched without trial, corpse pulped by the indignant masses, I pray?"

"Nay, at large," I coughed. "Terribly so. I caught wind of the plot with enough time to race to the theatre—but could not prevent the tragedy, and the villain escaped."

"Such a sorrowful waste of human life," the gruff one sighed. "The one man who could have brought peace to this horrid place and squalled these belligerent savages. *Why—couldn't—you—leave—him—alone!*" he cried—the later words punctuated by a blood-twisting series of *grunts*.

I wedged my eyes open enough to watch a portly man wearing the emblem of Sergeant-at-Arms deliver a final, meaty kick to the ribs of a figure lying on the sand. One of the prisoners from the ferry, I guessed—just a sallow sack of rags and bone, yielding not so much as a quaver once the body flopped to rest from the blow. Beyond that sad figure were a second and third, the former sitting and cradling the head of the latter, though the man upright looked no more able than the prone.

As I watched, Sergeant Portly checked the rifle in his hand and approached the pair. "This is for Richey," he growled, and in the instant before the seated man's head burst open like a blood-flower, his sunken eyes met my own, and I knew he was the one I had spoken with in the hold.

The first shot's echoes had not yet died away before a second shot put all doubt to rest regarding the prone man's chances of recovery.

His task completed, Portly turned back to me, working his rifle's bolt with such metallic malice that I feared once more for my own fate.

"Now, your Excellency—you are safe."

78: MASTER TACTICIAN.

THE SINISTER FACE OF THE PORTLY SERGEANT was the last image my eyes took in for some time. After collapsing on the shore I dreamt fitfully of Lara, brandishing a silver revolver, hanging lovingly on Tapiorca's shoulder as he slew rebels by the score with cannon-shot stamped with the emblem of the Crown. After that I dreamt of swimming in an ice-cream lake which I had somehow won the deed to in a raffle; I remember most clearly negotiating with a herd of caramel-pooping moose to work out an arrangement for our mutual benefit.

It was from that grand adventure in homesteadship that I awoke—to darkness.

How easy it was to slip back into that pleasant, ice-cream-filled slumber, where my only worldly concerns were of residual bodily stickiness and a chronic shortage of nuts! I tried valiantly to rejoin the reverie several times, dipping back and forth with varying measures of success until the moose-herd began to take on a decidedly sinister character, citing me for zoning violations and passing on pooping on my property pending my providing their posse with a particularly precious parcel of Papa's prized Polish antler-pomade. (Antler-*wax*, to be precise, but the ambrosaic allure of able alliteration o'erpowers even a stickler's desire for precision.)

But there was nothing to awake *to*—no light, no pain, no sense of place at all. Just an infinite, inky blackness. I briefly entertained the thought that, while in the roiling sea, I had been swallowed by a squid.

When the squid-option began seeming less and less likely, what with the lack of briny stench about, I admitted to myself that I might be dead. My last probable encounter with the after-life, back on the Isle of Yam-Runners, had been creepy enough—but I had seen Lara there, among the departed, when I knew now that she lived! What, then, to make of that old dream? *Had* it, in fact, been just a fevered product of an over-taxed mind? A simple hallucination brought on by the uninhibited consumption of barrel upon barrel of apparently-psychotropic Shamrock Shakes?

Perhaps it had been Fate telling me to let go of Lara.

It had been for Lara's sake that I had shoved the jade-knife into Rikah's throat. And for what? A book of lies, written by a crazy man smelling of salt and turnips.

"Wake up."

A woman's voice, guttural.

I opened my eyes, but no light flooded my vision. The lids felt heavy, as if pressed shut with wheat-paste. I moved my fingers—like swimming through maple-syrup, except lacking the sweet promise of pancakes at the finish—and patted my face numbly, only to find it wrapped whole-sale in cloth.

A burial shroud? No, not smelly enough. Bandages.

Oh God! I'd been *mummified!*

"Your eyes were badly burned," said the woman. "We did everything we could, but we have only so many leeches and tinctures of moon-shine on the island. Balms of harvested inmate-sweat have cooled the burns, but there was a shard of something in your right eye we were unable to remove. A green fleck of some

SAW THIS THING
ON OPIUM.

sort—we didn't dare disturb it for fear of damaging the eye further. Please don't sue us; we have no malpractise insurance." A sigh. "I shouldn't have told you that."

A fleck of jade from that accursed knife! My eye was already absorbing it into its own flesh! I would never see my handsome face in a mirror again!

She went on: "We've tried to send word back to Major-Leftenant Tapiorca"—at this, I clenched everything—"but it seems the telegraph is down, and there's too much fog for lantern-signals. Plus, we have never established a system of lantern-signals." I relaxed— the less Tapiorca knew, the better, that snake. He'd have his whole garrison after me if he knew I was free of the irons.

Which caused me to wonder—with no word from Tapiorca, I was still the ranking officer on this island. Could I yet turn this situation to my advantage?

"I order the garrison to arrest Major-Leftenant Tapiorca for multiple high crimes!" I commanded, though the words actually manifested at a volume somewhere between a whisper and a silent fart.

"He's delirious," said another voice—and I suddenly realised there were *two* women in the room. *This* one had awoken me harshly, and the *other* had soothed me with talk of leeches and broken telegraphs.

The latter voice continued: "No doubt—he's been given enough morphine to numb the whole of Parliament riding on wolverines. Our supply will surely be cut off; they'll think we have another huffer on staff."

"I'll minister to His Excellency; you should tend to the other wounded from the ship," the first voice cut in, presumably addressing the second person, or who knows, maybe some third or fourth person. Maybe there was a dog in the corner. Maybe I was in a surgery-theatre being watched by hundreds—I really had no way of knowing. I felt suddenly self-conscious.

Maybe I was alone. *That* thought was creepy.

The second voice laughed, and a burst of hot, stanky breath rolled past my face. If I *was* alone, someone was going to a lot of trouble to convince me I wasn't. "The wounded prisoner is in the *prisoner* infirmary," the woman said. "There's not much that can be done for him."

"I don't understand—wasn't he weak and starved almost beyond reckoning?"

"Yes, but...let me put it this way. The difference between a prison-*cell*—stone, iron-barred, with a chamber-thimble in one corner and abject misery in all others—and the prisoner *infirmary?* Is that the prisoner infimary has a wounded in it." The voice took on a sneering edge. "Better quarter than the blighters'd give our men."

"All the same—I'm sure you can find something to busy yourself with." A definite insistence.

The second woman got the hint—the air-quality noticeably improved as she left the room.

My skin prickled as I felt the heat of a body in proximity. The voice of the remaining woman dropped an affectation I hadn't even realised it'd assumed, and my blood froze in my numbed-out veins. "Now then. It seems that we've been left alone." *Ursula.*

"You've gotten your way, haven't you?" I asked as she manoeuvred me slowly across the infirmary cot. I felt her handling my body from far away, as if my arms and legs were attached to cords the length of curtain-rods, and I could perceive only second-hand accounts of their motion. She was dressing me, fitting my arms into familiar uniform sleeves, my feet into new boots. "You've manipulated me from the beginning. From the moment I met you till this, I've just been a puppet for you!" She set my legs onto something metallic, and hoisted my body through the air, paying no heed to my words. Could she even *hear* me? "Is the Countess on her way? Is Easthillshireborough-upon-Flats mere minutes from annihilation? *I don't care!* You can't get credit for manipulating me when I *would have done the same thing anyhow!*"

The squeak of metal wheels and a sense of momentum in the dark suggested that Ursula had seated me in an invalid-chair.

I managed to get my hands on the wheels and turn the apparatus sharply into a wall. "Ha ha!" I cried. "Can't manipulate me now!" I spun the wheels backwards, ramming her legs. "I'm in control now, you wretch!"

"Keep it down," she hissed. "You want to get out of here, or you want the whole place to come down on our heads?"

"What does it matter? It's all coming down any-how, isn't it? Peapoddy's air-ships are on their way, thanks to you, right? On *my* authority—first day on the job and it all goes up. Well, *good riddance!* I hope when she lets that lightning loose that the whole city alights like it's made of green-powder—and it takes you and her with it!"

Then, impossibly, something *clicked*. The air-ship's green flame—the stones that paved the tunnels beneath Easthillshireborough-upon-Flats—the powder on my boots that had blown a hole in Lara's ferry...!

"*That's* what she's after, innit? Blast-powder! The city's lousy with it below ground. And she wants to mine it for her armada, to power her weapons!" I had no I idea where I was going with this, but it seemed to be needling Ursula, so I kept it up. "She played you Yam-Runners like chumps all along. You bring her in, and she gets to wipe the site clean and harvest all that green gold, making herself more and more powerful. You'd better watch out—Easthillshireborough-upon-Flats is the master lode. She'll be the most powerful force in the world with a million tonnes of powder at her disposal. And she sure won't need any Yam-Runner help then!"

"Shut up!" Ursula was really bothered now. "The Peapoddys work for the Yam-Runners! *Not* the other way around. If you even *knew*—" She stopped herself. "Never mind. You're right—you've played a part in all this. But it's not like you haven't reaped the benefits as well!"

Blind, incapacitated, I laughed bitterly. "Benefits. You're right! Look at me—more benefits, please!"

She sounded like she wanted to say more—and then she did. "Listen," she whispered. "You need to listen to me now. Right now the only thing that matters is getting back to—"

"Your Excellency!" A man's voice rang out down the hall-way. Rapid footsteps heralded the approach of Someone Important. "So good to see you up and about!"

I spun my bandaged head toward the sound. "Here I am!" I shouted. Ursula, behind me, clapped a stern hand on my shoulder—forcefully enough that I knew this was counter to whatever sinister plan she'd set out for the both of us. *Fine.*

"If Your Excellency feels up to it—we have a briefing set up regarding the attack on the ferry," the man said. "We're still trying to establish contact with Major-Leftenant Tapiorca on the mainland, but in the interim, if you'd care to...?"

"Of course!" I swelled my chest with military fervour. "I can't wait to get some real strategic tactics going on. To the war room!" When nobody moved, I added, "Do you have a war room?"

"Er," the man replied, "we do have a *room*."

"To the room!" I cried. I could feel the anger mount and fester in Ursula's steely grip. *Good.* ✦

PRISON-ISLE ON PARENTS' VISITING DAY.

79: A BLIND BRIEFING.

I WAS ANNOUNCED AS "HIS EXCELLENCY, the Crown's Regent," and judging from the number of chairs I heard shuffling and boots I heard scraping, ten or twelve people must have stood as I entered.

"Your Excellency, may I introduce the command-staff of Prison-Isle," said the man whom I'd met in the hall-way, presumably indicating a roomful of figures I couldn't see. "First, our Minister of Operations, Nedward Duke Paddington-Boîtes."

"An honour, sir." Nedward sounded ponce. I nodded in the direction of his voice.

"To his right, our Secretary-General of Prison Up-keep, Sir Manfred of Glottis."

"Delighted of course, your Excellency." Sounded like Manfred went so far as to click his heels. The nancy.

"To his right, Head Armourer and Spear-Master, Captain Berkeblossom."

And so it went on, through Earl Duckingsham and Old Man Waddle-Bough III and the garlic-smelling Lord Biscuit-Tin or something, all around the room until I was thoroughly and completely introduced to a dozen strangers whose names I started out forgetting at once and graduated to never even hearing the first time. "Charmed, charmed, you all have done a capital job here, capital," I kept nodding, steepling my fingers in imitation contemplation.

"Now then," said somebody, possibly Biscuit-Tin or maybe the one before him (honestly, this was ridiculous), "we've deduced that the explosion aboard, and subsequent sinking of, the prison-ferry was the act of a prisoner attempting escape. We don't know how many were in the hold, but reports indicate that the holdouts from the siege were among the hardiest and most blood-thirsty of any combatants our men have faced on the battle-field. They may have been planning this assault for some time."

"But," interrupted another mystery voice, "we mustn't over-look the chance that the attack was related to the 'high-value prisoner' Major-Leftenant Tapiorca had the ferry pick up from Easthillshire-borough-upon-Flats Harbour. We don't know who that was, but we'll find out all those details as soon as our telegraph-link has been re-established. The cable seems to have been cut somewhere in the channel." *Excellent.* "In the mean-time, we have dispatched a messenger to rendez-vous with the Major, to clear all this up." *Crap-nuts.*

"Call the messenger back at once," I barked. "I know the culprit—the same that sank my un-announced ship at the same time, causing me to be mixed up with the prisoners from the ferry." Pretty sure I heard nodding. "It was a dastardly terrorist named Chin-Strap O'Flagnahan, and I bested him in hand-to-hand combat when I caught him trying to escape the ferry. He was good"—here I spread my arms to indicate my multitudinous injuries—"but I was better." A polite smattering of applause. This was going fairly well. "So, that wraps up that. Case closed on the ferry."

I swear I heard someone furrow a brow. "That doesn't quite match our intelligence," came a puzzled reply. "We've interrogated the surviving prisoners thoroughly. There's definitely a missing ele-ment—some operative who was able to smuggle explosives onto the ship. We believe there might be a conspirator among our staff."

I felt Ursula's grip tense on the invalid-chair, and I knew I had my chance. She had manipulated me long enough—it was time I took charge of this situation. Finally, I would be free from her twisting, sticky spider-web. "I'll tell you who it is," I said. "This woman behind me is not a nurse! She's a spy for enemies of the Crown!"

The room gasped, and feet shuffled angrily. I could hear people approach—but Ursula wasn't going without a fight. "This is non-sense!" she said. "He's delusional!"

"Is that true?" someone asked me. "Are you delusional?"

A knock sounded at the door. "Oh, bother—probably someone wanting the room," said the man I'd met in the hall-way. "But we've got it reserved till noon." He moved to the door and opened it. "Sorry, we're—"

It was at this moment that I was thankful for my blindness, for it imbued me with super-sensitive hearing, without which I certainly would not have over-heard the whispered words uttered by the lad who'd just knocked at the meeting-room door.

"It's the ferry-guard," came the hiss. "Viktor. He says he's got an urgent message. About the Crown's Regent."

I found the chair's wheels with my fingers and swivelled toward the doorway. "Ah, Viktor! How is my old school-chum? A vile prankster, he is. Last time I saw him, he was laughing about having a dozen pizzas delivered to me in the heart of the Saharan subcontinent—payment due! Oh, I swore I'd get that old rascal back, and I won't tell you what I've got planned! Say, what's he got to tell us? Spit it out, then—I'll bet it's a load of laughs!"

The messenger stammered. "He—he said it was for the Security Chief's ears only, Your Excellency."

"Spit it out, or face the stocks," I growled. "I assume there are stocks on this island? Someone see to it that my threat has teeth." Several chairs pushed back from the table at my command. Good. Those men, at least, were solidly mine.

"He said that—that the man posing as the Crown's Regent was the terrorist who blew up the ferry and freed the prisoners," the lad babbled.

I burst out laughing.

"Oh, Viktor!" I chortled, slapping my knee in delight, then grinning through the sharp pain that that ill-thought-out-move brought on. "Someone see that he gets a night in irons. That'll teach him to play pranks!"

The room started chuckling, then burbled over into genuine, tension-dissolving laugher. What a prankster, that Viktor! "Yessir," the messenger replied, skipping back into the hall. The door closed after the boy.

I seized the moment with them still on my side. "Don't forget the nurse," I said. "Traitor to the Crown! Take her away at once."

She tried to mount a feeble protest, but it was no use. *She* hadn't made them laugh. There was a rustle, the sound of sabres slipping from their sheaths, movement—and then Ursula was gone, and that was that.

It had worked. I heaved a copper breath of liberty. "Excellent work, Your Excellency," someone said.

"It's right there in the name," I said, and chanced a smirk. I don't know if it read through the bandages swaddling my entire head. "What other problems of yours can I solve?"

A shuffling of papers. "Er," began someone else, "there is the matter of the scout-ship sighting from the turret watch-men. A small aero-craft's been seen circling o'er the waters off the Easthillshireborough-upon-Flats coast—south of Northerly Isle but west of Boogeyman-Isle; east of Westington, but north of Santa-Claus-Isle. It flew no standard. We think perhaps privateers, or scavengers."

That would be a fore-scout from the Countess's armada. So they *were* on their way to obliterate Easthillshireborough-upon-Flats—a good thing I was safely here on Prison-Isle. "A French pleasure-skiff, no doubt," I proclaimed. "Package-tour hog-wash. Naught but pensioners and ill-behaved children. Pay it no mind. Is that all? Very well. Carry on, gentlemen; smashing work you're doing, expect bonuses all round at Christmas."

"But—that sighting was early this morning—"

"Sunrise sight-seeing; you know the French," I shrugged. "Let's be tolerant of their odd proclivities. What's the trouble?"

"It's just that now there are fifty of them," came the reply. "Massing directly overhead."

It was possible they heard the *chink* of my blood turning to ice all at once.

But I still held the room with steely command. "Fetch Lara the ferry-driver. Summon a ship to take me to London," I said, keeping so much beef in my voice you'd think I had swallowed a steer.

When no one answered, the horns came out. "So? Have you all gone dumb?"

"It's just that our ferry-boat's out of commission, as you know," came the reply—Waddle-Bough, I thought. It sounded like it came from a Waddle-Bough. "And until the telegraph's sorted we can't requisition another. The messenger we sent to Tapiorca's camp took our last—"

"That messenger cannot be trusted!" I shouted, rising half up from my seat before the phenomenon of totally non-functional feet plastered me back into my invalid-chair. "Is there no escape from this blasted place?"

A moment of silence. "Well," said Waddle-Bough, "it *is* a prison."

80: THE SCOUT, AND WHAT HE HERALDED.

BEFORE LONG, THE QUESTION OF THE scout-ship answered itself.

"Your Excellency!" A new voice peeped from the direction of the door. "The air-ships have sent a landing-craft bearing a messenger! Holding a *letter!*"

I turned to face that way, doing my best to sound commanding through my faceful of bandages. "What now? Why are there so many messengers in this place? Can't anyone leave a body in peace to wage war?"

"Of course, milord. Shall I discard their letter and have the interlopers imprisoned on specious charges? I'm sure we can think of—"

"Don't be bloody daft. A letter? You must read it to me. Clearly, and enunciate. Come—whisper it into my ear. It may be saucy, so let me have it privately first."

"It's..." *Another* blasted new voice! This must be the messenger. Were all the doors in this place standing invitingly open? "It's for your eyes only, sir."

"My eyes, my ears. Next letter'll be written on celery and I'll have to lick it clean. After that, I'll be bathing with the missive and calling it Sonny." The twang in this messenger's voice struck me as familiar, somehow—but I couldn't place it. Yorkish? No, too nasal. Harlotshire? Not sultry enough. Stamps-upon-Staves? Not infused with enough abject terror at the crippling terribleness of Life. Where was he *from?*

The weakness in my limbs was beginning to fade, and my general level of bodily misery had declined since I'd been able to exert a modicum of Authority. The act of shouting orders had a narcotic effect on me. (Of course, the pachydermite levels of morphine in my system were no doubt making some contribution to that effort.) I reached up and gingerly withdrew a layer of bandages from my eyes. The right orb began to throb upon exposure to the light, so I re-covered it in gauze at once—but after a few seconds' adjustment the left came into service quite nicely.

It was the first I'd seen of my surroundings—and I was sad to note that the room was shabby, built of brown bricks and apathy; clearly interiour-decoration had been last on the architect's mind when he received the glum news that he'd be designing a Crown prison on this desolate rock. Even a few flayed skins would have livened the place up lodge-style; surely they had a fresh supply. "What a dump," I muttered, and the assembled officers stiffened.

And what officers they were! I'd wondered what type of boot-camp washouts would have been assigned *this* miserable post, and now I knew. These were back-of-the-packs, fleshy, doughy, chicken-neck'd and bowl-cutt'd, unfit for proper military service by the looks of the whole lot—but pleased to fill their chests with tin-stamped breakfast-cereal medals and play Army-Time Soldier. They were stationed here to free up the *interesting* misfits for front-line fodder. These were strictly the mercy admits.

SIR MANFRED OF GLOTTIS.

"Let's have a look at that letter," I said. Whatever it was—auto-registration renewal, note from Grandmama, pre-approved credit-card offers disguised as official government mail complete with Royal signet (and not that I would be able to read any of it, in my illiteracy)—I'd claim it was my orders back to London, and somehow find the fastest way off this mossy boot-stone. The messenger stepped forward and handed me a folded sheet of parchment.

It was this fellow's wardrobe that clicked a latch in my skull. He wore a sheep-skin vest over a ruffled blouse and what appeared to be a steam-mechanic's jump-suit, all topped with a jaunty sombrero. His fashion sense was straight out of the Tardsborough Sanatorium. And he was a meaty lad, but fresh of face, wearing a blank geniality as if he simply didn't know any better.

He was a Yam-Runner. And the envelope bore just the merest traces of green powder in the seams.

It was an explosive. The signal to the Countess to begin her bombardment.

I looked up at the lad. He didn't seem to exhibit any malice or fear in the flare of his nostrils, just the *please-don't-ask-me-any-questions* anxiety of a newly-minted employee. "Whence does this letter come?" I asked.

He blanched. I watched his un-devious face cycle through the few possible answers he managed to come up with, but in the end he could only choke out the truth: "It's...it's from Larsenic the Lithe."

King of the Yam-Runners. Brother to Grenadine. The same man who'd pressed that jade knife in my hands and watched me drive it into Rikah's throat.

Surely opening the letter would blow us all, utterly, to meat.

A bead of sweat traced the back of my neck. The room was staring at me. "Let me take it in the hall-way," I said, and shakingly stood from my chair. Waving away half-hearted offers of assistance, I found my footing and hobbled to the door.

Corralling the Yam-Runner lad, I turned to the Prison-Isle messenger-boy who'd brought news of his arrival to the room. "Where did the air-ship land?"

"In the court-yard, by the irons," the whelp replied. "Shall I take you?"

The three of us emerged from the building into the glumness of twilight. Surrounded by guards bristling with rifles, in a roundish mass somewhat resembling a throughly under-trained hedge-hog, was a Peadpoddy aero-carriage identical to the one that had lifted Rikah and me into the air above the Isle of Yam-Runners. A rickety passenger-cage supported a steam-engine that turned a pair of air-screws, all suspended beneath a giant gas-sac. A leather-clad pilot leaned on the craft, nervously smoking a cigaret. A Peapoddy aviator, not a Yam-Runner himself.

The pudgiest of pudgy prison-guards saluted as we approached. "They flew a white flag for landing, but we thought it prudent not to allow him to leave again, milord." Then he shrank a little. "Did we do okay?"

"Fine, fine," I nodded, clapping him on the shoulder, grabbing a fistful of squish. Of *course* the air-ship would have orders to depart—so the ship and pilot wouldn't be lost in the coming bombardment! The messenger himself was expendable.

Clearly the pilot knew the score—he was white from fright, expecting the blast any second, despite trying to play it cool behind his mirrored-lens pince-nez.

I walked up and shook his hand. I needed him on my side if I was going to get out of here. "How are ya? Listen, no worries— we'll have you up and out in half a nit. Just a few seconds and you'll be safe and sound." He read my meaning. We were fast buds in an instant.

I looked at his passenger-cage, with room for two inside, then turned to the messenger-boy. "Lara. You know who she is? Good. Bring her here, at all costs." It didn't matter if she recognised me. I was going to save her.

The boy ran off. The Yam-Runner lad still stood there, the deadly letter in his hand. I tried not to look at him. I could sense shifting shapes in the clouds, high above, and even felt in my nerves the faint buzzing and thrashing of aerial engines, but a heavy fog hid the whole armada from easy view. Probably for the best—I was still shaky in my muscle-control, and the sight of that hovering terror would probably have filled my trousers with involuntary fear. Instead, I pretended the buzzing was far-off dragon-flies. I didn't care for dragon-flies much, but I could take them a far sight better than the Countess's massing dirigible-flotilla of doom.

I walked round the aero-carriage, past the nervous circle of lumpy-looking guards, and came across the irons. These were sets of heavy shackles staked to the ground, filled with prisoners of various shapes—most of whom I didn't recognise, but all no doubt guilty of innumerable crimes and deserved fully to perish in the impending cataract of flame.

But there was also Ursula, her wrists clamped into the shackles, her hair dirty and skin scratched, looking much the worse for wear since I'd last actually laid eyes on her back in Easthillshireborough-upon-Flats. She stared nails through me as I approached.

"This is your own fault," I said. "You called in the attack. You brought the armada here. Reap now what you have so carelessly sown. I understand that's how it works in agriculture—you should know that, *Yam*-Runner."

"You're going to die," she spat.

"Someday," I conceded. "But I've got ambitious plans yet."

She shook her head. "Before breakfast tomorrow." And then a sly, snake-like grin. "Feeling better, are you? The morphine helping much?"

"Capital, to tell the truth," I yawned, stretching my arms and twisting my trunk limberly. "Never better, in fact. Thanks to modern opiates!"

"No, thanks to Yam-Runner magic," she growled. "You were ten seconds from death when they brought you into the infirmary. And I saved you, with tiny bits of knowledge I recalled from the Tome of the Precious Lore." A shrug. "Admittedly, it was a physically wrenching process for you—hence the morphine."

"Impossible!" I would have kicked her face, if I didn't suddenly feel queasy like I'd swallowed a salamander wrong way first. "The Tome is a work of fiction!"

"So I told you," Ursula smiled.

The air-ships swirled above, ready to wreak their annihilation upon us all. I tried to likewise set her on fire with my glare, but did not immediately succeed.

I returned to the pilot, now on his third cigaret in as many minutes. A pile of ash at his feet told a longer tale. "Tell me your feelings on the Yam-Runners. Good chaps, or what?"

He searched my face, probably wondering what answer would get him aloft soonest and in the fewest number of pieces. "Tolerable in small doses," he finally said. "Bloody gits, in the main." I choked on the thought, but I was actually *glad* he was a Peapoddy man— he'd only a provisional loyalty to Ursula's people.

Next I approached the Yam-Runner lad and took the letter carefully from him for safe-keeping, before marching him to where Ursula lay in irons. "Do you know this lad?" I asked her.

"Never seen him before," Ursula said.

"Great-aunt Ursula!" he chirped. "It's me, Horace! Remember at Christmas, you got me a doggie puzzle? Well, I was unable to put it together."

"Your people sent him here to die," I said to Ursula. "Right?"

"Wait, what?" Horace said.

"You were dying yourself. I saved you," she said. "I racked my memory for you. I remembered enough to buy you these hours you're on now. *You're wasting your precious time!*"

"You sent him here with this letter," I said, "just like the one you gave me."

"You need the Tome to heal yourself fully, before the morphine wears off. You need to return to Easthillshireborough-upon-Flats, if you want to live. I need to read it to you!"

"You planned for the letter to kill him. He's dead to you already. So this won't bother you." I turned to the closest guard, and pointed to Horace. "Traitor to the Crown."

A shot echoed through the court-yard. Horace staggered. A second shot took his knee out. The third went wild and struck a pigeon, but the fourth wiped the fear from the lad's face, as well as everything else on his skull. He fell like a crashing log to the ground.

"*You* did this," I told Ursula.

Above us, the rumbling of the air-ships grew louder. The air felt stirred, like the hunger-burbles of a giant sky-beast, descending to gnash us with its terrible teeth and take us into its churning stomach, where we would be incinerated.

The messenger-scamp appeared around the corner with a flustered Lara in tow. The tension in my limbs released the instant her face emerged into the light. "I found her!" the boy crowed. "She was in the water-closet!"

Lara stopped short as a red ray of sunlight broke through the clouds to outline Horace's thick body leaking blood into the earth.

"We have to go," I said, and pulled Lara toward the aero-carriage. Ursula shouted something that Lara turned to hear, but the pilot was already cranking up the steam-valves on his ship and I didn't make out the words.

The guards looked upwards, and freaked out. The clouds were parting, and the air-ships were upon us.

81: AIR-BORNE AT LAST!

H OLD YOUR FIRE!" I SHOUTED TO THE
soldiers ringing the aero-carriage. The last thing I needed
was for some errant shot to provoke the lightning from above before
I and my love were safely absconded. "These ships are delivering
food and medicine! Hearty beef dinners for all to-night! Steady,
men! Ho!"

Who knew if they heard me through the din of a hundred
steam-engines belching with throttle-power, or were too paralysed
with loin-lubricating fright to squeeze the triggers of their weapons,
well-trained in battle as they clearly were—but in either case, with
a shudderous bump, the aero-carriage left the ground and Lara and
I were aloft. *Safe,* I thought, though the ships still hung above us.
Now, to flee this doomed land! "To London, and hastily," I called
to the pilot. "Or at least some shore far afield of Easthillshireborough-upon-Flats! Bugglesburg, Stamps-upon-Staves, Gloomswick
even—you can see its pouty spires on the horizon e'en now!"

The pilot wrenched back to steal a glance through the grate
separating the passenger-cage from his compartment. "Ye're flippin'
daft if ye think this racket can make London. We're barely gainin'
an inch a minute here wit' ye fatties! With this weight, we're lucky
if we can make altitude back to the Countess's flag-ship, an' I've got
a salt-beet ration tonight I dinnae intend to waste!"

"At least get us out of *here,*" I cried, banging on the grate. As
the craft strained to chew the air and spit it back out beneath itself,
like all known whales of yore, I turned to Lara. "It's not safe here,"
I said. "I can explain everything. I'm saving you, you see!"

She stared at me blankly, surprisingly calm for having been
rushed from her water-closet into this contraption with decidedly
less plumbing. There was no fear in her eyes—she did not seem to
recognise me as the one who'd blown up her ferry-boat. This was

good, as she may've still had her pistol upon her person; but she as
well did not seem to recognise me from the first time we had met,
back at the Police Bureau, when I had first fallen in love with her
graceful, g-g-g-ghost-loving form.

"We're friends, you and me," I added, just to be on the safe side.
"Total friends. Good relationship, us. Charming conversations we've
had. You'll remember. Really great stuff." To cap it: "Seriously."

I looked a wreck, I was sure. Still, *her* face had not faded from
my mind's eye these last months, except for the briefest of dalli-
ances with...well, never-mind; thus it seemed natural that *I* still
lived somewhere deep in the recesses of *her* memory.

I realised that I still clung to her hand from having ushered
her into the craft. I looked down at our clasp, and she withdrew, not
shamefully but simply, as if she'd set her fingers one place and now
wished to set them elsewhere. Was I slimy?

"You don't know me at all, do you?" I asked her. I suddenly saw
how this situation might be awkward.

She smiled politely. "You're the Crown's Regent," she nodded,
gesturing to my uniform. "At your service, milord." Her words
nearly swallowed by the thrashing of the air-screws behind us,
I snatched them from the furious wind, tucking each syllable safely
in a pearl-box for safety. I would draw them out later, to drink their
nectar; such were their sweetness to my chapped and blistered
inside-ache, and I liked them.

I could not touch her hands again; such would be untoward.
Vainly, I hoped that a sudden jolt of the carriage might toss me
guilt-lessly against her, and so I began to subtly exaggerate the
effects of its swaying movement upon my balance. I played it as
coolly as I dared, which is to say super-cool. "We met once, before
this unpleasantness," I said. "I was at your service as a loyal citizen,
when you were the Head Inspector."

"Oh! I know *him*," Lara perked. In the dimness it took a moment
to parse that she was gazing directly past my shoulder, at something behind me.

Down in the prison-yard passing barely a dozen feet below the carriage, I saw Viktor the ferry-guard, struggling against the efforts of several prison soldiers detaining him on my prior orders. He seethed against their grasp, held at bay only by the prodding of pointy rifle-tips; clearly he sensed the injustice being dealt him.

"Yoo-hoo! Viktor! What a lovely ride we're having," Lara screamed down to the prison-yard as we blasted past. I flinched at the volume cascading past my ears, but it was surely lost to the racket of the engine; Viktor would never notice a word.

Yet he did. Lara's voice pierced the distance in a register unoccupied by rival sounds. Viktor looked up, saw Lara, saw me—and that was it.

He threw off the guards in a feat of sur-human strength, dashing their skulls together like coconuts and drinking that milk for power. The rifle-tip at his back he bent into a shepherd's-crook, and though I wouldn't have thought it possible, a blast fired by the soldier in fear curved back through the hook-shape and nailed the man right in his own face. Snatching up that weapon before it fell, Viktor dashed its butt into the last guard's butt, then leapt to a run in an instant, trailing the aero-carriage at speed, bellowing inaudible curses and no doubt the most colourful of invectives through the darkening night. Men in his position always come up with the most creative things to say.

"Higher! Higher," I urged the pilot. The steam-engine strained in response, but though the craft vibrated more pleasingly with a corresponding increase in noise, altitude-response was sluggish at best and snailish at medium. Viktor was gaining on us, scrambling atop loam-barrels and the desiccated corpses of prisoners awaiting trial, straining and reaching with his hooked rifle, swiping at the aero-carriage's dangling wheels.

"He can't reach us," I reassured Lara, as an ominous *ka-thunk* pulsed through our seats.

"Cannae take it," the pilot shouted. "Watch yer arms—the cage-edge'll take 'em right off!"

With a roar that surpassed even the howl of the engine, Viktor pulled the aero-carriage from the sky and ripped the door from the passenger-cage. Nothing separated his fury from my face but a solid eighteen inches of mean-filled atmosphere.

"I anticipate your forth-coming objection," I said calmly, holding up one finger, "and since there is a lady present, I propose we settle this disagreement with a formal, gentleman's duel."

He grabbed me by my throat and wrenched me to the ground. The dirt tasted of shuffling desperation of the men who'd trod it in despair before collapsing in lonely abandonment—a bit chalky.

Lara let out a bull-froggy gasp. The pilot worked a lever for the steam-valves. "Ye stay an' rot," he spat, mashing the shaft to the stop—but something was stuck; he cranked a shift-rod back and forth several times. "Come on, Annie—don't leave me here with this-all!" The engine sneered in response, its overly-complex gear-arrays twisted out of alignment by the rough landing. A lesson to the smarties who thought that all-exposed brass mechanism made for prettier engine-works.

"A duel!" I cried again. "And we can settle this! Our hands as clean as our honour. A single, quick bout of Eton-rules satisfaction."

"I don't know those rules," Viktor growled.

"How handy that I happen to have them right here," I said, sitting up and handing him the parchment envelope from my coat-pocket.

Viktor stared at the paper.

"Now we each take fifty paces, and do what it says on the paper," I said. "Ah! No peeking. I promise the time spent reading will give you no disadvantage."

Viktor looked over at Lara. This stratagem would be hard to explain off to her, but it was the only way I was getting out of this.

"Fifty paces," he said. "You'll shoot me in the back."

"I have no gun," I said, standing and brushing sad-dust from my uniform. "Fifty paces. Turn, and march." I did so myself, and seeing me expose my vulnerable back-side to him, he did like-wise. A noble warrior, at least, this Viktor, if a bit thick.

As I ticked off steps I glanced to see if the air-ships were still blotting out the sky overhead. Yes, indeed. Some battle-drum within my breast began to beat a basso count-down to disaster. Twenty steps I had taken. Thirty, now. Thirty-five.

The steam-whine of the carriage's engine suddenly grew sharply in pitch. "There we go!" the pilot cried. "Annie, I'll never doubt you again!"

Thirty-seven. *Nuts to this jive.* I turned back and ran for the carriage. Viktor still plodded away, probably at forty steps now. Forty-two. Forty-four. There was no time to lose.

Lara still stood still, watching the whole affair blankly. "We have to go!" I hissed to her, and she obligingly settled herself in the passenger-cage.

"Oh no you donnae!" the pilot called, reaching to accelerate the craft from the ground. I powered into him at a full run, my whole weight stacked behind an outstretched fist. The shocking blow drove him straight out the other side of the craft, tumbling stiffly onto his head then flopping with boots skyward down fully onto the furrowed earth. I glanced back at Viktor. Forty-six. Forty-eight.

I pulled every lever I could find in the pilot's-cage. The craft left the ground like a fly tired of poop.

Viktor turned and opened the envelope. I turned away just as he disappeared into a swirling gout of flashing green flame, his body atomising into powder in the first bright second, only his feet surviving to tumble away like leaves in the blast.

I wrenched the carriage-tiller as hard as I could away from the island, knocking Lara against the side of her cage, thrusting me toward a gaping opening in my own. For the briefest moment I wished that I was back there with an excuse to fall into her—

—And then the sky filled completely with furious hot lightning from the air-ships massed above us. ✦

82: A DARING RESCUE.

A SEARING SHOCK-WAVE RIPPED MY hands from the aero-carriage's control-tiller and flung me sprawling clear out the far end of the pilot's-cage out into the open air. Instantly I was weight-less in a wave of heat, coat flapping in the burning wind, feeling Gravity bow to the massive fire-power that was the Countess Peapoddy and her deadly war-machines, floating, totally enveloped by some sort of terrible oven-womb.

That barrage lasted all of three seconds—and then the air was dark again, filled with the crushing thunder of rock and brick and flesh collapsing into itself, threatening to drown even the gnashing thrum of the hovering armada's thousand coal-engines. I could see nothing; the light had robbed even my un-bandaged eye of its sole faculty. Now it was loafing in my skull uselessly, taking up space like a free-loader. I would have chastised it severely were I not weeping, blind, falling screaming toward the destruction.

What had become of the carriage? Of Lara? Had they been blown to bits by lightning? Were they, robbed of my pilotage, steadfastly motoring toward the black sea below, thinking all was well until frigid water surrounded them?

Suddenly a deafening clatter was upon me, and a great heat swept past my body—then I was tumbling side-ways into something soft, some sea-creature, a horrid, squishy kraken awoken by the tumult in the skies above—

Lara.

I forced open my un-bandaged eye and beheld her at the controls of the aero-craft, working the tiller like a seasoned pilot. I was mashed against her utterly, a hand resting undecorously upon her knee, her heaving shoulder all but filling my vision. I could nearly make out the pores in her precious skin from this distance,

but I had little chance to marvel—for once I realised what had happened, I couldn't stop giggling.

She had snatched me from the air!

I scrambled to right myself, feeling my face redden and my skin
burn from the spark of her touch. What would she *say*? What would
she *think* of my impropriety? I'd have to be smooth. "Sorry, er, about,
uh..."

"Hang on," she said, banking the craft away from a billowing
dust-cloud growing over the island. I felt inertia slide me away from
her, toward that dangerous opening torn in the pilot's-cage—*was
she sending me a signal?* She could just as easily have banked the
other way, sending me tumbling back against her...!

Lara worked a lever and the carriage righted itself, then gently
leaned heavenward. In a lazy, twisting spiral it began to ascend,
smoothly and gracefully.

I fished for a good opener. "Hey, so...I didn't know you could fly!"

"THE CHILDREN ARE JUST DEAD WEIGHT."—[SEE PAGE 717.]

"I didn't know I would have to," she frowned, searching the sky around us. The Countess's massive bomber-dirigibles sat many and heavy in the air, moored o'er the island—we were level with them now, yet still we climbed. Betwixt the looming ships, smaller aero-carriages like our own traced glowing orange soot-trails across the night; I wondered how obvious we were, and if our own furnace would attract attention from the armada. Our coal-reserves were also a cause for concern, but Lara was the pilot now; I trusted she had a fair handle on the situation. I propped my feet up and peeked back at where we'd come from.

The island was gone—replaced by a smouldering cloud, crackling occasionally with green sparks but mostly settling into rubble. The bombers had laid it to waste, as they had Rikah's village. As they would Easthillshireborough-upon-Flats, and, potentially, the rest of the world; who could say?

I turned to Lara, trying to gauge the right words to employ. I'd just exploded her no-doubt dear friend Viktor before her eyes—yet she had saved me from falling; was she intending some grosser, yet more horrific punishment for me than death by simple Gravity?

Or...had she recognised me at last, and was now ready to start our new life together?

Best to get the obvious issues out of the way, at least. "About Viktor," I said slowly. "You may not have known this, but he was a child-molester."

She turned to me with the same blank look she'd sported all evening. "Who's...Viktor?"

Clearly she'd known the man five minutes ago; she'd pointed him out to me! Unless—"I mean the guard on your ferry," I said. "Perhaps his name wasn't...?"

"I don't know any ferry," she laughed, reaching between her knees to turn a brass crank. "Oh, it's shaping up to be a lovely night, isn't it?"

Indeed, a cool breeze ruffled our hair as the carriage continued its ascent. We'd left the bomber-ships behind now, and were approaching a cloud-bank, behind which the moon glowed wide and white. Brilliant clouds cast her face in shades of pale and heather, giving her skin a softness I'd not seen at sea-level. Her eyes twinkled with delight at the sight of far-off stars, and from this height, we could even glimpse the main-land—battle-field bivouacs burning tiny orange dots into the dark land-mass, and of course Tapiorca's headquarters were a blazing smear of yellow. The man burned more kerosene each night than a Madagascar oil-huffer so far off the waggon he'd forgotten what waggons were made of.

War was being waged, but it traced no worried lines into Lara's face. I recalled what Viktor had said, on the ferry-boat: *Not entirely still there, from the, you know. Had it rough, she has.*

She clearly seemed the type who would be concerned about such things as war, or the destruction of the island, or Viktor exploding. Only one explanation remained:

She had lost her memory.

"You don't remember me at all, do you?" I asked her, unafraid to be bold now. Even if I was wrong, I could still chalk it up to coyness.

She searched my face for the very first time, really stared into its crevices for what seemed like half an eternity, as the carriage continued screwing its way upward. "I can't say so," she finally said. "Were we friends?"

This was it—my chance to make history the way it should have been. The whole rakish-cheese-twirler-from-Beloochistan deal. I had been handed *yet another* opportunity to start the whole affair over from the start, to make Lara good and well my own. All I had to say was *yes, we were friends. Lovers. Married, even. Come home with me, my love. Come back to your own home, and let me teach you everything you've forgotten.*

White cloud-stuff enveloped us, and we were instantly cold and wet. I feared for the carriage's furnace, sputtering behind us. But Lara turned and quickly worked a bellows-handle I hadn't even seen was there—she knew this craft expertly, though she likely wouldn't know her own face in a mirror. Our coal-engine roared with healthy flame, and we continued to climb through dark fog, invisible to the world, invisible to each other, she invisible even to herself. I myself invisible to sky-ticks—I hoped.

As we rose through the cloud something deep inside me became afraid of something un-seen, of mist-dragons or star-narwhals or the like. I shushed that voice, reminding it that our team had done this before, risen through clouds with a woman—that we were old pros, that there was nothing up here to be afraid of.

Blind in the fog, but with Lara ten inches away, I began to stammer out some words.

I told her how we'd met in Easthillshireborough-upon-Flats when she'd become Head Inspector at the Police Bureau, and how she'd come to think my house was haunted by murderous spirits. How I'd coöperated fully with her investigation, only to have the treacherous Peapoddy enact violence upon her—and how I had then travelled the globe (or at least the Irish Sea) retrieving the Tome of the Precious Lore, with which, supposedly, to heal her.

I began describing herself to her, outlining the construct of her that I'd built in my mind, explaining to her all the qualities that she had embodied, at least so far as I was concerned. For that beautiful construct was truly who she could be, at her best.

I left out the bit about how I had blown up her boat and exploded her best friend. But I made sure to mention how I'd saved her from the island about to be destroyed by fire.

"Is any of that familiar?" I asked the mist, hoping that she had even been listening, that she hadn't fallen asleep or tumbled from the craft or turned into a monster squid while I wasn't looking.

For a moment, there was nothing. *Monster squids can't talk,* I thought; *this is a bad sign.*

Then her voice, seemingly from everywhere: "What was that name again? The man who hurt me?"

In that moment our carriage lifted through the fog-bank into the high clear black of the æther. Hanging pendulous from Heaven was the Countess's flag-ship, a massive, glowing dirigible with her grotesque face projected a hundred feet wide across its billowing gas-sac. No moon at all, this monstrosity out-shone the stars

around it—set into a back-drop of pure shadow, it exuded malevolence, smaller ships buzzing about it like flies at a rotting carcass.

"Peapoddy," I breathed.

The Countess's face reflected round and glassily in Lara's
eyeballs until she snapped her head to me, suddenly alert,
suddenly stern.

"I remember."

"She's going to destroy the city," I gasped. "She can destroy us
just as easily. Get us out of here!"

Lara looked at the flag-ship, then down at the fog-bank beneath
us, a wide, featureless sea of its own betraying no indication of what
lurked beneath.

"We have to warn Tapiorca," she said, and began to work every
lever in the pilot-cage simultaneously.

My gizzard lurched as the carriage suddenly banked. Panels
set into its structure began to extend and twist and fan around in
odd contortions. We dropped like a stone, screaming back toward
the fog-bank, then sinking through it, enveloped in darkness and
cold. "Stop!" I cried. "No! We can't go back! That's where they're
going next!"

REALLY HORRIBLE HORSE-CARTS.

"We're the only ones who know," Lara said with jaw firmly set. "Nobody escaped Prison-Isle. We have to warn the Crown forces!"

"Let's warn them in London," I growled, and reached for the controls.

I never reached the tiller. A spasm twisted my hand backwards, and I shrieked in pain. A jolt of fear spiked through my spine. The morphine was wearing off.

If Ursula had told the truth, I had to get back to Easthillshire-borough-upon-Flats myself—to retrieve the Tome of the Precious Lore.

"Fine," I squeaked, biting my thumb to avoid weeping with a sudden wave of morphine-shakes. "Back to Tapiorca we go."

We burst from the bottom of the fog and raced the armada toward the city.

83: FAMILIAR FACES.

ALL RIGHT, HERE'S THE PLAN," I told Lara, shouting over the wind as she pumped the bellows to the aero-carriage's furnace. "We land in Tapiorca's camp, give him the quick hey-ho, I make a stop back in my quarters to pick up a thing, and we're back up & out before the coal's cold, what?"

She shook her head. "We can't make shore near his camp—his cannons will make short work of what they'll think is an enemy craft. We'll have to circle round Laborious Point and come down the mountain-side."

Two minutes ago she didn't know her own mum—now she knew Tapiorca's defence strategies? "The Point's quite far, and a less direct route," I warned. "Full of brambles, probably. Nettles an' such, so I hear. Probably lousy with scorpions to boot, if this day goes on like it has, and at least one man I know from the area is just constantly covered in poison-oak." I glanced back at an inky smear in the sky, that mottled black absence of stars that was the smoke-cloud from the destruction of Prison-Isle. "Besides, Tapiorca must have seen the attack—it was visible Eton to Everest, no doubt."

"If he saw anything, he saw a lightning-storm," Lara said, her voice even, her eyes narrowed against the wind. She was steadfast of purpose, that was certain, and at the moment looked a bit like a dolphin racing to save some poor swimmer from problems, her skin sleek and blue in the false-moon-light. "Those air-ships will reach Easthillshireborough-upon-Flats before dawn breaks. He'll never see the attack coming!"

The carriage-furnace coughed and the craft shuddered, faltering in its flight for a moment before catching lift again. The gas-sac above us strained to inflate as Lara worked the bellows-control furiously. "How are we on coal?" I asked. "Should we have saved a body or something for fuel?"

"Do a favour," she said, twisting a knob with one delicate hand, keeping a firm hold on the tiller with the other. "For us to make it to land, I'll have to put the engine on manual aspiration. Can you take over the bellows? Pump it steady, with long, even strokes." She plucked my hand from my lap and set it on the bellows-handle, working it up and down.

When her hand left mine to the task, my skin felt suddenly cold. Abandoned. "How's it go again?" I asked, hoping for another lesson.

"I think you get the idea."

I worked the bellows. The furnace coughed, and a blast of bright orange flame fire-balled from the exhaust-stack. "Faster!" she cried. I worked the lever as powerfully as I could, even as the carriage began to sink—but then, with another sputtering blast of flame, we caught the wind and began to climb again.

"I can keep this up probably forever," I gasped mannishly, "but how long do you think it might be?" Already my long-suffering arms were burning with pain. I felt another morphine-tremor begin in my legs, and steadied my knees with my other hand. It would do no good to my wooing to get the junkie-shakes now.

"Not long, if they can help it," Lara shouted, and I turned to see where she indicated—at three orange soot-trails glowing against

the night, arcing our direction. The agents of the Countess had
noticed our escape.

"How much faster can we go?" I cried. "They're gaining on us!"

"We can go as fast as you can pump," she replied, grabbing
onto my hand with her own and joining me at the lever. Her strong,
sweat-slick grip pinched my skin against the polished wood of the
bellows-handle, adding weight and fury to my labour. Together we
pumped the bellows with mania, and our carriage spat fire and
leapt through the sky. It was one of those moments that you recall
decades later, and wonder how it ever even happened.

Behind us, the other craft were gaining. Our flaming path
made a clear beacon against the darkness. A snatch of ocean wind
brought the sound of far-off furnaces, and for a moment I thought
we were being pursued by a steam-train, chug-a-lugging into station with a friendly load of dry-goods and livestock and wide-eyed
passengers chock-full of happy Adventure-stories from the Big City.
What a lovely home-coming that would be, greeting Cousin Mamie
at the train-depot as she dug in her bag for trinkets and tokens
from her trip, and we'd all go back to the estate for an evening of
roast lamb and Story-telling. Such fun!

"Keep going!" Lara screamed as a swirl of hot soot in my face
brought me back. We were slowing. "Pump!"

I pumped, but still we fell, far-off in my mind, a dull, painful sensation preventing me from moving any faster. I knew
I should pump the handle as hard as I could manage, and I felt
my elbow bending back and forth, but my muscles suddenly
began speaking a different language, and I could not understand their songs. They were lovely, though, Old-World wedding
chants perhaps, and I thought what a lovely folk-dance they
would make, if only I could manage my dowry.

My head rolled to one side, and I saw the reflection of our carriage pacing us from the side—were we soaring side-ways over the
ocean, just ten feet above the waves? I hadn't even sensed us banking over. A figure who was apparently my own reflection gestured

at me, waving its arms, brandishing a rifle. That figure wore the uniform of Peapoddy's aviators, and it looked snappy on him.

From a far-away place, my stomach leapt to pull wildly on my dizzy-bells. "Made it over land," came Lara's voice, at the end of a tunnel somewhere. "Feel the up-draft? But it won't last."

A flash of sparks issued from my reflection—a deafening blast echoed through the tunnel—and our carriage shuddered. I tried to turn back to Lara, but my head weighed a thousand pounds and seemed made of crumbly cheese. I tried to feel if her hand still crushed mine against the bellows-lever, but I could sense nothing below my chin. My lips, oddly, felt very full and sore. I wondered if I looked bee-stung; people paid good money for that look.

Somebody knocked on the inside of my forehead. *Thump-thump. Thump-thump.* I was too tired to find the doorknob. "Nobody home," I tried to say, but it came out as "Nuhbvvuggh."

Then, another blast of sparks and sound...A rifle-shot! I snapped my eyes open. We were flanked by Peapoddy aero-craft and taking fire. Lara was twisting the tiller and pumping the bellows as fast as she could. The horizon outside banked zanily. She screamed into the wind, trying to move knobs and levers and fire a silver Colt at the pursuers and pump the bellows at the same time. I reached down, took her hand from the bellows, and continued to pump as fast as I knew could be possible. She took the opportunity to unload her Colt into the swirling shapes around us, but to no apparent avail.

Our carriage jolted skyward and whistled as hot steam met the cold exhaust-stack. Lara banked, and I became suddenly aware of trees underneath, moving fast and looming rapidly closer—then dropping away as we lurchingly swooped the other direction. The Peapoddy craft were just behind us. I pumped the bellows, ignoring the many carefully-reasoned excuses that my body put forth urging me to abandon the effort. I pushed myself aside and pumped the bellows.

One of the carriages behind us suddenly disappeared, taken up by the darkness. A blast of wind shot past us on both sides, along with the unmistakable sound of giant, leathery wings flapping fifty times a minute.

Bat-creatures.

"We must be over Stamps-upon-Staves!" I shouted to Lara, working the bellows-lever despite some burning pain I didn't even bother to locate. With each pump, the exhaust-stack whistled, a high-pitched screech not entirely unlike the shrieks of the horrid, man-sized flying beasts currently destroying the craft that pursued us.

As I watched, another of the enemy carriages plummeted into the bank of trees beneath, spraying glowing red coals over twenty yards of forest-floor.

"We're about to be *in* Stamps-upon-Staves," Lara shouted back. With a jerk, our furnace-engine seized; the exhaust-whistling dwindled and sighed into silence. No matter how hard I pumped the bellows, we fell.

The character of the land beneath us was impossible to determine, but at least it was land, and not ocean, or lava, or spikes, or Wales.

The third pursuing carriage shot overhead, its billowing orange soot-trail illuminating a clearing in the trees ahead. As the enemy banked around to approach us again, six or eight arrow-like shapes rocketed into the carriage at blinding speed, taking it apart in mid-air; great wings and flashing eyes surrounded the craft's billowing gas-sac and tore it to ribbons with deadly claws.

In the fading red light, Lara banked the craft to align us with the clearing, which appeared to be a rocky country road. "Do I need to keep pumping?" I asked, my fingers beginning to tingle—neither fire nor lift had resulted from any pump for a good minute now.

"All you can do now is hold on," she said, moving the tiller with minute adjustments. The road below began to fade into black as the blazing soot-trail above us dissipated into the night.

Unable to grasp anything with numb fingers, I searched for some protrusion to wrap my elbows around—but the options were either sharp (as in the torn-open edge of the seating-cage) or associated with the navigation of the vessel. I turned to Lara, her bottom lip bitten in concentration. "There's nothing to hold on to," I said, half-heartedly hoping she would volunteer her own self.

The flailing pilot of the disintegrated enemy craft suddenly fell screaming past our bow on his way to meet the Earth—we shot through his cry in the instant before it ceased, cut short by arrival at his ultimate destination.

Then *we* met the road. *Hard.* I was made painfully aware of the craft's lack of rich-man-car suspension as we struck a boulder and bounced back up and side-ways, caroming off the planet. For a dangerously vertiginous second I knew we would topple—

—But we smashed back down properly, on all of the carriage's wheels, and stayed pointed that direction. As we rolled jarringly to rest, there was nothing around but the bouncing crunch of the road beneath...and then, after that, there was stillness.

Lara's white hands clutched the controls. My feet pressed against the bulk-head, holding me firmly in my seat. My guts continued to roil, but then settled as some inner-self slowly came to accept that we had stopped. A general dull pain returned to my extremities, and I vaguely began to sense that I needed to use the facilities.

I ventured a leg slowly out onto the road, standing upright and stretching into the cool night. All was quiet. Insects called through the forest. Our furnace hissed and occasionally popped. There followed no sound of pursuit, or any evidence at all of any other persons within miles. The bat-creatures, as well, had vanished, save for a single, distant screech of fare-well—or perhaps, judging from the stains now marking the canvas of our gas-sac, love-lorn woo.

I rounded the carriage and extended a hand to Lara. She accepted, and stepped from the pilot's cage out onto the road beside me. Above us, the craft's gas-sac began to deflate, and in a moment it would cover us both.

In the heat of the moment I wondered if it would be appropriate to kiss her.

"Well," she said, *"that'll* make quite the story to tell Tapiorca, won't it?" As she said the words my spine painfully spasmed, and I began to wonder if my body was reacting not to the morphine, but to the mention of the Major-Leftenant himself.

84: A RACE AGAINST DAWN.

IN DARKNESS WE DRIFTED DOWN THE road, sometimes rolling along the path, other times floating a foot or two above the surface. Branches and leaves made poor fuel for a coal-furnace, but burned the stove hot enough to turn the carriage's air-screws, and so we shuddered our way along, Lara searching the skies for stars by which to navigate, I presumed, or else *totally* lost in thought. Meanwhile, I watched trees and meadows pass by and wondered how much the land values would plummet when the armada ultimately laid the country-side to ashes.

Lara had a notion that we could find Tapiorca somewhere in this dreadful night; that we could save him and his forces from the destruction sure to come. I felt sure that we were lost in the darkness, and might find, with the dawn, that we had at best described a circular path, or at worst were already several hours' travel into the impassible Buffoon's Gulch, the entrance and exit to which were rumoured to shift geographically with each phase of the moon, and which required for escape the performance of heroic tasks that were frankly just ponce—wrestling a bear while being drizzled with waffle-syrup, for example, or tickling oneself to the point of renouncing one's birthday.

But should we indeed be headed for Easthillshireborough-upon-Flats, with each mile traversed I felt my seat-parts grow more slick with fear and my thinking-parts more sour of opinion. Magnetic forces pulled at my body, urging flight from this country by any means available, whether it be aero-carriage, makeshift skate-board, or even the desperate hire of an unlicenced badger-cab—but my limbs and tendons were slow to respond to even the most fervently-whispered entreaties, and when they did move, they did so under vehement, painful protest and in the wrong directions. The morphine Ursula had administered had utterly faded, and should she be believed, the only hope for my recovery lay in that old, smelly book that I hoped still remained in Tapiorca's camp. If luck favoured us, the Major-Leftenant may have sent it out as a totem to the fore-front of his battle-lines, in the fashion of the Ark of the Covenant, and thus I might pluck it from potentially the first brigade that we encountered in the field; alternately, he may have tossed it as trash, and I could hardly blame him because it *did* look mouldy. I worried that my prospects in the whole affair were not great, but despite some initial overtures of politeness, prattling on about it at length began to elicit exaggerated moans and eye-rolls from Lara, so I eventually just shut the heck up.

Onward the both of us bounced, finding little to talk about in the awkward stretches. We chatted briefly about trivial things, favourite foods and the like (she fancied Indian spices and taco-flavoured Doritos, a palate I consider the hall-mark of a sociopath), but on the whole our small-chat fell disappointingly limp—Lara admitted to embarrassing gaps in her memory, and could offer no evidence that she recalled any of our encounters prior to this evening, to say nothing of that initial meeting months ago.

Of Major-Leftenant Tapiorca, though, she could bleat no end of praise; the man was a War Hero, to hear tell, and some sort of paragon of Gentlemanliness to be sure. Accounts of his dashing exploits about the Continent in service of the Crown and its ill-defined interests held little thrall for me, and I found myself nodding off continually during her monologues on the subject of his greatness. At one point I meekly offered a counter-point to one of her gushing plaudits, commenting that his much-commended moustache had seemed a bit frizzy when I'd had occasion to examine it up close, but this was met with such a hail of defensiveness from her that I reserved my harshest retorts for play silently in my seething imagination. Argument was effortful at the moment, and I had to save my energy for a hasty escape once the Tome of the Precious Lore was secured.

As the night drew on, the subject turned to gifts and tokens she'd received from the aforementioned officer; in this arena her memory was whip-sharp, and she could cite without pause every minute feature of each encrusted chalice, each gilded spork, each banal bejewelled bauble the Major-Leftenant had presented her with. Even the silver Colt revolver rated a mention, as a present for some no-doubt made-up holiday such as Ferry-Driver's Day or Besmitten-Lass Appreciation Week or Hero-Adulation All-The-Time (to be observed whenever Tapiorca was in the vicinity). In return for running the man's various errands, he'd presented her with no end of giggly gewgaws.

"So you're picking up his dry-cleaning, now, is it?" I snorted at this point, half-conscious enough to forget my wiser stance of silence. "Or are you cleaning his robes with your hands as well? Does he leave you trinkets of his hair within their folds?"

"It's nothing like that," she snapped. "Not *errands* errands. Just...well, that's what he called them." Her voice dropped an octave, and she looked around as if she suspected that in the surrounding darkness lurked eavesdropping owls, or Italians. "Tasks. Missions. You must know—you *are* the Crown's Regent."

Tapiorca was a more devious man than I gave him credit for, running various clandestine operations as a military commander might. I opened my mouth to say something likely to be dumb, but shut it again as Lara continued to speak, addressing the night flat in front of us.

"I'm sure he thinks you're doing quite well," she said. "It must be tough, coming into such a job—but you're a far sight more pragmatic than Richey was, that's for sure. The old man spent half his days lining his humidor with imported tobacco and the other half strutting; for him it was the *romance* of being at war that appealed. Tapiorca's a battle-field man, through and through."

Did she glance over at me then? It was hard to tell, in the dark.

We stopped several times as the night went on to forage for branches and stoke our furnace—or rather, she foraged and stoked, while I lay immobile and whimpering in the carriage. Anxiously she searched the sky for soot-trails that might mark the approach of the armada, while I mentally began to index my memories, to get all my affairs in order in case of my death, so that potentially someone could re-animate my brain—I figured my chances of success were greater if my thoughts were lined up in neat rows. I had a hard time of it though, because I hadn't been labeling anything these long years, and I'm sure I drifted off with the job un-done.

When I awoke, on the far end of more hours of silent travel, I realised I could now see Lara's face—and the road ahead, and the horizon beyond. The sun was rising, and the thick dark smoke-cloud that perpetually hung over Easthillshireborough-upon-Flats was closer than ever before. A few shuttered farm-houses passed us on the road; we were encroaching on Civilisation.

"How do you know you've stayed up too late?" Lara suddenly said, craning her neck back to search the reddening sky for air-ships, squinting through the haze shrouding the road-way. I was unable to move any muscle of my own, such were the pains and cramps that the night's travel had thoughtfully provided me with.

It took me a while to realise her question was the start of a riddle. "Uh...when you're too tired and miserable to function?" I asked, because it was true.

"When it *dawns* on you," she said, and almost—for the briefest of seconds—she started on the path to a smile.

It made her beautiful again, and for a moment I forgot how irritating she'd been all night long.

Then I realised where I'd heard the riddle before. It was a Carlton Rube line.

From the Bon-Mot gala.

Suddenly I was very aware of the silver Colt lying heavily in
Lara's possession, and my spirit clutched itself in soul-wetting fear.
Two things were immediately clear:

She had killed Field-Admiral Richey.

And if she thought *Rube* was funny, I would *never* be able to
love her.

85: FRIGHT AT
POOL-PARTY PLAZA.

"D O   Y O U   F A N C Y   E N T E R T A I N E R S   M U C H ?"
I asked Lara as innocently as I could pretend. I wanted to
know if she'd repeated the Carlton Rube riddle because she honestly
thought it was funny, or if perhaps she thought *I* might have found
it amusing. In the one case, she was a simpleton; in the other, a bad
judge of character—the latter could be rectified, perhaps, with a
fair measure of corporal training, but the former was a tragic flaw
even old Hippolychus the Tragic would find eminently scorn-able.

"Oh, I don't go in for too much frivolity," she tossed off. "I'd never
traverse the garish halls of an amuse-o-cade, or pay good money
to see a rubbish kinetograph, or read the wrapper of a Bazooka-
Joseph. Mother raised me to see value in hard labour and to take
joy from a job done strictly and well, and I just can't fritter time
away on idleness and vulgarity. Can you *imagine?* That there are
people in this world who earn their keep through *jesting,* without
engaging the mind or the shoulders for a single minute? I can't
reward such crassness, and I won't have it in my life."

A harsh strike against Lara, I cringed to admit. For *idleness
and vulgarity* was carved into my family crest, though the carving
had been done by me wielding the sharpened bone of an orphan

I had rent apart for a giggle. Still—"But that *was* a Carlton Rube line, wasn't it? Have you seen him perform?"

"Oh, Rube!" She stifled a laugh—*O double-faced wretch*, cursing the trade with one breath, but gifting the worst offender of all with a bird-song chuckle! "I *do* like Carlton Rube. What a card, he is! And a friend of the family—why, we're practically cousins. Our mothers were driven out of a nunnery together."

From that moment on, something *changed* in the thin space behind my one un-bandaged eyeball: Lara's shadowed form loomed suddenly *grotesque* to me, her laugh a maniacal celebration of all that was banal in the world, and I felt nauseous for ever thinking of her another way.

What had I done? I had spent so much, suffered so much, in the service of *this creature*? A *common-law cousin* of the man who trampled the integrity of every show-man in History? I felt my substantial cheese-twirler pride well up like bile in my gullet—I even tapped my thigh to discover, amazingly, that Abu Fromage's perfect cheese-wand still rested firmly and securely in my uniform's scabbard—but, agonisingly, I *could not* act against her. Too weak to move, too reliant on her for the moment; and besides, there was one more thing I had to know:

"Were you *there*—at the Bon-Mot gala?"

She glanced side-long, piercing my gaze in the dawning light with a four-inch crucifix-spike of a

DEALING WITH SOLICITORS.

stare. She seemed hesitant to speak, as if she was unsure how much to reveal.

If I was wrong I could always blame any ensuing confusion on more of her mental problems. So I pressed: "Field-Admiral Richey's last performance. Tapiorca's...*errand*."

"I thought Carlton was in top form, that night. I only wished I could have waited longer, to see more of the performance—but I had to catch the night-ship out. Besides"—and here she sighed, not resignedly, but rapturously, as if the thought of Tapiorca watching over her every move was somehow *pleasant*—"I was only there in his service."

"Tapiorca's?"

"Of course." Were her eyes narrowing? "As you are now."

"Of course." The uniform of the Crown's Regent hung heavy on my bones. "And a top-notch job you did, too—even sprayed his old wife with mind-matter. Really coated that whole seating-box. Crack shot, you."

"I—I don't really remember much about that part."

"It was the best bit of all."

We crossed the boundary of Easthillshireborough-upon-Flats proper and began a winding navigation of neighbourhood causeways. This part of town was cramped and shanty-heavy—it was where the paupers lived their pauperish lives doing pauperish things piled onto one another making thousands of horrible pauper babies all the pauper time. My skin prickled at the potential for ambush or attack—this would be a smashing time for renegades to leap from the burned-out skeletons of the endless miserable dwelling-spaces and do some smashing of their own on our noggins.

But we saw no one, for hours.

A few times I heard skittering, but it was easily explained away as weevils or weevil-like monsters feasting on rotted everything. Far-off rumbling may have been Tapiorca's cannons, or thunder. Or, the approach of air-ships; or the rumbling farts of the Earth. It was impossible to tell, with my sense of smell deadened by all the ash.

"I thought there was supposed to be a war on," I muttered.

"What's that?"

"Mmm? Nothing."

"No, you said something. What was it?"

"I was just talking to myself."

"Sounded like you were talking to me."

"I wasn't."

"Well, what were you saying to yourself?"

Anger roiled within. I would *never* tell her what I had said in that idle moment. This woman was *infuriating*. The silence that followed was maddening, each of us too annoyed to speak with the other, and all of it *her* fault.

We arrived at the smouldering ruins of Pool-Party Plaza to find only a few dead Crown troops guarding the entrance. I saluted them jauntily as we crunched through the yawning gates. "Capital defences, lads," I told them, and then caught my tongue in fear—was this another trick? Some possumish ambush-ploy? But no, they were stone dead, elephant-waste in their faces, smeared chunkily and arrogantly by a confident hand; I knew the assertiveness of the pattern. The men were cold to the touch, and even the golden crowns had been pried from their teeth.

"Get your hand out of that man's mouth and come along," Lara hissed.

I clutched a fence-post to steady my balance, determined not to accept any offer of her support; I wanted to never be in danger of touching her again, should her wretched taste in amusements somehow stain through my pores. But then I realised I should at least put on a good show for the moment, so she'd be inclined to help me find the Tome. As her warm arm encircled me I figured the matter of her horribleness could be tabled just for the time being.

"What's that?" She whipped round at a flash of movement, nearly sending me sprawling. A small shape had darted behind the carcass of an elephant, and I immediately began considering the various methods I knew of harpooning a child at this distance. I'd need a javelin, some sort of line, a bait-steak...I wondered how long it would take to saw a suitable sirloin from one of the guards behind us.

Lara began to coo, some sort of soft, motherly tone, and to my shock a little deformed boy came shuffling out into the open, looking like a regular human child that had been passed through a rope-twister and then given the clothes from a hundred-year-old buccaneer-corpse found washed up on a reef covered in putrefying whale-guts.

I was amazed. I'd have to learn this bizarre urchin-call, so easy it seemed for her—the child came right toward her! But how would she kill it? I looked around for suitable rocks, but she dragged me onward with the arm still supporting my weight.

Danger—the ugly thing was leaking water from its face, bawling like an unwanted peacock. "Where are they," it squealed. "Where is everyone?"

"Who are you looking for?" Lara said, treating the thing like some sort of sentient creature. It would be our last mistake, I feared. "Why are you here?"

A mangled claw-hand went into a soiled pocket. "It's got a bomb!" I wheezed. "Suicide whelp!"

Foolishly, she extended a soot-stained hand—and the thing dropped a slim brass canister into it, a few inches long, plugged at one end. It looked like a rifle casing stuffed with wax, or brains, or offal, or another semi-viscous substance; in such small quantities they were really only distinguishable by taste.

One hand still supporting me, Lara examined the canister with the other, and despite a vocal protest I was convinced to ease the plug from the casing. As I flinched, she dumped the contents into my palm—but it was not, as I had feared, miniature scorpions; it was instead a curled wisp of paper.

Together we unfurled it, and to my dismay I found it covered entirely with *writing*. Useless! The squiggles taunted me with their incomprehensibility.

But Lara had no such handicap. The blood drained from her face as she read.

She turned to me with eyes wide. "Do you think it's genuine?" she gasped.

Ah. She clearly thought I could read. "Uh, eye problems," I said. "Can't focus on the...what are they? *Letters.*"

She turned away, searching all around the camp. "Help me gather wood," she told the child-thing. To me: "It's a message. Tactical communiqué from the front. I know where Tapiorca is."

"Are—are we leaving?" I stammered. "There's just this *thing* I want to look for while we're here, if we could—"

"He could be walking into a trap," she hissed. "There's no time to lose!"

I split my jaw to respond, but my breath tripped and fell sharply in my throat, and suddenly my sense of balance tilted a full half-turn. My ankles gave way, and she was unable to stop me from collapsing onto the rocky ground in a manner to which I was becoming accustomed.

From this height, the twisted child-thing was even more terrifying; its curious, deformed visage filled my vision, and it looked like mocking, ironic Death. So many of these things I had dispatched in my time, and now I had the bad fortune to find one that possessed psychic murder-powers!

Or perhaps I was just, at long last, exhaustedly succumbing to Fate. I slumped to one side, and caught sight of a huge, growing puddle of blood marshaling around my head. This had potential to be a thoroughly sour development.

Was that rumbling in my skull the furnaces of an attacking armada, the thunder of a hostile cavalry, or simply my o'er-taxed brain rotting gloopingly through my ears to leak onto this accursed soil?

"You're right," I somehow choked. "There's—there's no time at all."

The last thing I saw was her running away, and I was too weak to even appreciate the view. ✦

86: HORRIBLE
OLD FRIENDS.

F ROM THE SHADOWS OF ENDLESS
night stepped dim figures, luminous and familiar: though
I could not lock a gaze on their slippery features, I knew their wiggly
forms. These were the shades of murdered souls—Ursula the Yam-
Runner, and Rikah the village-girl. Mortal enemies in life, united in
death by my hand. No need to thank me.

When last I had visited this bare space, spooky and far from any
known country, I had thought it the realm of Death; but I had lived,
that day, and so this place must be short of that ultimate, croak-some
horizon. Perhaps it was merely a tourist-trap on the road to that
ultimate destination—one I could buy some Skittles at, use the facilities, and *escape*. "I'm dreaming," I told the approaching shapes, as if
heading off any impending claims to the contrary.

"So you are," said Ursula, suddenly becoming a hippopotamus
for some reason that seemed perfectly understandable even if
I couldn't place an extremity on it at the moment.

"I can do whatever I want in my dream, can't I?" If I concentrated hard enough I could make them both into puppy-dogs,
perhaps, or ice-cream treats or party-balloons or anything I wished.
They could become *anything* my subconscious desired.

Ursula looked at Rikah, and suddenly they both were Lara—
one the Lara from before, the rose-lovely, slightly schoolmarmish
Head Inspector of the Police Bureau; the other became the Lara of
today, fan of the awful toad Carlton Rube and suck-up to the awful
moustache-fiend Tapiorca. The older was faint, and seemed wobbly
at the sharp lines and corners; the newer was twisted in a manner
that seemed somehow appropriate, though I consciously knew it
was not how she actually appeared. It was how she *should* look,

though—not beautiful. Not knees-quakingly charming. These were her deceptions.

"You *can* do whatever you want," they both said in creepy unison.

"But first you have to want something," the beautiful one said, to which the twisted one cackled, a sound like gravel being destroyed in a threshing-machine built by blind imbecile children as part of a work-study programme.

"You ran away from me," I shouted at the twisted one, wondering if my words would penetrate past her malformed goatish ear-nubs. "I fell to the ground bleeding, and you ran away from me to go save your precious Tapiorca!"

Between one blink and the next, she became Rikah. "I saved you, on the beach," she said, a knife-wound suddenly opening in her throat, blood staining her sporting-wardrobe, her voice growing harsh and burbly. "I brought you to the village. And you killed me." She fell, white and bled-out.

When I turned to the other Lara, she was Ursula. "I saved you on Prison-Isle," she shrugged. "You'd be burst-open dead on the shore if not for me—or else burned in the bombardment for certain." She looked skyward, into nothing-ness—then *foompf*ed into fire, writhing within a bright green burst of flame, the shape crisping quickly down to a blackened skeleton. Though I knew I was dreaming, the heat still blistered my eyes, and the smell was *distressingly* appetizing—

My eyes! I touched my face—the bandages were gone, and I stood perfect and healthy. I moved my arms and legs with wonderful ease. Though it be a dream, I cherished this moment of mobility. Perhaps I could go for a jog before I awoke.

When I looked back to the women, both were mere heaps of remains—but a third figure had joined them: the *real* Lara, crouching and examining them both, touching black bone or white skin with a Police Inspector's keen eye, and also with her fingers. She appeared exactly as she did in life to-day: stern, strong, and lovely; a bit be-sooted; harried; starting on some cankles.

"I've seen what saving you earns a woman," she said. "You'll forgive me if I don't make the same mistake."

I *wanted* her again, suddenly and achingly—but she turned and ran away as I fell to the earth, bleeding from my ears, the blackness above resolving into the shape of a million descending air-ships.

A stinging pain speared my cheek. Had I fallen on a jelly-fish? I moved to brush it away, but my arms did not move. Was I so weak, now, even in a dream?

I tried to open my eyes, but one seemed fastened shut. The other burned sharply with light.

Another slap twisted my face to its stop—I bit my shoulder. "There he is," I heard. "And a bonus, just for good-morning."

Slap! My neck wrenched in its socket. Ants seemed to burrow through the skin of my face. "Stobbit," I croaked. "Blasded stobbit."

"You are enjoying the key benefit of a long life," came the voice. "The joy of recognising patterns. For we've been here before, haven't we?"

I forced my good eye open—to find myself supported at the arm-pits by a pair of strong, awfully-dressed figures. My shoulders ached with the twisting they gave my limbs. "I'm getting bloody tired of this *pain* situation," I mumbled.

"Don't we all, eventually," came the response. I fixed eyes on the speaker for the first time—and knew him at once.

It was Larcenic the Lithe, King of the Yam-Runners, brother to Grenadine, keeper of the Tome, bearer of the knife that I had driven through Rikah's throat.

"Not even a proper welcome?" he said, the wrinkles around his mouth contorting into a sneaky smile. "We are guests in your home town, after all. But don't worry—we've brought something familiar to do."

I shifted my gaze to the long view. We stood in Pool-Party Plaza, surrounded by rotting elephants and dead Royal guards. A new addition was a cadre of Peapoddy aero-carriages, parked at awkward angles, as if having landed quite bumpily; their furnaces still hissed with steam. A small heap of rags was likely the remains of the urchin from before. It appeared that Larcenic had either taken that creature's mussy wardrobe for his own, or else had ransacked the closets of a Renaissance meat-peddler. Did he really think that *ruffles* made him look scary?

Behind Larcenic, two equally-hideous Yam-Runners had arms clasped on Lara, who stood sulkily without struggling. I knew they must have knives or pistols at her back.

In her hands was the Tome of the Precious Lore.

"She quite rudely barged into our study, looking for something you misplaced," Larcenic smiled. "Which struck me as the perfect opportunity for a little game."

He held up the jade knife, gleaming green in the sun. "You left this behind as well."

"I won't do it," I said. "The book's worth nothing to me."

Larcenic turned to the guards holding Lara. "Burn the book," he said.

Lara twisted her body to protect the Tome, but the guards were stronger. "No!" I cried, damning my own voice as I felt the word wriggle free unbidden.

"Ah," Larcenic said.

"The air-ships are coming to blast this place to the ground," I spat. "We'll all be dead within the hour."

"The air-ships under my command?" Larcenic templed his fingers. He must have taken a correspondence-course on How to Look Evil. "You may have misunderstood. The Countess works for *me*."

"The Countess is after the powder beneath the City," I said. "She's using your petty battles to mine the most powerful explosive on the planet. She'll roll over you like a rolling-pin with a steam-engine affixed!"

"I assure you," Larcenic said, leaning close enough to take my chin in one spindly hand, "everything is sternly under control. The Countess is mine. The air-ships are mine. Soon"—at this he theatrically checked a gaudy pocket-watch emblazoned with fish-bones—"Major-Leftenant Tapiorca and his army will be dealt with as well. And you?" He tilted my head from one side to the other, as if examining a servant on the auction-block, or a horse fit for toil, or a Yam-Runner wife. "You're the Crown's Regent, and I might have had use for you, if you had coöperated with Ursula. As it stands, however, you cannot be trusted."

"I can be trusted to bash your forehead in," I growled, lunging my brainium at Larcenic—but was held back firmly from behind. Nothing at all affectionate in their grasp, these two.

"Such a propensity for violence," Larcenic clucked. He held the knife up again. "Care to re-earn my trust?"

Through my one good eye I saw Lara, pleading at me with her face—and, with her fingers, flipping pages in the Tome.

"What are my options," I sighed. Perhaps I could buy her some time, for whatever she was planning to do.

Larcenic hurled the knife into the dirt like a lawn-dart—it stuck, quivering, into soil still moist from my ear-blood. The men holding my arms tensed at the impact, squeezing gouts of pain through my shoulders down to my fingertips. I resolved to return the favour as soon as practicable.

"Well, you can kill her," Larcenic said, ticking off his fingers as if he was discussing choices for supper. "If you do, I'll let you live. Of course, if *she* kills *you,* I'll let *her* live." He turned to her, making sure she understood, then looked back down at his fingers—but stopped short of announcing another option. "That's it. That's where we're at."

"And the Tome?"

Larcenic laughed. "My brother really had you fooled, didn't he?" He walked up to Lara with four great strides and yanked the open Tome from her hands. She lunged after it, her lips moving rapidly, but the Yam-Runners held her firm.

Larcenic put a finger against her forehead and pushed her back to where she had stood. "*It doesn't work,*" he snarled.

Her eyes burned holes through the man. I'd seen that glare before, and I didn't envy the King of the Yam-Runners.

He fought to match her glare with an equivalent of his own. It took a minute or so as he scrolled through his repertoire of scowls, but finally he found one suitable. That task accomplished, he marched to the nearest aero-carriage and threw the book into the furnace, slamming the grate shut with a *clang* that seemed to resound in the deepest recesses of my marrow.

BARCLAY THE EARWIG-TRAINER.

The vessel's chimney-stack coughed up a flurry of white, paper ash.

It was like snow-fall, except instead of water frozen into flakes, it was millions of dying bits of my every hope for survival.

87: UNTOLD POWER.

H E'S LED YOU HERE FOR A STACK OF RUBBISH, better fit for water-closet reading," Larcenic spat at Lara. "You can't save Tapiorca, but you could have saved yourself! No longer, thanks to *him*." He jabbed at me with a bony finger, then turned back to Lara, dialing up the charm like a pit-viper might attempt to seduce a developmentally-disabled bum-badger. "Though, of course, you still have one path out of here alive."

Lara turned to me, her eyes narrowing into something resembling Terrifying Purpose. "You're right," she said. "Let me at him."

I scrambled to push away as the guards released her, but my own guards held me fast. With a crafted disinterest, she plucked the jade knife from where it sat staked into the ground. "Jade can't

cut Yam-Runner flesh," Larcenic called after her. "Just in case you
have any ideas."

"That's not true," I bellowed, but my guards clapped strong,
dirty hands over my mouth. I contemplated eating my way to freedom, but a trial-tonguing of that heavy palm yielded overtures of
waste-oil, rancid yams, and radishes—and not in the most appetizing possible proportions.

She approached me, lips quivering, and pressed the gleaming
green stone into the flesh of my neck. I tried to swallow, but was
prevented by the blade. She whispered something—praying, perhaps? To Benji, the Yapping Dog-God of Sour Betrayal? Or to one
of the *bad* gods?

"*Abalasta walabanishifa,*" she said, so softly that only I could
hear. Then, when nothing happened, she said it louder: *"Abalasta
walabanishifa!"*

Larcenic, behind her, laughed. "It *doesn't work!*" he cried.

"*Abalasta walabanishifa,*" she repeated. *"Abalasta walabanishifa. Abalasta walabanishifa."*

"Even if it *could* work, it'd take *weeks!*" Larcenic barked. "And
training! And *practise!*"

"*Abalasta walabanishifa, abalasta walabanishifa, abalasta
walabanishifa,*" she sobbed, pressing the knife into my throat
with increasing pressure, as a warm, orange wave seemed to wash
through my veins, crashing through my humours like an energy-
drink made from electric-eel ooze. When I blinked, the pores in
her face were suddenly very clear—as if a spotty gauze had lifted
from my vision, and the dulling effects of pain shimmied from my
muscles like a flaky snake-skin being coyly shed for shillings.

I felt *strong* again.

I yanked my head away from the blade, smashed my temple into
the guard on my left, stomped the toes of the guard on my right,
then kicked his knee backward when he stumbled. His grip slack-
ened on my shoulder, and with no thought for any stiffness, I pulled
up my feet and let my whole weight rest on the other guard's arm.

The guard on my left staggered, and I kicked his knees side-ways. He clutched to me, dragging me to the ground as he fell.

I put my hand out for the knife, and without so much as a traded glance Lara set it solidly against my palm. In half-a-gasp it was through the guard's eye-socket, but his grip lasted a firm five seconds longer before I could peel his dead fingers from my arm. He clung to me desperately as he passed to the next world, but I threw that horse and sent it sailing. I would not be trailing along.

The two who'd held Lara rushed us, urged on by angry screams from Larcenic. Lara dodged their grasp, but I, fallen, could manage no such feat; my clown-training was ably rushing back in spurts, but as of yet my muscle-memory had only returned so far as seltzer-antics, and tumbling was still a semester on. One mighty, yammy fist missed my face but glanced along my ear, sending the world spinning crazily. As another blow landed in my chest I managed to cough back to Lara: "Say it again!"

"*Abalasta walabanishifa*," she shouted. At the sound my ear knit itself together in an instant, and my chest swelled with strength. "*Abalasta walabanishifa*," she cried, and my foot found Yam-Runner groin. The heel of my hand found Yam-Runner nose. A few stomps with the boots and they were finished; then it was Larcenic and Lara and me, and he was furious.

"Oh, well done on adrenaline," he sneered. "Now you're weak for the *real* fight. Where does it hurt? Shoulders, still? Eye?"

"I feel great," I said, flexing my arms and beaming at the old man.

"We'll see," he said, bum-rushing me.

The bright silver Colt spat noise and flame from Lara's hand; from whence it had been produced I knew not, and could hardly give my mind over to wayward imaginings under these circumstances. She was a crack aim against a big target, but Larcenic took all six shots in stride—plowing through the impacts like a harvester mowing down corn-stalks or a Scotsman weltering against chavs. She spun the Colt's cylinder open and dumped the hot shells to the ground—but her hands were trembling; she'd never reload in time.

I raced at the man, aiming lightning-light feet at the bullet-wounds in his chest, kicking him full with both boots and stopping us both still as a brick wall. The impact raced up my legs and rattled my teeth in their face-sockets, so much so that I worried a few'd shaken loose from the ol' chew-hole.

He fell as well, landing with a solidity usually reserved for cartoon anvils and belly-flop-contest winners; yet he stumbled back upright without pause, and I scrambled crabbily away to avoid his growling, stomping attack.

Crack! Crack! Crack! More blazing kicks from the Colt. Larcenic swatted in Lara's direction as if brushing away a particularly bothersome flea. The shots had hurt him, but indignant fury made him stronger; I rushed to scoop up the jade-knife, and we faced each other like Aztec blood-fighters, sworn to battle for the honour of having our hearts eaten by the Sun, and also to get some chocolate-drink.

"The armada is on its way," Larcenic laughed, flexing, his lips becoming red with his own liquid innards. "The time you've spent here has been lost. Your Royal army will be burned to ashes before sun-down tonight."

"Your shoes don't match your trousers," I spat back. "Your reliance on cackling is annoying. Your yam-based economy is absurd."

With a roar, he charged.

"Abalasta walabanishifa," Lara said, and Larcenic fell down dead, his face carving a furrow in the earth before coming to rest a full yard from my feet.

I turned to her.

"He was right, in a way," she said. "The chants don't work on *them.* They actually *take* life *from* them, and give it to you."

I looked at the aero-carriage where the Tome had been incinerated like so much evidence. "Then you'd better remember that incantation."

"Abalasta walabanishifa," she muttered to herself. *"Abalasta walabanishifa.* Got it. Won't forget it."

"Lordy, what a pick-me-up," I grinned. My mind was clicking and working with a clarity and precision I'd not felt in ages, and my muscles moved with more power than I'd ever recalled. I felt I could leap to the clouds and punch out a pelican, if I wanted to. "How are you feeling? Will it work if I say the words to you?"

"I'm okay," she said. "A little hungry. Sore, perhaps. No major complaints."

"*Abalasta walabanishifa,*" I said. "There? Feel better?"

"One more."

"Why not? *Abalasta walabanishifa.*"

She smiled. "Top-notch." As she surveyed our situation her features darkened: the many corpses littering the grounds could not feel the benefit of the Tome's incantation, though I could tell she wished to try it.

Hesitantly, she approached the urchin-child, that mangled mess of poor-flesh wrapped in burrito-stained rags. Slowly she knelt, leaning close to the skin-wad, whispering into its ear.

Nothing happened, of course. She whispered again, again, *again,* repeating the magic words a dozen times, until finally— I thought it a trick of the light at first, but unmistakably—the thing's fingers moved! Some spider had weaved a marionette-style web, certainly—but no! *Its fist clenched!*

What power over life and death had we lost with the destruction of the Tome?

"*Abalasta walabanishifa,*" she wept at the small creature, "*abalasta walabanishifa.*"

Then it *lunged* for her, all teeth and finger-nails and maniacal blood-rage, and she screamed and batted at it and put three slugs from the Colt through its chest before it slumped to the ground again, hissing with fury, hissing with stale demon breath, until gradually, finally, eventually not hissing at all.

After a quiet minute, Lara found me where I'd taken refuge behind one of Tapiorca's aero-carriages, cringing in fear and shielding my precious face with my hands. "Did it work?" I asked.

She stared at me numbly, then dumped the brass from the Colt's cylinder and reloaded with trembling fingers.

"We still have time to warn Tapiorca," she said, "but we can't do anything for these here."

"How in the world are we going to find him?" I stood, taking a cautious peer back at the crazy child, then doing a few jumping-Jacksons to limber my newly-wonderful body. "If we make it back to London we can get word to the Crown's Regents—maybe General Hap 'Happy' Happydie can dispatch an infantry battalion to defend the county. But we're of no use here, cut off from everyone, wasting time scouring the city for Tapiorca when he can't even fight back!"

"The Crown's Regents are corrupt," Lara spat, working the catch on the aero-carriage's pilot-cage. "You know that. Tapiorca's the only one strong enough to save this city—a year under Richey's what *brought* it to this state." She sat herself in the cage, unfurling the ribbon of paper she'd taken from the urchin earlier. "There's no time to lose. He's walking right into a trap."

The carriage's furnace alit with a rumble as she twisted valves and worked the bellows. The gas-sac above began to inflate like a giant slug rousing from a particularly restful slumber. I scratched at my face and discovered the bandage covering my eye starting to peel away. It came off easily, though my eye remained sensitive to light.

"If you're not coming, clear away from the smoke-stack," she shouted. A black ball of rolling soot belched from the exhaust-pipe, and I stepped back.

"I don't owe Tapiorca any favours," I said. "All the same, I'd rather head back to London while I've still got my health."

"I understand," she said—then uncorked that brilliant, un-walk-away-from-able smile. "But you owe me one. So get in."

I cursed my envigourated loins.

Like it or not, I was in for a penny, in for a pound—and at this rate, she'd have my whole purse invested in fool-stocks before I could flee the coming crash of the market.

88: A RIDICULOUS PLAN.

T HE WHOLE SAD WAR-SCAPE OF
Easthillshireborough-upon-Flats spread itself beneath us
like a soot-stained street-tart as Lara took the aero-carriage aloft.
She seemed to know where to look for Tapiorca and his soldiers, so
I simply sat in the rear passenger-cage watching the city drift past
in great ugly blocks of destruction, spotting streets I'd traversed in
happier times—shops I'd driven out of business with my merciless
haggling; parks I'd chased impudent servants through before they'd
been reduced to brown smears of burned-out ash (the parks, as well
as the servants); factories now silent and still, no industrious smoke
painting the sky with Progress or children working feverishly to
make products for their betters to conspicuously consume. Life really
had been ground into miserable un-snortable death-powder here, and
with each second that we flew deeper into the heart of the ruin, I felt
my wisest organs constrict with anxiety.

On the up-side, my jade-pricked eyeball felt now fully recovered; there remained a slightly-annoying irritation, as if a tiny
curmudgeonly dust-mite had taken up permanent squattership in
my cornea, but otherwise my vision was perfect. I amused myself
for some time comparing the relative colour-balance of my two eyes;
the left gave my sight a reddish hue, and the right cast the world a
bit green. Winking back and forth amused me for a full half-hour,
before I began to notice something unusual.

"What's that sparkling?" I asked Lara over the thrumming
roar of the furnace. Pointing to a hillside ahead, I indicated a
row of dancing green lights, fading and twinkling as our craft
swayed, faint but unmistakable. "Fires? Torches?"

"I don't see anything," Lara said. "But the rebel forces may
be massed up ahead—the message indicated they'd moved into
this area." The act of following the information from her precious

message was starting to give her a bloody high estimation of her tactical abilities.

But sure enough, wisps of battle-smoke began to cloud the sky ahead; perhaps we'd detect the thunder of elephant-cannon, were we able to hear anything at all over the thrash of the air-screws. The green lights didn't seem to be flames; more like the reflected facets of jewels or glass—as if a massive emerald had shattered at high altitude and rained minute fragments across the country-side. "You can't see that at all? All along that ridge-way?"

"No," Lara said, and I frowned. The colours were dim, but certainly present. I began to wonder if her persistent head-injuries had affected her vision as well; perhaps she was colour-blind, or even all-the-way-blind—the latter seemed unlikely, given her facility with things like the pilotage of an aero-carriage, but it was possible that she was merely supremely functional despite her handicap. I began to pity and respect her in equal measures, such that my overall estimation of her remained at about the same level.

Out of habit, I did the ol' winky back-and-forth, and was surprised to discover that the green specks only revealed themselves to my right, injured eye.

"Lara," I said calmly, trying to keep my voice from cracking with restrained excitement, "I believe the splinter of jade in my eye has given me super-vision."

"Oh, it has, has it?" she asked. "Are you suddenly able to see the dire gravity of our situation, and ready to stop mucking about with winking at the scenery and help me watch for Tapiorca's battalion?"

"No. Nothing like that. I can see green dots *everywhere*."

And they *were* everywhere—now that I searched for them, I could see faint green sparkles in every patch of earth, concentrated in great veins along the hillside ridge, spreading and branching in great lines across the whole of the valley. What they were, I could only imagine—the cast-off scales of dirt-dragons, perhaps? Those burrowing wurms of the planet's core, shedding precious dust as they rushed to hide from Mankind's ever-deepening mining-endeavours?

Or perhaps I was seeing a visualisation of the encroaching Irish influence into Britain—those squealing marshmallow-maggots were a growing threat to the forces of Righteousness here at home.

"Tell me if the dots point to Tapiorca," Lara grunted, "because we're out of time for sight-seeing."

I craned to look behind us—and startled in alarm at a fiercely sparkling dance of green on the far horizon, shimmering like a cloud wearing a sequin-encrusted belt fitted with a rhine-stone buckle in the centre. Not a good look for Fall, but shocking in its presumption. "It's all green!" I called to Lara. "What is it?"

She looked at me like I was the dumbest porcupine in a hedge-hog wedding. "It's the armada."

Of course! I closed my right eye and the dancing green van-ished, replaced by a dark smudge of far-off shapes. Whatever the green signified, the air-ships were lousy with it.

I rolled back to face forward in the carriage's cage, to find the battle-field looming ever closer. A moaning stomach protested of a lack of supper, as well as the approach of certain death from both front and rear. "This doesn't sit well," I moaned. "Say the thing, the feel-better words, will you?"

Lara glanced over blankly. "The feel-better what?"

"The incantation. The Tome of the Precious Lore—say it; I don't feel well."

"You're not making any sense." She glanced back at the armada—"Oh, they're faster than we are," she moaned.

My stomach flat-out double-flipped in alarm. "The incantation! What was it—*alibasta waloshafina,*

"...ITS EVERY BLOSSOM, I WOULD SNORT."—[PAGE 710.]

something like that, oh, I don't remember! You were supposed to remember it!"

"Stop babbling and start looking for weapons," she snapped. "Unless you're about to be possessed by the flame-wielding power of the Holy Ghost to save our seat-cheeks, I don't want to hear any nonsense babbling. In that case, though, it's okay."

The world swam. *Curse her sieve-like memory!* She'd *forgotten* words that could close wounds, heal the infirm, even raise the dead into horrifying killing-beasts! As I fumbled with the latches of the cargo-trunk behind the passenger's-cage, my mind spun up to speed like a recently-repaired sewing-machine, *click-clacking* its way to mending the rift in my memory, but taking its time chewing through the thick denim-like folds of my absent-mindedness. *What were those words?*

A squealing burst of sharp noise jolted my train of thought from its fat-slick rails. Lara and I both jerked up to stare at a tiny gauge set in the carriage's instrument-dash, and at a needle that leapt with each burst of spitting sound. "The Marconigraph," Lara said. "They're hailing us. What've we got for weapons?"

I fumbled through the trunk, finding only the terrible accessories of Yam-Runner fashion: stiletto-boots, velvet leg-warmers, the odd feather-headdress, a catcher's-mitt. "Just awful clothes," I said. "Yam-Runner wear. Nothing to fight with."

Steadying the carriage's tiller betwixt her comely knees, she spun open the cylinder on her Colt, then counted the cartridges in her belt-pouch. "Barely a dozen left," she said, shaking her head. "No match for the armada—our only hope's to make it to Tapiorca's artillery. What's our coal look like?"

Abandoning a test-fitting of the feather-headdress (quite a dashing look with my uniform, really), I checked the coal-larder. "Looks like little black rocks," I reported. What a stupid question to ask *now!*

She shot me a dark look for some reason and began to work the bellows to stoke the furnace. "I'm going to climb so we'll have more gliding-distance."

With a lurch, the carriage began to rise. My ears crackled, and I worked my jaw to clear the sensation. We were passing through the ghost-stratus.

Lara clutched at her ear. "Oh, that hurt!"

Instantly the words were at my tongue. "*Abalasta walabanishifa.*"

She sat upright, shivering.

"That's it," she said, smiling. "I remember."

Abalasta walabanishifa. Abalasta walabanishifa. I couldn't forget them now. I worked the sounds like rustwater-taffy, forming them into a rhythmic pattern, impressing them firmly into my memory. As I turned them over in my mouth, the syllables began to suggest a fun little song. "*Abalasta walabanishifa,*" I chanted. "*Abalasta walabanishifa, abalasta walabanishifa.*"

She repeated it as well. "*Abalasta walabanishifa, abalasta walabanishifa.*" Between the two of us, we'd *never* forget these magical words. Over and over we sang them, chanted them, made them part of our lives forever-more.

With each utterance, a power filled us—strength poured out from some invisible, bottomless chalice, seeping into every nook of our finger-prints and o'er-flowing out our crowns like a cascading cataract of pure envigouration. If this was what the Yam-Runners felt like every day, it was no wonder they'd decided to try conquering Britain.

"Keep saying it," I murmured to Lara. "Let me feel it some more."

She giggled. "*Abalasta walabanishifa,*" she breathed, almost too softly to hear. "*Abalasta walabanishifa* for you, and *abalasta walabanishifa* for me, right?"

"*Abalasta walabanishifa* for you, indeed," I moaned as unending majesty filled me from toes to tip-top.

Suddenly the world darkened as a shadow swept over our craft. "Clouds moving in?" I asked. "About time for some rain—clear this ash out nicely."

The bone-rattling rumble of the Countess's flag-ship shook
every joint in my body and our carriage. A swarming mass of buzzing aero-craft approached, like bees sent from their hives to murder
invading strangers in bee-costumes.

The Marconigraph chattered with a needle-bobbing spasm of
long and short bursts of noise. "Should we answer?" Lara asked,
but I sure as Gehenna didn't know what we could possibly say.
Whomever was manning the Marconigraph aboard the Countess's
dirigible *probably* didn't want to hear Lara's Morse-code rendition
of a Carlton Rube routine, and I doubted she would transmit my
earnest plea for a hundred-mile head-start before the shooting
could begin.

With a crackling roar, twin green-lit streaks flashed past our
ship. A searing heat-trail of furiously-burning light surrounded
us with a bucking cloud of turbulence, nearly capsizing our flimsy
carriage, swinging the riding-cages violently, throwing the both of
us from our seats and filling my passenger-cage with a wild cyclone
of garish Yam-Runner garments. A dinner-vest seemingly made
of yellow spotted giraffe-hide wrapped itself about my jaw. "These
Yam-Runners are *too much*," I shouted through a daze of light-
spots, giraffe-spots and perhaps a few fresh up-chuck spots on the
vest itself. Who could tell with all the commotion?

By the time I'd blinked the light-ghosts from my vision, sending
them moaning to the after-world behind my eyeballs to plague me
with their complaining on some other day when I had more time on
my hands to chat, Lara had recovered the craft. "What *was* that?"
I cried, bridging nearly to a whine before catching myself and suitably deepening my tone back into the register of Man. "All I could
see was that blazing green light!"

"Close your magic eye and look again," Lara said, pointing at
and tracking a moving object. "Gliders, by the look of it—radically
advanced, I've never seen Jackson-squat like them! Four or five
layers of wings, powered purely by gravity and air-currents. No
gas-sac, no weight of a furnace or boiler—I'd wager they're the fast-

est beasts in the sky." A tinge of wistfulness crept into her voice. She sounded like she wanted a ride, but *too bad.*

With my right eye closed and covered, I could make out twisting shapes below us, bristling with wings and trailing a spinning, billowing cable that seemed to lead back up to the dirigible. "Are they tethered to the air-ship?"

"Seems that way," she said, working her brow into corn-rows. We watched one craft spin gently down to the end of its line—and then the cable began to retract, winching the vessel back to its roost. The Countess was casting the world's largest fishing-pole, and *we* were the fish—so it was a good thing we didn't much care for the taste of wood-and-canvas flying-machines. "They're drawing back for another run," Lara breathed.

In that instant the Marconigraph squawked again. The dancing needle captured our attention fully; we fixed it with baleful glares in unison. To my ears, it sounded like rats being squeezed for juice, but the staccato noises clearly had meaning to Lara: "Now they're asking if Larcenic is with us." She twisted a knurled knob, and a tiny telegraph-button sprang from the panel beneath the gauge. "What should I say?"

I heaved a bundle of Yam-Runner-wear back into the trunk, watching the gliders rise past us as they were reeled back up to the dirigible. With both eyes open, those craft left shimmering green dust in their wake; sighting through only the left, I could see the hateful stares of the leather-clad pilots, clearly relishing the chance to dive at us again. One of them made machine-gun fingers at us, so I shot a single finger of my own right back. (Solomon's Pinky, of course.)

Once the glaring pilots had passed my eye-line, I dug madly through the trunk. They contained absolutely zero weapons of any kind, only bale after bale of the most ludicrous clothing imaginable. Perhaps the Yam-Runners were used to stunning their enemies with eye-watering clashes of colour? Before us, Tapiorca and his artillery remained miles away; around us, the skies above and below teemed with enemy aero-carriages, closing in on us fast. There would be no escape.

I examined Lara's build. It was hard to judge in the shaking carriage-cage, but with several layers of costume and a quick accent-lesson she might pass for a Yam-Runner. I trusted I was broad-shouldered enough on my own to be convincing, and of course I was a master of all known dialects of English, having taken a back-of-the-pulps mail-away course one idle fort-night between cricket-season and locust-season. "Tell them we're coming in," I said, fishing through the trunk for the most outlandish, and thus most appropriate, items of all. "Tell them we'll give a full account on board. You can dock us with that ship, right?"

Lara's eyes popped so wide I thought they would fall into her lap, which would send this whole plan spiraling right back to Earth. *Put those things back in!* "The whole ship's crawling with Yam-Runners and the Countess's men! Are you daft in the dafter?"

"If we can't warn Tapiorca, we'll just have to save him ourselves," I heard myself say as I pulled on a purple mayor's-sash I thought made me look particularly authoritative. "And you forget we have a secret weapon against Yam-Runners. *Abalasta walabanishifa.*"

I watched the tingle-worms climb her spine at the sound of the words. "All right," she said, snapping the telegraph-button on the Marconigraph like she was dribbling a novelty miniature basketball in the championship game of our destinies. "But at least find me something that matches my eyes."

"My dear, you are missing the point entirely," I smiled, as our vessel banked and started to climb. We aimed head-long into the danger.

89: ABOARD THAT TERRIBLE CRAFT.

T HE APPROACH TO THE FLAG-SHIP was terrifying, our carriage bucking and bobbing as it pierced the varied and swirly aero-currents agitated by the larger craft's travel, but Lara's firm hand on the control-tiller led us safely to the dirigible's docking-bay. In the light of day, the Countess's grotesque visage was not projected across the great blank expanse of the ship's flank; up close, that canvas was beige and stained, flapping loose in some corners, and on the whole it gave off a rather less-than-scary vibe, like a haunted-house at high-noon when the costumed malarkeys are stumbling in still warped from their benders and all the mirrors have yet to be charged with evil juiced from the souls of vagrant children.

But the weaving flight itself was vertiginous enoough without need for further frightening visuals, and I was happy when leather-clad dock-crew snagged our tie-lines and made fast our carriage on the landing-bay aboard ship. I worried that we'd encounter Yam-Runners straight-away who'd reveal us as impostors, despite our regionally-accurate hideous garb; yet we were met only by stone-faced Peapoddy crew, all with the lean look of pirates or Spaniards about them, and were led quickly through a narrow doorway into the ship's cabin proper.

The first thing I noticed were dead Yam-Runners, everywhere, lying in heaps like wilted flowers. (To be precise, wilted flowers that had been wrapped around hunks of decaying meat and then dropped unceremoniously in the hall-ways of a dirigible.) They lay where they had fallen, at gun-emplacements or map-stations or, in one memorable case, the loo. The Peapoddy men gave them as wide a berth as possible in those narrow straits, stepping over the mounds when necessary with over-dramatic sighs and great, exasperated strides.

I dared not ask what had afflicted these chumpy saps, and Lara, having proven herself an awful study at the peculiar Yam-Runner brogue, was under strict orders to remain silent; so we simply followed the dock-men briskly through the hall-ways, feeling the eyes of all the other crew fall sharply and heavily against us as we made our meddling way along. For *we* were the only Yam-Runners still breathing.

As my guts roiled with burbles, I thought of perhaps asking Lara to sneak-whisper the incantation at me, just to settle the ol' bowel—and then, in that instant, I knew what had happened.

We had killed the Yam-Runners, with our constant invocation of the Tome verse. We had drunk their power, and they had fallen over one by one, drained like dried timber, their mightly muscles relaxing into licorice. *Oh Jehu,* I thought, *that's it. That's the end of the incantation. With their life gone, it's done.* I tried to catch Lara's eye, to see if she'd had the same realisation, but she was lock-step straight-ahead, and I had to scramble to follow.

With little fan-fare, the dock-men ahead burst through a door like any other—this led to a wide chamber, lined with view-windows and bright with mid-day sun. Silhouetted before us was a seated figure, with a kneeling shape to its side; before we'd even resolved our peepers on the duo properly, a quick *slam–latch–lock* from behind let us know that we were in for keeps.

"I want to know what's happening," came a voice from the dark mass ahead, "before the rest of you follow suit, hmm?"

The Countess Peapoddy was short but solid, her figure un-shaped by corsets or bustles or puffy, chenille ball-gown bits; she wore a snug leather pilot's-vest over a barrel-chest, the only ostentatious elements to her ensemble a lizard-green velvet cape and a nosegay of posies in a jewelled holder about her neck (not at all unbecoming on a woman of her age). I suddenly felt foolish in my bold headdress, mayor's sash and clown-suit, but such was the Yam-

Runner way. Perhaps it taught them courage, or perhaps they were simply, as a people, insane.

Crouched beside this commanding figure, a skinny Indochine delicately cleaned the Countess's ears with thin combs, feathers and brushes. As we neared, the Countess waved the man away and stood to approach us. "What's afflicted your people?" she boomed, a presence that filled the room despite her short stature. "I've lost my gunners and half my navigators; I can't go into battle like this. Are you contagious? Where's Larcenic? Who are you?"

Despite myself, I liked her immediately. She was straight-forward. I almost regretted that it was time to lie to her. "I'm Larcenic's chief lieutentant, and this is our mute section-chief," I said in the looping Yam-Runner way, indicating myself and Lara respectively. Lara glared at me, but *she* was the one who couldn't pronounce a Yam-Runner "b" without making a sound like a deaf child breathing through a garden-hose. "And not contagious. Larce-nic's dead—not from this ailment, but by rebel bullets; I'm in charge of the contingent now." I hoped this assertive declaration would be taken at face value, as it was a mask with no substance behind it. Otherwise I could try to take the woman out at the knees—I just hoped the Indochine wasn't deadly with that ear-kit.

"The contingent is *you*," the Countess laughed, turning to pace the room, staring out the broad windows at the battle-field approaching on the horizon. "All your kind aboard this ship have perished, one after the other, fallen lifeless just this past hour. So odds are you'll be dead in a moment from the same—the foul pox has made my men afraid to touch the bodies even to dump them overboard. They claim your kind are cursed, and won't lay fingers on the meat; they want to burn them, and I've only just been able to convince them that the hall-ways aren't the place for't. You need to get those heaps off my ship, and fast, before you succumb yourself."

Such *authority!* My body wanted to obey that assertive tone at once, but Lara's presence made me hold firm. Without interven-tion, the armada would be over the battle-field in a few minutes' time, and would likely make short work of both the rebel forces and Tapiorca's Royal troops; Lara would prefer the latter be spared, but my mind worked diligently at the loom of planning to weave a stratagem warm and tight enough to embrace us all.

"Fear not contagion, for this is simply the Yam-Runner Blight," I said dismissively. "They were un-prepared for the rank grasses and pollens of this country, far from our home, and neglected to drink rancid taint-weed as I urged them to. This weakness is their own obstinate fault, and do not fault our whole people for it—I am pleased to assume command over myself and Paolina, here, however, and place ourselves fully at your service."

"I'm sure you do," the Countess droned. "Were I a suspicious woman, I would see this as a coup. I will have you know that my fee was paid fully in advance by Larcenic, and nothing will stop us from our assigned task, which you see just ahead." She indicated the battle-field through the windows. "As you've volunteered for service, however, I believe I'll take you up on the offer. You shall deliver our marker-beacon."

I turned to find the Indochine standing uncomfortably close, holding a simple piece of folded parchment atop up-turned hands. My blood suddenly churned in its canals—for this was the explosive that would allow her to target the armada's storm of lightning, and any who opened it would surely perish. She was trying to send me on a suicide mission!

Stop liking her style! I urged myself.

It was time to play her frankness game up-front and against her. I looked out the windows, allowing my eyes to focus through the brightness, and closed my left eye. Instantly, sparkling green lines jumped into relief, shimmering dully through five thousand feet of air and smoke, and I knew what she was after. "There is a rich vein of jade-powder in these hills," I said. "Your attack will blast through the surface, so you can mine and collect that mineral for refining into explosive. But the concentration near the battle-field is too great—if you fire lightning into the Earth, it may ignite the powder and obliterate us even at altitude." A capital assertion! She'd be on the defensive now for sure.

"You've lost your accent," she said.

Caught.

But she said it with a smile. There was something about this Countess—her awful son must have gotten his unalloyed annoyingness from his father, I did my best to convince myself.

"Tell me what you want," she went on. The battle-field drifted close enough to make out the forms of figures at war.

I looked back at Lara, staring through the windows at Tapiorca's troops engaged with the enemy. She flicked her eyes to me worriedly—*safe to speak?*

I nodded. *Why not, at this point.*

"Were you paid to eliminate all factions in the field?" Lara said tentatively. "Or—or merely to fight the Crown?"

"I cannot engage one enemy without the other," the Countess said. "Look at them swarming like ants—our weapons are powerful, but blunt. A strike against one will hit both, and destroy both. That's what it's designed to do, you know."

Lara approached the windows, her fingers pressed against the glass, studying the terrain, the cloud formations, the patterns of the men on the battle-field. "So you're going to unleash that fire, regardless of anything we say, aren't you?"

"That's what we've been paid to do," replied the Countess. "And my men will not be turned easily away from the promise of combat." She took a considered look at my outfit. "But historically my allegiances have been somewhat...fungible."

"Sounds like *fun dirigible*," I noted.

The Countess spread her arms wide. "It's an environment I've tried to create. People enjoy coming to work here!"

When Lara spun around, her eyes burned with the cold coal light of an *idea.*

"I can make this work for us all," she said. "Just give me a glider." ✦

90: A CUNNING STRATAGEM.

"A BSOLUTELY NOT!" THE GLIDER-PILOT scoffed, his impudence even in the company of the Countess a testament, perhaps, to the management-style employed by the Peapoddy matriarch—were he one of *my* servants, in any context up to and including a glider-pilot on a mercenary dirigible commanded by myself, I'd have given him quite the what-for. As circumstances stood, however, the Countess seemed merely bemused. Standing, her head came barely to my shoulder, but her presence filled the entire room.

"Hear out the plan," she said in a reasonable tone that seemed to indicate she'd read far too much Enlightenment philosophy. Next she'd be according inalienable rights to all peoples (Imperial subjects or no) under the sun, like those nancy Yanks. "If it won't work, fine, say so. But if it will—"

"It will," Lara said, wiping grease from her hands onto now-black-smeared Yam-Runner wear. The colourful costume hung from her in bunches and bolts, the layers of padding I'd advised in order to enbulk her frame into Yam-Runner proportions now drooping pendulously from sleeves and skirts, making her look like a particularly mal-designed puppet intended to represent a tumourous medical condition in some vulgar medical-school production of *Those Maladies That May Befall You*, in the days before that particular drama was banned from Britain for propagating new and intriguing vices amongst the shame-organs of the monocled class. And each new grease-smear made it worse, adding to the titillating rubbish-bin aesthetic. "It's just as I hoped—the tether's made of copperized Tesla-wire!"

"I know what you're trying to do," the pilot sneered; it was the same homebody who'd given us the stink-eye whilst being reeled back into the ship. "But these tether-cables are under far too much pressure as it is!"

"For the sake of those of us *not* residing purely in the realm of presuppositions," the Countess said, "why doesn't somebody explain the idea?"

Lara took the floor commandingly, no doubt intending to flavour her plan with positive idioms before the pilot could have his nay-say. "The gliders can be made into weapons as powerful as the air-ship itself—but much more precise and targeted," she gushed. "The tether can be used to channel the mother-ship's electric energy into a focused burst—making the gliders into mobile firing platforms able to attack from any angle."

"Bollocks and poppycock," the pilot scoffed. "You'll set the bloody thing ablaze. It's made of *wood*, for Thor's sake."

A Norseman—those blokes knew their electricity, as exemplified by the Mjolnir-powered street-cars canvassing Oslo. But I bit my tongue, waiting to hear the rest of Lara's explanation. A hint of frustrated desperation had tinged her voice; the battle raged below us this very second, and lives were being lost while we dithered. But she was fine in the moment: a persuasive figure despite being clad ridiculously, and fascinating to watch slither through the convolutions of her evolving plan. Her words meant nothing to me, but I admired the fervour with which she thrust out their syllables.

"The blast doesn't run through the craft itself," Lara insisted. "The craft is like the needle on a piece of thread. The thread does the actual work of binding; the needle simply points the thread where it needs to go."

"Women!" the pilot lamented to the echoing corners of the hangar. "She wants to use my glider to sew a pair of trousers!"

Lara beckoned us all to follow as she indicated the dangling form of the glider suspended from the hangar's ceiling. Like a giant dragon-fly it hung from its tether, a thick black rope that passed through a pulley in the ceiling before winding about a massive reel bolted to the bulk-head, the entire spool the height of a small man and likely the weight of a large one. The glider itself was a wood-and-canvas contraption of six bristling wings jutting from a coffin-shaped pilot's berth; two rusty blunderbuss rifles bolted and hinged to the craft's sides like antennae bespoke the thing's purpose as an instrument of war. But Lara, like most ladies of sheltered breeding, didn't seem interested in the blunderbusses.

We rounded the glider's suspended form and watched Lara clamber atop a crate to reach the craft's under-belly, where the tether-line, as thick as a man's arm and twice as salty, was bolted to the pilot's-berth with six iron brackets. In the dimness, tiny green sparks and glowing mites dusted from the line like chalk from a surveyor's plumb; but these were visible only to me, and only through my super-powered jade-eye.

"Anything you do to weaken that connexion is going to give you one great flight before the whole array comes loose, and then you've punched a one-way ticket to Crash-Towne," the pilot warned. "It's taken us a goodly long time to master the easy-fall so there's no tough jerk on the end of the length. We'd like to be able to use these again once you're done, if you don't mind, Miss?"

"YOU TELL THAT DANG OLD MISERABLE COOT I AIN'T PAYIN'
NO DANG RENT TILL HE FIXES THAT DANG OLD AIR CONDITION,"
HERMOLINA SPAT AT THE THE COWERING WOMAN.—[PAGE 874.]

Disappointingly, her rejoinder didn't build on the concept of a "tough jerk on the end of the length." My own mind tossed off a half-dozen clever ripostes in the time it took me to cough "wanker," but Lara didn't bite. I reminded myself that, despite her apparent facility with mechanics, she wasn't much of a Bon-Mot candidate herself.

But my cough *did* provoke a glimmer of recognition from the Countess, I noted with surprise; the matriarch was surprising me more with every likable moment. I wondered, not for the first time that day, if her ill-begotten son had passed through an icy waterfall on his path from her womb into the world at large, so much colder was he than her. A shock like that would never wear off a man, I reckoned; that must be it, then.

"This is the way a veterinarian would wire this together, or a soap-maker, or an improvisational-clarinetist," Lara said, tugging on the iron brackets while the pilot sucked in his breath. "Not anyone with any knowledge of electrics or aero-dynamics. Why in the world did you use Tesla-wire for a tether instead of spring-cord or even straight hemp-hawser? Did you simply have a reel of it collecting dust?"

The pilot bristled. "Look, I think we did pretty well making the best of a collection of spare parts. We've shot down more than two enemy craft with these gliders—and my partner's nearly half-completed the patent-forms, so don't go getting any ideas."

"You did a fine job for a bunch of coal-burning gas-drivers," Lara shrugged, "but gliders hammer the air in a wholly different way. No matter—the Tesla-wire's the secret to our plan. Because you already pick up electrical interference from the super-structure of the dirigible, right?"

The pilot blanched, and looked at the Countess in the first expression of deference I'd seen from him. Was this a sore subject? But the Countess nodded. "It's no secret that our power-plant is jade-powder, rather than coal," she said smoothly. "All the Tesla-wire in the ship picks up some interference from it. To properly shield the furnace would make us far too heavy."

"That's perfect," Lara said. "So we take advantage of that—and connect the tethers directly to the discharge."

The pilot fell to his knees. "Odin, Thor, Freya," he sobbed. "Deliver us from this ignorance before she burns us all to death where we stand!"

Lara shot him a look like she was trying to burn *him* to death with her brain-power, but she was really there to convince the Countess, not the pilot. "It's all in the attachment," she said. "If you insulate the join between the line and the glider—you direct the charge outwards, into the air and down to the ground. As a weapon." She cocked her head at the pilot. "Why don't you join the tether to the glider with a pressure-piston? Then you don't have to worry about hitting the end of the line with a jerk."

"Pressure-piston," the pilot sneered. "Oh, sure. Let's just go to Frankfurt and pick up a crate of them. We're five thousand feet in the air! Where are we going to get a pressure-piston with that kind of weight rating?"

"There's two of them in the aero-carriage I landed in," she said. "And in every aero-carriage in your landing-bay. Part of the furnace-bellows. You just ignore the steam-fitting and attach your brackets to the clamp-ears."

By now it was clear the pilot simply wanted to win the argument. "We can't just disassemble the aero-carriages! What if we need them for transport? To get down to the surface?" His voice was taking on a faint, but distinct, tone of whinging. "And how do you direct the electrical charge, anyhow? You're just bringing the blast closer to you!"

The Countess didn't even acknowledge the pilot—she clearly understood the plan now. "The nozzles we have on this craft, and the others," she said. "We use them for the large blasts, releasing the charge generated by the furnaces. But if we funnel that charge down the line and out to the gliders..."

"...Each charge can be smaller and more precise," Lara said. "You just make sure the enemy's between the glider and the likely ground-point for the lightning."

"How will you ever do *that*," the pilot moaned.

At this, Lara and the Countess looked at me.

"*He* tells us where the powder-deposits are in the ground," Lara said.

"Ridiculous!" I sputtered. "I can't see anything at all! You said yourself it was poppy-cock! Eye-floaters or worse—you can't count on *me* for this!" But the Countess seemed not to have heard a word.

"Get to it," she smiled. "I'll have the crew bring you the nozzles, the pistons, and whatever tools you need."

"I still get to fly it," the pilot said desperately, looking at me as if I were the child that had been unexpectedly awarded the last cookie in the house. But I was just happy to get a cookie instead of a swift kick in the trousers; I nodded sagely, as if I'd understood a single word of what had just been discussed.

The Countess patted the pilot on the back motheringly. "You can help pile up the bodies of the Yam-Runners," she said. "I think they'll make for a fine initial bombardment while we prepare the glider attack." They both ducked through a doorway, leaving Lara and I scandalously alone in the hangar.

"You really convinced her," I said. "You're quite the handy-woman." Lara had become lovely to me again, a Lady with a Plan she wasn't afraid to Argue for, and I took a slow step toward her, aware of the creaking Aloneness all around us.

"I can't believe it," Lara beamed. "To think—instead of warning Tapiorca, we'll be coming to his aid! We can end this war once and for all—with the Crown utterly victorious."

Tapiorca. Of course she was still obsessed with him. "I wonder if he's been killed in battle," I said hopefully.

She seemed to sober at the thought. Fishing through her voluminous pockets, she retrieved, cloaked in lint, the ribbon of parchment she'd received from the urchin-thing.

"One way or another, this is the last battle of this war," she said, so seriously I thought she was joking, until I realised she had no sense of humour.

It was a strange sentiment, this steadfast insistence of hers that the battle between Tapiorca and the peasant-monster cabal was of great moral import. As far as I was concerned, irritating folk were killing irritating folk; they could all mash each other to jelly, so long as I was a goodly distance away with a fresh pot of ambergrass tea. But she—she was supposed to be *better* than I. "You're quicker on the trigger than I'd have guessed for an officer of the law," I told her, perhaps more bitingly than my well-known diplomatic acumen might have predicted.

"Evil should be defeated no matter who defeats it," she shot back. "A cockroach can be smashed with a boot or with a hammer; does it matter?"

This belligerence rankled me, because it was drawing me into a conflict that I had made clear I would rather let thunder along without me. She had roped me into joining her on her crusade, when I was by weight more a cavalier than a crusader; but *thinking too much* and *being clever* had gotten me into this mess, and I didn't see any sense in continuing the practise lest it lead me down further roads far more treacherous and annoying even than this.

Any exuberance imparted by the Tome's incantation had worn off by now, and suddenly I felt heavy and tired. It was hot in the hangar, beneath my dumb mounds of Yam-Runner clothes, and I made for the doorway, aiming to find an observation-deck or other escape to fresh air. One hand on the doorknob, I thought desperately of something to say to Lara, anything at all.

But all I came up with was more "jerk on the line" puns, of no real use in the present situation. I filed them duly away in case I encountered the pilot later, so we could bond.

As I shut the door behind me, I looked back—and in the split second before the wood met the jamb, I saw her watching me, oddly, searchingly, as if she didn't know what I was, as if I were a strange animal in a menagerie who'd suddenly changed colour in a bold and unusual way to match its surroundings.

Which was odd, because I felt the same way about her.

91: CALM BEFORE
THE FIGHT.

A NARROW DOOR SET WITH THREE HEAVY latches led to a windy walk-way circumscribing the bulging watermelon of the dirigible's exteriour. From this breezy vantage-point I could watch the canvas sides of the craft buckle and ripple like a fat man's jowls on a carriage-ride; shadows of clouds passed across them like vague worries, and joists and buckles creaked with the wind like old bones asked to take up arms in elder-age. Shedding my hideous Yam-Runner clothing, I let the fabric flap in the wind, then released it to the world. My tight Crown's Regent uniform was rumpled but cooler, and Abu Fromage's cheese-wand still dangled by my side. I wondered if I would ever use it again, to twirl cheese or any other viscous substance, but it was impossible to predict, and also depressing to think about. I was *no longer* simply a cheese-twirler; I was now a warrior-vagabond-scoundrel-officer, and it was complicated.

Around the air-ship flew the fleet: a fistful of other craft not quite the size of this, each drifting and buzzing in the wind, dusting the world with sparkling green flecks only visible to me through my crazy jade-pricked eye. Between them flew aero-carriages like the one we'd fled Pool-Party Plaza in, noisy and reckless contraptions burning coal to turn air-screws, the whole mess held aloft by bulging gas-sacs pulled this way and that by currents and ghosts and sun-beams and Fate. The air was thick with soot, the ground below as invisible as the walls of an opium-den on any of the lonelier holidays—but the occasional echoing blast of elephant-cannonry was a dreadful reminder that war was still being waged far below my feet.

"Do you think it'll work?" The Countess was suddenly beside me, attended by her wispy Indochine, braving the gusts to file away at her finger-nails even as she leaned on the railing. I was struck with a torso-pang for Thigton, whom I'd last seen in the waters off Prison-Isle. *What had become of him? Did his veins pump Yam-Runner blood...and if so, had we killed him along with the others of that tribe by over-using the incantation?* Did he even have veins at all?

It was possible, I realised, that Thigton was an animate spirit of some sort, or visiting demi-god sent to test my mettle. I was suddenly upset for not having thought of him lately, and wondered after his fate. *Perhaps he's found a pleasant mer-woman to settle down with,* I reassured myself, *and I'll soon receive a dripping post-card from his happy, scaly family.*

To the Countess's question, I nodded professorially. "You mean the glider-plan? I suppose it will; Lara's craftier than most who talk as much, and she's found novel ways 'round most of the scrapes we've landed in recently. I'm sure it'll all go just as she's aiming."

The Indochine whispered into the Countess's ear like a lizard sipping from a bird-bath, and the woman nodded. "Come along, if you would," she said to me, striding quickly along the long walk-way describing the circumference of the ship. Glad to have some instruction, rather than relying on my own decision-making as I'd been doing (which had led swiftly into a morass of self-doubt and melancholia), I chipperly followed.

"You don't seem particularly charged about the whole thing," the Countess continued as I matched her pace. "You'll find no sym-pathetic ears on this ship if you don't speak your mind, and freely."

It was true that she'd cultivated an unusual standard of *frank-ness* aboard this vessel that was a surprising departure from the malevolence I'd assigned her from afar. She seemed as forth-right as a new breed of merchant, insistent on using proper weights and fair dealings to ensure repeat business, rather than conniving as many pennies as possible from every rube off the street as was the practise along Avenue T in Easthillshireborough-upon-Flats. "I've a hard time casting in lots with either Yam-Runners or the Crown," I began, banking on this understanding of her character, "and, if you'll forgive the sentiment, Peapoddy folk as well." I cringed, but she didn't seem inclined to slap me at the insult; another small point in her favour.

"I sense you've had poor dealings with us all," she said, with a pause and straight-on look-in-the-eye I'd never seen from any Yam-Runner, Ursula included. The Indochine nearly fell over his own feet, so sudden was her halt. "The Yam-Runners can scarcely deal any other way, cloaked in duplicity and scheming as is their nature. My late husband had secured their acquaintance before I met him, and it was only with great reluctance that I ever took commission from them—but for many years, they paid well, provided provision and training for my crew, and only asked of me tasks that were easily accomplished. You tell me what I should have done."

The Indochine opened a hatch-way door, and she gestured for me to precede her back inside the ship's cabin. Taking this as an invitation to continue the conversation, I went on. "You can hardly be faulted for working under contract. But the power you wield on these ships..." I didn't even know what to complain about. She'd killed *so many* people! But this was war. People were *expected* to die; in fact, the fans booed the whole proceedings if the body-count didn't climb daily. Politicks!

"The power allows me and my crew to live outside the stifling embrace of the Crown, or its analogues around the world," she said, her words echoing from the narrow walls of the corridor we now threaded. "The Yam-Runners had wanted for many years to conquer the island where they lived, but felt constrained. Their King was afraid his brother would return to oppose him. But then the brother died, and the last obstacle fell; so he hired my crew, and we did our work, same as any demolition crew hired to collapse a building or raze a tenement or flatten an orphanage." The Indochine opened another, smaller door, and we entered the chamber where I'd first met her, the deck ringed by bright windows. "Buoyed by their success, their ambitions grew; they asked if I'd help them move to the main-land, and their coins bit as true gold, so I accepted."

"Knowing that Easthillshireborough-upon-Flats sat on thick deposits of jade-powder," I added. "I'm sure it's expensive to keep this fleet flying."

She nodded, unfazed as ever. "It pays to take all factors into account." She sat herself in the chair centred between the windows, and the Indochine began to wheel a large cart from one corner of the room.

I stood there feeling stupid, trying to reconcile warring emotions, until she spoke again: "Tell me your concern. Do you hate the Yam-Runners? They are dead, it seems, from some strange malady you claim to know nothing about—and even should some of their ilk remain in the world, my crew will never sail with them again, so shaken are they by this plague. Do you hate the Crown? Clearly you are in league with this Lara, who is on their side; you must either then support her in her aims, or else subvert them, or flee. Do you hate me? I have given you no cause, so far as I know, and if I have, please describe it. My husband and the worst of my sons made many enemies in their lives, but I have found it more worth-while to make allies—and I have many other sons you likely have not met: Peapoddy the Missionary, in Dutch Africa now, building churches; Peapoddy the Literacy Advocate, working with the Ministry of Education; Peapoddy the Explorer, racing to the far reaches of the Arctic as we speak. My youngest son was of jealous temperament, and took after his father in his cruelty; but I raised three sons to be fair and kind, and have only the one to count against me." She stopped for a breath, and to look out the windows. "Finally, do you hate the monsters threatening to overrun this city? Then take up arms, as Lara wishes, and fight with her against them. I shall be your ally in this, for I wish the Crown as my enemy no more than anyone. The Crown has hired me many times to clean up its more complicated messes, and I hope to do business with them in wars to come."

The Indochine was working quickly around the room, setting up giant mirrors at angles near the windows, and soon I could see myself reflected in odd directions, speaking to a myriad of

Countesses, looking each time like quite the loser in a tattered Crown's Regent uniform, still with the cheese-wand at my side. "But you were on your way to *kill* Tapiorca, weren't you?"

She sighed. "My weapon is blunt and merciless," she said. "It would not have been the first time a wrecking-ball would have been used to kill an ant. Why, just last month, we were contracted to exterminate a band of termites from a Gallic monastery; despite my descriptions of our power, the monks were insistent. So we flattened the whole place but good, the monks with it, and they could scarcely complain I'd not warned them. This is why I demand payment in advance." She watched the Indochine move from the mirrors to a sprocket-powered device, to which he attached a wire pulled from a spool in the wall. "I don't know you, but I know men like you. Many have served on my crew, and many I've fought against. What you need to do is to *stop thinking.*"

Stop thinking? I thought about what she might mean, but couldn't puzzle it out. "I don't understand."

"Of course you don't," she said, settling into her chair, finding a comfortable position as the Indochine adjusted the sprocket-machine. She turned delicately as if sitting for a portrait. "If your choices are to fight with Lara, or abandon her to her own devices, which will it be?"

"I...I don't know," I stammered. "I don't want to abandon her, but I can't in good conscience abet the forces of Tapiorca after what they've done to me—"

"Stop it," the Countess barked. I wondered how many of the crew-men accidentally called her *Mother.* "Help her, or leave her?"

My voice did that thing again, where it spoke up without waiting for me. "Help her."

"Then help her," the Countess said, "and go to it quickly. It's nearing night-fall, and the monsters are massing for a final assault on the troops. Vien Dhuc!" This last was directed to the Indochine. "Bring Karolinga's mask."

"BUT THE WORM REFUSED TO TAKE HOLD OF THE LONGBOW."—[PAGE 913.]

The little man scampered away. "How do you know what they're planning?" I scowled at the Countess.

"They *also* enlisted my aid," she smiled, "but be thankful that they couldn't raise the requisite purse."

The Indochine returned in a chittering burst of energy, holding a leather aviator's cap with a set of thick goggles affixed. The lenses were dusky violet; for a moment I took them for Yam-Runner wear, such was their unusual fashion. "This," the Countess said, "will help you, I think. We had a man, once, with your same affliction."

Puzzled, I worked the leather over my brow and around my ears. It was tough, and cold, but fit well enough. The goggles I set over my eyes, and could instantly see her meaning. The faint green sparks dancing through the windows outside became sharp points of light; their detail burst into perfect relief. Suddenly, staring through naked air seemed debilitating, like trying to walk with eyes plastered open through the atomised lard from a continually-burning wheel-barrow. "This is extraordinary," I breathed.

"Go and fight," she said. The Indochine turned a switch, and light burst from the sprocket-device. Through the windows, the face of the Countess suddenly reflected from the clouds. She would be watching.

92: SCREAMING
TO EARTH.

M Y STOMACH TRIED ITS WRIGGLING BEST to crawl out my nose as our glider swung back and forth from its tether, suspended from the roof of the dirigible's hangar. My face swelled hot with blood; my skull throbbed menacingly. The terrible sight of our first enemy might burst my head open like a pressurised mosquito-bladder.

Lara and I sat shoe-horned into the coffin-shaped glider body like buttered salami-hocks in a Christmas eel; after a fair amount of clucking and wrangling with propriety, it was discovered that the only way to fit us both in the cramped space was for us to tandem, my legs flanking hers like trouser-cloaked parentheses. This was a terribly awkward arrangement to suggest, of course, and it was only through a truly valiant exercise of euphemisms and mumbles of "er, you know" that the plan took shape at all—but I would be a damnéd Cornish liar if I denied the smallest throat-closing thrill at the pressure of her back against my ventrals. It was a sensation nearly as tingle-sparking as the Tome's incantation.

I nearly whispered those melodic words to her in the shuffle as we arranged ourselves, but found myself holding my ashy tongue. That chant had turned hollow somehow, its giddy energy having been siphoned from a hundred desiccated Yam-Runner jerky-heaps...but while it wouldn't have hurt to try, for some reason I had no stomach for't. Perhaps—who knows!—Thigton was still out there; perhaps he would be affected.

Having arranged ourselves in the craft, Lara's hands set firmly on the flight-controls and mine on the newly-installed lightning-weapon handle-bars (nicked from a delivery-boy's bicycle, I wouldn't wonder, with awhooga-horn and sassy streamers still attached), we were winched to the ceiling of the hangar in preparation for our

drop o'er the battle-field. The thrumming of the dirigible's engines
had softened, and I knew the air-ship was descending to attack-
altitude; between the soft sinking and our ratcheting rise in the
glider, my insides-equilibrium had been scrambled all to Dizzy-
Ville, and I thought the whole enterprise doomed to chunk-blasting
from the start.

But the winching leaned me heavily into Lara, Gravity conspir-
ing to thrust us together at last, and thusly was I convinced to at
least afford the endeavour a stay of judgment. Perhaps Newton's
other children would intervene in still-naughtier ways—Inertia, I'd
oft been told by rocket-testers in husky, gin-tinged whispers, was
the very sauciest of minxes.

Then we sat waiting, our hot breath filling each others' ears
like candle-smoke 'twitxt fetishists. Below us, the Countess's
crew piled Yam-Runner bodies onto the bay-doors—burly men
given way to imaginary boogy-fears, they handled the remains
with gloves and sticks, afraid to come into closer contact with
those colourful corpses than strictly necessary. Among the cadre
was the bitter glider-pilot whose craft we'd commandeered and
repurposed for Lara's own aims, and he shot us as many stares
as he could afford to lose as we all waited in cough-spackled
silence for war.

"Here's how I see it working," Lara whispered. "The lightning
will seek the ground at its most-charged point—so when we see an
enemy, you need to indicate where I need to steer so that when you
squeeze that handle, the discharge will destroy the enemy."

"I don't know what makes you think I would have the slightest
idea how to gauge that."

"You'd better learn. Tapiorca was directed to amass his entire
force here, thinking he could ambush the rebels and crush them
with one decisive blow. But it was a trap! He's encircled now, fighting valiantly, desperately, muskily for his noble life. The whole
bee-hive hangs in the balance, and we are the weights that will
tip the row-boat into the Crown's own back-yard."

"Do Tapiorca and his cannons know we're on his side?" I had no desire to ride a cavalry charge directly into the flight-path of an artillery shell, despite the potential for being rammed even closer to Lara.

"They'll figure it out soon enough," Lara said, and I didn't have to see her face to make out the set in her jaw. It was evident in the way she tensed between my knees.

"Hope so," I muttered, just to have the last word, if nothing else.

But she quashed even that minor goal. "Look, thank you," she murmured. "For everything. For...the things you've done. For the Crown. And for me. We wouldn't be here, saving Tapiorca's skin, if you hadn't."

This was it. The moment that months of voyages and struggle and hardship had led to.

"I didn't do any of it for the Crown," I breathed directly into her ear. "From the first moment I saw you, I did it for you."

A terrible *whoosh* of wind obliterated my words, sucking them from my lips and scattering them in component syllables to the far reaches of the non-English-speaking world. I knew not whether they had passed her ears on their way. Below us, the hangar's wide bay-doors fell open like the jaws of an aghast Hephæstus having just seen his wife dally with a not-especially-handsome tapir; without so much as a confetti-blast of fan-fare, great heaps of Yam-Runner bodies fell from the belly of the ship like crumbs from the tapir's bread-munching face. They would soon be followed by Lara and I, the quavering tapir-quills of vengeance.

Below us, flares and explosions of cannon-fire illuminated the twilit world in blinks and rumbles of blasting-fire. "It's dark!" I cried. "I can't possibly be expected to—"

With a dry *clunk*, the winch's catch released, and we dropped like a fat stone at the fray.

I struggled to fit the suddenly-too-tight violet goggles properly over my face as we fell. My gut was set off spinning, but Lara's mass was a comforting presence to my nethers, and soon she'd pulled us up level, Tesla-wire falling in great loops and coils behind our tail.

She steadied the craft into a gentle banking turn as we gathered our bearings against the landscape. Though the air was still hot, it was dark out, and my eyes struggled to make out any form or shape through the thick tinted lenses.

"There!" Lara's voice was mostly punched away by the wind, but she tugged at my knee for emphasis. "They've got him trapped against the ridge-line!" With that, the glider dropped out from beneath us, Lara pitching us into a screaming dive toward the hills.

The discharge-controls felt suddenly leaden in my grasp. Each slick hand gripped a tinsel-adorned handle connected through the craft's belly to a pivot, which aimed a nozzle below our seats; somehow I was expected to use the approximately four degrees of rotation afforded by the pivot to target this nozzle at the blurry shapes racing by below us. My eyes were hot and foggy inside the goggles, and I was suddenly very aware of my breathing. Each inhalation was more laboured than the last, requiring absurd levels of effort to snatch individual atoms of air from the rushing stream like a thirsty man with lips fused at birth doing his level best at a water-bubbler. *At least we're already in a coffin,* I thought; *this'll be convenient.*

"Fire!" she said, and I squeezed the spring-loaded handles, too late I was sure, un-aimed, too weakly, all wrong. The sky erupted in brilliant green, and through my goggles I watched a thousand crackling hairs of electricity flare through the sky around us. Something *boomed* near the ground, and Lara whipped around to track it—"Not quite on target," she moaned, belying a disappointment that I wished I could suck out of her with bravado I did not, in this unusual moment, seem to possess. I was out of my league, and this was the play-offs.

Then we reached the end of our tether, and I nearly bit her head in half as the glider jerked to a halt. Facing downward as we were winched back up to the dirigible, I gained perspective on the field for the first time; that shower of sparks in the hillside would be where our lightning had met the earth, and the churning, ant-hill quivering of the terrain would be the overrunning monster army, shadowy and beetlish. Beyond, I made out a few of Tapiorca's elephants pinned against a ridge-line; torches blazed and rifles flashed in skirmishes all around. *Now* I could see what was happening.

"This time let's try to herd them away from the elephants, so their cannons can be brought to bear," Lara shouted. The dirigible loomed large behind us, and soon we were at the top of the tether...

Then we fell again, and all gave way to blurry vertigo. I'd count us lucky at the end of this campaign if I'd managed to not shake my eyeballs out to rattle loose in the goggles.

But as confidence continually whistled from the ever-floppier balloon of my spirit, it was Lara's surety that filled it again with the rigid yellow insulation-foam of insistence. "Keep a close eye on that group up ahead," she pointed, gently drawing the glider into a bank, following a torch-bearing mob as they stampeded across the brush. "I'll take us around—let's head them off!"

Don't think. Don't think. Lara's instructions washed over me and I simply acted on her command. The next lightning-blast elicited an aggregate cry from the forces below, piercing and audible even at altitude, and I even understood *why*. I was maybe—possibly—a little bit—getting the hang of this.

"What's your overall plan?" I shouted to Lara as the tether drew us up a second time. "We can't just pick off individuals all night long!"

"We just need to scurry them away from Tapiorca's line," she called back. "If we can get them massed in any area where you see a powder deposit, we should be able to take out a greater number by igniting the powder underground."

The jade-powder deposits! Through the goggles those luminous green earth-veins were sharper: I picked out one running parallel to our most recent flight. "There!"

She squinted. "I can't see it," she said. "You'll have to guide me."

We flew for the vein, my hand gently pressing her shoulder left or right as the enemy squalled underneath us, and when I squeezed the lightning-trigger this time, I knew it was on target. The earth erupted in a volcanic gout of flame, a blast-wave pushing at our wings and sending us spiralling back toward the heavens, as rock and terrain and pulverised bits of evil flesh misted the sky around us.

Tapiorca's cannons were silent; Lara and I were not. With great whoops and increasingly-targeted strikes, we lit the night ablaze with lightning, bursting great veins of explosive like pimples on the oily face of Easthillshireborough-upon-Flats. We came under light rifle-fire from spotty pockets of rebels, but no artillery threatened us. With each run it became less like war and more like sport, reminding me of nothing more than heady days at the Manor filled with munchkin-chasing and orphan-tetherball and great marathon sessions of that most popular amusement from the Sub-Continent, Land-Mine-the-Monkey.

It was violent, it was vicious, it was *fun,* and by blazes, Lara enjoyed it too.

LOOKS NOTHING LIKE THE BROCHURE.

93: THE AFTERMATH.

THE FIGHT RUNG IN MY EARS LONG AFTER it was over. The giant face of the Countess Peapoddy shone on the battle-field like a wandering moon, round and pocked with cheese-crumbs. Her flag-ship drifted low to the ground, the mammoth visage projected on its distended surface shining a white light of terror over the silent war-scape like a hideous search-beam of scary.

To me, watching with my jade-pricked eye, the ship's superstructure sprayed a constant stream of green sparks; without the Countess's goggles the colour seemed blurry, now, and it was hard to clasp the shape sharply in my vision. The craft floated rumblingly through the dark air like a glowing whale seen from underneath, scouring the sea-bed for plankton by the glow of luminous magical whale-skin, barreling through and vapourising any nailed-together metaphors hastily constructed for it.

I sat on the frame of our glider, perched gently on the hillside like a dragon-fly dropped dead sweetly of old age. My fingertips felt dunked in swamp-ice, cold and tingly with a hint of frog's-tongue ickiness. Whether afflicted from the endless string of numbing aero-sorties or my just-now sprint up the embankment, I couldn't judge, not being the sort of trivia-nerd that could describe the difference between the various types of finger-fatigue—but the climb had surely slurped the wind from my personal sails, and having seated myself, I felt up to naught but shoving one ragged breath down the gullet after the next. What I wouldn't give for the sound of that healing Yam-Runner incantation now!

The night was a long, smeared-together frenzy in my memory; as we flew, Lara and I had melded into a diligent destructive team, and of such totality was the enveloping reverie that I could recall almost no discrete instant from the entire shrieking affair. So many times had we been dropped over the battle-field, and so many times had we unleashed crackling power on the shuffling forms below; so many times had we been winched back up to the dirigible, and so many times had I purposefully down-shifted the clanging gears and bobbins and rattle-sprockets in my skull that fought to make sense of it all. *Don't think* had become my mantra, and thusly had I become a fighting unit with Lara: the lightning had flowed from my hands all night long, and all night long had our enemies fallen, disintegrating all and every into dusty black bits of background. The whole thing was wild.

I didn't recall the Tesla-line snapping in twain at the end of one screaming run at the Earth, but I *had* noticed the sudden fade in brilliant green power surrounding us. I remembered Lara shouting something, and as if watching from far-off through a tube of some kind I remember distantly observing our glider coming to rest on the hillside, shuddering and snapping and shaking our bones. I had tightened around Lara in that moment, I remember most vividly, because of course I had not the room to form a ball of strictly myself.

The instant the glider had found rest, Lara had been up and out and running, and before I could struggle free from the craft she had disappeared. I'd set off aimlessly after her, stumbling over stones in the blackness of the unlit field, and quickly found myself winded and trembling in the loneliness of night.

All around were mounds that might have been either earth or bodies; this smell of up-turned soil was riper than I'd recalled from my last, disastrous trip to a farm during a day-exercise at The Young Snide Chap's Dairy-Mocking Sleep-Away Camp.

And so, wheezing like a tuberculotic Laplander with nowhere else to venture besides, in a few certain seconds, the malodourous uncertainty of the lumpy ground beneath, I'd affixed my gaze to the lumbering flag-ship above and ascended the hillside back toward the glider. Certainly Lara would return here; certainly I could, if nothing else, have something less completely soiled to sit on. Already I'd trod on something disgustingly squishy, and in the darkness it could have been *anything*. It could have been Ferdinand Magellan's *brain*.

As I stared now across the empty plain, lit here and there by fading embers still obscured by dust and ash and all the smoky after-bits of warfare, I was hard-pressed to call it a *battle-field*. It was a *field*, certainly; it was an undeveloped tract, with few trees and a largely flat profile. But as I racked my memory, I could scarcely label what had occurred tonight a *battle*. A *rout*, perhaps, or surely a *thumping*. I was toying with the idea of going ahead and applying *massacre* when suddenly Lara's voice spiked the sombre stillness of the scene:

"I've got the Baron!"

94: A RECKONING OF SORTS.

IT WAS THE BARON OF THE ALLEY-WAYS: that black-wire beard, the haughty gleam in his coalish eyes despite (or perhaps due to) his eye-line only reaching to Lara's trunk. She held the Colt on him as alighting aero-carriages blasted sand into gusts all around us; it wasn't long before the Baron was flanked by Peapoddy men holding Peapoddy torches and Peapoddy guns, marking an orange ring of fire in the jet-black landscape. I wondered if we were setting up a tribal ritual, or perhaps a circus of some sort; but no, as it turned out, we were awaiting the arrival of a different sort of clown.

The ground quivered with the heavy approach of an elephant, and the torches parted to allow the triumphant entrance of none other than Major-Leftenant Tapiorca, Fiercest Heart in the White Realms, Commander of Her Majesty's Tenth All-Round Heavy Brigade & Tea-Club. He looked more gaunt than I recalled, and he swung from his dirty steed with a graceless *stomp* that struck me as somehow *sadder* than the swooping fluidity he'd showed-off at previous encounters. Lara, of course, was prideful to bursting, beaming through her decorum as Tapiorca swaggered his suddenly-saggy red uniform to her side.

"It's over, Your Powerfulness," she said. "I have delivered you from the murderous aims of these rebels and miscreants. As you once delivered me."

Whatever adoration she poured through her eyes at Tapiorca, he kept and did not return. Instead, he spread a disgusted glance around the gathered assembly of Peapoddy crew-men; if he recognised me in that mass, he made no sign. Which was frankly just as well.

"*Delivered* me?" he spat. "Delivered me up-right & centre into the claws of these flying barbarians! What a bloody mess you've whipped up, and left the kitchen a right disaster at the tail of it. This—this *cadre* has aims running straight *orthogonal* to you, me and the Crown, missus, and I don't know what half-cooked egg-salad they've cracked and fed up to you but *this*—this en't the way to end a war, y'see? This is how you *start* a war, laying fire to the soil of God Almighty's own Britain!"

Lara's enthusiasm never so much as flinched in the face of the blusterous assault. One hand still grasping the Colt in the King of the Alley-Ways' back, she extended the other toward Tapiorca, cast orange in the torch-light, smooth and gentle, loving. A touch I'd never felt, in waking any-how. "You look so tired," she said. "So hurt. Come here—just listen for a second. Just listen."

I knew what she was going to do, and I cringed.

"*Abalasta walabanishifa*," she said, and Tapiorca grunted like some cranky old ox taking offence at everything.

"What in blazes is that?" he growled. "Persian? Chinee? What ducky sorts 'ave you been cavorting with?"

She frowned. "*Abalasta walabanishifa*," she tried again, reaching to brush his chin with her fingertips, but he avoided the slightest contact like a moth circling a steam-iron. She went on: "*Abalasta walabanishifa*. This—this will help. Where are your soldiers? Bring them here—let me talk with them. Any that are wounded, let me talk with them. *Abalasta walabanishifa.*"

I couldn't take watching her like this, deluded and hopeful as a blind kiwi-vendor with a basketful of tennis-balls. "It's gone," I said, stepping into the ring of orange light. "The Yam-Runners are all dead. We've slurped-out all their power. There's none left for us anymore."

Lara whipped her head to me, then back to Tapiorca. "No," she said to him. "Bring out your soldiers. Wh–where are the rest of your soldiers?" Her hand holding the Colt began to quaver, and the Baron of the Alley-Ways tensed, his beard plumping itself in instinctual defence.

"They're all *dead,*" Tapiorca snarled, shaking a sooty finger at the aero-carriages now cooling some yards beyond the torch-line. "We was tricked. Hood-winked by falsified orders that brought the whole Regiment the whole ways out here—*here,* out-numbered in a fight over land of no value, the whole tract not worth half a dram o' pig's spittle on Sunday. All so we've our backs turned to *that.*" The hand shot up, pointing an accusing arrow-finger at the Countess's flag-ship, now banking for another searching pass over the field. A green spark arced from the craft to a cloud, but no one saw that. "So we can't defend Prison-Isle. And Hamburger-Isle. And Limburger-Isle. And Pool-Party Plaza. And our own *bloody* skins, so it seems from a particularly foul yesterday."

"All that mess was the work of the Yam-Runners," she said. "But the Yam-Runners are dead, now. You don't have to worry about them."

"Who in bloody blazes are the Yam-Runners?" Tapiorca screamed at her. He reared back to strike a blow, but veered on delivery and instead caught the Baron square on the pate. That squat figure tumbled to the ground as Tapiorca continued to screech like a hawk with a roofing-nail driven through the liver. "I *trusted* you. And now you've *turned* on me—*why*? Why destroy Prison-Isle? Why send my men to their deaths?"

Too stunned to respond, Lara gasped for air like a fish flopped into a row-boat expecting a birthday-cake but rewarded instead with a face-stomping. The Baron clutched his head with stubby fingers, moaning and fighting his way back to his feet. Before Lara could fumble new sounds together into words, the Baron lashed out at Tapiorca himself.

"*You're* the one that brought this calamity upon all of us," he bellowed. "You and your *planning!* It was *I* who trusted *you* all too foolishly—and now my people are destroyed, battered and blasted like ducks in a duck-barrel, and all is in ruins. We have once more fled to our catacombs and tunnels—and we'll rebuild, regrow, stronger than ever before. You were nearly rid of us, Tapiorca, trai- tor—but you will never see the end of us now!"

Lara stared at the Baron as if he'd just grown a third, medium- sized head. "You—you—"

I understood. I didn't care for all the shouting and blathering, but I was suddenly so *pleased* with myself simply for understand- ing how it all fit together that I opened my fool mouth as wide as I could manage.

"You folks are too much," I said. "The two of you in cahoots! Pass- ing little ribbon-messages back and forth like school-girls plotting love-spells against Donny in Maths. What did he tell you, Baron? That he could prevent even greater, *more* wanton blood-shed by coördinating the 'war' with you? Oh, but Tapiorca's not interested in preventing blood-shed—he wanted to *extend* the war. He *likes* being on the battle-field, Sir Commander-In-Charge. Leading worth-less souls to their doom for the sake of a story in the smoking-lounges of London. *That's* why you killed Richey, eh? Because he would have *ended* the war!"

The snapping torches were the only sound as I circled the ring, really working my spirits up now as I watched Tapiorca's shoulders slump in defeat. "She was right, you know—the Yam-Runners were after this territory too. They sent you *both* false messages, I'd wager, leading you out here to fight each other, massing you in one spot so the air-ships could destroy you both. It's true! They *did* destroy Prison-Isle. They *were* coming after you. *But Lara and I stopped them."*

Lara shook her head. "Wait, first what's all this about Prison-Isle?" she said. "What happened to Prison-Isle? Did something happen to Prison-Isle? All my stuff's there!"

"I'll explain later," I lied. "All of you were *played* by the Yam-Runners. Because *that's what Yam-Runners do.* And they played you without you even realising it, until *we* came along." A shrug, here. It was pretty obvious. "You owe us your lives."

The Baron of the Alley-Ways spat into the dirt. "I take it you're not talking to me," he hissed. "You've just spent the last six hours systematically annihilating my grass-roots people's revolutionary army. Except for the, uh, *millions of additional troops* we have massing in the tunnels," he added quickly.

"Not worried about it—as far as I'm concerned, we're going to blast this whole place to bed-rock with the big ships before we leave," I told him. "Give it all a good spring-cleaning. So no, I'm not talking to you directly."

The Baron of the Alley-Ways nodded. "So long as we're clear."

Then, before we could blink or even so much as half-wink, he snatched the Colt from Lara's feeble hand. First to fall was Tapiorca—two solid shots to the neck, grouped well. Another bullet found elephant-flank (eliciting a trumpet of alarm), a fourth dropped a Peapoddy man, and then the gun swung around to me.

"Sandy had such faith in you," he sighed. "But *money* made you forget all of the—"

A fusillade of rifle-fire from the Peapoddy crew cut him short and in half. The Colt dropped into the dirt, and Lara scooped it up, emptying the last two rounds into the ground-meat husk of his remains for good measure. Then she ran to Tapiorca, who lay bleeding into the dark dirt like a wuss.

"There's an old story about why the Crown's men wear red," he rasped. "So when we're bled, our comrades can't see it. So they don't lose heart in battle."

"Abalasta walabanishifa," Lara sobbed over him, *"Abalasta walabanishifa."*

But it had no effect.

"Thing is, it don't work," Tapiorca coughed. "On this getup... blood's black."

Indeed it was. A black stain ran along his shoulder and grew rapidly across his chest.

"Before you die," I piped up, "a curiosity. Some Yam-Runner showed up with falsified orders to lead you into this trap; that much is clear. But why did you *listen?* I mean, I'm the Crown's Regent. Your legitimately superiour officer. And you never even listened to *me."*

"Didn't know he was a Yam-Runner," Tapiorca wheezed. Lara shot me a glare for making him exert himself—but this was important. After all, I was curious. "Thought he was an emissary from the rebels, with a new message from the Baron. Looked like one of them monsters. Freak."

With his last breath, Tapiorca raised a quivering hand, and pointed to his elephant.

There, tied spread-eagle across the animal's rump, was Thigton.

95: THE FINAL CHALLENGE.

GET ON THE MARCONIGRAPH. CALL the Countess," Lara cried o'er the glistening mound that until recently had been the Crown's own Major-Leftenant Tapiorca. "She must have a medical officer. Get me bandages, sutures, whisky— oh, why are you just *standing* there, to blazes with you all!" She strained to tear the sleeves from her too-well-built coat, then finally hacked at them with a small pocket-knife until they rent from her shoulders. Holding them to Tapiorca's neck, she glared at the rest of us, apparently because we weren't spontaneously generating surgical-equipment from our foreheads.

"The Countess is on her way down," one of the crew-men said simply, their group huddled around the one of their own fallen, staring dumbly at his corpse as if afraid it had fallen victim, in death, to the dreaded Yam-Runner disease.

"Here then, men, help me, will you," I called to the crew-men; "unless that man's clothes start turning colours you don't have to worry about him. Help me with this blasted animal!"

The elephant was skittish at my approach, snorting and stomping the ground as if counting apples in a side-show, receding from me as I came after Thigton. Perhaps it was my wide-eyed amazement that set the creature off; I likely resembled one of the crazed capuchins or gob-smacked ourang-outangs the beast had no doubt fended off prankish attacks from in the wild. "Come back here, you brute—for the love of Babar, will you stand still?" Still it snuffled and wagged its vulgar trunk in my direction, as if fending off some impending crop-blow from a stern, o'er-moustachioed ring-master or too-forward ape in heat. "Tapiorca! Blast it all, man, tell your wretched pachyderm to hold his stance!"

"He can't hear you," Lara said simply, as if stating that the math-berry bush was all out of maths for the season.

"Well, *somebody* do *something*, come on then, don't just stand there like a mass of dunder-noggins!"

At this prodding, the crew-men shouldered their rifles and brought down the beast—it took quite the barrage to end its porcine squalling, but when it ultimately began to stumble, I directed the crew to lean their collective might against one leathered flank. Unleashing a final, bellowing curse in some ancient elephantine language, the creature toppled, the earth letting out a brief shiver with the blow not unlike the usual chamber-pot spine-tingle. The cannon-bell tumbled from its mooring atop the animal and fell to the earth with a dismal, deep *clong*, and I wondered if it would be the last church-bell ever sounded o'er this plain, and then wondered if the bat-creatures would come and eat us where we stood if it turned out to be.

As the sound echoed away, a calm descended. I hadn't realised how much raw malice the elephant had been exuding, twitching and sneezing off in its corner, but now we were clear of it, and something akin to hope began to well burblingly in my breast as if I'd eaten a full balloon of fresh blue-bird juice then swallowed a tack to burst it. What of my man Thigton?

The fellow was bound by ropes to the rear of the elephant, his impish joints stretched beyond their natural limits, his garb tattered to threads by the constant friction of pachyderm-burn. Back at the Manor, I'd had a Hindoo balm for just that affliction, but of course that whole vast store-house of overly-specific unguents was no more. A priceless trove, destroyed; I doubt the Norse even *made* Svalbardian igloo-tonic anymore, given the difficulty of importing Freon in the current economic climate. "Thigton, my lad, it's me," I cried. "Cut him down! Who's got a blade? Lara, let's have that knife!"

Lara held her makeshift bandage to Tapiorca's neck, not moving a muscle even to glance at us with disdain, which women can do without changing a tick of their expressions. "No."

The crew-men looked awkwardly to me for direction, until I remembered noticing a particularly snaggled tooth on a nearby war-corpse and dispatched the gang to investigate. The bright white projection-light had faded from the Countess's dirigible rumbling overhead, making our snapping torches the only illumination, which was lame.

I held one of those flickering lights to Thigton's face, searching for the heroic stoicism in the face of horrific abuse that had marked his time in my employ. "Come on, man, you've grinned through tougher challenges than this," I muttered at him. "Show us some spirit!"

He moved! Alive, he wriggled in his bonds like a giant frog caught in a rope-trap designed for animals of quite different anatomy. "Not of Yam-Runner blood, are you?" I smiled. "Whatever stinking cocktail of parentage runs through your twisted veins, thank heavens it's not of that accursed line."

Thigton opened his cracked lips, perhaps to speak, perhaps (who knows) even to beckon for a kiss—but Lara let out a wail that curdled all our skin on our bones. She shook Tapiorca vigorously, kneeling now in a mud-puddle of black, moonlight-drinking blood. "No, no, no," she sobbed. "Get him out of here! We need a medical officer! He's got to get to a hospital!"

One of the Peapoddy men turned to watch, holding the head of the war-corpse I'd indicated cracked open like a pistachio-shell as one of their lot pried at its jagged teeth with a rusty pair of pincers. "I've had a bit of medical training meself," he shrugged. "I could have a bit of a look—"

"No!" she screamed at him, as the wind from the dozen mighty air-screws of the dirigible washed over all of us, whipping her hair and mine and the dust and the ashes into a furious cyclone of eye-stinging tumult. The ship took twenty long seconds to pass through the space above our heads before drifting to meet the earth a Kensington-rules cricket-pitch away.

When my eyes found Lara again, she was snapping shut the cylinder of her reloaded Colt. Her clothing black and wet with Tapiorca-juice, her eyes unreadable in the darkness, she crossed the space to Thigton in five rapid strides, betraying a determination of purpose I've only ever seen in jilted women ready to let loose a slappin' or worse, and Heaven help any organism near their path. *"He's* the one who did it," she said. *"He's* the one who killed them all!"

"This is Thigton!" I cried, wanting to wrestle her for the gun, but afraid it might go off in the struggle—and also afraid of what Tapiorca's presumbaly-acidic blood might do to my delicate skin. "He's my very own man, saved my life more times than I can count. He saved me from *you,* in that boat explosion on the way to Prison-Isle!"

Her eyes slid to me and locked calipers of fury about my shape. "What do you know about that?" she spat. "There, were you? What else have you been keeping from me? Were you my third-grade bully,

as well? My first awkward romance? My father's leering business-
partner? All of these and the school-nuns too? Tell me!"

And then her face softened, as a sweet cherub of realisation
alighted on her nose.

"You," she breathed. "You gave the orders all round. *You* killed
everyone on this battle-field! The trap was *yours!*"

"Er, no," I said quickly, watching the wildly-swinging gun-
barrel point in dangerous directions as she began to shake with
rage. "I can understand the confusion, given what I've, perhaps
foolishly, shared of my history, but that in particular was the
Yam-Runners—"

"*You* told me everything about the so-called Yam-Runners," she
said. *"How* did you get appointed Crown's Regent? *Why did you kill
everyone on Prison-Isle?"*

"Ah, you've remembered that now, have you," I swallowed.

"I'm through being *lied to,*" she said, pressing the Colt against
Thigton's chapped face. "I want someone to start talking."

"Look, you know who I am, I've told you everything," I said hur-
riedly. "We've had loads of conversations about all of this. And this
is really conduct quite unbecoming an officer of the law, because as
you'll recall you've sworn to uphold and protect the—"

"I don't remember anything!" she shouted, firing a round at some
constellation high above. I flinched at the sound, and she jammed
the Colt into Thigton's cheek—he tensed as the hot metal touched
his skin, though it was surely cooler than the various implements
he'd suffered the touch of in course of his normal duties for me back
in London. "Someone had better start telling me what's going on!"

"What's going on is that Tapiorca played you for a fool," I barked.
"Running a scheme with the rebels to prolong the war, so he could
stay in power longer! And you ran all around and did his little bid-
ding, thinking you were serving the Crown—well, sorry. Tapiorca
wasn't in business for the Crown, he was in business for himself.
And he strung you along like a little rat-dog, one of those irritating
toy models that thin women with too-large sun-glasses carry in
their purses. It was his own deceit that brought them down, not me

or you or anyone here still breathing. So calm down, and give me the gun."

That last bit might have been over-reaching my influence—I reached for the gun, and she swung it at me. "Don't touch me," she said, and the Colt might as well have mouthed the words itself.

"Hoshifelaffa parotanselaba," Thigton whispered, and Lara fell in a heap, silent and solemn to the earth. The gun fell limply from her fingers without so much as a sigh of regret, and all was suddenly, shockingly quiet.

I jumped back in alarm, then looked at Thigton's weary visage—"What the bloody arse-bucket was that?"

"She sleeps. Hurry," he said, his voice barely a zephyr in a dry river-bed of sadness. "You won't have long."

I debated searching Lara's person for the pocket-knife, but the Peapoddy lads were already standing at the ready with the extracted snaggle-tooth. It was short work to free Thigton, and he

STUDYING MAGAZINES FOR INCIDENTAL NUDITY.

slumped wearily into my arms, a tangled mass of strained tendons and aching. His skin had the rough, sort of dry texture that it always had, so he wasn't exactly nice to the touch, but the sentiment of the embrace was somewhat pleasant.

"No time," he coughed. "Write down what I'm about to say. The Tome of the Precious Lore—"

"Gone," I moaned, "destroyed by Larcenic the Lithe in fire!"

"Just as well," Thigton said. "But its powers still exist—and I remember a few of its words. Quickly, before my breath escapes: write these down!"

"Thigton," I said sadly, mournfully, in as weepy a tone as I could manage so he would be clear to understand the gravity of the situation, "you know I was never called to literacy. O drat my pride!" For I knew not how to write!

I looked at the crew-men for help; their cretinous expressions confirmed they'd never written anything longer than the names of their dingles in fresh snow-banks. I looked to the dirigible, moored some fifty yards away o'er rock-snotted terrain; but Thigton would never survive being moved, I was sure. And Lara, for all her vaunted intellectualism, lay slumped at my feet. Some help *she* was.

"Then all is lost," he said, "for my heart is fading by the moment. I'm simply glad that...I die in your arms." He coughed, a phlegmy blast that landed mostly on my coat-sleeve, and I despaired.

I would not—*could not*—let it end this way.

"Do you remember any words that can heal you? Tell me, and I'll repeat them back," I said desperately.

But Thigton shook his head. "My folk are cross-breeds of Yam-Runner stock and of mine-dwarves," he said. "The incantations do not work on the Yam-Runners, and so long as a Yam-Runner heart beats in my chest, I am immune to their power."

"But..." I was suddenly sure of everything. "What if that were not the case?"

He looked at me, seeming to read my meaning. "There is one, very dangerous verse I know," he said. "Most of the incantations take power from the Yam-Runner race—and even from me; see my weakness now—but this one takes power from the race of man. Any one of you could die if you utter it."

"I'll take those odds," I said, and he understood. He whispered a phrase that I seared into my memory with the hottest iron I could imagine, and it *burned so good.*

The three Peapoddy men stood dumbly, the mock-doctor still holding his rusty pincers, and it was to him that I directed an imperative: "You. Doctor. Have you ever performed a heart-transplant?"

He scratched his head. "Only once, on a llama, on a bet. Worked out pretty well, as I reckon. Llama lived a few days, long enough to carry our packs to Cabul."

"Don't need your life story. You, the dirty one—run to the dirigible, get the Countess, whatever medical supplies you have, alcohol's the most important. Go! Now!" The urgency of my tone stood in for any proper rank or authority, and the man dropped his rifle and took off at a sprint. "And you, Third-Man. You're going to be my moral-support."

He nodded sagely. "You can do it!"

"Also my nurse. Clear a space on the ground," I said, and both the doctor and Third-Man helped me gently lay Thigton down. A thin sliver of morning was beginning to peek o'er the horizon, but the wan light in Thigton's eyes wouldn't survive un-fanned till dawn. "Listen," I told him, "this is going to hurt. But there's no reason I can think of that you won't pull through, if you just stay with me."

"Ever yours, Master," he said with a tight smile, and for a moment I thought of Sandy, the hunch-back, dead by my hand. The same fate would not befall my Thigton.

"Right," I said, and stood. I jogged in place to psych myself up, then went to work.

First I found the knife in Lara's blood-soaked pocket, and was proud of myself for not even pausing at the touch of round thigh-meat beneath the fabric. It wasn't particularly sharp—nor was the knife—but it'd do for hackery. It would be tough going in the darkness, but I would have to manage.

Major-Leftenant Tapiorca's body was still warm. His ridiculous uniform was covered in so many sashes and buckles that it was tough to get through them all, but a combination of disrobing and knife-disrobing finally yielded soft, furry white chest-flesh. Without even a sigh to savour the moment, I dug the blade into his throat and quickly revealed his rib-cage. The judicious use of a rifle-barrel as a lever broke his ribs from his sternum—*that* is a sound that you never forget, and *boy* did it bring me back.

Soon his steaming viscera was revealed. It was a bit more red than I'd anticipated—I'd figured someone of his treachery would have humours running gangrenous and jaundiced with mouldy bile—but all the same, it was a heart. The strongest heart in the Royal Regiments, if you believed rumour, and to be honest it was a bit over-kill for just little Thigton, but hey, we'd come this far.

I handed off the knife to the Doctor. "Let's make this as fast a transfer as possible," I said. "I'll wait to pull this one out until you've opened him up—we've got just barely a moment to make the switch before air-ghouls eat the meat, or however it works."

"This whole thing looks a bloody disaster to me," he said, but my tone let him know I was serious. "Right. I'll make it jack-quick. Can't see a drat thing, though—hold that torch steady!"

"It's burning out," said the Third-Man. "Our torches—they're about spent!" At this news, I set my jaw—it was hard enough carving up Tapiorca by torch-light, but now, with no light at all, our chances looked grimmer than a taxman on Christmas. Thigton coughed, each moment weaker than the last.

The dirty crew-man returned from the ship, out of breath and heaving, carrying a barrel in his arms, somehow even soilier than before. "Wasn't much," he gasped. "But I brought what I could find." Behind him, a larger group of crew-men were approaching with torches and rifles. "And I told the Countess what's on."

With a rumble, the dirigible began to lift off again—and slowly, like the sun emerging from the sea, the projection-light flickered to life, bathing us all in brilliant white illumination.

The Countess's face filled the side of the ship, beaming down like a jovial goddess high on speed-balls, and we turned to our work.

Dirty-Man had found no whisky, but had located a bottle of pear schnapps, which I downed to steady my nerves. He'd also brought a few towels and a hotel sewing-packet complete with replacement plastic buttons—hardly a doctor's kit, but it'd have to do. With a spray of spit on the blade for luck, the Doctor opened up Thigton's chest—the imp sucked in his breath and clutched stones in his hands, but never let out a cry. What a trooper.

"Bring that heart," he called to me, and tossed me the single knife—deftly I snatched it from the air, and quickly severed the vessels. Gingerly I lifted out Tapiorca's heart, then rushed it over to the kneeling Doctor.

"Bloody mess," he whistled. "It's too big. Got to make some room. Hold it clean!"

With the knife out of reach, he found the snaggle-tooth and began to saw at Thigton's abdominal-cavity. I stood to vacate his light, Tapiorca's heart cooling in my hands and draining onto my shoes, and already I felt its walls begin to collapse beneath my fingers.

"It's falling," I said. "Got to get this in place!"

"Need a minute," the Doctor growled. "Turns out it's a bit tighter in here than a llama."

With the heart dying in my grasp, I knew what I had to do. Juggling its weight into my left hand, I reached down with my right and retrieved Abu Fromage's perfect cheese-wand.

Don't think, I told myself—*for God's sake, don't think!*

Without even knowing why, I touched the wand to the heart, and began to float it around. The control afforded me by the weight of the wand allowed me to keep the heart perfectly balanced at the tip of the instrument, bouncing, twirling, spinning around from one side to the other, making sure no more of its precious blood leaked from its cut vessels. In the bright whiteness of the dirigible's light, I was alone on a stage—the horizon vanished from view, and it was just me and the cheese-wand, dancing like a hummingbird flirting with a flower, the heart held perfectly to the wand-tip like a Globe-trotter's basketball to a glue-gun.

For the briefest of instants, I became scared that I didn't know what I was doing—and in that moment, the heart faltered. As its weight tipped, an instinct took over and I fell back in that zone, working without thinking, acting without reasoning.

It was the zone I'd striven for my entire life, I suddenly realised, in my many acts of violence—watching my victims fall to my blows, I'd been yearning for *this*, this perfect abandon, this moment of clarity where the world simply fell away and all that existed was the act of being wondrously, beautifully *deft*.

And I was *good* at it—the *best* at it, in this moment, in the time of not thinking.

"Now!" the Doctor cried, and in the most fluid motion of my career I knelt, swivelled, turned, and deposited the heart into the gap in Thigton's chest. The inertial motion of the blood within the heart suddenly sloshed forth and into Thigton's veins, and as the imp's eyes opened wide in sudden shock, I breathed into his ear the phrase he had taught me, and he lived.

96: LOOKING DOWN
ON IT ALL.

WHERE DO YOU THINK SHE'LL GO?" the Countess asked. Thigton, the Countess and I watched the ground recede beneath the dirigible as we ascended from the ash-heap of Easthillshireborough-upon-Flats. Below us, Lara still lay sprawled and asleep; an aero-carriage fully stocked with coal sat not far away. Sunlight revealed the plane of battle for what it was: horrible. Just horrible. Ugly and horrid. A blast-land of misery. It looked a bit like Wales.

We had taken the liberty of re-closing Tapiorca's chest and shrouding him with cloth—after some debate, it was decided that finding him in his current state would be less shocking to Lara than not finding him at all. Her figure was tiny now; it was hard to make out anything at all but a black speck on the hillside.

"London, probably," I said. "To report to the Crown, no doubt; but who knows, really." I was done trying to solve the lives of others. She would awake, Thigton assured us, in full health; then, she would have to assess her situation on her own, and take appropriate action. I would allow her to do this on her own behalf. It was my parting gift to her.

"Pity," the Countess replied. "She'd be a fine pilot in a fight. Hate to lose such a skill."

"She remembers Prison-Isle," I said. "She'll never come aboard this ship again."

"Also hate to lose the Crown as a client," the Countess went on. "Might be high time to make the rounds again, cross the Channel and see what's what on the Continent. Always a few scrapes worth getting into, if you know where to look. Where do you want us to drop you?"

And that was it—the ultimate question. Easthillshireborough-upon-Flats held nothing for me, of course; but neither did London, anymore. The waggling tongues of the Bon-Mot gala seemed so far away and prattling, now, and with Thigton steadfastly by my side I was already assured of never having to perform any manual labour that I chose to eschew. The only pursuit that held the least interest for me now was...

"Almost at altitude," a crew-man told the Countess. "Standing by for the signal."

"We'll wait until Lara wakes and flies out of range," the Countess said gamely.

The armada was preparing to unleash the lightning on East-hillshireborough-upon-Flats, to eradicate any rebels that might remain in the hillside caverns. And, of course, to mine the land of its jade-powder, to fuel the massive ships and their weapons.

So while Lara lay sleeping we waited, hanging softly in the air over the ruined town I had once called home. There was Waverly Hill, topped with cratered estates; beyond was the light-house, and in the other direction Pool-Party Plaza, and the wharves. On the horizon, Prison-Isle and the others thrust up from the sea. Behind us, on the other side of the ship, were empty factories, where children had toiled ceaselessly to make novelty over-sized boot-laces and the like; those hardy days of industry were gone, now, forever. The town was good and surely *dead*.

"How far are the Himalayas?" I asked the Countess. "There's a monastery there, where I once met an old friend. I might want to go check in on the place, see if it's occupied." The cheese-monks might be long gone, now, but I might like having the place to myself—practicing the twirl, fermenting my own spices, perhaps even tutoring any acolytes that might make the long climb to the top as I once had.

"Whoof, a ways off," she said. "If you ride with us that far, you'll have to do some work on ship—with that eye of yours we could use you, for sure. We'd welcome a joiner—just don't mind the glares from the crew; I'll knock 'em around a bit, and they'll warm to you soon enough. Give it a week and you'll all be in an adorable pile in the pilin'-hold, keepin' warm at night."

"I'd like that," I smiled. "I'm keenish on warmth."

From below, a muffled *pop*, like a paper-bag bursting. I looked down—and where Lara had been was a greenish cloud of fire.

The armada fired—and the ship bucked like a dinghy in a squall as the sky erupted in furious, searing green lightning. The Countess held fast to the railing, but Thigton and I were tossed from our feet, landing in a heap on the deck as great, sizzling power coursed through every inch of the vessel and poured into the landscape below as *burning*.

Then it ended, as suddenly as it had begun. When I managed to look over the railing again, I saw green gems sparkling everywhere—it was as if the lightning had unearthed a lode of emeralds, cut and shimmering like the scales of a giant, buried dragon. I saw land burned black, and then slowly the gathering smoke-layer hid the ground from view as if embarrassed by the naughtiness it had revealed.

The dirigible's mighty furnace moaned into operation, and we began to climb. I gaped at the Countess.

THE SUN-RISE IN QUESTION.

"Someone must have left her a letter to read," she said coyly.

"But—but she—"

"I hated to lose her skill," the Countess said, "but I'll be damned if I'm ever going to let her come up against me in a fight." She cocked her head. "And I'd hate to lose the Crown as a client."

Ruthless.

"We'll head to sea for a bit," she told the vista beyond, "and return when the smoke's cleared for our mining." She turned to me. "Can we count on you?"

There were eight hundred things to consider about the offer, but I stopped that train short with a blink. "I'm yours till I betray you," I told her honestly, and she laughed.

"Same here," she said. "Same as always."

With that, the ship began to rise, climbing to join the sun.

Epilogue.

T HE SNOW BLEW LIKE A YETI HORDE clearing their black noses in concert: sharply, aggressively, indelibly tinged with regret, occasionally with solid-matter enclosed. Karolinga's mask saved my eyes from a blinding batter-ing of ice-dust, but that old leather was cracked now from fierce use in battle, and I feared its oily buckles would give way any moment, leaving my precious eyes defenceless in the storm. That would be bad—I, like so many others nowadays, needed my eyes, for many of the Modern Pursuits.

And I needed those lenses—I'd dropped a jade-flare from the air-ship on our last pass overhead, and though the blizzard had swallowed the signal-smoke with the eagerness of an addict for whom the opium-patch proves less and less effective each day, I trusted that through the violet Karolinga glass I would still make out a glimmer, some sharp beacon of colour to beckon me like a pre-paid lover through the white. For I had dropped my gear after the flare, and the ship had flown on with haste; there would be no return, no extraction. No matter if the tooth of my journey turned rotten, it could do no else but stay firmly rooted in the jaw of this miserable place—and oh! would the land cry when I jabbed it in the skull-nerves. I would not be bested by simple *chunky water*.

Sure enough! there! a gleam through the gusts! and Time forgot its ticking as I scrambled over icy ridges with the pep of a new-foaled springbok. *Springbok* was a new word I'd learnt on our expedition to the Veldt; others had been *man-limb gourd* and *hash-ish by the pound*. (I knew the latter, but now it could be said I really *knew* the latter.) The Peapoddy armada had crossed land and sea with me aboard, and I'd earned my weight in sabre-rustling along the way; but after dallying too long in the Sub-Continent I could no longer ignore the call of that far-off earth-tit, ever-peeking through the mists, ever-caressing in surprisingly erotic dreams, ever-maddening in every other type of dream, ever...ever *waiting*.

Tall-Mount.

I'd concocted excuse after excuse, side-scheme after dalliance, and had middling adventures (of a thoroughly un-satisfying sort generally) along the way. I'd avoided the snow-capp'd stare of that destination for years, never sure what I might find, or what I might hope to find, or what I feared I would find, or what I wanted to want to find, or what I feared I might want to hope to find against all odds. An ice-covered monument to emptiness and despair? Or a thriving cheese-monk community, with its own cheese-based economy and salty, cheese-flavoured passports? I wasn't sure which would be worse—being the only one there, or arriving and finding myself utterly unnecessary.

But soon it became high time to find out, as I'd begun rustling against some rather sharp corners aboard the narrow confines of the air-ship, and so with no major measure of fan-fare, as soon as I espied the sodden flags of the defunct skunk-farm I knew to be near the monastery, I tossed a flare and my belongings overboard and arranged to be dropped into the snow-storm like a dafter. To their credit, they let me go.

If I survive, I had thought on that long, cold glider-flight down, *then this will have been a good idea, right? I mean, logically.*

Sadly, my puffed chest had drained of a bit of its bravado since then, and I quite wished I'd saved some of that hot ichor in a mason-jar to keep me warm, as my fingers were beginning to tingle in their yak-fur mittens. But I'd seen the glimmer of the flare and knew it was just ahead, surely as a timber-wolf poots on its young.

And there it *was*—rising out of the snow, grey-stone and impassive, a mighty bulwark against the raging horror of The World Outside. With stumbling steps I navigated the twisting labyrinth that kept the snow from drifting into the court-yard, clambered o'er the icy steps that stymied the slithering frost-wurms endemic to the region, and vaulted with the last dregs of my strength up the

Yeti-befuddling clock-work escalator. (It was emblazoned with the silhouettes of owls, to keep those mythic beasts at bay—related to rodents in their hind-brains, they craved the cheese boiling in the great underground vats of the monastery.)

With each foot-fall closer to the sanctuary, I searched the air for cheese-scent. Was I dead to that sensation? Had my nose dulled from too many days breathing ozone, soot, gunpowder-smoke and empty Herbal-Essences bottles?

No—the fault lay not with my acuity. The bitter tang of despair still lay sharp in my nostrils. There simply was no cheese cooking here. The place was empty.

I felt my heart down-shift. I would have to rebuild that great, deep furnace myself, or else die in the coming night.

I looked around and found a quiet hill-scape of snow. The entrance to the sanctuary was buried here, somewhere, and I would have to find it and burrow in—then find matériel to build the flame and start the tradition anew.

It would be a long slog, and lonely.

Behind me came crunching in the snow—Thigton, with my pack. "Come hence, Thigton," I barked, "we'll need to create shelter. Gather what wood you can, if any; otherwise, we'll start burning Sherpas." Following the imp trudged a line of indigenous sorts he'd picked up somewhere-or-other, who might be useful for fuel in a pinch.

Thigton said something to the furry fellows and they began to shuffle about looking busy. "Put the kettle on," I reminded them, and began a great circuit of the grounds, searching for the sanctuary opening beneath the rolling blanket of snow. The sun spat cold at this elevation, and we'd need to move underground if we'd hope to save any of the Sherpas for later in the week.

As I rounded one particularly heaped mound, something moved—I reached for the sabre at my belt and came up shy; my yak-mittens made it hard to grab things. Still, I pawed at the blade a few times to show I was serious.

Before me, a pelt of fur emerged from the white; red and black in a pattern that looked hardly natural. Loom-weave for sure; no animal wore such regular checkers. Beneath the blanket was a long parka, and beneath the parka a coat; then by slow layers was revealed to me a person, a woman by the looks of it, smiling to boot.

"Hullo," she said. "Here for the cheese?"

"Er," I said, lifting my Karolinga lenses as she rubbed her face until her cheeks burned crimson with warmth.

"I'm just waiting for the monk to emerge," she said. "Sometimes it takes a while, an' you have to show you're dedicated."

I looked at her, then at the feature-less mounds around us. From this angle, one of the hills had a squarish profile; suddenly I knew the layout of this place, could feel the brick beneath the many layers of ice, knew this plaza exactly, and knew how I would make it my home. We would open the sancutary to-day, and re-light its lamps and furnaces, and set cauldrons on stoves and begin to milk whatever we could and make cheese. We would start this place right up again. It would be *great.*

Further-more, I knew the feeling of waiting; my first and, for so long, *only* glimpse of Abu Fromage had been as just such an acolyte as this woman. Her dedication played a note that I recognized, on a long-silent organ.

I extended my hand.

"Well," I said gamely, "here I am!"

The End.

Further Reading
by David Malki !

Mr MALKI'S style is very much like that of the discerning citizen's favorite author, the late lamented Rev. Herve Pandersnatch-Gumps, but unlike that jerk, his tales are thoroughly up-to-date. The stories are as sturdy as they are shrewd, and will prove of absorbing interest to folks in fine fettle everywhere.

Bindings vary. All volumes illustrated. Price per volume on par with market rates. Available from your local bookseller or via WONDERMARK.COM.

Beards of our Forefathers
A collection of Wondermark comic-strips—hard-bound and featuring vibrant Colour. The recipient of many Lauds and much fervent Acclaim.

ISBN: **978-1593079840**

Clever Tricks to Stave Off Death
A newer strip-collection, hard-bound as well and delightful. Also contains many Tips to help extend your own life.

ISBN: **978-1595823298**

Dapper Caps & Pedal-Copters
Not only a collection of comic-strips, but also a Journal of Inventiveness and Progress, as well as a Guide for children.

ISBN: **978-1595824493**

——————— ALSO, THESE THINGS: ———————

Hey World Here Are Some Suggestions
(A Tweet Me Harder Collection)
David Malki ! and Kris Straub solve every problem in the world, over and over and over again.

ISBN: **978-0982167113**

Machine of Death
Edited with Ryan North & Matthew Bennardo. A collection of stories about people who know how they will die. Fun!

ISBN: **978-0982167120**

BEARSTACHE BOOKS;
DARK HORSE BOOKS;   } Publishers.

Author's Note.

IF YOU HAVE ENJOYED THE TALES I HAVE recounted, may I kindly suggest that you be examined by a medical professional at once?

However, should you discover, upon doing so, that there simply *is no cure* (as I have so discovered), I would recommend for your further enjoyment the twice-weekly Humour-Strip "Wondermark," which can be found at WONDERMARK.COM. You will find Comics abundant at that address, as well as the opportunity to peruse further works by myself.

Finally, in my own defence—the accounts you have read are true to the best of my recollection, however it should be mentioned that I took no notes at the time, and have written wholly from memory.